EYE OF THE CAT

EYE OF THE CAT

A. L. McWilliams

Five Star
Unity, Maine

Five Star First Edition Romance Series.
Published in 2000 in conjunction with The Seymour Agency.

Cover photograph by Robert Darby

Set in 11 pt. Plantin by Rick Gundberg.

Printed in the United States on permanent paper.

Library of Congress Cataloging-in-Publication Data

Williams, A. L. (Audra LaVaun)
    Eye of the cat / by A. L. McWilliams.
        p.   cm. — (Five Star standard print first edition romance series)
    ISBN 0-7862-2495-9 (hc : alk. paper)
    1. Texas — Fiction. I. Title. II. Series.
PS3563.C927 E94   2000
    813'.6—dc21
                                                                00-028847

This novel is dedicated to the memory of my dad, Bill McWilliams, and to my mother, Linda McWilliams, two people whose love and support and faith never once faltered. Without you, this would not have been possible.

CHAPTER ONE

Pima County, Arizona: July 13, 1877

The Sonoran Desert lay before him, silent, awesome, a mosaic of brittle, resinous shrubs, cacti, and gravel patches. A shred of cloud drifted slowly eastward, while down below, heat waves shimmied, making the horse and rider in the distance appear warped. The sun suspended all other movement, everything either dead or dormant, waiting, it seemed, for something to happen. Waiting for rain.

Slipping the black patch from his left eye, Catlin Myers wiped the sweat from his brow, and lifted the field glasses. He watched the horseman a moment, still over eight hundred yards away, then shifted the glasses to his left and down and held them on the crumbling adobe. It served as a line shack for cowhands of the Avra Valley Ranch. Near the adobe were a rickety corral and a windmill, the first he had seen in this far-flung country. All were in plain sight of his ridgetop lookout.

Dividing the intervening desert into one hundred yard units with his eye, he estimated the distance at about a quarter of a mile.

The set-up was perfect.

Lying belly-down in a little hollow among the blistering rocks, Catlin put the field glasses away and rolled over onto his side. The Sharps .50 lay next to him. He slipped the monstrous gun from its leather scabbard, handling it almost lovingly, slender brown fingers caressing the walnut stock as he

7

rested the barrel across his folded jacket.

He raised the leaf sight, set it for four hundred yards, and drew a brass cartridge from his bandolier. He thumbed it into the rifle's open breech.

Snapping the lever shut, Catlin settled down to wait and watched the horse and rider draw nearer the line camp. He could make out more details now through the glasses—the horseman's dust-colored Stetson, mousy brown hair curling around the brim, the young, unworried face—and he knew this was his man. This was the man he had been hired to kill.

A troubled frown creased Catlin's forehead. The job at hand seemed no different from any other he had pulled off in the past. He came, somebody died, he left. Yet something didn't feel right.

It began a week ago when a gentleman by the name of Arnet Phillips contacted Catlin in Tres Alamos. His message was simple: "Come to Tucson. Easy job. Good pay." More out of curiosity than a need for money, Catlin slapped a saddle on Chico and pointed him west.

Of course, he had heard of Arnet Phillips. Few in this part of the country hadn't. Phillips came to Tucson, Arizona, fifteen years ago and now owned the second largest business in Pima County. Phillips's fortunes rested upon freighting—transporting goods by wagon train into Arizona via Guaymas, Yuma, and Kansas City. Two years ago, he married Inez Robles, the daughter of a prominent Mexican *ranchero,* and his fortune more than doubled.

As it turned out, Phillips's present dilemma centered around his young wife.

Seated in the study of Mr. and Mrs. Phillips's Spanish-colonial mansion, Catlin smoked one of Arnet's expensive cigars and waited to hear why he had been summoned.

"I want a man killed," Phillips had stated. No beating

around the shrubbery whatsoever.

Catlin remembered smiling. "You and half the world want somebody killed. If you want me to do it, you'd better have a good reason." He was not, he explained, an indiscriminate killer.

Resting his arms on the polished oak desk, Phillips laced his fingers together and looked Catlin square in the eye. "This man raped my wife."

His name was Johnny Keaton, and he rode for the Avra Valley Ranch west of Tucson. When Catlin asked when and where the incident had occurred, Phillips grew evasive. It happened, he said. That was all that mattered to him, and the details were none of Catlin's business.

Catlin put on his hat and prepared to leave. "Sounds like a job for your sheriff then. Not me."

"Wait." Phillips made a hasty gesture of apology. "Please, have a seat. I'll explain."

His wife, he said, had not spoken of the rape in any great detail, and she was now in the care of her mother and sisters. The terrible experience had left Inez emotionally unstable. For this reason, Arnet Phillips had refrained from contacting the proper authorities, feeling to do so would only make matters worse for his wife.

Listening patiently to his tale of woe, Catlin finally replied that he would take the job, warning Phillips in the same breath that his services did not come cheap.

"Money, Mr. Myers, is not an obstacle."

Later, they shook hands, and Catlin took his leave, carrying with him a down payment of one thousand dollars and the unshakable notion that he'd just been hoodwinked.

Now, lying in wait for Johnny Keaton, the feeling crept over him again, though he wasn't sure why. He had no reason to distrust Arnet Phillips. And the deal was already made.

Keaton dismounted at the corral, led his horse through the gate, and began to unsaddle. Trapped like a gnat in a spider's web. Catlin pressed his right cheek against the stock of his Sharps .50. The metal parts of the rifle burned his hands, heated by a glaring, afternoon sun. Pulling back the rear trigger to set the sear in hair-trigger position, he gazed through the leaf sight's peephole, aligning it with the globe front sight on the tiny figure of Johnny Keaton four hundred yards away.

Whatever doubts or misgivings he might have had were forgotten the minute he prepared to shoot, his every sense, every nerve and fiber, centered on his gun and the man and nothing else.

Sucking in a deep breath, Catlin exhaled slowly, slowly, and squeezed the trigger.

There was a whoosh of sound as the .50 caliber slug exploded out the barrel, a deafening boom, and seconds later, Johnny Keaton toppled tail over teakettle into the dust at his horse's feet.

Waving gunsmoke from his face, Catlin saw the horse half-rear and shy away from Keaton's body. The man did not move. Old Poison Slinger had spoken. Still keeping an eye on Keaton, Catlin sat up, ran an oil rag up and down the barrel of the Sharps, and returned the big gun to its scabbard.

He rose, propping a booted foot on the rocks, and flipped the empty brass cartridge up and down in his right hand. Another man dead. He felt no remorse for his victim, no guilt. He hadn't felt either of these emotions in a very long time and almost regretted the loss.

Suddenly restless, he slipped the cartridge into his pocket and swept the desert landscape again with his field glasses. While it was his custom to simply leave once a job was completed and have his client pay any money due him to his account in El Paso, Arnet Phillips had insisted that he report to him personally with proof of Keaton's death. Catlin had made no promises.

Another line rider would be coming in any time now from the south, and Catlin had no desire to be caught rifling through a dead man's pockets. Yet he saw no sign of the rider through his glasses. He decided to risk it.

Collecting his gear, he walked back to where he had left his horse ground-tied out of sight behind a craggy upthrust of rock. Chico spotted him and nickered, impatient at having been left alone so long in the hot sun.

Catlin scratched the long-legged bay behind the ears, lashed the Sharps snugly to his saddle and mounted up.

They left the ridge and struck out across the open desert through yellowed creosote and saguaro. A whiptail lizard dashed before them, making for a patch of shade. The smell of sun-baked earth and the dust churned up by Chico's hooves tickled Catlin's nostrils.

They approached the line camp by a roundabout route, Catlin keeping a wary eye on the adobe house, looking for anything suspicious. He had been watching the camp since early morning, had seen no one in all these hours, but remained cautious.

He dismounted and climbed over the mesquite-pole corral. Johnny Keaton lay sprawled on his back, his hat in the dust several feet from his head, eyes and mouth gaping open in an eternal expression of astonishment. Squatting beside him, Catlin noted the position of the bullet hole. His aim was a mite off today; the .50 caliber slug that should have struck Keaton's heart had ripped through the young man's throat instead and exploded out the back of his neck.

Catlin's gaze moved back up to Keaton's face and held there, intense, searching. Keaton's smooth young face was dirty from work, mousy hair sticking in wet curls to his forehead, reminding him of someone . . . someone. It came to him finally, painfully. Brad Gilley. His best friend during the late War Between the States. Dead now. His bones scattered, bleached beneath a Mississippi sun.

Catlin felt his mind slipping back over the years to another place, another time. He was lost for a moment, staring into space, his slim form so still he might have been dead, as well. He remained so for a full minute before some inner caution roused him, and he struggled back to the present, to Arizona, clawing his way through the old memories and regrets.

He glanced around him and brushed a shaky hand across his face. Sometimes he went away. A sight, certain odors, a sound even, might open the door to his memory, and his mind would take a walk. It was happening more often lately. Too often. Catlin pulled himself together and returned to business.

He searched Keaton's pockets for papers or keepsakes, looking for anything that might prove his identity and death to Arnet Phillips, short of cutting off his head. There was a plug of chewing tobacco, an old watch that had ceased to keep time at precisely 9:35, a stub of pencil, and an envelope freshly stained with blood. Johnny Keaton's name was written in small, neat script across the front.

The envelope was torn, as if Keaton had opened it in great haste. Catlin withdrew the folded letter, shook it out, and immediately smelled the sweet, alluring scent of a lady's perfume. Not a cheap perfume either, by the smell of it. Like roses snipped fresh from the garden.

Catlin sat back on his heels and scanned the letter. It began with a passionate oratory of the lady's undying love and longing for Keaton, written in the flowery, gushing style of a very spoiled, very foolish young woman, and he skipped down to the last paragraph where the tone abruptly changed.

Frowning, his lips moving silently, Catlin read her final words: Please be careful, Johnny. I am almost certain Arnet suspects us, and there is no telling what he might do . . . Love forever, Inez Phillips.

The name jumped out at him from the page, and he stared at it for a long moment, his usually nonchalant features drawn into hard, sharp lines.

Phillips had lied, after all. The realization sank in without difficulty, for hadn't he suspected something shady all along? Yet, like a fool, he had disregarded his gut feeling, relying instead on the knowledge that Phillips was known far and wide as an honest and upright businessman. A real square-shooter, he was called.

"Lying son of a bitch!" The words burst from his lips with a bitterness that startled him.

Keaton couldn't have been more than nineteen or twenty years of age, not even old enough to vote, hardly a man at all, and in love with some big bug's spoiled-brat wife. Neither could have suspected the true depths of Phillips's jealousy.

A strange sadness washed over Catlin, mingling with the anger, and he closed Johnny Keaton's eyes and covered his body with a saddle blanket. The second line rider would find him before nightfall.

Catlin smoked a cigarette beneath the skimpy, latticed shade of the windmill, taking time to gather his thoughts, and let Chico drink from the dirt tank. Green scum and skimmers covered the water's surface. The windmill turned its cheek to a sudden gust of wind, its wooden blades thrashing, churning, clattering, while dust and dry leaves performed a mad dance on the ground below. Catlin shielded his face from the swirling grit.

Cramming Inez's letter into the back pocket of his pants, he swung into the saddle and touched a spur to Chico. Arnet

Phillips wanted proof of Keaton's death. Well, he'd found that and more.

And he had a good mind to shove it down the bastard's throat.

CHAPTER TWO

The temperature was over one hundred degrees in the shade when Catlin Myers rode into Tucson the following day. In the church plaza, the bells of San Augustín cathedral began to clang, and Catlin supposed it must be high noon, time for dinner and a short *siesta* 'neath the shade of a brush ramada.

He rode into town with care, alert to the strange sights and sounds that surrounded him. Tucson reminded him a little of El Paso—dusty streets littered with chicken feathers, one-story, flat-roofed adobe *casas,* and jackasses, hogs, and packs of skinny mutts roaming the streets and alleys. Like El Paso, Tucson was isolated and still predominantly Mexican, though a handful of Anglo merchants and freighters also called this tough little community east of the Santa Cruz River home.

Catlin knew of one gringo in particular who would catch hell before the day was over, and walking Chico down the main street, he considered where would be the most likely place to find Arnet Phillips. Catching sight of the Shoo Fly Restaurant, he decided to start with it.

There were a number of horses tied along the hitch rail in front of the Shoo Fly, it being dinnertime, and Catlin left the bay tethered to a crooked cedar post at the corner of the building. A Mexican leaning against the wall near the open doorway eyed him beneath his sombrero while pretending not to and carefully rolled a pinch of tobacco in a shred of corn shuck. He wore dirty, striped trousers and an equally

15

dirty shirt, half unbuttoned to reveal a brown, hairless chest. He had a shifty-eyed appearance that Catlin distrusted.

The rich aroma of fried chicken hit Catlin midway to the door, as did the clamor of plates and utensils and the constant murmur of voices, punctuated occasionally by a burst of laughter. Beating the dust from his pants with his hat, Catlin ducked through the door and stood there a moment, angled so that he could keep an eye on the Mexican outside and still check out the dinner crowd.

The Shoo Fly was a long, low, narrow building made of adobe with a rammed earth floor and a ceiling of white muslin. There were ten tables of varying sizes and homemade chairs with rawhide seats. Nothing fancy by any means, but the food was good, and it was cool here and hospitable.

Catlin scanned the crowd, and his keen gaze settled on the man in the gray, tailor-made suit seated near an open window off to his right, a man with muttonchop whiskers and thick, auburn hair streaked with silver. It was Arnet Phillips. Across from him sat Estevan Ochoa, Tucson's mayor.

Catlin started toward their table, taking his time, feeling his anger of the day before returning, building, though to look at him, no one would have guessed it.

Enthralled in discussions of business and the latest Apache scare, Arnet Phillips didn't notice him at first. It wasn't until Catlin pulled up a chair beside him and helped himself to the man's cup of coffee that he looked up, and the shock and displeasure on his face were priceless.

Ignoring Phillips for the moment, Catlin thrust out his hand to Estevan Ochoa.

"Mr. Mayor, it's a pure pleasure to meet you," he declared, overemphasizing his natural Texas drawl to the point of absurdity. He was grinning so hard his face hurt. "Saw your picture in the paper the other day and said to myself,

'Now there's a man I'd like to meet!' "

Ochoa smiled graciously and shook Catlin's hand. "The pleasure is mutual, Mister . . ."

"Myers. Cat Myers."

"Cat Myers. Your name is familiar to me somehow. Do you live here in Tucson?"

"No, sir," Catlin replied. "Just blew in with the tumbleweeds a few days ago." He swallowed another gulp of Phillips's coffee and gave the businessman's shoulder a friendly clap with his free hand, using more force than was necessary. "Arnet here probably told you all about me."

Clearly amused by Catlin's obnoxious behavior, Ochoa cast a sidelong glance at Phillips's reddening face and chuckled. "You didn't tell me you had a friend from Texas, Arnet."

"He didn't?" Catlin feigned surprise. "Why, we're practically blood brothers." For the first time since he had sat down, Catlin looked Arnet Phillips in the eye, a hard, direct stare that would have cowered a lesser man. "Ain't that a fact, Arnie old boy?"

Phillips glared back at him, his face stiff as a plank, and didn't say a word.

Perhaps detecting the sudden edge to Catlin's voice, Estevan Ochoa picked up his plate and coffee cup and pushed back his chair. "I'll leave the two of you to talk privately," he said, rising. "Mr. Myers, should you need anything during your stay in Tucson, I'm at your service."

Catlin nodded. "Much obliged, sir." He watched Ochoa walk away and turned back to Phillips. "Nothing like politics to make a man friendly. Hey, come to think of it, you've got political ambitions, too, don't you?"

"I did until you showed up," Phillips replied, his voice low and growling. His hands were resting on the table and

17

clenched into tight fists. "What in the hell are you doing here, Myers? And what was that little performance you put on for the mayor? Have you lost your mind? What if someone recognizes you?"

Catlin flashed him a wicked grin. "That's your problem, not mine."

He reached over, selected a chicken leg from Phillips's untouched plate of food, and took a bite. He chewed slowly, savoring the first woman-cooked meal he'd tasted in three months, while Phillips glared at him and silently fumed.

Catlin understood the reason for the man's annoyance and reveled in it. They had originally agreed on a clandestine meeting, for Phillips didn't wish to be seen in public with a known hired killer. He had his good name to protect, after all, and high hopes for a seat in the territorial legislature. Furthermore, Catlin Myers had acquired a reputation for solving his clients' troubles in an efficient and confidential manner. His conduct today was anything but normal.

Phillips leaned toward him. "Well? Did you get the job done or not?"

"I did it." Still eating, Catlin flicked his gaze up to look at him. "Give me one good reason why I shouldn't do the same thing to you."

"If you're worried about getting paid, Myers, I assure you . . ."

"I don't want your damned money. Save it for the funeral of your wife's lover."

Phillips cast a cautious look around him to make sure no one had heard the remark and drew away, tipping his chair back. He drummed the fingers of his right hand on the table and stared at Catlin with sudden apprehension.

"You know."

"Yeah, I know." Catlin pitched the chicken bone into his

plate. "And before I get done with you, so will everybody else."

Not giving Phillips time to react or say a word, Catlin hooked his toe around one of the back legs of the man's chair and gave it a hard, quick jerk. It was an impulsive move that caught Arnet Phillips wholly unprepared and sent him toppling over backwards, chair and all. Phillips was heavyset, and when he hit Mother Earth, everyone in the restaurant seemed to feel the concussion. A shocked silence spread across the room as all eyes turned to look at him.

His face red and puffed with anger, Phillips swore at Catlin and untangled himself from his broken chair. He was halfway to his feet when Catlin rose, grasped him by the hair, and smashed his face against his lifted knee with brutal force. Across the room, a woman shrieked as blood spurted from the man's broken nose and lips.

"That's for lying to me," Catlin said, and still holding Phillips by the hair, he sank his fist into his stomach and threw him back to the dirt floor. "And that's for wasting my time."

Moaning softly, Phillips rolled over onto his side, his body curled in agony. Estevan Ochoa knelt beside his friend and offered him a handkerchief.

Catlin slipped Inez Phillips's love letter from his back pocket, spread it out flat on the table, and stabbed it with a fork, pinning it down. "I didn't take this job so's I could solve your wife troubles," he said to Phillips. "Now an innocent man's dead, and you're just as guilty for that as I am."

"You'll pay for this," Phillips gasped.

Catlin nodded. "We both will."

He turned and headed for the door. Before he had taken five steps, a small crowd of men had already gathered at the table to read Inez's letter.

At the door, Mrs. Wallen, the Shoo Fly's proprietor, shot him a disapproving look.

He reached into his pocket. "I can pay you for that busted chair."

"All I want you to do is leave," she said. "This is a peaceful establishment, Mister. If you want a barroom brawl, go to the Quartz Rock Saloon. I'm sure they'd be more than happy to accommodate you."

"Yes, ma'am." Catlin touched a finger to his hat brim and stepped out into the heat and glare.

At the corner of the building, he paused next to Chico and glanced up and down the dusty street. Except for a passing water wagon, the town was sleepy and still. A scantily clad whore lounged in the doorway of the cantina across the street, fanning herself and wiping the sweat from between her breasts.

Catlin watched the woman and sucked the chicken from his teeth and thought about another woman who waited for him in El Paso. He felt a deep weariness settle over him and again experienced that strange, empty sadness of the day before. He had a sudden yearning to go home. Catlin Myers was a Texas boy, and he missed his native land. He missed that woman in El Paso.

"She's *muy hermosa,* that one. And willing."

At the sound of the man's voice, Catlin dropped his hand to the butt of his revolver and turned to find that it was the same Mexican who had been loitering here when he first arrived.

He gave Catlin a knowing look and cut his eyes to the saloon girl. "You like Mexican *señoritas?*"

Catlin studied the man, trying to remember if he'd ever seen him before today and decided he hadn't. Relaxing, he gathered the reins and swung into the saddle.

"I like all *señoritas*."

He reined Chico into the street. Tucson didn't possess anything in the shape of a hotel, which was just as well, for he had no intentions of staying. He had made more enemies in this town than friends, an unhealthy circumstance he generally tried to avoid.

Riding eastward out of Tucson, Catlin braced himself for the long, lonesome ride through Apache country, knowing he'd be lucky if he reached Texas soil with his scalp still intact. He decided he didn't like Arizona. The aversion had been growing in him for some time now, brought on by the mid-July heat no doubt and clinched yesterday by the wrongful death of young Johnny Keaton.

He had left his mark here, and it wasn't a good one.

CHAPTER THREE

Eladio Moreno had seen many things and had met many people in all his years of aimless wandering, and he considered himself a good judge of character. This man who wore the black patch over his left eye was a bad one. Bad clean through to his bones.

Loitering in front of the Shoo Fly, rolling a cigarette, Eladio had watched the man on the bay ride up and dismount at the corner of the building, and he said to himself, This could be him.

Certainly he fit the description. Tall, slim, sandy-haired, early or middle thirties. Good-looking but hard. Very hard. He had a scar on his face, a knife scar that began at his right eyebrow and streaked upward to disappear into his hairline. Judging by his gear, namely the double-cinched saddle and split reins, he was also a Texan.

And there were the guns he carried—a Sharps .50 in the saddle scabbard, a Winchester carbine slung loose to the saddlehorn, a Colt on his hip and another stuffed down the back of his black pants. Slanting across his chest was a bandolier studded with big brass .50 caliber cartridges. The man was a walking arsenal.

From the doorway of the Shoo Fly, Eladio Moreno watched in silence as the gunman publicly humiliated one of Tucson's most influential citizens, ate his dinner, and left him bleeding on the floor, and he envied him. He envied any man who showed no fear, for when sober, fear was Eladio Moreno's constant companion.

Now, watching the horseman ride out of Tucson, he was certain that this one-eyed gringo was the man for whom he had been searching. Fear stood behind him and whispered urgent warnings in his ear.

At sound of footsteps, Eladio turned, and he saw Arnet Phillips stagger out of the restaurant and into the street. Swaying slightly, the businessman shaded his eyes and squinted at the horse and rider in the distance.

"He has gone," Eladio said, his voice soft and laden with a thick Spanish accent.

Frowning, Phillips turned to look at him. Blood still oozed from his nostrils and lips. His suitcoat and silk cravat were rumpled.

"Did he say anything to you? Where he's going?"

Eladio shrugged. "He say he likes *señoritas.*"

"What did he mean by that? Is he headed for a whorehouse or something?"

"No, I don' think so." Eladio pushed away from the wall and stepped into the street to stand beside Phillips. "I think he has a woman in El Paso. Me, I think he will go there maybe."

Phillips studied him with sudden interest. "You know Catlin Myers?"

The name sent a chill through Eladio's body. Fear tapped him on the shoulder.

He drew a deep breath. "*Si,* I know of him." He cast a furtive glance at Phillips. "I plan to kill him."

Phillips looked him up and down, taking in the shabby clothes, the slumped posture, and appeared skeptical.

"Is there any particular reason why you want to kill him," he asked, "or do you just not like his looks?"

"It's a matter of . . . How do you call it? Honor?"

"I see." Phillips turned his back, dismissing him, and pressed his handkerchief beneath his swollen nose. He started to walk away. "I'd like to shake the hand of the man who kills that son of a bitch," he mumbled. "Hell, I'd give him half of everything I own."

"*Señor.*" Eladio took a step forward, waited for Phillips to turn and look at him. "*Señor,* do you mean what you say?"

Phillips squinted at him, impatient. "What?"

"I'll kill him. I'll kill Cat Myers."

Phillips approached him, stopped two feet away, and gave him a long, searching look. Eladio's quick eyes darted up and down from the man's face to the ground, his gaze shifting and bouncing.

Reaching into a pocket of his trousers, Phillips drew forth a handful of change. He held the silver and gold coins in his open palm, letting them wink in the bright sunlight, and then tossed them at Eladio's feet.

"There's more where that came from," he said quietly. "You bring me Cat Myers's filthy scalp, prove to me he's dead, and I'll give you anything you want. I'll make you a rich man."

Without waiting for Eladio's response, Arnet Phillips turned and walked away, leaving him standing alone in the middle of the street.

His heart pounding, Eladio stooped and picked up the dusty coins, wiping each one on the front of his shirt and counting. There were sixty-two dollars and fifty cents, more money than he had held in his hand all at once in a very long time, and he counted them again to make sure.

Gripping the coins in his fist, he glanced toward the cantina across the street. He was tempted to go there. It had been many weeks since he had tasted anything stronger than alkali water. He could buy a whole bottle of tequila, spend the night with the whore, maybe give her a dollar tip if she pleased him . . .

Thinking about the prostitute made him remember his

wife in El Paso. It was because of her that he was here in Arizona. Everything was her fault.

Eladio remembered again the painful reunion with his wife two months ago. It had been ten years since he had seen Zella. Ten long, lonely years. Many times, he had wished to return to her, beg for forgiveness, promise to change his ways and be a good husband to her, but he was afraid, afraid of rejection. His reasons for leaving in the first place had been foolish, for she was a good woman and beautiful. Perhaps, he thought, that was the problem; he couldn't measure up to her standards.

Finally, homesick for El Paso and flat broke, Eladio had been forced to go back. His reception had not been a pleasant one. Zella at first had seemed shocked that he was even alive, then angry, and he remembered the contempt in her eyes, the stinging insults she had flung at him when he tried to apologize. He wasn't sure now what he had expected from his wife. He had, after all, abandoned her.

It was his discovery of Zella's infidelity that had saved Eladio Moreno from total disgrace. It provided him with an excuse for his own failings and gave him a chance to redeem himself. He could say to people, See? See what I have to put up with? Now I will be forced to kill a man all because I have a whore for a wife.

Eladio thought about the man, Cat Myers. That Zella had dared to share their bed with this gringo made him tremble with indignation and jealousy. He would show her! He would prove to her that he was the better man and then she would plead for his forgiveness!

His mind made up, Eladio strode toward his horse and stuffed the coins into his pocket. There was more money where that came from, Phillips had promised. Much more.

All he had to do was kill Cat Myers.

CHAPTER FOUR

El Paso, Texas:* August 8, 1877

"This town consists of two classes of men," Judge Howard proclaimed. "Ignorant rabble and spineless cowards. You and I, of course, being the rare exceptions."

Catlin Myers's gaze flicked up from the month old Santa Fe newspaper he had been trying to read for the past twenty minutes to look at Charles H. Howard, District Judge. Would the man ever shut up?

They were seated across from each other at a table in a dingy saloon on West Overland Street. When Catlin tossed off his drink, Howard motioned to the bartender to refill his empty glass.

"I tell you, Myers, something's got to be done. The Army won't lift a finger, and the Texas Rangers are always too damned busy. What does that leave me with? A handful of Americans to fight off a horde of border thieves and cutthroats."

"How about the sheriff?" Catlin ventured and turned to the *New Mexican*'s editorial page.

"The sheriff?" Howard smirked. "He wouldn't make a

---

* In 1877, the name El Paso referred to present-day Ciudad Juárez on the Mexican side of the Rio Grande. Until 1888, El Paso, Texas, was known as Franklin. The author has taken some historical liberty in this instance, however, and has used the name that is most familiar.

bump on a lawman's butt."

Catlin glanced up from his paper again, a cynical smile curving one corner of his mouth. "Maybe he figures you're a border thief yourself."

The judge frowned and rubbed a thick forefinger back and forth across his lower lip. "Don't be absurd. The Salt Lakes belong to me. Any man, woman, or child caught taking salt from my property without paying for it is stealing, pure and simple." Howard rested an arm on the table and leaned toward Catlin. "If Sheriff Kerber won't enforce the law, then by God, I will."

"You've got salt on the brain, Judge."

"Me and everyone else. Everyone, that is, but you."

Catlin sighed wearily, for he knew where this conversation was leading.

The Salt Lakes lay in the desert at the base of the Guadalupe Mountains one hundred ten miles from El Paso. Charles Howard, a man of great courage and little scruple, had recently laid claim to the deposits and was now attempting to levy a fee for gathering salt there. Mexican settlers on both sides of the Rio Grande who had obtained free salt from these lakes for generations were indignant over Judge Howard's new business venture.

Fueled by dirty politics, greed, and the natural distrust existing between the Mexicans and the Americans along the border, the Salt War was heating up rapidly and feeling was running high. Catlin had been home only two weeks and was already looked upon with suspicion by both factions for failing to take sides.

Folding his newspaper in half, Catlin dropped it on the table and glanced out the window, seeing the late afternoon shadows stretching longer and longer. He downed his third shot of whiskey and watched in amusement as Charles

Howard snapped his fingers at the bartender.

"Trying to get me drunk, Judge?"

Howard blew out his breath in a gust and leaned back in his chair, tugging at his collar and necktie. "What I'm trying to do is loosen that infernal tongue of yours."

Catlin nodded. "Find out which side of the fence I'm on?"

"Precisely."

"I'm neutral."

Howard scowled. "It doesn't work that way, Myers. If you're not for me, you're against me. Besides, I have a job to offer you," he said and lowered his voice. "There are two men here in El Paso—Cardis and Borajo—who are responsible for the Mexican uprising. If these two people were to . . . disappear, my worries would be over. Do you catch my drift?"

"I do," Catlin replied, "and I'm not interested."

"Damn it all!" Howard shook his head, at a loss. "It's the Moreno woman, isn't it? She's turned you against me."

"I promised Zella I'd stay out of it," Catlin admitted, though this was only part of the reason for his reluctance to become involved. He had an idea Charles Howard was as much to blame for the Mexican insurrection as were the two men he wanted killed.

"Oh, well," Howard grumbled. "I doubt I could afford your price anyway."

Catlin's curiosity was piqued. "You know what I am, what I do," he said. "How did you find out?"

Howard smiled. "Your guns, your fancy saddle gear, the expensive trinkets you buy Zella Moreno. You're no thirty-a-month cowpoke. Then you stay gone for three and four months at a stretch. On business, you say." He tapped his temple. "It doesn't take a genius to figure out you're either a bank robber or a gun for hire. I chose the latter."

"Why?"

"Call it an educated guess." Howard left some coins on the table to pay for their drinks, scraped his chair back, and stood up. "Killing's your life's work, Myers. You'll get drawn into this fight sooner or later. I just hope you're on my side when the shooting starts."

Catlin watched Charles Howard leave and thought about what he had said. He supposed he was right. The dispute over the Salt Lakes would touch everyone in El Paso before it was settled.

With the approach of evening, men began to trickle into the saloon, and the bartender lit the wall lamps. Catlin took a final drag on his cigarette, dropped the butt on the floor, and glanced toward the crude plank bar where a few men had gathered to drink and talk. Off to himself at one end of the bar was a Mexican patron Catlin hadn't noticed until now. Dirty, haggard, and unshaven, he looked as if he had been riding the trail for many days.

The Mexican bought tequila, flashing a great deal of coin in the process, and drank straight from the bottle. Liquor dribbled from the corners of his mouth, leaving muddy trails down his neck to his collar. Wiping his mouth on his sleeve, he shifted around and looked Catlin square in the eye.

Their gazes held briefly, long enough for Catlin to glimpse an expression of hatred cross the Mexican's face before he averted his eyes and turned back to the bar. Catlin noticed then the double-barreled shotgun on the man's right hip, looped to his belt. Both the barrels and the stock had been sawed off so that it wasn't much larger than a revolver.

Without drawing attention to himself, Catlin reached down and casually slipped the rawhide thong from the grip of his holstered sidearm. He recognized the man at the bar, or thought he did, remembered him from somewhere. But who was he?

Not fond of surprises, he considered forcing the issue,

maybe walk up to the Mexican, friendly-like, and ask him whether or not they'd met before, but decided against it. Judging by the way he was working on that bottle of tequila, he'd be down to the worm pretty soon and mean drunk.

"To hell with it," Catlin muttered, and he rose and left the smoky saloon, turning up the street toward home.

He and three other El Pasoans with money to burn had planned to meet at the store of E. Schutz and Brother for a private game of poker. Catlin, however, felt out of sorts tonight and decided a quiet evening alone with Zella might better serve to ease his restless mind.

The town lay tranquil beneath a reddening sky, the sun gone now, bright stars popping out one by one. The nearby Franklin Mountains provided a dark, rugged backdrop to the cluster of adobes hugging the banks of the Rio Grande.

But for the bullet-riddled posted notices announcing Charles Howard's ownership of the Salt Lakes, the atmosphere was peaceful, giving no indication of the trouble sure to come.

Catlin lived with Zella Moreno on a nameless side street just south and east of the town plaza and El Paso's main business district. They had few neighbors, the street consisting mostly of vacant lots with gardens and small fruit trees, and nearby their house ran one of the several irrigation channels that crisscrossed the town. A large cottonwood shaded the front yard.

Though larger than the many poorer dwellings in El Paso, the house was nondescript, a simple Mexican adobe with four rooms and a portal. Within its walls, however, was a whole other world.

Inside were floors of native stone, Navajo rugs, Mexican pottery, and fine Victorian furniture upholstered with horsehair and made of elegantly carved black walnut. All of this together created an odd mix of cultures and traditions, a reflection of the Southwest itself and an example of Zella's eclectic taste. Freighting the furniture all the way from St. Louis by wagontrain had proved to be an expensive endeavor, and Catlin was one of the few men in El Paso who could afford to do it.

The furniture was still the object of much gossip among their friends and neighbors, not all of it kind. Some felt they were living too high, not to mention living in sin, and refused to have anything to do with either of them. Most, like Charles Howard, merely wondered where the money came from.

Catlin and Zella ignored the speculation and the occasional disapproving glance they received while walking down the street together. They minded their own business and expected others to do the same.

When Catlin arrived home there was a light burning in the parlor, and he found Zella busily sweeping the floor. Startled, she looked up as he was hanging his hat on the hook by the door and passed the back of her hand across her forehead.

"What happened to the poker game?"

He shrugged. "Wasn't in the mood."

"You haven't been in the mood for much of anything lately," she observed. "Are you hungry? We have tacos."

"Sounds good."

Glancing around the room, he noticed the books scattered on the sofa and in one of the chairs, the paper trash on the floor, and didn't have to ask Zella how she'd spent the afternoon. For the past few months, she had been teaching six or seven of the neighborhood Mexican children how to read and write and speak proper English. They dropped by every other day or so.

This was, he knew, her way of filling the void left ten years ago by the deaths of her own children, victims of smallpox, two boys and a girl laid to rest in the El Paso cemetery. Zella visited them faithfully each Sunday and adorned their graves with wild desert flowers. Catlin never accompanied her on these Sunday morning outings, sensing she wanted to be alone with her memories.

"How'd the lesson go?" he asked.

"Good," she said and smiled. "Some are quick, some are slow, but they all work hard, and that's all I ask of them."

Catlin stood out of the way by the door and watched her sweep. "I got suspended from school when I was eight years old. Did I ever tell you about that?"

"No, but it doesn't surprise me. What did you do?"

"Dipped Janie Bowen's pigtails in an inkwell." He flashed her a roguish grin. "I always did favor black-haired women."

"You're terrible," she said, though he knew the remark pleased her.

He held the dustpan for her and dumped the trash into a waste basket. "Are we the happy homemakers, or what?"

Something in his tone of voice, a hint of wry sarcasm, made Zella look up at him. "Catlin, what's wrong?"

"Nothing."

"Don't lie to me." She followed him into the bedroom. "Ever since you came home, you've talked more in your sleep than you have to me. I'm tired of it."

Catlin took off his black leather vest, unbuckled his gunbelt, and draped them over the back of a chair. His gaze settled momentarily on the statuette of the Virgin Mary sitting atop the chiffonier near their bed. Sometimes after making love to Zella, he would lie awake in the darkness and imagine the Virgin's sorrowful eyes looking down on him, watching, always watching. Even now, he could almost feel her disapproval.

He turned to Zella. "I've been doing some thinking," he said.

"About what?"

"How would you like to leave El Paso for a while?" Stepping toward her, he pulled her into his arms and held her close, resting his forehead against hers. "Maybe go back East, like to Chicago, New York, or Boston, see the sights, meet new people."

"Why?"

"Why not?" He bent his head down and kissed her, taking his time about it, and murmured, "We need a change of scenery."

Zella frowned. "Something went wrong in Arizona, didn't it?"

"Now what gives you an idea like that?"

"I know you. You can't run away from your problems, *querido*."

Avoiding her searching gaze, Catlin played with her hair, twisting a long, blue-black strand around his forefinger. He had never been able to hide much from Zella Moreno. She read him with the same ease with which she read all those novels and books of poetry cluttering the parlor.

Catlin had every intention of telling her about the unfortunate tragedy in Tucson but wasn't ready to talk about it just yet. Zella hated his work, hated his long absences, and he dreaded her reaction. Furthermore, the killing of Johnny Keaton had forced him to stop and take a long, hard look at himself and the man he had become, and he wasn't so sure he liked the view. He needed time to think.

"I'd like for us to stay out of El Paso until this Salt Lakes mess blows over," he said finally. "You don't want me getting mixed up in it, do you?"

"No. No, I don't." She smiled at him in understanding.

"How soon can we leave?"

"How soon can you get your bags packed?"

"By tomorrow morning. Where will we . . ."

Catlin suddenly touched a finger to her lips, silencing her, and looked toward the bedroom door.

"Did you hear something?" he whispered.

She stared up at him. "No."

Moving away from her, Catlin picked up his gunbelt, slid the Colt from its holster, and glanced at Zella as he sidled toward the open doorway.

"Wait here."

CHAPTER FIVE

Hooking his thumb over the hammer of his .45, Catlin cocked it before gliding soundlessly through the door to the parlor. Except for the soft flutter of a moth bouncing against the lamp's glass chimney, the house was silent. Yet Catlin was almost certain he had heard something, felt something, a sixth sense telling him they were not alone.

Walking carefully so the spurs on his boots wouldn't jingle, he crossed the living room and paused just to the side of the door leading into the kitchen. He listened a moment, his back hugging the wall, gun muzzle lifted. There was no sound.

Catlin cast a quick peek around the corner. The light from the parlor lamp spilled into the kitchen, and in the dim glow, he didn't notice anything out of kilter. Perhaps he had been mistaken.

Relaxing a little, Catlin gripped the door jamb with his free hand and was about to enter the kitchen when a tremendous roar sent him hurtling backwards, away from the open doorway. Stray fragments of buckshot seared the left side of his face and pelted his arm. He dropped to one knee and threw four blind shots into the kitchen, his ears full of the hard blasts of gunfire and Zella's screams.

When several seconds passed and no one returned fire, he stole into the kitchen, body crouched low. Gunsmoke and dust filled his nostrils. Sliding his left hand along the wall, he felt where buckshot from the intruder's shotgun had ravaged a large area to one side of the doorway. Crumbling adobe dribbled to the floor.

Catlin found the room empty, the back door gaping open. Wary, his muscles tensed, he peered outside. Night was not fully upon them as of yet, and he could see the small corral and shed out back, his horse standing with his head over the top rail, staring toward the east side of the house. From that direction, Catlin heard a hollow clink, the sound a man's boot might make striking against an empty tin can. He slipped out the door and edged along the back wall.

Roused by the shooting, dogs howled and barked, and somewhere a man called out in Spanish, his voice lifting in a question. Catlin ignored the ruckus. At the corner, his gaze swept the vacant lot to the east, and he was surprised when he didn't see anyone. That meant one of two things: The shooter had either sprouted wings, or he had headed for the street. How else could he have disappeared so quickly?

Swearing under his breath, Catlin sprinted along the side of the house to the front yard, still cautious but hurrying, tired of running in circles. What if this man, whoever he was, had decided to go back inside? Zella wouldn't be expecting him to return. And she was alone.

The front door was ajar. Stepping beneath the portal's deep shadow, Catlin edged toward an open window and peered inside it at the parlor.

The tall lamp on the center-table was still burning, the gray moth still fluttering in its soft yellow light. Beyond it in a corner of the room stood Zella Moreno.

They were partly concealed from Catlin's view by a high-backed chair, but he could see the man behind her, his forearm curled around her throat, shotgun pressed to her right temple. The sawed-off barrels glinted in the light whenever he shifted his weight. The man's features were lost in shadow, but the straw sombrero hanging down his back by the chin strap around his neck told Catlin he was probably Mexican. Could it be the same man he had seen in the saloon earlier?

"Cat Myers! Come here, you dirty *cabrón!*" The Mexican's voice sounded thick, his words slurred. "Show your face, Myers!"

Catlin hesitated, not sure what to do and afraid for Zella. He suddenly remembered his gunbelt was in the bedroom. That left him with only the two rounds still in his gun. He'd better make them count . . . if he got the chance.

The Mexican rested his head against the wall, face tilted up, and shouted, "Come on, *Gato!* Come see the happy surprise I have for you!"

Catlin realized he had little choice in the matter. From his position in the corner, the Mexican had a clear view of all the windows and doors, so getting the drop on him was out of the question. It was the cocked scattergun aimed at Zella's head, however, that convinced him.

Drawing a deep breath, he swung the door open and stepped into the parlor.

At his entrance, the Mexican's hold on Zella's throat tightened, and he stared at Catlin with wide eyes, clearly shocked, as if he hadn't expected his invitation to be accepted so quickly, if at all. His face appeared taut in the lamplight, the skin stretched across bone like hide on a drum.

"You're bleeding, *Gato*. Next time maybe I don't miss." His gaze dropped down to the gun in Catlin's hand. "Throw your *pistola* outside and shut the door."

Catlin studied him momentarily, making sure he was, indeed, the man he'd seen in the saloon and said, "You don't like me much, do you?"

"Throw your gun down! Do it now!"

"Why? Are you afraid?"

Sweat beaded the Mexican's forehead, and Catlin could hear the uneven hiss of his breath. Drunk he might be, but he was scared, too, and Catlin got the feeling that breaking into people's houses wasn't his favorite pastime. It would, he hoped, make this situation easier for him to handle.

Standing with the .45 dangling muzzle-down at his side, Catlin glanced casually around the room, appearing relaxed. His gaze touched Zella. Her face was unnaturally pale, her dark eyes fixed on him and filled with dread. She clutched the arm around her neck with white-knuckled fingers.

"Tell you what," Catlin said. "You let Zella go, and we'll talk."

"No, I don' think so. I don' think I like that idea." The Mexican thumbed back the other hammer on his shotgun, both barrels cocked now. "How about you do like I say, throw your gun outside." He paused, wetting his lips with quick darts of his tongue. "Do like I say, or I blow off her head. Uh? Sound good?"

Zella squeezed her eyes shut.

Exhaling slowly, Catlin clicked the Colt's hammer forward, turned, and pitched the weapon outside. He kicked the door shut with his foot and saw both Zella and her captor flinch at the loud slam.

"I'm unarmed," he said. "You can stop hiding behind her skirt."

The Mexican made no move to release Zella, and Catlin shook his head in disgust. He took a step toward them, stopped. "Who are you? What do you want?"

The Mexican smiled. "Ah, now we get somewhere." He pressed his mouth close to Zella's ear. "Tell him who I am, *puta*. Tell him about us."

Zella's eyes cut to the side to look at him. "This is your

38

show," she said in a low voice. "Tell him yourself."

Angered by her words, he changed his hold on her, gripping her throat with his hand, fingers digging into her flesh. She gasped for air and clawed at his hand.

"Tell him who I am!" He thrust the shotgun's stubby barrels against the side of her head. *"¡Hable!"*

"No!" she screamed. "You're nobody!"

Catlin took another step toward them, feeling the matter was slipping out of his hands, out of control. The Mexican saw his movement and swung the shotgun to bear on him.

"Tell him, Zella, or I kill him now!"

"Eladio, *por favor* . . ."

"Say it!"

"Eladio . . ."

"Louder!"

"Eladio Moreno!"

"Who am I, Zella?"

"My husband." She broke down, sobbing. "You're my husband."

The revelation left Catlin with a sick feeling in the pit of his stomach. Shocked, he looked from Zella to the grimy, weak-jawed face of Eladio Moreno and tried to imagine these two as husband and wife, tried to imagine Eladio Moreno as the father of Zella's three children.

It suddenly came to Catlin where he had first seen this man and why he had seemed familiar to him in the saloon.

"You were in Tucson," he said softly and drew closer, one slow step, then another, head canted a little to the side. "You knew who I was. You had a chance to kill me. Why didn't you?" The deadly black bores of Moreno's shotgun stared Catlin in the face, almost within arm's reach now. "Isn't that what you want? To kill the gringo who stole your woman?" One more step.

"Stop!" The whites of Moreno's eyes flashed wildly. "Don't come no closer!"

Catlin smiled, eyebrows lifting in mock surprise. "What's wrong, Moreno? What are you afraid of? You've got the gun, not me."

He glanced at Zella, saw her watching him, her face tensed and still. She was ready for whatever happened.

"Have you ever killed a man, Moreno?"

Eladio Moreno stared at him, lips pulled back from his teeth in a pained grimace. His body trembled.

"You kill a man from a distance," Catlin said, "and it's not so bad." He eased forward, the shotgun scarcely two feet from the tip of his nose. The smile still lingered in his one eye and on his lips. "Up close now—it can get pretty nasty, 'specially with that ten-gauge you got pointed at me." He gave a soft, easy laugh. "Back home, there's some folks don't think I've got any brains. Hell, my brains'll be splattered all over this room pretty soon . . . the instant you pull the trigger."

"I never killed nobody," Moreno whispered. "I never . . ."

"You'll smell me," Catlin continued. "The stink of blood and raw meat. It's a smell that'll stick in your nose forever."

Moreno swallowed noisily in the silence that followed Catlin's words. He let the shotgun barrels drop a little, his resolve slipping, while the fingers of his left hand tap-danced nervously along the smooth curve of Zella's throat. Catlin made his move.

He struck out viciously, lightning swift, grasping the shotgun in both hands, jerking it to the side just as it exploded. Gunpowder stung his face, and he lost his hold on the barrel. Across the room, a wall mirror shattered into a million pieces, the fragments showering to the floor with a tinkly crash.

Releasing Zella, Moreno swung the empty gun at Catlin's head. Catlin ducked the blow, managing at the same time to get a grip on the barrel again, and he wrenched it out of Moreno's hands and flung it aside.

Moreno stood half-crouched, cornered. Panic filled his eyes as Catlin moved in.

"You just bought yourself seven years of bad luck," Catlin said and backhanded him across the face.

The solid slap almost broke Moreno's neck. He fell against the wall, stunned, bloody saliva stringing from his open mouth. Grabbing the front of his shirt, Catlin straightened him up and bashed his head against the wall a few times to get his attention, and then punched him in the gut. Air whooshed from Moreno's lungs, his soured breath steaming Catlin's face.

Moreno doubled over, bracing himself with one hand on Zella's small parlor desk, breath huffing. He cut his eyes up to look at Catlin.

"Hijo de puta."

He took hold of the desk with both hands and flung it in Catlin's direction.

A corner of the desk struck Catlin in the thigh, staggering him, and Moreno made a frantic dash for the door. Ignoring the pain in his leg, Catlin hurdled the center-table to cut him off and dove into him from behind. The two men landed heavily on the sofa, Catlin on top, and tumbled off it punching and kicking to the floor.

A shard of broken mirror clutched in his right hand, Moreno stabbed at Catlin, missed, stabbed again and sliced him across the chest. Catlin gripped the man's wrist. Teeth gritted, he squeezed the weak point at the base of Moreno's hand with his thumb and forefinger, gaze fixed on the razor-edged shard pointed his way. Moreno groaned in pain and finally dropped the shard, and Catlin knocked it out of his reach.

Jabbing Moreno in the face with his elbow, he raised himself to his knees, straddling the man, pinning his back to the floor. He balled up a fist and smashed it into Moreno's sweaty face.

Catlin pounded away at Moreno, swift, brutal, his darkly tanned face drawn hard with rage. He didn't feel Zella's hands gripping his shoulders as she struggled to pull him off her husband, didn't hear her pleading voice. Moreno's body went limp beneath him like a puppet whose strings had been cut. Catlin drove his fist into the unconscious man's nose.

"Myers! That's enough! Myers!"

Two pairs of rough hands dragged Catlin off Moreno's body and held him down.

"Myers, damn it, cool off!"

Surprised, Catlin gazed up into the faces of Sheriff Kerber and Charles Howard.

"Looks like somebody butchered a shoat," Howard commented, eyeing the blood spatters on the floor.

Breathing hard, Catlin passed the back of his hand across his mouth. "Let me up," he gasped.

The sheriff nodded at Howard, and they let him go. Catlin staggered to his feet.

"You all right?" Kerber asked.

Catlin waved a hand toward Eladio Moreno. "Drag him out of here, will you?"

"All the way to jail," Kerber said, and he stepped over the Mexican's prone figure. "Did he break in?"

Catlin nodded and touched his fingers to the gash on his chest, only now beginning to feel the raw pain of his wounds.

Howard grinned at him. "I guess he'll think twice before bothering you again."

The sheriff grasped Moreno beneath his arms, Judge

Howard grabbed his feet, and they carried him outside where a crowd of people were gathered and quietly talking. Zella closed the door behind them, turned, and sagged against it to look at Catlin.

He stood in the middle of the disarranged room, arms hanging at his sides, bloody shirt sticking wetly to his chest and belly. A worried frown clouded Zella's face as she crossed the room to him and started to unbutton his shirt.

He struck her hands away, green eye blazing. "Don't touch me."

Startled, Zella flinched and glanced up at him. "Catlin, you're hurt. Let me help you."

"Go help your husband," he said angrily.

"Catlin, I . . ."

"You lied to me." He spit the words. "You told me he was dead."

"How was I to know he wasn't? Catlin, he abandoned me years ago! I never heard from him again. It wasn't until . . ." Her voice faltered.

"It wasn't until what?"

She closed her eyes a moment and bowed her head.

"Zella?"

"He came to El Paso two, almost three months ago," she confessed. "Not long after you left for Arizona. All these years . . ." She shook her head, drawing a weary breath. "He found out about you and me. We had a terrible argument. He told me he'd kill you and left."

Catlin studied her, letting it all soak in, mulling it over in his mind. "So what you're saying," he began and stopped. His voice sounded strained. He started over, too loudly this time. "So what you're saying is you knew as of three months ago he was alive but still didn't tell me!"

She lifted her hand to his face, fingers caressing his blood-

43

smeared cheek. "I was afraid to tell you. I was afraid I'd lose you."

"What if someday I'd asked you to marry me? What would you have done then?"

Zella's lips parted, and for a moment she was speechless. "I didn't . . . I never thought you'd ask me, Catlin."

"Yeah, well, that's your problem. You didn't think."

Catlin turned away from her and limped into the bedroom. He gathered his few personal belongings—guns, saddlebags, canteen—forgetting in his turmoil that the house itself was his, and brushed past Zella without looking at her. She caught him by the arm.

"Please don't go. We can work this out."

He met her gaze. "It's already worked out, Zella. Can't you see that?"

CHAPTER SIX

Catlin saddled Chico in the dark. He yanked the latigo straps hard and tight, taking his frustrations out on the horse, and Chico repaid his rough treatment by knocking him for a loop the instant his butt hit the saddle. Catlin guessed he should have expected it. Chico hadn't been ridden in several days and was ready to work out his kinks.

Dusting off, Catlin climbed back aboard and spent the better part of thirty seconds getting his brains joggled. The bay's hooves hammered the hard-packed ground, each buck ending in a solid, jarring jolt that rattled Catlin's teeth and made his nose bleed again.

Chico finally simmered down and stood motionless in the center of the corral amid a swirl of dust.

"You finished?"

The bay swivelled an ear toward him, and Catlin reined him out of the corral gate and past the house.

There were a couple of places to spend the night in El Paso if a man suddenly found himself homeless, the best being the St. Charles Hotel on the corner of El Paso and Overland streets. Or if he was broke as well as homeless, he might bed down in the livery stable.

Neither choice appealed to Catlin. There was always a number of men loitering at the St. Charles, and his blood-soaked appearance would draw attention. He'd be bombarded with questions, and he'd have to muster up his smart-ass grin and wisecrack his way through the lobby while evading their questions.

But not tonight. He wasn't up to it.

Catlin rode southward down Durango Street. The road had been pulverized to fine powder by many hooves. Nearing the river, he breathed in the cool, damp air and listened to the guitar music. A fandango was in full swing down on the north bank.

Durango Street ended in a cul-de-sac less than a hundred yards from the river, and near the dead-end was a tiny jacal where Catlin sometimes spent the night, following an argument with Zella. The jacal belonged to a saloon whore named Hattie Diller. While Catlin wasn't one of Hattie's customers, her house afforded him the privacy and solitude he desired during his infrequent fits of anger.

He dismounted in front of the jacal, led Chico to a patch of dry grass, and hobbled his front legs so he wouldn't wander too far. In the short time Catlin had lived in El Paso, Chico had been stolen twice. Each time, the bay gelding had mysteriously reappeared, trailing his lead rope. It seemed he didn't take to his new owners and decided to come home.

Catlin shouldered his saddle and was walking toward the jacal when the door creaked open and lantern light splashed across him. Hattie Diller filled the doorway and lifted her lantern higher.

"Is that a stray cat I hear?" she called.

"Yeah, it's me."

"You and Zella must've had a lover's quarrel."

"Something like that." Catlin stepped past her into the house and dumped his gear on the floor. "Why aren't you at work?" he asked, for Hattie seldom got home before three or four in the morning.

"My night off." She set the lantern on the kitchen table and turned to look at him. "Gosh a'mighty," she exclaimed.

"What happened to you?"

"Nothing a strong shot of whiskey wouldn't cure."

"Looks to me like you already got a shot of something," she said, and grasping him by the chin, she tilted his face toward the light. A pellet of buckshot had seared his left cheekbone, and three more were embedded in the muscle of his upper arm. "Buckshot?"

"Just a spattering."

"You were lucky," Hattie remarked. "I seen a man drop dead once when a piece of shot stuck in his heart. And that was birdshot." She planted her hands on her mighty hips and regarded Catlin with disapproval. "I guess you expect me to dig them chunks of lead out of your hide, eh? Haul and heat your bath water, mend your torn shirt. I always did say a man was about as helpless as a newborn baby."

"All I want is a bottle of whiskey."

"This ain't a damned saloon," Hattie grumbled, but she lumbered over to the cupboard where there was quite a collection of liquor, all of it filched from the saloon in which she worked. She selected a quart bottle of hundred proof whiskey. "Your usual," she said and tossed it to him. "Two dollars."

He paid her and tucked the bottle under his arm. "You still rent out that back room?"

"Yeah. Cost you fifty cents for one night. Five-fifty if you want me, too."

Catlin dug a half-dollar from his pocket and dropped it into her open palm.

Hattie accepted his rejection with grace. "You don't know what you're missing, sugar. Well, the bed ain't made up. You wait here and keep out of my way."

She disappeared into the back room, a robust, big-boned woman stuffed into an old gingham dress at least one size too small. Like the dress, Hattie Diller was a bit frayed around the edges, a result of time and wear, but most of her customers were too drunk to notice. Catlin figured before the night was over, he wouldn't notice either. He popped the cork from the bottle of whiskey, raised it to his lips, and swallowed a long, hot swig.

"Room's all yours," Hattie announced.

The whiskey hit Catlin's empty stomach like a ball of fire. He hissed through his teeth and walked into the back room, slapping Hattie on the rump as he passed by her. Cackling, she shut the door and left him alone.

Catlin glanced around him, took another drink. While the room in front was Hattie Diller's combination kitchen-bedroom, this back room was reserved strictly for boarders. A plain, narrow bed pushed against the wall filled one corner, and two whiskey barrels turned upside down served as tables: one next to the bed to hold the oil lamp and another across the room holding a chipped wash basin. A small window looked out on the alley behind the jacal.

Hattie kept the room clean—as clean as one could expect of a house with dirt floors and a roof made of straw and mud—and she kept a sharp lookout for bedbugs.

Catlin crossed the room and inspected his face in the small mirror hanging above the wash basin. He had managed to duck most of Eladio Moreno's sluggish punches, but at least two had found their marks, leaving him with a fat lip and a sore nose. The gash across his chest and the buckshot wounds were more serious, however, and needed tending, yet Catlin put it off.

He slipped the eyepatch from his left eye, dropped it on the upturned barrel, and leaned closer to the mirror, studying himself critically. The pupil of his blind eye was abnormally large, the once green iris appeared murky, and he had noticed in the past year that the eyelid was beginning to droop.

It had happened a little over two years ago in Fort Griffin, Texas. A big-footed cowboy kicked him in the eyeball during a brawl, and Catlin hadn't seen daylight out of it since. A trifle vain, he was bothered almost as much by the disfigurement as he was by his loss of sight and chose to hide it with the patch.

Tonight, though, he didn't care much one way or the other. He looked bad, felt bad, smelled bad, too, he guessed, with all the blood and the sweat, but made no move to clean up. Pulling the shirt tail from his pants, he unbuttoned, tossed the bloody shirt on the floor, and sat down. The bed creaked beneath his weight.

Normally quick to react and quick to recover, Catlin's mind was working at a snail's crawl tonight. The full impact of his loss was only now starting to sink in. Zella Moreno, the one good thing in his life, was his no more, for where she was concerned it was either all or none. He wouldn't share her even in name with another man.

They had been together two years, the longest Catlin had ever stuck with one woman, and he had just recently begun to think they ought to get married. How difficult could it be? True, he'd made her no promises, no declarations of love, but had felt sure that she understood. As it turned out, his only consolation tonight was that he hadn't poured his heart out to her.

Catlin took another pull on the bottle and touched the back of his hand to his lips, thinking, You should've left her a long time ago. He ground his teeth together, brooding, jaw muscles knotting. Crafty bitch. She didn't want you for nothing but the money anyway.

He sprawled out on his back, dusty boots sticking out over the end of the bed, and stared up at the ceiling. Through the open window, he heard crickets chirping in the weeds, and up the street, a pump handle rattled, a door slammed. Life continued even while his own seemed to be floundering.

Time passed. Thoroughly soused by now, Catlin's anger began to sputter and finally burned itself out, only to be replaced by something worse. The depression that had laid hold of him in Arizona had followed him across three hundred miles of desert to Texas. He recalled what Zella had told him, that he couldn't run away from his problems. Perhaps she was right.

Catlin turned over onto his side, drawing his knees up and hugging the whiskey bottle to his chest. He remembered how one man had put an end to problems of a different nature during the war. Both his legs had been blown off by Yank artillery, and rather than go home to his family sporting nubs, he thrust the barrel of his big Dragoon Colt into his mouth and pulled the trigger. So calm, so resigned. Blew his brains out as if it were the most natural thing to do. The incident stuck in Catlin's mind because it was the first time he'd ever seen anyone commit suicide. It wasn't the last.

Catlin had been fifteen years old, a skinny kid from Texas wearing a ragged Confederate uniform and worn out brogans, a kid who should have been at home hoeing his pa's cornfield, or fishing with his brother in the Clear Fork of the Brazos. But farm life was too tame for young Cat Myers.

He enlisted when he was fourteen. Told the recruiting officer he was eighteen, clearly a lie, but they issued him a uniform and a gun anyway because the Confederate Army couldn't be too choosy, and a boy could stop a bullet as easily as a man.

The war still haunted him. Blue and gray ghosts tortured his nights, polluted his dreams. Sometimes he awoke screaming, trembling, and Zella would comfort him while the reek of blood and smoke and human decay lingered in his nostrils, and his ears rang from the thunder of cannonfire.

Tonight, alone in Hattie Diller's stuffy little boarding room, old ghosts came calling.

Bullets and cannonballs plowed the earth around Catlin, men shouted, and the big guns roared. His mouth was full of gunpowder from biting the ends off paper cartridges and so dry he couldn't swallow or even speak.

A little over a hundred yards away, the Union line blazed away at them, and Catlin lifted his musket to his shoulder and fired into the solid wall of soldiers. The smoke of battle filled his vision for an instant, then cleared, blown by a breeze, and he glimpsed his best friend, Brad Gilley, lying on the ground several feet away and frantically tearing at his clothing, searching for the source of the blood that had soaked the entire left side of his jacket and trousers.

Horrified, Catlin dropped his musket and scrambled toward Gilley on hands and knees across the bodies of the dead. A panicked voice pierced his consciousness like a bayonet: "My God, they're flanking us!" and suddenly Catlin's whole regiment was running, yelling, cursing. Brad Gilley turned to look at him, smoke-blackened face pleading, Don't leave me behind, and Catlin reached out to him, almost touched him . . .

Catlin hit the ground hard on his stomach, lay still a moment, and finally rolled over onto his back, moaning. He had fallen out of bed.

The room reeled as he sat up. Eyes closed, breath labored, he leaned against the bed for support and slid his right hand down to the Colt on his hip. He slowly drew the gun from its holster.

Catlin would never have considered suicide an option had be been sober. But whiskey coupled with self-pity and a troubled mind gave rise to drastic notions. Thumbing the hammer back, he lifted the .45 to his temple.

CHAPTER SEVEN

"Is this Mexico?"

The question had been uppermost in Ray Myers's mind all day. It worried him. He was bound for El Paso, not Mexico. But rather than risk embarrassing himself with his ignorance, he had kept his fears private . . . until he could stand it no longer.

The Mexican gentleman seated across from Ray in the hot, cramped confines of the stagecoach smiled in amusement. "Look to your left," he said. "See the trees in the distance? That, my friend, is the Rio Bravo. Beyond the river's banks is Mexico."

Feeling foolish but relieved, Ray murmured his thanks to the man for straightening him out and gazed through the window at the dry, hateful land.

For days, the stagecoach had bounced its mail bags and wayworn passengers across the most rugged country Ray had ever laid eyes on. From Fort Griffin, in Northwest Texas, they had kept to a roughly southwestern route, following the military road to a string of forts scattered across the far reaches of West Texas. By the time their stage forded the Pecos River at Horsehead Crossing, Ray was thoroughly lost. Surely this burned out land, salted with alkali, peppered with volcanic rock, could not be Texas!

After reaching the adobe stage station on the Pecos, Ray hadn't seen a single wooden building for over two hundred miles. The reason was simple. There weren't any trees.

Ray had been on the road for six days and five nights through countless changes of horses and drivers and very little rest in between. For a man of thirty-three years who had never traveled more than eighty miles from home, this was an unwelcome experience.

He owned and ran a general merchandise store in Fort Griffin, and his day-to-day life, on the whole, was routine and uncomplicated. He had looked forward to this trip to El Paso in the same way a man with a toothache might look forward to a trip to the dentist. Painful but necessary.

Yet the journey had provided some instances of excitement, most of them caused by the half-wild horses pulling the stagecoach. Ray also saw his first Apache, a decrepit old man squatting outside a swing station near Fort Davis, begging the male passengers for "bacca." Ray, who didn't smoke or chew, gave him a lemon drop instead.

To see real mountains had been his most fervent desire, but where he had expected to find lush pine forests and sparkling streams there were instead barren, gloomy mountains of rock and dirt and thorny brush and cactus. Moreover, the Guadalupes, the highest mountains in all of Texas, were far to the north of the stage route, and he never got so much as a glimpse of them. The disappointment was still very much with him.

Ray sighed wearily, shut his eyes to the grit boiling within the stagecoach, and massaged his throbbing temples. He was prone to headaches. Sometimes the mere mention or thought of one would cause his head to pound. Ray reflected on the fact that he'd suffered from only one headache since leaving Fort Griffin . . . and it had lasted the entire trip.

Mary warned him to stay home. He had a business to run, a four-month-old baby girl, and an ailing father, and this was no time for him to be gallivanting across the country.

His father's health began to fail around the same time Beth was born. Ray, at first, had felt sure that his condition would improve, but as their family doctor's optimism waned, so did Ray's. He realized it was time he summoned his younger brother.

He supposed that if he had been born of a normal family like everyone else, a simple letter or telegram would have been sufficient. But unfortunately, this was not the case. It wasn't going to be easy convincing Catlin he should come home, and Ray dreaded the inevitable battle.

He hadn't seen or heard from Catlin in over two years. Their father had ordered him away, had disowned him after finding out how he earned a living, and although the old man was too proud to admit it, Ray knew he had regretted the deed ever since. Catlin was past praying for, but he was still family.

Last winter, a freighter had mentioned to Ray, in passing, that he knew of a Myers who lived in El Paso. Further questioning by Ray had confirmed that this Myers was indeed his brother, Cat Myers. Yet Ray had already considered the possibility that he might not find his brother in El Paso. Catlin was a wanderer, after all, and apt to be anywhere.

Thinking about him, Ray felt a sharp pang of guilt. His reasons for wanting Catlin to come home weren't entirely selfless. In all honesty, he probably would have settled with sending him a telegram if it hadn't been for the threat he had received three weeks ago. He drew the crumpled note from his suitcoat pocket and read again the words that had chilled him to the bone:

"Your time is drawing near, Ray Myers. Cowards die many times before their deaths."

The hair on the back of Ray's neck prickled. Who would want to hurt him? The note appeared to have been hastily written, the words scribbled in pencil on a torn scrap of paper. He didn't recognize the handwriting.

He had found the note while opening the store early one morning. Someone had evidently slipped it beneath the door during the night. Not wishing to worry Mary, he never showed it to her but took it to the sheriff instead and discovered he wasn't the first to be threatened. Three other men in Fort Griffin had also reported receiving similar notes.

Summoning Ray and the others to his office to discuss the matter, Sheriff Luger pointed out that each man shared a common bond: All had served as members of the Fort Griffin Vigilance Committee a couple of years ago.

Whether or not this had anything to do with the threats, no one knew for certain, but Ray wouldn't be surprised if it did. Nothing good had ever come of his involvement with the vigilantes. He insisted that Sheriff Luger and his deputy keep a close eye on his family while he was away.

Ray would be relieved to have his brother return with him to Fort Griffin. Catlin's presence would most certainly make anyone think twice before causing him trouble.

"Is El Paso your destination, *Señor* Myers?"

Ray looked up at the Mexican gentleman across from him and tucked the note back into his pocket. "Yes, sir."

The man nodded. "Then you are almost there."

Ray poked his head out the window, craning his neck to see the town, and felt a sense of accomplishment. He had made it to El Paso in one piece. At last!

The sun was a gold medallion setting on the horizon, slowly sinking, leaving the sky above cloaked in gilt-edged layers of purple and red. A range of mountains loomed black and menacing northwest of town. It would be dark soon, but Ray could see the adobe buildings in the distance, the groves of ash and cottonwoods. Nearby flowed the muddy waters of the Rio Grande, or the *Rio Bravo del Norte* as it was called by the Mexicans, and irrigation channels fed orchards, vineyards, and gardens. There was a hint of moisture in the air. Its cool essence caressed Ray's sunburned cheeks.

El Paso appeared smaller than he had expected and differed little from a couple of other border towns they had passed through earlier that day. This entire river valley, the Mexican passenger informed him, had been settled long ago by the Spanish, and their language and customs still predominated. It was all foreign to Ray.

At the stage station, Ray shook hands with the Mexican gentleman, the only passenger he had exchanged more than five words with the entire trip, and picked up his bag. The ticket agent pointed out the hotel to the passengers who were staying overnight in El Paso. Besides the hotel, there were two stage stations, three stores, three saloons, an open-air market, and nearly two hundred people.

Standing in front of the station, trying to work the stiffness from his aching muscles, Ray was startled by the sound of gunfire. One of the lady passengers squealed with fear.

"Settle down, folks." The ticket agent sought to reassure them. "There's a big fandango going on down by the river. Most likely it's just some drunk shooting his pistol into the air celebrating."

"Excuse me," Ray followed the agent into the station. "Do you happen to know where a man named Catlin Myers lives?"

The agent slung a mail bag onto the counter, mopped his brow with a dingy white handkerchief, and studied Ray curiously. "Who wants to know?"

"My name's Ray Myers. I'm his brother."

The agent gave him a strange look, a reaction Ray had come to expect, then surprised him by laughing. He slapped Ray on the shoulder.

"You poor devil! I pity you."

Ray smiled uncertainly and pulled at his earlobe. "How come?"

"Because being kin to the likes of Cat Myers has got to be a fate worse than death," the agent declared, still grinning.

This was true, at times, but Ray hesitated admitting as much to a stranger. The ticket agent seemed to sense his bewilderment.

"Don't worry," he said. "I wouldn't play poker with the bottom-dealing devil if you paid me, but I like him well enough." He flipped out his pocket watch and checked the time. "You being a stranger and all, I hate to see you strike out across town in the dark. If you don't mind waiting, I'd be glad to take you to his house."

Ray smiled in relief. "I'd appreciate that very much."

While waiting for the ticket agent's shift to end, Ray washed the sweat and grime from his face, neck, and hands at a nearby water pump, changed into a clean shirt, and returned to the station to watch eight Santa Fe–bound passengers board the stagecoach behind a team of fresh horses. He waved goodbye as the stage lurched forward into the night.

An hour and forty-five minutes later, Ray climbed up beside the ticket agent in his two-wheeled gig, and they set off at a smart clip through the darkened streets. The saloon-gambling houses were the only businesses open at this late hour, and the town was quiet. Ray breathed in the pungent aroma of woodsmoke and another less pleasant odor, a fishy smell he had noticed earlier in the town of San Elizario.

"It's the river," the agent told him. "I can't smell it any more, I'm so used to it."

Ray looked at the flat-roofed, single story adobes lining either side of the street as they whisked past. "I figured Catlin would have a room at the hotel," he said.

The agent nodded. "He did at first. It was Zella's idea to buy the house."

"Zella?" Ray's mouth dropped open in dismay. "Zella Moreno?"

"Yep." The agent leaned toward Ray, lowering his voice confidentially. "The best looking woman in El Paso. But don't you tell my old lady I said that."

Her name brought back a flood of uneasy memories. Zella Moreno had lived in Fort Griffin for a time with her lover and business partner, Eddie McCall, and they had kept the Starlight Saloon. Not long after Ray allowed his brother-in-law, Sid Lane, to coerce him into joining the Vigilance Committee, he voted in favor of hanging McCall for a double murder, then discovered later that they'd lynched an innocent man.

The incident had ignited a blaze of anger and vengeful feelings among Fort Griffin's rougher element that was extinguished only after the deaths of two vigilante members and the imprisonment of Ray's brother-in-law. Ray managed to escape incarceration, but McCall's death still weighed heavily on his conscience, and he dreaded another meeting with Zella Moreno.

"Here we are," the agent announced, and he steered the horse and gig to the edge of the narrow street. "I'll wait here while you check to see if Cat's home. He plays poker most nights, I think."

"Thank you. I won't be long."

Leaving his carpetbag in the gig, Ray walked beneath the dark shadow of a towering cottonwood to the house, noting the light shining through the windows. Someone was home, at least.

A tangle of rose bushes grew on lattices across the front of the portal, and in his nervousness, Ray blundered into them and caught his sleeve on the thorns. He was trying to disengage himself when the door opened, and Zella Moreno looked out at him.

"Catlin? Catlin, is that . . ." Her voice trailed off, and she took a swift step back, a shocked expression widening her eyes. She started to close the door.

"Wait!" Ray stumbled beneath the portal. "It's me. Ray. Ray Myers." Suddenly remembering his manners, he jerked his hat off his head and clutched the brim in both hands. "Ma'am, I'm looking for Cat. Is he here?"

Recognizing him, Zella's face stiffened. She had changed little in the two years since Ray had last seen her—a trim, voluptuous woman with flashing black eyes, and hair of the same color flowing loose down her back. Her dress was of black silk and looked expensive.

Ray had always considered Zella Moreno rather intimidating, and tonight she reminded him of a wicked witch. A very beautiful witch.

"Catlin's gone," she said, her voice toneless.

"Well . . ." Ray fumbled for words. "When do you think he'll be back?"

"He won't."

Fully aware of her dislike for him, Ray thought she might be lying. He looked past her into the parlor, noticed the pieces of broken mirror littering the floor, the room's overall disorderly appearance, and felt increasingly uncomfortable. Was this Catlin's doings? Ray suspected so, for like a Texas twister, his brother had a way of leaving behind him a trail of destruction.

"Do you know where Catlin is, ma'am?"

Zella stared at him without expression.

"It's important I find him," Ray added. "Our father . . . he's sick, and I . . ."

"Hattie Diller."

Ray frowned. "Huh?"

"He'll be at Hattie Diller's," Zella replied. "Go there. You'll find him."

She slammed the door in Ray's face before he could thank her.

CHAPTER EIGHT

Ray climbed back into the ticket agent's gig, happy that his encounter with the witch woman was over, and asked, "Do you know where Hattie Diller lives?"

"Yep, but I wouldn't admit that to just anybody."

"Why?"

"Hattie's a wheeligo gal."

Ray lifted his eyes heavenward. "Good Lord."

Chuckling, the agent slapped the reins, and they were off again.

Drunken whoops of joy, peels of laughter, and guitar music met Ray's ears as they approached the river. The agent pulled to a halt in front of a primitive looking shack and pointed to a horse grazing nearby.

"Cat's here all right."

In the moonlight, Ray could see the animal's black mane and tail and black-stockinged legs, and nodded, recognizing Catlin's horse, Chico.

He hefted his carpetbag and offered to pay his benefactor for helping him track down his brother, but the agent wouldn't hear of it. Bidding Ray a cheerful farewell, he hollered a "git up" to his horse and rolled away in a swirl of dust.

Ray walked to the shack, glancing around him uneasily, and noticed a light shining somewhere in back of the tiny, crude house. The front windows were dark. It was too late to be dropping in on people uninvited, but Ray saw no way to avoid. Catlin might be here in El Paso one day and gone the next. He didn't want to risk missing him.

He knocked three times on the door jamb, waited a full minute, and knocked again. A woman's voice called out in exasperation.

"Can't a lady get no beauty sleep? Go away!"

Ray sighed. "I'm sorry, ma'am, but I need to speak with Catlin Myers."

"You the law?"

"No. I'm his brother."

There was a grunting sound from within, a moment of silence, then a flicker of light as Hattie Diller struck a match and touched it to the lantern's wick. Ray could see the big woman clearly through the window by the door. No sign of Catlin.

"Door's open," she said, yawning. "Come on in."

Ray stepped inside and almost tripped over the gear piled near the door. He glanced down at the saddle, noting the Texas rigging, the ornate, hand-tooled scrollwork and silver trappings, and figured it belonged to Catlin. He fancied elaborate frillery.

Hattie Diller looked Ray up and down with sleepy, dull gray eyes. "You favor the Cat a mite," she said and slapped him on the stomach with the back of her hand. "Only he ain't got any fat on him." She jerked her head toward a door leading into the back room. "He's in there. Probably drunk, too, so watch it."

"Yes, ma'am."

Leaving his hat and bag with Catlin's gear, Ray edged past Hattie Diller, trying not to look at her too closely. She wasn't wearing anything but a loose, skimpy shift, and he could see more of her than he really cared to. Her indecency embarrassed him.

He had taken hardly four steps across the room when a

deafening blast caused him to stumble backwards in alarm. Loose chunks of dried mud dropped from the ceiling, jarred by the reverberations.

Exclaiming in surprise, Hattie Diller charged fearlessly past him and threw the door open.

"What in all hell's going on in here?"

Ray followed her more cautiously and peered into the back room.

He saw his brother sitting on the floor beside his bed, legs sprawled out in front of him, head slightly bowed. Sweat darkened his sandy blond hair, streaking it. Across his thighs rested a revolver, its barrel gripped in his left hand, its butt in the other hand, and Ray's first conception was that someone had shot at Catlin through the open window, and he was slowly bleeding to death. This notion was rejected, however, when he noticed that the dark red streams running down Catlin's bare stomach were crusted and dry.

"My floor!" Hattie cried.

Across from Catlin on the other side of the room, the hardpacked ground was broken up where a bullet had evidently plowed into it. More concerned about her damaged floor than Catlin, Hattie tried to crush the hard clods of dirt with her bare feet.

"Just look at this mess," she muttered and turned on Catlin, hands on hips. "What were you shootin' at?"

Unaware of Ray's presence as of yet, Catlin lifted his head to look at her, a slight movement that seemed to take the utmost effort, and heaved a shuddery sigh.

"Rats," he hissed.

Hattie scowled. "Are you sure? I ain't seen any rat pills."

"Big sonsabitches."

"Oh, p'shaw." She waved a hand at him, dismissing him. "You're so cockeyed you're seeing things. When you sober up, you wet that tore up floor down and tromp it good and flat like it was. And don't piss on it. Use water."

Catlin gave her a two-fingered salute, rested the back of his head against the straw-stuffed mattress, and closed his eyes.

Leaving, Hattie shook her head at Ray. "He don't seem to be in no talking mood. I'd try him tomorrow if I was you," she advised and glanced over her shoulder at Catlin. "He ain't been here two hours, and he's already swilled down a quart of bug juice."

"Was he in a fight?"

"What else?" Hattie replied and left.

Ray shut the door behind her, brow wrinkled with concern, and cleared his throat.

"Cat?" He took an uncertain step toward him. "Cat, it's Ray. Are you all right?"

Stirring, Catlin looked around at him, squinting a little, focusing, and showed no trace of surprise or recognition, no pleasure or displeasure. Ray wondered if he even knew who he was.

"I couldn't do it," Catlin said softly, his words deliberate, careful. Raising his arm, he grasped the edge of the bed, started to push himself to his feet, then sagged drunkenly back to the floor. "I couldn't do it," he whispered, talking more to himself than to Ray.

Ray crossed the room to him, glancing at the same time at the empty bottle lying on the bed. He noticed where whiskey had spilled and soaked into the mattress. Most of it, however, seemed to have soaked into Catlin.

Not sure how badly his brother was hurt, he squatted down beside him to look at his wounds. There was a deep, five inch gash across his chest, still open and raw and sticky wet, as were the buckshot wounds on his face and arm. Dried blood matted the hair on his chest and stiffened the front of his pants where it had run down his belly.

Afraid he was going to vomit, Ray turned his face away and swallowed hard. His stomach settled finally, its contents sinking again to the bottom, heavily, like liquid metal.

"I'll get you a doctor," he said.

At his offer, Catlin uttered a couple of choice four-letter words and shook his head.

Ray frowned. "Those wounds need to be cared for. You'll get lead poisoning."

"Well, bully for me."

Not sure what to do, Ray stared at him and tugged on his earlobe. "What's the matter with you?"

Catlin looked up at him and wiped the back of his hand across his mouth, fingers quivering. Ray noticed his knuckles were swollen and bloody.

"I think I'm losing it, Ray."

"Losing what?"

"Control, my mind, everything."

Ray sighed wearily, thinking, *I could have told you that a long time ago, little brother,* and felt bad about it as soon as the thought crossed his mind.

He studied Catlin a moment, it having been a while since he'd seen him, and was struck by how much he resembled their father. He supposed if Catlin lived to be a hundred he'd still have a full head of hair. Oddly enough, in this age of beards and handlebar mustaches, he remained clean-shaven. Ray's own neat mustache and short-clipped beard were his source of pride. Mary said they made him appear more distinguished.

Unconsciously comparing himself to Catlin, however, old feelings of inferiority rose within him. Catlin had always been better looking, quicker, more daring. He was a clown at times, too, making people laugh, most often at someone else's expense. Ray was the serious one, quiet, almost shy, and had borne the brunt of Catlin's annoying sense of humor throughout their childhood. Little had changed between them since then except that they were no longer forced to live under the same roof.

Ray realized his jealousy was childish. Whereas Catlin had expressed the fear that he might be losing his sanity, Ray was merely losing his hair and his waistline.

He sat down on the dirt floor beside Catlin, gently pried the gun from his brother's hands, and shoved it beneath the bed.

"I wasn't gonna shoot you."

Ray smiled at this. "Maybe not, but you know me. I've never cared much for guns."

"Yeah." Catlin looked at him, the usual cockiness gone, his face serious. "If you were gonna kill yourself, what would you use?"

The question shocked Ray. It brought to light an unsettling possibility. The sick feeling returned to his stomach.

"My God."

"What would you use?"

"I wouldn't . . . I wouldn't use anything."

"Because you don't have the guts," Catlin stated, nodding, as if he had given much thought to the matter and had finally come to a conclusion. "Neither do I." A wry smile touched the corners of his mouth. "We're more alike than I figured."

Ray kneaded his right earlobe between thumb and forefinger, appalled, disturbed. What if Catlin really was cracking up?

He was reminded of an incident that had occurred when they were children and still living in East Texas. Catlin had been nine years old, Ray twelve. Their father was the not-so-proud owner of a yellow-toothed nag named Hammerhead, the kickingest, bitingest brute in the country, and had warned the boys countless times to stay away from him.

Ever the dare devil, Catlin got it into his head one day to play broncbuster, threw a leg over old Hammerhead, and was tossed forked end up in the same split second, cracking his noggin in the process. It marked the last time Ray ever saw his brother cry. For years after the accident, whenever Catlin pulled some harebrained stunt, their mother would blame his behavior on that bad spill for lack of a better explanation, half-joking, half-serious, never quite sure what to make of her wild young son.

Ray thought he knew how she must have felt.

Letting his breath out in a gust, he massaged his aching forehead and said, "Cat, don't you think you've got it backwards?"

"Got what backwards?"

"Suicide's a cowardly, selfish act. An unforgivable sin. You could go to hell for it."

Catlin seemed to mull that over, his mind working slowly on account of the booze, and carefully rolled a cigarette with fingers that still quivered a little.

"You should've been a preacher," he said at length and regarded Ray suspiciously through a haze of cigarette smoke. His good eye glittered like an emerald in the lamplight. "Why are you here?"

"I want you to come back with me to Fort Griffin."

Catlin gave a short, humorless laugh.

"We need you at home, Cat . . . Pa's sick."

"Sick? What's wrong with him?"

"His heart's giving out on him," Ray replied and shrugged. "I thought you two might like to make amends before it's too late."

"You thought wrong." Catlin spit the unsmoked cigarette

from his mouth, angry now, his face hard and unforgiving and strangely wild. "I got better things to do than watch some old man die."

"He's not 'some old man.' He's our pa. And he wants to see you."

"Then he must be senile, too."

Ray shook his head. "He hasn't been the same since you left that last time, but it's not senility. Regret maybe. I don't know. But he wants you to come home."

Catlin was silent a moment, head bowed, and when at last he spoke, his voice had lost its sharp edge.

"Did he tell you that?"

"Yes," Ray lied, hating himself, for Ocie had made no such claim. "Pa said for you to come on home," he added, clinching it. "How about it?"

"I don't know."

"I'm not leaving without you," Ray warned.

Elbows propped on upraised knees, Catlin cradled his head in his hands, fingers buried in his hair. "Seems like everything's going wrong all at once."

Not everything, Ray thought. At least Catlin had had sense enough not to end his problems with a bullet. He wondered what had distressed him so much that he'd consider such an extreme measure. A break-up with Zella perhaps? Though he didn't wish any unhappiness on his brother, Ray couldn't help hoping that he and Zella were finished. The woman possessed as much warmth as an icicle.

On impulse, he slung an arm around Catlin's neck and gave him a rough, good-natured hug. "Cheer up, Cat. By the time we get to Fort Griffin, you'll have forgotten all this and be looking forward to seeing Pa, the store, mine and Mary's little girl . . ."

"Y'all have a kid?"

"Elizabeth Jane Myers," Ray said proudly. "She's four months and two weeks old."

"Guess that makes me an uncle."

"Yes, and it's about time you met Beth."

Catlin nodded and rubbed his eyes. "Sure as hell nothing keeping me here." His voice sounded heavy with fatigue. "When do we leave?"

"Well, not tonight. You need a doctor first, and I need some sleep."

Grasping Catlin around the waist, Ray helped him up and into bed and tugged off his boots, careful not to stab himself on the sharp-rowelled California spurs. He remembered the revolver then, and not thinking it wise to leave Catlin alone with a gun in his present condition, he retrieved it from beneath the bed.

"Do you want anything before I go for the doctor?" he asked.

"Uh-huh . . . Tell Hattie she's got rats," Catlin murmured, already drifting off. "Big sonsabitches . . ."

CHAPTER NINE

Clear Fork of the Brazos River: August 23, 1877

Northwest Texas was a land of broad, rolling prairies, grassy valleys, and vast distances; a land of wide, blue skies that could turn black and threatening in a twinkling of the eye, of violent thunderstorms, and glorious sunsets, and coyotes yipping and howling in the night. This was home to Ray and Catlin Myers.

The aorta of the land in which they were reared was the Clear Fork of the Brazos, and so it was only natural that, upon reaching the river, they should tarry here a while before riding the few remaining miles to Fort Griffin.

In the sweltering summer heat, the shallow waters glided over a bed of white limestone and gravel like a muddy-red serpent winding through the prairie, seeking the path of least resistance to the Gulf of Mexico. Channel catfish sometimes left the deeper holes to gorge on big yellow grasshoppers as they fell into the water from overhanging trees.

Sitting relaxed astride his horse on the high bank, Catlin watched in amusement as Ray dismounted, hobbled stiffly down into the bottoms, and collapsed on his back inches from the water's edge. For Ray, who was unused to riding horseback, the past two weeks had been torturous.

Pillowing his head on his forearm, he looked up at Catlin. "I hurt in places I never even knew I had."

"Another couple of weeks of riding and those blisters on your ass would turn into callouses, and you wouldn't feel a thing," Catlin assured him.

Ray groaned.

Even though it would have made their trip both safer and quicker, Catlin had flatly refused to leave Chico behind and take a stagecoach to Fort Griffin, suggesting instead that he and Ray make the trip separately. Clearly not trusting Catlin to return home, Ray opted to keep an eye on him and bought a good mount, a packhorse, a secondhand saddle and rode with him.

When it came to getting where he was going, Catlin possessed a relentlessness that neither foul weather nor rough, dangerous country could squelch. It was his theory that if you were going to get from Point A to Point B, you took the trail most closely resembling a straight line and you stuck to it come hell or high water. In this instance, he chose the old 1858 Butterfield Overland Mail Route. The trail had been abandoned years ago and was miles north of the scattered military outposts that would have provided them some protection from marauding Apaches and *bandidos*.

The only good thing about the trail, from Ray's standpoint at least, was that it passed beneath the very shadow of the Guadalupe Mountains and the colossal prow of El Capitan. Ray would never again think of Texas as flat.

Still sitting his horse beneath the shade of a tall hackberry tree, Catlin gazed around him at the familiar countryside and gently massaged his injured arm. The buckshot wounds were beginning to heal, but the surrounding muscle remained stiff and rather painful. As he tried to knead the soreness out with his fingers, he sang a little tune he'd picked up somewhere in New Mexico:

"I am a lonely cowboy, I work all the time;
I can whip the son of a bitch that stole a cow of mine;

I'll climb up on his hocks, you bet your life I'll try,
Comb his head with a six-shooter, root hog or die . . ."

The name of the song was the "Ballad of Root Hog or Die." To the dismay of his traveling companions—both human and equine—Catlin had whiled away the miles singing his unique rendition ever since they'd left El Paso. What stanzas he couldn't remember, he simply made up as he went along, occasionally adding an off-color verse here and there to liven it up. It was not a pretty song, and Catlin couldn't have carried a tune in a bucket.

"Don't you know any other songs?" Ray demanded, exasperated.

"Let me think," Catlin said. He dug a half-pint whiskey flask from an inside pocket of his vest, took a drink, and nodded. "Got it. You want to hear it?"

"Do I have a choice?"

Catlin pressed a hand to his heart in melodramatic fashion and sang loud enough to be heard across three counties:

"Farewell to the girl that I no more shall see,
This world is wide, and I'll spend it in pleasures.
I don't care for no girl that don't care for me,
I'll drink and be jolly and not care for no failures.
I'll drown my troubles in a bottle of wine . . ."

Here he paused, trying to remember the rest of the song, and finally shrugged.

"Thank God," Ray murmured.

"No ear for music, uh? Well, I dedicate that song to Mrs. Zella Moreno," Catlin said and returned the silver flask to his vest pocket. "I hope she's happy with herself."

"You never did tell me what happened between you two."

"I left her."

"How come?"

Catlin frowned down at him from his perch on the river bank. He saw no reason to discuss the matter, believing if he poked around in that wound too often it might never heal.

He turned his attention instead to the two horsemen that had just guided their mounts down the opposite bank and were now splashing across the river toward him and Ray. In case they weren't friendly, Catlin lifted the beat-up Winchester rifle he kept slung to his saddlehorn and laid it across his lap.

"Who do you reckon that is?"

Ray stood up, settled his hat on his head, and squinted across the glaring water at the two riders. "Looks like Sheriff Luger."

"Luger? R.D. Luger's the sheriff?"

"The best Shackelford County's ever had," Ray said and glanced up at him. "He takes his job pretty serious, Cat, so don't give him any trouble."

"Who? Me?"

Sheriff Luger and his companion drew rein on the gravel spit next to Ray, and Catlin let the Winchester slide back down to its usual position. Noting the movement, Luger nodded and barely smiled.

"Good afternoon, Sheriff," Ray greeted him.

"Howdy do, boys." Luger gazed up at Catlin. "Was that you singing a minute ago, or a gut-gored buffalo?"

Catlin ignored the cut. "R.D., you old goat. I always knew you were nothing but a lawdog at heart. When did you decide to quit cowboying?"

"When I found myself with a wife, six youngsters, and an

empty cupboard," Luger replied. "If you boys don't mind my saying so, you look like you just rode through a sandstorm."

"We did. Got caught in one this side of the Pecos and ain't had a bath since. How many days ago was that, Ray?"

"Too many."

"Ray warned me you might be coming home," Luger said, still studying Catlin with keen, blue eyes. "He said you'd be on your best behavior, but I can see you've done got in one scrape. What happened to your face?"

Catlin touched the scabbed-over wound on his left cheek, compliments of Eladio Moreno's ten gauge shotgun, and grinned. "Cut myself shaving."

"Thunder. Are we gonna set here and gab all day, Sheriff?"

"Wasn't planning on it," Luger replied. He bobbed his head in the direction of his impatient young deputy. "Cat, you remember Virgil."

"Hey!" Catlin leaned forward in the saddle to better see the narrow-shouldered, black-haired man with the handlebar mustache and thumbed his hat off his forehead. "Hey, is that Virgil Shinbone?"

Ray's already sunburned face flushed redder with embarrassment, and R.D. Luger ducked his head to inspect the tie strings on his saddle, hiding his smile.

"The name's Virgil Bone." The deputy glowered up at Catlin, his lean face screwed up against the sunlight filtering through the trees, revealing the gap between his two front teeth. "B-O-N-E. Bone."

Catlin laughed, enjoying himself. "Virgil, you never could take a joke. How's your health these days?"

Of course, it was the wrong question to ask a hypochondriac. Virgil Bone's former animosity melted away, and he told Catlin and Ray all about the sharp pain he'd been experiencing lately. He was taking liberal doses of Hostetter's Celebrated Stomach Bitters to no avail and worried that he might have contracted something fatal. In an effort to reassure him, Catlin expressed the opinion that it was most likely a gas pain, a diagnosis that forced the sheriff to inspect his saddle strings again. Deputy Bone failed to see the humor in this and wisely changed the subject.

"Shouldn't we be on our way, Sheriff? That note sounded serious."

"I reckon." Luger turned to Ray. "I hate to welcome you home with bad news but . . ."

"Are Mary and Beth all right? And Pa?"

"They're doing fine. It's you I'm worried about."

Luger dug a piece of paper from his vest pocket. It was limp with sweat. He handed it to Ray. "Virgil found that on the floor of my office. Recognize the handwriting?"

Catlin saw the color drain from his brother's face as he read the note. "What's it say?" he asked.

Without answering, Ray compared the sheriff's note to another scrap of paper he'd taken from his own pocket and grimly nodded.

"It's the same. The handwriting's the same."

"What does it say?" Catlin asked again.

"Figured as much." Luger lifted his battered Stetson and wiped the sweat from his forehead. His wispy, gray hair was plastered to his skull. "The person that slipped that note under my office door is the same person that threatened you and the others."

"Who threatened who?" Catlin demanded.

Ray glanced up at him finally, a distracted look in his eyes, then turned back to the sheriff. "I hope Charlie's all right."

"So do I. His wife reported him missing two days ago. I

figured he'd show up sooner or later and didn't worry about it too much till today."

"Charlie and his old lady's been having some domestic troubles," Virgil added, as if this explained his disappearance.

"Y'all don't mind me," Catlin called out. "I'll just busy myself swattin' flies while you fellas chew the fat. Just pretend I'm not here."

Luger's leathery face creased in a grin.

Frowning, Ray climbed back up the steep bank to his horse and gave Catlin the two notes before mounting up. "I'll explain on the way to the bend," he said. "Sheriff, do you mind if Cat and I ride with you?"

"The more, the merrier."

CHAPTER TEN

R.D. Luger and Virgil Bone lunged their horses up the bank, and the four men headed south to a curve in the Clear Fork known locally as Baby Head Bend. Reading the message the sheriff had found in his office, Catlin saw the reason for Ray's change of direction:

"Charlie Conrad awaits your arrival at Baby Head. Give him my best regards."

He read Ray's ominous sounding message next and noticed that neither of the two notes was signed.

"What do you think?" Ray asked, watching him closely.

Catlin shrugged. "Somebody doesn't like you. What's the deal with Conrad? Was he threatened, too?"

"Charlie, Frank Wyman, Ben Fletcher, and I all received similar threats," Ray told him. "And at one time, we were all members of the Fort Griffin Vigilance Committee. What does that tell you?"

"Maybe one of those horse thieves you lynched has a vengeful partner."

Ray sighed. "That's what worries me."

"Whoever it is, he's had some education," Luger commented. "Not many horse thieves I've met up with could write their names, much less a complete sentence."

"And he likes Shakespeare," Ray added. At Catlin's strange look, he repeated a line from the note he had received. " 'Cowards die many times before their deaths.' It's a quote from *Julius Caesar*."

77

Catlin took him at his word. He guessed any man who spent half his time with his nose stuck in a book ought to know a quote from Shakespeare.

It seemed odd to Catlin that Ray had not mentioned any of this to him before now, and he wondered if perhaps this was Ray's true purpose for wanting him back here instead of their father's illness. What if Ocie Myers had not, in fact, asked for his return? The possibility made him queasy.

The truth was, he was glad for this little side trip to Baby Head, welcoming any diversion that might delay his meeting with Ocie. Though he hid it, he had been suffering from a nervous stomach all day. The hard-eyed old man always gave him a case of the jitters.

"You shouldn't make fun of Virgil," Ray said abruptly.

They were riding well behind the sheriff and his deputy, having dropped back to give their jaded horses a breather, and were out of earshot.

"He's awful touchy, you know."

Catlin agreed. "He always was the serious type."

"Yes, but he's changed in other ways," Ray said. "Virgil's more confident than he used to be, more mature. He may be afraid of disease, but he's not afraid of you or anyone else. I know. I've seen him arrest some real tough characters since he's been deputy."

Catlin looked at him, half-smiling, thinking surely he must be pulling his leg. "Are we talking about the same Virgil Bone? The clumsy oaf who'd wet his pants if you hollered boo?"

Ray nodded. "People change, Cat. So don't take Virgil too lightly, and for God's sake, try to be more respectful of him and Sheriff Luger." He paused, then added more quietly, "They both know what you are."

"Yeah? What am I, Ray?"

78

Ray gave him a quick look, as if the question had startled him.

"You can't even say the word, can you?" Catlin asked, and he was gripped by a sudden, unreasonable anger. "You think you're too damned good to even say the word!"

Shocked, Ray opened his mouth to utter a response, then seemed to think better of it, and looked away.

They rode together in silence after that, and Catlin's anger subsided enough for him to regret his flare-up. He guessed Deputy Bone wasn't the only one who was easily offended these days.

Catlin had known Virgil Bone for years. They were the same age and had grown up together in Clear Fork country. Virgil joined the Confederate Army when he turned seventeen, contracted a severe case of measles, and was discharged before he even had time to warm up his uniform. He had been dying ever since, and so it struck Catlin as strange that he should choose such a dangerous profession. Stranger still that R.D. Luger had chosen him to be his deputy, though if Virgil was as fearless as Ray claimed, that would certainly explain it.

Like Virgil, R.D. was no newcomer to Fort Griffin. Prior to pinning on a sheriff's badge, he had worked as a cowhand for one of the area ranches and had bossed a number of cattle drives up the trail to Kansas and as far west as California. He was pushing fifty now, a tough, capable man and honest, but still no match for a county full of cattle and horse thieves, killers, and con men. Catlin didn't envy him his job in the least.

The men followed the river to Baby Head Bend where Catlin and Ray caught up with the two peace officers. On a rocky bluff, they rested their horses and gazed south and west across the valley to the opposite curve of the river. Towering elm, pecan, and hackberry trees lined the banks, and the intervening valley was broad and level and grassy. Sunflowers grew tall here, their brown, yellow-fringed faces swaying in the slight breeze.

"Where do we start looking?" Virgil asked.

R.D. pointed to the tumbled, partially burned out ruins below them in the valley. "Guess we could start there . . . John Zimmerman's old place."

Virgil nodded. "If Charlie's hiding out by the river, he might spot us when we cross that open ground and give us a holler."

"If he's alive," R.D. added.

They left the bluff, riding single file down a hardpacked cattle trail, and struck out across the valley to the ruins.

John Zimmerman, his wife, Ellen, and their three children had moved here from Ohio in 1857, the same year Catlin's family left East Texas to settle in new country. Like Ocie Myers, Zimmerman was a farmer, and in this bend of the Clear Fork, he found fertile soil with no trees to clear and an abundance of good water and wild game.

The northern Comanches were attracted to this region for some of the same reasons, and in 1858, a small war party raided the Zimmerman farm, killing all but the two young girls whom they took hostage. Before leaving, the warriors mutilated the bodies of the dead, ransacked the house and outbuildings, and set them afire.

Today, all that was left to remind folks of that raid was the stone section of the house, the chimney, and the grave site of the three Zimmermans, marked by oblong piles of rocks and crude headstones. The two Zimmerman girls were never seen again.

Riding toward the ruins, Catlin noticed a couple of buzzards circling low over what remained of the house, sinking,

sinking, disappearing from his sight behind the crumbling stone wall. This was not a good sign, and they all knew it.

"Maybe it's just a dead cow," Ray said.

They were downwind of the ruins, and nearing the stone wall, Catlin caught the first emanation of rotting flesh. It was a horrible odor and indescribable, and he recognized it instantly for what it was.

This was no dead cow.

They found the object of the buzzards' interest in what had once been the Zimmermans' kitchen. Fly-blown and partially eaten by coyotes, the dead man lay among the weeds and rubble, and a single brazen buzzard stood hunkered over on his chest with a shred of meat dangling from its beak. The bird watched the approaching riders with beady eyes while four or five of its confederates swung in slow circles above them all.

Looking as if he might topple from his horse any minute, Ray grasped the saddlehorn with one hand and his nose with the other. "Oh, no," he moaned. "This is going to give me a headache."

The smell was so foul, they were forced to ride around the body and approach it again from upwind. Deputy Bone dug a bottle of Dr. Bristol's Neutralizers from his saddlebag, ate four tablets on the spot, and gave the rest to Ray. Both men's faces were a pale shade of green.

Dismounting, Catlin and R.D. stepped over the building's foundation to get a better look at the mangled corpse. Though the clothes were torn apart, it appeared the dead man had been wearing a black, three-piece suit and a white shirt. A nice, low-heeled boot still encased one foot. Charlie Conrad, who owned a large mercantile store and ran a banking business on the side, dressed similarly.

Catlin waved his hat at the buzzard, shooing him off, and

noticed then that the dead man was headless. He and the sheriff exchanged shocked glances.

"Well, I swan," R.D. muttered. He pressed his red bandana tightly against his nostrils. "Where do you suppose his head went?"

"Coyotes probably drug it off," Catlin said.

Deputy Bone called out to them. "Sheriff, is it him? Is it Charlie?"

"Hell if I know! Look around some, see if you can find his head."

"Thunder! You mean, it ain't there?"

Catlin gazed down at the headless body, standing relaxed and somewhat slouched, the voices around him sounding hollow and far away in his ears. The stench of human mortality and the mid-afternoon heat wrapped around him, smothering him, and he felt himself slipping away again into that black, nameless tunnel . . .

It was so dark! He stumbled through the moonless night, scared, alone, an unlit lantern gripped in his left hand, his musket in his right. It had been two days since the terrible battle in which he had lost his best friend and messmate, Brad Gilley, and the death smell washed over him in waves as he recrossed the killing ground. Except for an occasional hooting owl, the woods were sad and silent.

Risking severe punishment, telling no one of his intentions, he had slipped away from his regiment's bivouac shortly after nightfall and returned to the battlefield, to the muddy ditch where Brad Gilley was shot and killed. Off in the distance, he saw splashes of lantern light as other soldiers searched the darkness for their fallen comrades in the hopes of laying them to rest. Fearful they might be Yankees, Catlin did not light his own lantern, but occasionally struck a match to peer into a dead soldier's face, recoiling from the distorted,

decaying features that stared back at him in the feeble light
. . . "I can't find him," Catlin whispered, anguished. "Why
can't I find him?"

Sheriff Luger glanced over at him. "You say something?"

"I can't find Brad."

"Can't find who?" Luger regarded him strangely, frowning. "Myers, you feel all right? You look sorta dazed."

Catlin's mind snapped back to reality. He looked up at
R.D. Luger, blinked, his good eye glazed over with grief,
emotion, weariness, and managed to pull himself together.

"I'm fine. Forget it."

But he wasn't fine. The flashbacks took him places he
didn't want to go, made him remember and think about
things he wished to forget. And they were uncontrollable.

Suddenly dizzy, he thrust a hand out, pressed his palm
against the rough, sun-warmed wall, caught himself before he
fell flat on his face. The feeling came and went swiftly, and he
found himself staring down at an empty cartridge shell
gripped in R.D. Luger's thick, square-tipped forefinger and
thumb.

"Take a look at this," R.D. was saying. "The sick bastard
shot Charlie in the chest. Stood him up against the wall and
shot him."

Catlin nodded, glancing over at the wall where the dead
man lay, seeing the darkened spatters of dried blood. He took
the big brass shell from R.D.'s hand. Fifty caliber. Studying it
more closely, he noticed there were two firing pin dents instead of just one. The shell then had been reloaded, a practice
not uncommon among buffalo hunters . . . and himself, on
occasion.

"You think it's Charlie Conrad?" he asked.

"I know it is," R.D. replied. "While you were day-
dreaming, I found some papers on him." He gave Catlin a

perplexed look. "I told you that already."

"Sweet Jesus! Sheriff, come here! Hurry!" Deputy Bone's voice reached them, shrill with excitement. "Oh, Jesus! I think I'm gonna be sick . . ."

R.D. made a face. "Sounds like he stumbled onto Charlie's head."

"Or a fresh pile of cow shit," Catlin said and laughed at the thought of it.

Walking out past the untended graves of the Zimmermans, they found Ray and the deputy and Charlie Conrad's head, all three looking quite ghastly.

"See!" Virgil exclaimed. "Somebody chopped off his head!"

It was true. Conrad's killer had courteously impaled the head on a stick so a coyote wouldn't carry it off. The grotesque visage leered at them over the sunflowers.

Afraid it might trigger another flashback, Catlin was careful not to look directly at it.

R.D. blew his breath out and shook his head. "It's days like this that make me wonder why I ever ran for sheriff." He turned to his deputy. "Guess you'd better ride back to town and get a team and wagon out here."

"Who'd do a thing like this, Sheriff?"

"That's what we have to figure out . . . before he kills again."

Ray shuddered. He was sitting on a rock a little distance away, his back turned to Conrad's head. "I could be next," he said and unconsciously touched his throat.

"I bet you fellas twenty dollars whoever knocked off Conrad has lived around these parts his whole life," Catlin said. He flipped a double eagle into the air, watched the gold coin flash in the sunlight, and caught it in his palm. "He ain't just passing through."

R.D. studied him. "What makes you so sure?"

"Think about it. You were living here in '58 when the Zimmermans got massacred. All four of us were, and we all know how Baby Head Bend got its name. But we're in the minority. Most folks don't even call it that any more."

R.D. slowly nodded, soaking this in, understanding. "Everybody calls it Zimmerman's Bend," he said. "Everybody except us—the ones who saw the baby's head."

It wasn't a sight one easily forgot. Of the three Zimmerman children, the smallest had been a mere baby of five or six months. The child was too young for the Comanche raiding party to take with them, so they killed it instead and impaled its tiny head on a stick as a warning to the other white families who had dared to settle on their lands. Though it failed to frighten away the Myers family, it did inspire the name of this sharp bend in the Clear Fork, a name only a handful of people knew, or remembered the origins of.

"That narrows the list of suspects down some," R.D. said. "The killer possibly lived around here in 1858, and he carries a .50 caliber rifle. A buffalo gun."

Virgil Bone eyed Catlin with a touch of suspicion. "Hell, Myers, that description fits you," he declared and glanced at R.D. "We all know it ain't buffalo he kills with that Big Fifty of his."

Catlin hawked and spat on the ground, standing hipshot amid the sunflowers with his thumbs tucked into his pants pockets, his head cocked a little to the side to better see the deputy through his good eye. "But I mainly just kill snakes with my .45," he said casually. "And rats."

Ray stood up. "Cat, that's enough."

"You calling me a rat, Myers?"

"Now whatever gave you a crazy idea like that?"

"Cat! I said that's enough!"

R.D. stepped between the two young men. "Virgil, if you

want a fight, do it on your own time. Right now, we got a murder to solve. Ray, you and Cat go on home."

Catlin flashed the deputy a cocky grin. "See you around, Virgil. You take care of that gas pain."

Following Ray back to where their horses were grazing, Catlin's smile vanished, leaving his face hard as granite. Virgil Bone's suspicious remark annoyed him. This was one killing they couldn't possibly pin on him, yet there were a number of people around Fort Griffin who disliked him enough to take such careless talk straight to heart.

Glancing up, Catlin saw a buzzard light on the old chimney of the Zimmerman house. He drew his .45, took quick aim, and fired. The big carrion bird fell to the ground with a heavy thud, its powerful wings beating the earth in a last futile effort to fly.

Catching his brother's watchful eye on him, Catlin blew the smoke from the barrel of his gun, gave it a fancy twirl, and dropped the weapon back into its holster.

"God," Ray muttered, "what a showoff."

CHAPTER ELEVEN

Riding northeast to Fort Griffin, Catlin and Ray crossed a stretch of open prairie where some lucky buffalo hunter had made a stand; bleaching bones were visible as far as the eye could see in every direction. A quarter mile away, two men were collecting the scattered buffalo bones and tossing them into a wagon.

"Bones are selling for six dollars a ton now," Ray remarked.

"What are they good for? Fertilizer?"

"They're shipped to a sugar refinery in Louisiana where they use them in the refining process." Ray sighed and rubbed his nose. "I'm afraid one of these days there won't be anything left of the buffalo but just that—bones."

"That's what the Army's counting on," Catlin said. "No shaggies means no Indians. Sounds all right to me." He faced Ray and touched a forefinger to the thin, white scar extending from his right eyebrow to his hairline. "See this? A Comanche buck jumped me five years ago north of the Canadian. Son of a bitch tried to take my scalp."

"I remember you telling me about that. You killed him, didn't you?"

"Yeah. Finally. I'm sort of partial to my hair."

"Me, too. But the Indians were here long before we were. So were the buffalo." Ray paused, looking around him at the bone-littered prairie. "I don't think this is what God had in mind when He gave us dominion over the animals."

"If you feel that way, then why do you sell supplies to the buffalo hunters?"

Ray frowned at him and didn't reply. There was no need, for Catlin knew the answer. He did business with the hunters for the same reason they killed the buffalo: He liked the money.

With the approach of fall, business would be booming in the town of Fort Griffin as the hunters made preparations for the winter kill. Fort Griffin was the principle hide-buying and supply-distributing point for Texas buffalo hunters. Each spring, the town's narrow side streets were lined with stacks of hides hauled in by ox-team outfits and grizzled hunters from as far away as Palo Duro and Yellow House canyons.

Catlin found himself looking forward to Fort Griffin's hustle-bustle and rough and rowdy atmosphere. Seldom a week went by that there hadn't been a lynching, stabbing, or shooting. He was sure he'd feel perfectly at home. He hoped R.D. hadn't tamed the town too much.

Riding easy in the saddle, reins held loosely in his left hand, Catlin took a long drag on his cigarette and glanced sideways at Ray's troubled face.

"Have you told Pa and Mary about that threat you got?"

"No, not yet. I'll probably tell Mary tonight."

"Pa's liable to blow his stack."

"I know. That's why I'm not going to tell him and neither are you. His heart can't stand too much excitement."

Catlin laughed softly. "Hell, if he don't keel over when he sees me walk through the door, it'll be a damned miracle."

"Just try not to rile him."

"I'll try."

The brothers reached the outskirts of Fort Griffin in time to hear the 4:30 bugle call, announcing stable duty. The military post was situated atop a broad plateau overlooking the town and the Clear Fork of the Brazos to the north. Catlin and Ray cut across the post's western edge, riding past rows of wall tents and small, frame huts where the enlisted men lived. The post grounds were neatly kept, with stone walks and transplanted trees.

Among the soldiers stationed at Fort Griffin was Company G of the 10th Cavalry, one of several regiments staffed entirely by blacks. Called Buffalo Soldiers by the Indians, black troopers had proven themselves to be some of the Army's best fighting men and deserved much of the credit for the Comanche-Kiowa defeat of 1875.

Yet the threat of Indian raids was far from over. Ray told Catlin about the party of Mescalero Apaches that had raided Texas last July, plundering and burning as far east as Shackelford County. They led a company of Fort Griffin soldiers on a merry chase into the waterless sand hills, taking with them several thousand dollars worth of stolen stock.

After giving the fort a hasty inspection, Catlin followed Ray down a dusty, heavily traveled wagon road that joined the town's main thoroughfare below the plateau. His first glimpse of Griffin Avenue assured him that nothing had changed since his last visit home.

Wide-open, thriving, utterly shameless, the town sprawled without order on the sandy flat between the post and the Clear Fork. Known as just that, the Flat, this little metropolis of the Texas frontier catered to a rough, independent lot and attracted anyone who yearned for excitement and fast money. From hide hunters and merchants to cutthroats, shady ladies, and slick-talking speculators, they all came, pushing the population in excess of two thousand.

The town was nothing very attractive to gaze upon—a few false-fronted frame buildings, adobe and picket houses, corrals, and wagonyards—but to a man who had just ridden across the uninhabited, semi-desert expanse between here and El Paso, it looked like paradise.

Keeping a tight rein on the skittish Chico, Catlin waited for an ox-drawn freight wagon to pass before turning onto Griffin Avenue. Between the rattle and creak of wagons and the shouts of the teamsters, someone could be heard pounding away at a rinky-dink piano in Doney's Saloon, limbering up for tonight's crowd.

Catlin gazed past the telegraph office at the saloon's open doorway and licked his dry, wind-cracked lips. Were it not for his pending visit with old Ocie Myers, he would have been in hog heaven.

He caught up with Ray. "How about we wet our whistles first?"

"Your whistle's wet enough already," Ray replied, referring, no doubt, to Catlin's occasional nips from the silver flask tucked inside his vest. "If you're thirsty, drink some water."

Catlin rasped a palm across his grimy, unshaven face, thinking of ways he might delay his visit another hour. "Guess I should at least clean up," he said.

"Pa's seen you dirty before."

"I was thinking of Mary. She might not love me any more if I smell like a billy goat."

Ray suddenly pulled up short and turned his horse half around in the middle of the street to face Catlin. "Mary's my wife now, Cat. My wife," he repeated, spacing the words for emphasis. "The days when you had any claim on her are over. Understand?"

Surprised and rather amused by Ray's sudden fit of jealousy, Catlin gave him a blank look and let it go at that. Of course, he understood.

Mary Lane had been his sweetheart for a time after the

war, a fact that clearly stirred up feelings of insecurity in Ray. Catlin wasn't sure why it worried Ray so much. Mary despised him now and blamed him for her brother's imprisonment.

Worse, Sid Lane had contracted consumption in prison and was dying. When Ray gave Catlin this dose of bad news, he felt remorse, not for Sid, but for Mary. He hoped she didn't hold that against him, too.

Catlin and Ray drew rein in front of Myers's Mercantile, a frame, L-shaped building with glass display windows and a loading platform. The store was located on the corner of Griffin Avenue and Third Street, next to Charley Hatfield's Restaurant. The building's front section was weathered gray, whereas the boards of the rear section were still yellow and oozing sap in the hot sunshine.

"You added on," Catlin observed.

Ray nodded. "I had to. It got so we didn't have room to turn around."

Ray's hired man caught sight of them, lifted a hand in greeting, and hefted a hundred pound sack of flour into the back of a waiting wagon.

"Looks like everything's running smoothly," Ray said.

Catlin dismounted in front of the store and tethered Chico to the hitch rail. "How's business? Good?"

Smiling, Ray replied modestly, "It beats farming. Although, I doubt I make as much money as you do."

Catlin shot him a quizzical glance. "What makes you say that?"

"I saw your house in El Paso. I saw the way Zella Moreno was dressed. That takes money." He frowned at Catlin beneath knitted brows. "Business must be good for you, too."

"I think I have a corner on the market," Catlin admitted, making light of it.

Still frowning, Ray shook his head. "I'll never understand you, Cat. Not as long as I live."

Catlin was dreading the reunion with his father too much to let Ray's fault-finding unsettle his nerves. They walked into the store together, the little brass bell on the door tinkling pleasantly, and Mary Lane Myers looked up at their entrance. Her face lit up when she saw them.

"Ray! You're home!" She hurried from behind the counter and flew into his outstretched arms, paying no mind to the ogling customers.

Mary Myers would be around twenty-six, Catlin remembered, and as perfect in appearance as ever. She reminded him of a china doll. Mary was Ray's second wife. He had married his first wife when he was nineteen, a young lady named Lucy Watson whom he had met while he was attending McKenzie College in Red River County. Lucy was bitten by a rattlesnake shortly after they were married and now lay buried near their mother's grave at the old homestead.

Ray waited eleven years before he remarried. Catlin didn't know if the long interval was out of deference for his first wife or something more concrete. Marriageable women were a scarce commodity in this part of the country.

Giving Ray and Mary some privacy, Catlin walked around the store looking things over, half-expecting to see his father sitting in a corner somewhere, glowering at him over the top of his newspaper. But Ocie was nowhere in sight.

Myers's Mercantile was filled to bursting with everything a body could ask for, from boxes of ammunition to Borden's canned milk, all of it displayed in a neat, organized arrangement. Mary's work, to be sure. An odd mix of odors overwhelmed Catlin—warm, spicy aromas, the heavy scent of molasses-cured tobacco, the mingled smells of leather, soap, apple cider, and fresh-ground coffee.

In back of the store, past the counter, was a closed door with a sign above it that read: DO NOT ENTER. That would lead to the family's private quarters, Catlin guessed. After Ocie fell ill, Ray had decided once and for all to move into town and had leased the farmland to a neighbor. Catlin wondered how his father was taking the change.

Eyeing the candy jar on the counter, he helped himself to a piece of peppermint and ambled back to where Ray and Mary were quietly talking. They fell silent at his approach. Mary turned to look at him.

"How you doin', Mare?"

Mary's smile was cool, reserved. "I'm doing well," she replied, "especially now that Ray's safely home."

Catlin nodded and glanced at his brother. "Ray told me about Sid being sick. I'm real sorry."

"You should be," she said tartly and changed the subject. "Do you want to see Ocie?"

"Is he around?"

"Yes, taking a nap, I think. He spent most of the afternoon across the street playing checkers."

"Well, at least he's stopped brooding," Ray remarked and glanced at Catlin. "Pa's not been too happy about the move."

Catlin wasn't surprised.

"I'll show you to his room," Mary offered and led the way to the door in back.

Trailing behind her, Catlin watched Mary's dark blue dress swish. Her full skirt was pulled to the rear where it puffed out at least a foot or so and just naturally drew his eye. He felt the fluttery sensation return to his stomach, his mind on two things at once, Mary's physique and bitter old Ocie Myers.

At the door, Mary reminded him to remove his spurs and wipe his feet. He obeyed without a word and stepped into the Myerses' living room, a neat, modestly furnished room with calico curtains at the windows and a puncheon floor. Catlin recognized his mother's what-not shelf in one corner, his father's old armchair by the window. A child's Noah's Ark set, hand-carved and brightly painted, was arranged on the windowsill.

Mary saw him looking at the yellow, red, and blue toy animals. "Beth's much too young for them," she explained, "but try convincing Ray of that."

"Where is Beth?"

"With my Aunt Cora. She keeps her when I need to work in the store."

Catlin studied her a moment, half-smiling, absently clinking the spurs together in his hand. "You make an awful pretty mama."

She ignored the compliment. "Don't touch anything until you've bathed. You're filthy."

"That's what I told Ray, but he said you wouldn't mind the dirt since it just makes more of me to love."

Mary gave him a sharp, skeptical look. "That sounds like something you would say. Not Ray." She turned her back to him. "Come along. You've wasted enough of my time."

Catlin followed her down a short hallway to the first door on the right. Mary knocked, heard Ocie's gravelly response, and glanced up at Catlin.

"He's awake," she said and took her leave, squeezing past Catlin in the narrow hall, making an obvious effort not to touch him.

Catlin drew a slow breath and opened the bedroom door.

Ocie Myers was sitting up in bed, fully clothed except for his socked feet, which were crossed at the ankles. He had been about to fill his pipe with tobacco until he saw Catlin. His fingers froze.

Catlin had prepared himself for a change in his father's appearance but was shocked nonetheless by the pallor of his skin, the hollowed out eyes and cheeks. He appeared to be slowly wasting away. Catlin took off his hat and gazed down at it, too shocked to speak.

Ocie's own surprise seemed to dissipate quickly, and he cast a stern eye on Catlin, watching him fumble with his dusty black Stetson. "Well, don't just stand there like a damned deaf mute," he said gruffly. "Sit down somewhere. And put your hat back on. I ain't dead yet."

Catlin smiled, heartened by his father's customary surly temper. Nothing wrong there, at least.

"Glad to see you're in a pleasant frame of mind, Pa."

"I stay that way," Ocie said. He set his pipe and tobacco pouch on the bedside table. "When did you and Ray get in?"

"A few minutes ago."

Ocie gestured to the chair near his bed. Crossing the room, Catlin sat down and dropped his hat and spurs on the floor.

"Fiddlefooted as you are, I didn't figure Ray'd ever find you."

"I'm living in . . . I was staying in El Paso."

Ocie nodded, studying him. "Why'd you come back, Tom Cat?"

Catlin frowned. "Ray said you sent for me."

"I never sent for you."

Biting his bottom lip, Catlin stared out the window at the traffic, pedestrians, and boiling dust of Third Street. It was just as he had suspected earlier. Afraid for his life and in need of Catlin's protection, Ray used the one argument he felt would get him to come home, and it was a bald-faced lie.

Jaws knotting, Catlin picked up his hat. "I should've known better," he muttered and rose. "I won't take up any more of your time."

"Plant your ass back in that chair!" Ocie commanded.

Catlin looked at him, a concerned frown wrinkling his forehead. "Easy, Pa. I'd sure hate to cause you to pull your picket pin."

"Don't coddle me, boy." Ocie ran a shaky, claw-like hand through his white hair, standing it on end. "Sit down. I'm not finished with you."

Catlin eased back into his chair, tensed up, sitting on the edge of his seat.

Ocie resumed filling his pipe. "If it'll make you feel any better," he said, "I'm glad to see you."

This grudging admission was uttered so low, Catlin had to strain to hear it. Lips parted in surprise, he stared at his father without speaking.

"Close your mouth, Cat, before you catch a fly in it."

A faint smile brightened Catlin's face. He leaned back in his chair. "You mean that? I mean, what you said about being glad to see me?"

"I said it, didn't I? Now make yourself useful and get me some water."

Catlin took his glass and filled it from the water pitcher on the washstand. Giving the glass to Ocie, he became aware of his father's close scrutiny of his scabbed-up face.

"Got into a little trouble in El Paso," he explained.

Ocie scowled. "With the law?"

"No, a woman." Catlin suddenly grinned. "The woman's husband actually."

Ocie eyed him a long, silent moment and pulled on his pipe. He shook his head finally, appearing almost sorrowful.

"How old are you, Cat?"

Catlin had to think, adding up the years in his head. "Thirty," he answered. "Thirty as of last March."

Ocie nodded, and his tone of voice hardened. "Thirty years old and still just as dumb and worthless as you were ten, fifteen years ago. Have you given any thought to what you're gonna do with your life?"

Realizing he had already fallen into disfavor again, Catlin didn't reply.

"Me and your ma always hoped you'd settle down someday," Ocie continued. "If not in her lifetime, then in mine. Maybe get married, raise a family, show folks you got some sense."

Catlin started to remind Ocie that he had been almost forty years old before he got married but wisely kept his mouth shut, sensing his father wasn't in the mood for contrariness. Ocie Myers had spent his whole life toiling behind a plow and a team of work horses, too tired at day's end for saloon brawls and poker and women. There could be no comparison, and Catlin knew it.

Ocie set his pipe aside and swallowed a drink of water. "I have just one regret," he said. "When that cowboy kicked you in the face that time, I wish he had put out your right eye instead of the left one."

Catlin gave a short laugh. "What for?"

"Because your right eye's your shootin' eye," Ocie replied. "Maybe if you'd lost your sight in it, you'd have to do some honest work for a living."

Catlin's body stiffened slightly. Propping an elbow on the arm of his chair, he traced the scar on his forehead with his middle finger and tried to think of something smart to say. Again, words failed him, a rare occurrence only his father could bring to pass.

Ocie sighed. "That's the last time I'll mention it. You already know how I feel." He rested his head on his pillow. "I'm tuckered out. You'd better go."

"Do you want me to leave Fort Griffin?" Catlin asked, his voice quiet.

"You can stay . . . for a little while anyway." A touch of humor showed on Ocie's face as he closed his eyes. "I like them comers and goers but dang them comers and stayers."

He was softly snoring before Catlin reached the door. Looking down on the sleeping old man, he felt a pang of sadness. In his father's eyes, he was a failure, a source of shame. Catlin remembered again his killing of Johnny Keaton, the young Arizona cowboy.

Ocie didn't know the half of it.

CHAPTER TWELVE

Following his visit with Ocie, Catlin bathed, shaved, and changed into clean clothes in time to make a good impression on Mary's aunt, Cora Lane. A gray-haired, unsmiling woman, she peered through her pince-nez spectacles at him and sniffed, apparently expecting him to stink. The Lanes were a well-to-do family, owning not only several businesses in town but a large and prosperous ranch, as well, and held the belief that they were several notches above common grangers such as the Myers family. Mary's involvement with Catlin and her later marriage to Ray had scandalized the entire clan.

"Well, well. Look who's here." Cora Lane plucked the spectacles from her nose and let them dangle by the black cord around her neck. "Your brother tells me you'll be staying in Fort Griffin for a spell."

Catlin glanced at Ray. "My brother says a lot of things. Some of it you have to take with a grain of salt, though."

Ray made a face, as if he'd been sucking a lemon, and tugged on his earlobe.

"Hmph. I'm surprised you'd dare set foot around here after what happened two years ago," Cora snapped, and she regarded Catlin with a waspish leer. "While poor Sidney wastes away in that horrid prison, you . . . you of all people . . . remain free. It leads me to wonder what this country is coming to."

Catlin wrapped an arm around her bony shoulders and planted a loud, smacking kiss on her left temple. "Aunt Cora, you're beautiful when you say things like that."

Horrified, Cora Lane's eyes and mouth gaped wide, and Catlin thought for a second she would faint dead away. She struck his arm away and pressed a hand to her bosom.

"Heavens!" she exclaimed. "Of all the nerve!"

Tying on her sunbonnet, Cora Lane hurried out of the store, banging the door behind her. Catlin watched her flounce across the street, and burst out laughing.

"Look at her go, Ray! Did I shock her drawers off or what?"

"Hers and mine both," Ray said. He locked the door behind her and put up the CLOSED sign. "Now she'll really hate us."

"Don't it just break your heart?" Catlin winked at him. "How much you want to bet I'm the first man that's ever laid a finger on the frigid old biddy?"

Ray smiled sheepishly, rolled his eyes, and turned to gaze out the display window. "Mary's family will never forgive you over this mess with Sid, especially now that he's sick."

"Not even Mary, huh?"

"No. She realizes Sid overstepped the law, of course, but she's still loyal to him."

Catlin thought about that, harking back to his last visit home, Ray's brief involvement with the Vigilance Committee, the lynching of Zella Moreno's then lover, Ed McCall. Mary's brother, Sid Lane, had been the ringleader of the vigilantes at the time and was enjoying the power of his position. When one of the committee members revealed the vigilantes's identities to the sheriff after McCall's murder, Sid killed him for breaking his vow of secrecy.

Zella Moreno later tried to hire Catlin to put a stop to the vigilantes before they murdered another innocent man. Though Catlin declined the job offer, his relationship with Zella stirred up suspicion among Sid and his followers. They beat him unconscious and threatened to finish him off if he ever showed his face in Fort Griffin again. His sight gone in one eye and his pride wounded, Catlin shelled out his own brand of justice, resulting in the deaths of two more vigilantes and the eventual imprisonment of Sid Lane.

Catlin considered the problem at hand. Ray Myers, Charlie Conrad, Ben Fletcher, Frank Wyman. All had been members of the Vigilance Committee prior to Ed McCall's hanging, all but Ray had turned state's evidence against Sid Lane in order to save their own necks, and all had received threats recently. Who would be the most likely person to want these four men dead? There were any number of possible suspects, the Lanes being the most obvious, but Sid was the only known murderer in the family, and he was doing time in Huntsville and dying besides. That left a myriad of suspects to sift through, a task for which Catlin lacked the patience.

"Mary took Beth to her room," Ray said suddenly. "I'd like for you to see her as soon as you tell me how your visit went with Pa."

"I survived it. Not much else to tell."

"I guess he told you I lied."

"Yeah, he told me."

Ray sighed wearily and turned to face him. "I needed you here, Cat."

"But not because of Pa."

"Yes, because of Pa. And other things."

"You should have told me the truth."

"If I had told you the truth, would you have agreed to come home?"

"That's beside the point." Catlin eyed him haughtily. "I could leave right now. Maybe I will."

Ray threw up his hands in exasperation. "What do you want me to do? Fall on my knees and beg you to stay?"

Not answering, Catlin leaned against the store counter and watched his brother sag into a straightbacked chair and massage his forehead. Suffering from a headache, he guessed, suffering from worry and taut nerves, wondering when the head-chopping murderer who likes Shakespeare would come calling.

"My reasons for wanting you here aren't all selfish," Ray insisted. He looked up at Catlin. "After that night in El Paso, I don't think it's a good idea for you to be alone."

"Spare me, all right, Ray? I was drunk. So what?"

"You were about to blow your brains out! That's what!"

Catlin cast a hasty look at the door in back, making sure it was closed. "Keep your voice down," he said. "You want Mary to hear you?"

Ray shook his head. "No. No, we'll keep this between the two of us. Just promise me the next time you get some crazy notion into your head, you'll come to me first. Will you?"

Catlin glowered at him, not liking this kind of talk. He remembered just enough about that awful night to feel an acute sense of embarrassment at the mere thought of it.

"Promise me," Ray said again.

Catlin nodded grudgingly. "Yeah, fine. Whatever you say."

Pushing himself to his feet, Ray walked toward him and extended his hand. "Shake on it."

Catlin hesitated a moment before complying and was thankful for the approaching dusk, not wanting Ray to see his face. This was much too personal for comfort.

"You've eased my mind a little," Ray said, and he rested his hand on Catlin's shoulder. "Now I want you to come and meet my daughter."

Catlin found Elizabeth Jane Myers to be a helpless, doll-like creature that laughed and gurgled the instant her blue eyes focused on his face.

Laughing with her, Catlin glanced up at Ray and Mary. "I always knew I had a way with women," he joked.

While Mary hovered close by and Ray gave out needed instructions, Catlin picked Beth up from her tiny bed and cradled her in his arms. It was the first time he had held a baby, and he found the experience rather nice. No wonder Ray had talked of little else during their trip home. It gave him an odd feeling, as if he were missing out on something he had not known existed until now.

Catlin ate supper with the family and spent some time catching up on local happenings—last year's flood, the latest shootout in the Flat, the numerous marriages and funerals. Before Ray got around to breaking the news about the threatening message and Charlie Conrad's death, however, Catlin put on his hat and announced his intentions of taking a stroll through town.

Ray frowned at him. "I should think you'd be too tired after that long ride," he said, and he yawned so hard his face almost split. "I know I am."

Ocie struggled to his feet and slowly followed Catlin through the kitchen to the back door. His breath wheezing a little, he touched a hand to his chest, the unconscious gesture of a man with a bad heart, and braced himself against the kitchen table.

"Pa, you all right?"

"I'm fine, damn it. Quit asking me that." Ocie glanced back once to make sure they were alone. "Don't say nothing about this to Ray or Mary, but here in a day or two I want you to take me home."

"Home?" Of course, Catlin knew he was referring to the farm but pretended otherwise. "You're already there, Pa."

Ocie impatiently thumped his cane on the floor. "Don't act dumb. I'll tell you when I'm ready to go."

Not waiting for Catlin's reply, he turned and rambled

back into the living room. Catlin watched him, troubled, and heaved a gusty sigh. He didn't like the sound of that.

It was warm outside and still, the night dimly lit by a star-studded sky and the light spilling from windows and open doorways. Next door, Charley Hatfield's Restaurant was closed, yet the smell of food still lingered in the air.

Pausing to light his cigarette, Catlin walked past the storage shed and outhouse, making for the narrow passageway that opened onto Griffin Avenue. The sound of footsteps stopped him. He spun around.

A black, indistinct shape appeared briefly against the glow of lamplight less than fifteen feet away from him before it vanished, swallowed up by the shadows. Hugging the side of the store, Catlin closed his right hand over the leather holster on his hip.

"Who's there?"

There was no sound, no movement. Catlin waited. A slight breeze kicked up, carrying with it the hubbub and laughter from one of the saloons.

Catlin called out to the shadows in a friendly voice. "Come on out, and I'll buy you a drink! Don't be shy!"

Silence followed his invitation. He waited a few more dragging minutes, finally decided he was imagining things, and whistled a tune as he left the darkened passageway.

Catlin walked half a block up Griffin Avenue and crossed the street to the nearest watering hole, a cheap, rat trap shebang of upright cottonwood pickets and a faded sign that said simply SALLOON, misspelled. Catlin paused in front of the small building, standing just to the side of the light slanting across the boardwalk from the open doorway, still thinking about the occurrence outside Ray's store. He glanced back the way he had come but saw nothing suspicious.

"Hey, mister. You coming in or not?"

Catlin turned. A saloon girl peered out at him, her yellow hair falling limply over bared shoulders. She smiled when he looked at her, recognition in her eyes.

"Long time no see, Cat. Remember me?"

Though he didn't recognize her, Catlin grinned and said, "I sure do. Buy you a drink?"

Taking his hand, she led him into the saloon where a dozen or so men were drinking and discussing the gruesome death of Charlie Conrad. Most of the saloon's patrons appeared about as prosperous as their surroundings. The bar consisted of a warped plank suspended across two barrels where drinks were sold for nine cents apiece, too cheap to be anything but rotgut.

Catlin made room for himself and the girl and caught the barkeeper's eye. "Two whiskeys."

The greasy, sour-faced little man slopped amber liquid into two shot glasses and passed it to them in return for Catlin's eighteen cents.

Turning to the girl, Catlin lifted his glass for a toast. "May this tarantula juice go down painlessly." They clinked glasses, and he drained his in a single swallow.

It was indeed rotgut. Though it hardly fazed Catlin's cast-iron goozle, he gasped and choked and screwed up his face. The girl giggled at his overly dramatized reaction. Taking her drink from her, Catlin tossed it off, as well, wiped his mouth, and inspected the few drops of liquor still rolling around in the bottom of the glass.

"Strychnine," he decided and gazed down into the girl's laughing eyes and dirty face. "Where do you live?"

"River Street."

Catlin nodded. That would be the Red Light District.

She puckered her lips into a pout. "You don't remember me at all, do you?"

105

"Maybe you'd better refresh my memory."

"You spent the whole night with me last time you was here," she said and walked her fingers up his chest. "You told me you liked my nose."

Catlin studied her, trying hard to remember. She did have a very nice nose. It was small, turned up, and freckled. It reminded him a little of Mary's nose, minus the freckles, and he was admiring it when Virgil Bone entered the saloon.

Catlin glanced around at him. "Evenin', Mr. Bone."

Virgil cast a covert look at the half-dressed girl glued to Catlin's side before averting his eyes. "Myers, I need a word with you."

"Yeah? What about?"

"Charlie Conrad."

Virgil spoke the name louder than was necessary and glanced around the smoky room. Conversation died as the men turned to look at him.

"I'm investigating Charlie's murder," Virgil announced, and his gaze settled on Catlin. "If I was you, I wouldn't be making plans to leave Fort Griffin any time soon."

Catlin's face hardened. He flicked the ash from his cigarette. "Am I a suspect?"

"I never said that. I'm just telling you not to leave town."

"Was this your idea or the sheriff's?"

"All mine." Virgil smiled triumphantly as he turned to leave. "Have fun, Myers."

The murmur of voices picked up again following his departure, and Catlin sensed a change in the climate, felt the muggy weight of suspicion settling on him as the men talked and drank and glanced his way.

One thing was certain: Deputy Bone had learned how to play dirty.

Suddenly disliking the atmosphere, Catlin jingled the

coins in his pants pocket, slung an arm around the girl's waist, and steered her toward the door.

"Let's take a walk down River Street," he suggested, "and get reacquainted."

CHAPTER THIRTEEN

Catlin awoke the following morning in unfamiliar surroundings. Buck naked and severely hung over, he squinted at the cheap, pea-green wallpaper, rubbed his eyes, and very carefully turned his head. Sunlight streamed through the east window. Its brightness dazzled him. Perhaps that was why he didn't notice the woman standing at the foot of his bed until she hurled his wadded up clothes at him. They struck him full in the face.

Gasping in surprise, Catlin raised up on his elbows. "What the hell . . . ?"

"You're taking up space, cowboy. Get your duds on and get out. I got clients waiting."

Her face was only a bloated, ruddy blur to Catlin's unfocused vision, but he had sense enough to know that this was not the woman he had left the saloon with last night. Suddenly aware of his state of undress, he covered himself and glanced around the small room. The girl with the pretty nose was gone.

When the woman left him, Catlin sat up and held his head in his hands. He waited for the nausea to subside and slowly dressed and tugged his boots on. There was a vase of wilted wildflowers on the table beside his bed. Catlin pulled the flowers from the vase, dropped them on the floor, and leaning out the open window, he splashed the cold water over his face and head. It did little to assuage the dull throb inside his skull.

Water dripping from his nose and chin and hair, Catlin

looked down at the ground below him and realized he was hanging out of a second story window of Hunter's Hideaway, a bawdy house on River Street. The revelation left him feeling out of sorts and sullied. Dirty inside and out. This was not like old times at all. Something was missing.

He gazed unhappily out the window, peering through the tall pecan trees and elms at the sluggish, muddy waters of the Clear Fork.

"Damn," he muttered. "What am I doing here?"

Weak in the stomach, his head pounding with the even tenor of a bass drum, Catlin wandered down Griffin Avenue toward his brother's store. There was a mean look in his eye this sunny Wednesday morning, and men loitering on the boardwalk were quick to step out of his way when they saw him. Their caution and gawking stares didn't help Catlin's mood, for he understood the reason for it. Clearly, word had gotten around.

That hellion, Cat Myers, was back in town. Trouble would surely follow.

Crossing the street to Myers's Mercantile, Catlin climbed the steps to the loading platform, opened the door, and found himself face to face with the last person he had expected to see in Fort Griffin. It stopped him cold.

Long hair sweeping across her face in the breeze blowing through the open doorway, Zella Moreno brushed it back with her hand and stared up at Catlin, an expression of uncertainty showing in her dark eyes that was not characteristic of her. She looked beautiful to him, clean and strong and good, and it took all his will power not to let on how glad he was to see her.

"Catlin?" She touched his hand. "Catlin, I was hoping to find you here. Can we talk?"

He looked past her at Ray and Mary, both of them

watching him from behind the store counter. Ray frowned and shook his head, discouraging him from speaking with Zella. That made up Catlin's mind.

"In there," he said gruffly and gestured to Charley Hatfield's Restaurant.

Zella followed him in silence to the building next door. Choosing a table in a secluded corner of the restaurant, they sat across from each other, separated by a barrier of red and white cloth, salt and pepper shakers, and overlooked breakfast crumbs.

"You look as if you had a hard night," Zella remarked. "Coffee might help."

Catlin nodded, then remembered with a twinge of shame that he didn't have a dime on him. Last night's visit with the ladies of River Street had wiped him out in more ways than one.

"I guess the coffee'll have to wait," he said. "My walking around money walked plumb off."

Zella smiled and started to open her purse. "I'll pay for it."

"I said it can wait."

At his sharp tone, she glanced up at him, sighed deeply, and snapped her purse shut. "You don't have to bite my head off."

"Why did you follow me here, Zella?"

"To warn you."

This was not the answer he had expected from her. "Warn me of what?" he asked.

"I think we have a problem, Catlin." She met his intent stare, a worried frown clouding her face. "Two days after you and Ray left El Paso, the sheriff let Eladio out of jail and . . ."

"Hold on." Catlin stopped her. "If this is about your old man, I don't want to hear it."

"I'm past caring about what you want," Zella shot back.

Her eyes flashed in sudden anger. "You'll shut your mouth and listen to what I have to say!"

Catlin smiled, amused by the way her Spanish accent, hardly noticeable most of the time, strengthened whenever her dander was up. He liked the sound of it. He liked her fire.

"As I was saying," Zella continued, "the sheriff released Eladio." She shrugged. "Why, I don't know, but the first thing he did was come to me."

"Did he hurt you?"

She shook her head. "No, he was sober this time. He told me he loved me still and wanted me back." She closed her eyes a moment, as if trying to remember Eladio Moreno's exact words. "He said that he would prove to me that he was the better man."

"By killing me, right?"

"Yes. He said if he killed you, he'd be rich, and I would learn to love him again."

"What makes him think he'd get rich by punching my ticket?"

"That's the interesting part." Zella leaned toward him. "Eladio told me that while he was in Tucson, a man named Arnet Phillips promised him a lot of money if he would kill you." She reached across the table and gently gripped his forearm. "Catlin, what's going on? Who is Arnet Phillips?"

His face thoughtful, Catlin avoided Zella's prying eyes and idly played with the salt shaker, spinning it on the table top, watching it whirl and wobble. So Phillips wanted him dead. That wasn't surprising. What surprised him was the fact that he had chosen someone as incompetent as Eladio Moreno to do the job.

Zella ordered two cups of black coffee from one of the waitresses and turned back to Catlin. "I want to know what happened in Arizona," she said. "You owe me that much."

"I guess I do," Catlin conceded.

His voice lowered, he started from the beginning, relating to her his first conversation with Arnet Phillips, how Phillips had claimed that Johnny Keaton had raped his young wife. He told her of Phillips's desire to punish this man for his crime, quickly and permanently.

"I did the job," he went on. "Afterwards, I found out Phillips lied. His wife and Keaton were lovers."

"You killed an innocent man then," Zella murmured.

"Yeah. When I figured it out, I went back to Tucson and confronted Phillips." Catlin sipped his coffee and gave her a tired, halfhearted smile. "Phillips had political ambitions, I think. I guess I must have dashed them all to hell."

"And now he wants revenge."

"Looks that way."

Zella was silent a moment, then, "I'm so sorry for Johnny Keaton . . . and for Phillips's wife if she loved him," she said, and the genuine sadness in her voice served to renew Catlin's own feelings of regret. "This is what was bothering you when you returned from Arizona, isn't it?"

Catlin admitted it was and gazed down into the black, steamy depths of his cup of coffee. Talking about his shooting of Keaton was not easy. While Arnet Phillips was partly to blame for the man's death, Catlin blamed himself most of all. He had been careless. He had taken Phillips at his word, taken the whole situation for granted, something he rarely did.

He was believed by many to be a coldblooded killer, worse yet, a bushwhacker, yet Catlin didn't consider himself as such. He was not, as he had explained to Arnet Phillips, an indiscriminate killer. A lone mercenary, he chose his missions carefully, selecting only those he considered to be justifiable causes.

Many of the states and territories west of the Mississippi remained lawless, and folks were forced to protect themselves. Even in those regions where there was some pretense of law and order, one peace officer might be expected to patrol an area as large as entire states back East. In these instances, Catlin Myers's services were not only in demand, they were indispensable.

Following the tragedy in Arizona, however, Catlin had begun to wonder if perhaps it was time to retire his guns and learn a new trade.

"Tell me something," he said suddenly. "How much am I worth to Phillips?"

Zella shook her head. "Eladio didn't say."

"Does he know I'm here in Fort Griffin?"

"Yes. Your brother didn't exactly make a secret of where the two of you were going. For all I know, Eladio may already be here." When Catlin showed no signs of concern, Zella's worried frown deepened. "I think you should leave Fort Griffin. Today."

Catlin looked at her in surprise. "You're taking this awful serious."

"*¡Claro que sí!* Of course, I take it serious! Sometimes, Catlin, you are so thick." Her natural Spanish accent began to assert itself again. "Eladio fears you, yes, but he's also very desperate. He wants the money Phillips promised him. He wants to show me what a big man he is."

"I understand all that, Zella, but I'm not gonna run from him. Besides, Pa told me yesterday he wants me to stay."

Zella's expression softened. "How is your father?"

"Not good."

She nodded and regarded him a moment, searching his face. "I didn't just come here to warn you," she said at length. "We need each other, *querido*. Especially now. I'm

113

willing to start over if you are."

Catlin lolled his tongue around inside his mouth, thinking about it. God, it was tempting! Seeing her here, smelling the faint flowery essence of her perfume, hearing her voice, low-pitched and melodious, was almost more than he could bear. Then he thought of Eladio and how Zella had sworn the man was dead, and his heart hardened.

He spoke without looking at her. "I don't kill women and kids, I don't spit on the sidewalk, and I don't mess with other men's wives."

"You're so moral," Zella said sarcastically, rolling her eyes. *Qué risa.* She left some change on the table to pay for their coffee, pushed her chair back and rose. "Watch your back, Catlin. Eladio won't confront you alone again. He'll find someone who hates you as much as he does, and together, they'll try to kill you. I'm sure of it."

"Are you going back to El Paso?"

"Not yet."

Catlin nodded, gazing up at her, drumming his fingers on the table. "Do you need any money?"

"Money isn't what I want from you," Zella stated. "I can take care of myself." She started to leave, then turned to look back at him. "Charlie Conrad was murdered. Did you hear?"

"I heard."

"Justice is slow sometimes, isn't it?" He didn't answer, and she shrugged and turned away. "When you finish sulking, come see me. I'm staying at the Occidental. Room six."

Listening to the fading rustle of Zella's petticoats, Catlin finished off his coffee and followed her with his eye as she left the restaurant. She crossed the busy street, and he lost sight of her then, his view blocked by a passing team and wagon.

Room six at the Occidental. He wouldn't forget it.

CHAPTER FOURTEEN

That same morning, following a short visit with his father, Catlin wandered into the kitchen where Mary was making preparations for dinner. Without saying anything to her, he stepped outside for a breath of fresh air.

In an effort to beautify an otherwise ugly backyard, Mary had planted geraniums along this side of the house and went out daily to pull weeds and pick up blowing trash from around her flowers. A trumpet vine slowly creeping up the side of Ray's small storage house attracted bees, butterflies, and hummingbirds with its bright orange flowers, and farther away, a two-holer outhouse attracted flies. Catlin could hear them buzzing in the static August heat.

Vaguely bothered by his conversation with Zella, Catlin wondered if Eladio Moreno was, in fact, here in Griffin. That was all he needed, a jealous husband dogging his heels, trying to kill him. He remembered the shadow he had seen outside the store the night before. Had that been his imagination or not?

Catlin approached the narrow passageway between Ray's store and the restaurant, walking slowly, scanning the ground for tracks. Thanks to Mary's war on weeds, the earth was bare except for a random patch of grass, and he easily recognized his own boot tracks in the loose dirt. There were other footprints besides his own, all of them too old and ill-defined to have been made last night. He paused near the corner of the building, sure that this was approximately where he had seen

115

movement of some sort, and searched the surrounding area for sign.

He found what he was looking for, a single set of fresh prints. He knelt down to study one particularly clear foot-print and knew instantly that the man he had seen here last night was not Eladio Moreno. The size of the boot was too short, the heel's cut in the loose earth too shallow, suggesting to Catlin that the man who had made this track was below medium height and light in stature.

He examined the imprint more closely and noticed a star pattern etched into the bootheel.

"Looking for something?"

Catlin glanced up to see Mary watching him from the kitchen door. Wiping her hands on her apron, she stepped outside and walked toward him. Her hair was pulled back as usual in a loose chignon, and stray, pale blonde tendrils clung wetly to her neck and forehead. Her cheeks were flushed from the heat of the oven, giving her face a rosy glow.

Catlin pointed to the track he'd been studying. "Take a look at this. Somebody was out here last night when I left the house."

"Really?" Hardly glancing at the print, Mary frowned at him. "Any idea who it could have been?"

"No, not yet. It's probably nothing to worry about, but you'd better keep the doors and windows locked just in case."

"I don't need you to tell me how to care for my family," Mary retorted. "We were doing just fine before you got here."

Catlin rose and smiled uncertainly at her. "I never said you weren't."

Mary folded her arms together and watched him in si-lence, a shadow of distrust and hostility lurking behind her eyes that made him uncomfortable. She had changed. He saw it in her eyes, in the tightness around her mouth. He felt her coldness toward him.

"Ray told me last night about the threat he got," she said at length, and with the toe of her shoe, she idly brushed out the footprint Catlin had found. "He told me he thought you still had the note. I'd like to see it."

Having forgotten about it until now, Catlin felt inside his vest pocket, drew out the two messages Ray and Sheriff Luger had received, and gave them to her. He watched Mary unfold the crinkled scraps of paper, watched her face change, her skin blanching, tensing up. She stared for a long moment at the note given to Ray before at last looking up at him. Her left eyelid twitched uncontrollably.

"Mare, are you all right?" He reached out to touch her shoulder, genuinely concerned, but she shrank away from his hand. "Mary, what's wrong?"

"Keep your dirty hands off me!" she exclaimed.

Catlin pulled back, perplexed. Why was she behaving so strangely? Yet even as the question crossed his mind, he sensed that her agitation was more a result of the messages than anything he had done or said, and he wondered at it. It didn't make sense. Ray had already told her about the threat.

Drawing a shaky breath, Mary seemed to regain her composure. She crammed the two notes into her apron pocket.

"Mary?" He spoke her name gently. "Mary, do you recognize the handwriting?"

She met his gaze with a look that cut right through him. "I want you to leave Fort Griffin," she whispered. "You're not wanted here."

Catlin frowned. "I see." He sighed, trying to think how to respond. When nothing came to mind, he told the truth. "I thought Ray might need me," he confessed. "Hell, he's the only brother I've got, and maybe we haven't always got along, but that doesn't mean I don't care about him."

Mary gave a mirthless, mocking laugh. "You stupid fool. The only person you've ever cared about is yourself. How could Ray possibly need you?"

Stung by her words, Catlin looked away, hiding the hurt. It wasn't often he ventured to express his personal feelings, and Mary's harsh mockery was both humiliating and painful. Never before had she laughed at him, and he realized the extent of her hatred.

Recovering, he met her gaze, cold, withdrawn. "If Ray and Ocie tell me to leave," he said, "I'll damned well wipe the dust of this town off my feet and never come back. Until then, though, you can forget it."

"I can make your life very uncomfortable if you stay," Mary warned him.

"Why? Because of what's happened to Sid? Or is it something else?" He took a step toward her, watching her face closely. "Do you know who's threatening Ray?"

White-faced, Mary backed away from him. "How could I possibly know?"

"You tell me."

"Even if I knew something, I wouldn't confide in you," Mary declared. "You've caused my family nothing but grief. You and that filthy Mexican tramp."

"Mexican tramp?"

"Zella Moreno!" Mary's lips twisted. "That heathen! She's as much to blame for Sid's troubles as you are."

Catlin felt his anger mounting. "Sid caused his own trouble!"

"Oh, and of course, you've never taken a life, have you, Mr. Myers?" Mary's tone was caustic. She turned sideways to open the door and glanced back at him. "Stay out of our lives and stay away from Ray. He doesn't need your kind of help."

"I'll let Ray decide that for himself."

"Then I'll make your life miserable, Catlin." Angry tears glistened in Mary's eyes when she looked at him. "I'll turn this whole town against you," she promised. "Count on it."

She went inside, slamming the door behind her. Catlin heard the metallic snap of the lock.

Left alone, he drew the silver flask from his pocket, unscrewed the cap and took a drink, rolling the whiskey around inside his mouth, savoring it before swallowing. He needed it, needed the burning jolt.

Disturbed, confused, he leaned against the weathered plank wall of his brother's store, feeling the sun hot on his face, the whiskey's warmth in his belly. What was going on with Mary, if anything? Had she recognized the handwriting of the person who wrote those messages?

Catlin had never doubted Mary's love for Ray, yet if she was attempting to conceal the identity of the person who had threatened him, likely the very same person who had killed Charlie Conrad . . .

Catlin shook his head, smiling a little, realizing he was being foolish. There had to be some other explanation. Mary wouldn't risk the life of her own husband to protect a killer's identity!

CHAPTER FIFTEEN

The next few days passed quietly for Catlin. No more was said of his and Mary's quarrel, though he caught her glowering at him more than once in a manner that suggested the incident was not forgotten. Catlin had intended at first to move out of the guest room and into one of the hotels or a boardinghouse but soon changed his mind. He found himself deriving a certain perverse pleasure from Mary's disapproval.

Odd to think they had once fancied themselves in love with each other!

Charlie Conrad was laid to rest on Thursday, and most of the town and at least half the families from outlying ranches and farms attended his funeral. Conrad had been well-liked and respected, and his murder was a shock to everyone.

According to Conrad's widow, a hangman's noose was found dangling from their front porch the day after her husband's disappearance. This was yet another clue affirming Sheriff Luger's theory that the man's death was directly related to his involvement with the vigilantes two years before.

The sheriff had already interrogated two men and was keeping a sharp eye out for yet another. All three men were former partners of a known cattle rustler who had been hanged by the vigilantes. R.D. believed they might have decided to avenge the death of their friend.

There was much speculation as to the killer's identity. In spite of a sound alibi, Catlin's name was mentioned frequently in these quiet discussions, proof that Virgil Bone's attempt to make him the target for suspicion was working. Catlin found the gossip annoying, but so long as no one was pushing for his arrest, he managed to ignore it most of the time. The rumors, however, worried Ray to distraction.

Ray's hired man hurt his back, and Catlin filled in for him at the store. His days were spent loading supplies into waiting wagons and buckboards and giving advice to the numerous would-be buffalo hunters who passed in and out of Fort Griffin each day.

His knowledge of the attributes and flaws of various gun makes and ammunition made him quite popular among these greenhorns, many of whom were wealthy Easterners who had come West in search of adventure. Catlin discovered them to be as gullible as they were enthusiastic, and with tales of Indian raids, outlaws, and buffalo herds twenty miles long and ten miles wide, he generally talked them into buying enough grub and ammunition to outfit a small army. Ray expressed the belief that this might be slightly unethical but didn't complain.

A regular paragon of virtue, Catlin had steered clear of River Street since that first night and spent his evenings playing poker at the Beehive Saloon. The Beehive was a two-room adobe building with a saloon in front and a dance hall in back and was one of the better drinking establishments in the Flat. Painted on the building's front wall was a huge beehive with a witty verse that read:

> In this hive we are all alive,
> Good whiskey makes us funny,
> And if you are dry
> Step in and try
> The flavor of our honey.

Catlin found the honey was made sweeter by the presence

of the Beehive's new barmaid, Zella Moreno. Hired for her prior experience working behind a bar, as well as her ability to attract new patrons to the saloon, she soon became a favorite among the sporting crowd, and she filled Catlin's nights with longing and jealousy. He conjured up maddening mental images of Zella falling for another man, perhaps even spending her nights with him, and these fervent imaginings gave him no rest. While he rarely said more than two words to her at a time, he felt the hurt and anger toward her gradually melting away.

August faded into September, and the nights grew cooler, less stifling. Catlin had been home a little over a week when he made his usual evening pilgrimage to the Beehive and settled in for a game of five-card stud.

As the night wore on, his thoughts began to stray to the black-haired, brown-skinned woman behind the bar, and he lost more hands than he won. Five hundred dollars in the hole, he paid up, shoved his chair back, and walked to the bar where Zella was drying glasses. It was nearing one o'clock and the end of her shift. Her face appeared tired in the smoky light.

"Long day," Catlin remarked.

She looked up at the sound of his voice. "How did the game go?"

"Bad. Luck's gone sour, I guess."

Zella gave him a knowing smile. "Since when did you start relying on luck alone?" she asked and lowered her voice. "Mike said if he ever catches you cheating . . ."

"Mike can kiss my rear," Catlin broke in, referring to Zella's boss. Catlin believed the man was taking a shine to her and resented him for it. Changing the subject, he picked up a deck of cards lying on the bar and shuffled them. "How about a game of blackjack?"

"I'm tired, Catlin."

"So am I. Just one quick hand."

"What shall we play for?"

"Ahhh, let me think." He gave the cards another fancy shuffle. "If I win, I get to ask you a personal question," he said finally. "If you win, you get to ask me one."

Zella frowned slightly. "Are you drunk, Catlin?"

He wagged his finger at her like a displeased school marm and grinned roguishly. "Uh, uh, uh. You don't get to ask a question unless you win."

Dubious, Zella folded her arms together on the bar and leaned toward him, watching his hands closely as he riffled the deck, then shuffled.

"Cut 'em," he commanded.

She cut the cards. Catlin picked up the deck, and with a simple sleight of hand, switched it back to its original position and swiftly dealt, fingers and cards softly whispering as they touched and slid past each other to the bar.

Zella examined her hole card, then glanced at the card lying face-up on the bar.

"You've got a nine of hearts showing," Catlin commented, his voice and features inexpressive. "Want another card?"

Zella bit her lip and looked across at Catlin's face-up card, a jack of spades. "I'll try one more," she said.

A little smile ticced one corner of Catlin's mouth as he slapped the card down. It was a ten. Zella's face fell.

"Hmmm. Nineteen showing," Catlin mused. "You want another card?"

She shook her head.

"Me neither." Catlin flipped his hole card over, revealing an ace, and added it to his jack. "Twenty-one."

Zella sighed and turned up the four of diamonds. "I went over," she said. "Twenty-three. You win." Gathering her cards together, she tapped them against the bar and regarded him with suspicion. "You cheated, didn't you?"

"No questions, Zella. You lost, remember?"

"You cheated."

He smiled at her. "You stood right there and watched me. Did you see me cheat?"

"No, but that doesn't mean anything. The hand is quicker than the eye. Next time, let me deal."

Ignoring her accusation, Catlin set the deck of cards aside. "Now for my question," he said, "and you have to tell the truth."

"All right."

"Did you sleep with him?"

Shocked, Zella stared at him for several long seconds, her face close enough to Catlin's that he could see the little freckle at the corner of her mouth and feel the warmth of her breath on his skin. His gaze wavered a little, sliding down to the gold locket positioned between the soft, double rise of her breasts. He had given the locket to her when he returned from Arizona, and she had placed within its metal case three precious locks of hair tied together with silk ribbon, all that remained of her children, children born to herself . . . and Eladio Moreno.

She spoke in a quiet voice. "Who do you think I slept with, Catlin?"

"Eladio." Drawing a slow, silent breath, he met her intent stare. "You said he came to El Paso not long after I left for Arizona."

A tender smile curved Zella's lips and softened her eyes. "Silly man," she whispered. "What makes you think I'd sleep with him? I don't love him."

"You loved him once."

"Yes, once," she admitted. "Before he left me."

"You should have told me the truth about him."

She sighed softly. "I realize that now. But I never expected to see him again, and it seemed best at the time to pretend he was dead and forget him. I'm sorry I lied."

"And I'm sorry I acted like a jackass." Lowering his gaze, Catlin drew imaginary circles on the bar with his forefinger. "Anybody courtin' you yet?" he asked huskily.

Zella's laughter was pleasant and mildly teasing. "I've had several marriage proposals," she said, "but none have interested me . . . so far."

Catlin watched her a moment, searching her eyes, her face, making sure she was telling him the truth. Finally, his fears pacified to some degree, he straightened up and pushed away from the bar. He looked past her at Mike the bartender who, for several minutes, had been standing with his back turned to them, pretending to be busy while spying on them in the backbar mirror.

"Hey, Mike."

Startled, the man turned to look at him.

"Did you hear all of that," Catlin asked, "or should we talk louder?"

Mike Forgerty shot Zella an apologetic look, ashamed that he had been caught eavesdropping.

"Tell you what, Mike." Catlin collected the playing cards he and Zella had been using earlier. "How about a game of fifty-two card pick-up? Ever hear of it?"

"No. How's it played?"

Zella smiled in amusement. "You shouldn't have asked him that."

Catlin gathered the cards into his right hand, arched the deck between his thumb and forefinger, and let them fly. Fifty-two cards scattered across the bar and onto the floor.

"Now," he said, laughing, "pick them up."

CHAPTER SIXTEEN

Later, leading Chico by the reins, Catlin walked Zella safely home, a job Mike the bartender usually reserved for himself, and paused with her on the darkened street in front of the Occidental Hotel. A mosquito whined in Catlin's ear, and he swatted at it with his free hand.

"Thank you for walking with me," Zella said. "You didn't have to, you know. I would have been fine."

Catlin glanced up and down Griffin Avenue. It was a Friday night, and there were many more men in town than usual, cowboys, drifters, soldiers, and the like. Their horses lined the hitch rails.

"Wouldn't want nothing untoward to happen to you," he mumbled.

Zella stood on her tiptoes and kissed him lightly on the cheek, and in that instant, Catlin would have gone with her to room six had she only asked him, Eladio Moreno be damned.

She didn't ask.

"*Buenas noches,* Catlin."

"G'night, Zella. See you tomorrow."

Catlin waited for her to disappear into the hotel lobby before he turned away and walked back up Griffin Avenue. He had gone almost a full block when he felt Chico's nose bump him between the shoulder blades and remembered he owned a horse. Silently chiding himself for his absentmindedness, he swung into the saddle.

Catlin put Chico up at the livery stable nearest Myers's

Mercantile and headed for home. Home. He laughed to himself. Home was sipping Madeira wine with Zella and listening
to the sounds of crickets chirping outside their window and
distant guitar music, listening to Zella's quiet voice as she
read aloud to him from one of her books.

Catlin missed very much this aspect of his life. Could it
ever be the same between them as long as Eladio Moreno
lived and breathed? He doubted it and almost wished for another encounter with the slack-jawed coward, this time to
take care of him once and for all. So far, however, Moreno
had yet to show his ugly face in Fort Griffin.

Fumbling in the dark for the house key Ray had given him,
Catlin let himself in and walked softly through the kitchen to
the living room. He was surprised to see a light burning in the
hall and Mary Myers standing in front of Ocie's bedroom
door. Hearing him, she turned to look at him and frowned, at
the same time drawing the blanket she had wrapped up in
more tightly around her body, as if the very sight of him
chilled her.

"Well, should I faint?" she asked him. "How did you
manage to drag in so early?"

She spoke in a hushed voice so as not to awaken anyone,
but her sarcasm was loud and clear.

Catlin didn't let on. "What are you doing up?" he
whispered and glanced down, noticed she was wearing a
dress and black shoes instead of a gown and house slippers.
The toes of her shoes were dusty. "You been somewhere?" he
asked.

"I got up to check on Beth," she said shortly. "That's all."
She flipped the single long braid of hair off her shoulder so
that it dangled down her back, reaching almost to her waist.
"I thought I heard something, a crashing sound." She gestured impatiently at Ocie's closed door. "It came from your

father's room, but he won't tell me what happened, and he won't let me in."

To demonstrate her point, she tapped on the door, and Ocie's voice rumbled like distant thunder.

"Go away, damn it!"

"Ocie, I'm losing patience with you," Mary said. "Must I wake up Ray?"

"Go away!"

"Let me in this very instant," Mary demanded. "Unlock the door."

Her manner annoyed Catlin. She addressed Ocie in a way that made one think the old man was either ignorant of the English language or hard of hearing, speaking slowly and enunciating each syllable. She treated him like a child.

"Go to bed," he told her.

"What?"

"I said, go to bed. I'll make sure he's all right."

"How dare you tell me what to do in my own house!"

"Somebody needs to," he muttered, his voice rough. "Now go to bed."

Mary flung him a seething look and held up a brown glass bottle and a teaspoon. She thrust them toward him.

"He refused to take his medicine this evening," she said, "and I'm fed up with being responsible for him. He's your father. You take care of him. God knows you're just like two peas in a pod, so you should enjoy it!"

She whirled away and disappeared into her and Ray's bedroom, quietly shutting the door behind her. Catlin was glad to see her go.

Mary had left the oil lamp on the floor, and he picked it up now and approached his father's bedroom door. "Pa, it's Cat. Are you all right?"

"Is Mary gone?"

"Yeah, she went on to bed. It's just me."

"Good." There was a long pause, then, "I can't make it to the door, Cat. You'll have to crawl through the window."

Catlin picked the lock instead. Using a long, steel key he'd dug from a pocket of his jeans, he gently probed the lock until he felt the moveable part give. Straightening up, he lifted his lamp and opened the bedroom door.

He found his father lying on the floor beside the toppled bedside table amid a clutter of broken glass, spilled water, and scattered red and black checker pieces. Grunting, propping himself up on one elbow, Ocie bent his neck back to look at him. His face was sweaty and ghastly white.

"Pa, what happened?" Catlin strode across the room and knelt beside him. "Are you hurt?"

"Just help me back into bed," Ocie gasped.

Feeling thoroughly incompetent to handle a situation like this, Catlin helped his father sit up, felt the old man's arm circle his shoulders, and clumsily hoisted him into his bed. Exhausted, Ocie lay flat on his back, eyes closed, his left hand pressed to his heart. Blood smeared his white longjohns, and Catlin noticed then that he had cut his palm on the broken glass when he fell. He sat on the edge of the bed and wrapped a clean towel around his father's hand, his efforts awkward but well-meant.

"Thanks, Tom Cat." Ocie's eyes slitted open. "You can go now. When I make an all-fired fool outta myself, I don't crave no witnesses."

"What happened?"

Ocie sighed. "I got up to raise the window. Head started spinning, and I lost my balance and fell." He scowled ferociously. "Then here comes Mary, squawking like a gol'derned chicken." He slanted his eyes over to look at Catlin. "I'm glad you come along when you did. I'd just as soon die as to have Mary see me splayed out on the floor in my underwear. It's bad enough with you."

"Don't you be worrying yourself none about that," Catlin said, hoping to squelch not only his father's embarrassment but his own, as well. "You need me to do anything for you, Pa? Get you something?"

"I need you to take me home," Ocie said.

Catlin frowned. "You're not gonna start that again, are you?"

"I want to go home," Ocie insisted. "I want to visit your mama's grave one more time and see the farm. I want to sleep under my own roof."

"I don't know, Pa." Catlin absently scratched at a mosquito bite on his arm and considered his father's request. What to do? He drew a deep breath. "Guess I could ask Ray what he thinks . . ."

"No!" Ocie shook his head, glowering. "I'm a grown man, Cat. I don't need Ray or Mary's permission to do a damned thing! They forced me to come here after I got sick, and by God, I won't take it no more!"

Catlin understood his father's anger, for Ray and Mary had used his illness to their own advantage. They had wanted to move into town ever since they got married, but Ocie refused to come with them, and Ray was reluctant to leave the old man alone. Now, too sick and weak to fight them, Ocie was languishing away in unfamiliar surroundings.

At the same time, Ray was not being entirely selfish, and his reasons for not wanting Ocie to return to the farm were legitimate ones. The rough, five-mile trip by horse and wagon could be enough to kill him in itself.

"Stubborn cuss that you are, you've never done anything I ever told you to do," Ocie said at length. "I wish just this once you'd break with tradition. I got a feeling I won't be around much longer."

Catlin listened to his father's words, saddened by them, for he knew he spoke the truth. It helped him to make up his mind.

"When do you want to go?" he asked.

"Ray and Mary are going to a church picnic this Sunday," Ocie replied. "They'll be gone all day. We'll set out as soon as they leave."

"All right. If that's what you want to do."

"It is." Ocie reached over and covered Catlin's hand with his, squeezing hard, something he had never done before. "You're a good boy, Tom Cat." Smiling at the surprise on Catlin's face, he picked up his bottle of medicine and the tea-spoon. "This crap's about as tasty as gyp water," he commented, "but I guess I'd better take it, seeing as how I've got something to look forward to now."

CHAPTER SEVENTEEN

Ray knew the instant he opened up for business Saturday morning and saw the dead rat dangling in the doorway that this was not going to be a good day.

In fact, the realization had dawned on him already. Mary was out of sorts, had been for weeks, and hardly said two words to him all during breakfast. Even little Beth acted cranky this morning and wouldn't stop squalling. To top it off, he suspected someone was stealing from him. Yesterday, he discovered a sack of flour and a can of coffee missing and was certain he hadn't sold them to anyone. This wasn't the first time items had turned up missing from the store in the last month or so.

The rat was just one more reason why he should have covered his head with a pillow and stayed in bed.

The dead rat was dangling at eye level so that it was the first thing Ray noticed when he opened the door. It was fat and gray, the kind he sometimes glimpsed scuttling through the rubbish in the alley, only this one had the unfortunate luck to be hanging by its neck from a rawhide pigging string. The rat's black eyes bulged out of its head like small, glass beads.

Not quite sure what to make of this new development, Ray gazed at the critter and pulled at his earlobe, lips moving silently. He felt Catlin draw up beside him, heard the crackly crunch of his teeth as he bit into a piece of toast.

"Nice decoration," Catlin remarked. "Think it'll attract any new customers?"

"He's back," Ray murmured.

"Who's back? The rat?"

"No, the killer. Charlie Conrad's killer."

Either something Ray had said or the sight of the strung up rat tickled Catlin's funny bone, and he burst out laughing. Not amused, Ray turned to look at him and frowned. As if Catlin's weird sense of humor wasn't aggravating enough, there was that underlying touch of wickedness in his laughter that always made Ray uncomfortable.

"What's so derned funny?" he demanded.

Catlin drew his pocketknife, stepped outside, and cut the rawhide string. Still grinning, he held the rat by the end of the string and twirled it so fast it was only a gray blur.

"Son of a bitch left you his visiting card, Ray."

"You think so, do you?" He watched Catlin hurl the dead rat into the street. "Good riddance then."

Thinking the killer might have left a note behind, as well, Ray searched for one but came up empty-handed.

Fear and dread weighed him down inside. He saw the rat as an ominous sign, a warning of pending danger. Could this be the killer's gruesome way of letting Ray know he was next? The likelihood made him sick to his stomach.

Catlin slapped him on the back, jolting him from his dark thoughts.

"Hey, stop worrying," he said. "As long as you stick close to the store, I doubt anything'll happen. R.D. Luger said Conrad was probably on his way to Jacksboro when the killer nabbed him. He ain't got the guts to kill you in your own home."

"I don't know," Ray said doubtfully. "He had the guts to come and hang a rat on my door."

Catlin couldn't argue with that.

Setting his brother about the task of sorting a shipment of

canned goods he had received the day before, Ray swept the loading platform and paused a moment to survey the town. Though it was light, the sun had not yet risen, and Griffin Avenue was quiet, with only a handful of people stirring, most of them merchants like himself who were preparing for the Saturday rush.

This peaceful hour of the day always made him think of the farm. He missed the old home place at times. He missed the peace and quiet.

Reflecting that he had some free time before the first customers of the day began to trickle in, Ray decided to have a talk with his wife. His concern for her grew stronger with the passing of each day. Mary seemed so distant lately! Of course, she was upset about her brother's failing health. Thinking it might cheer her, Ray had offered to take her to Huntsville to visit Sid two months ago, but she had simply shaken her head and turned away from him. He thought he understood the reason for her refusal. Sid Lane had asked his family not to visit him, too proud to be seen in prison stripes, but Ray felt sure the man would make an exception just this once. Mary needed him.

The door separating the store from their living quarters was slightly ajar, and Ray was about to push it open, when he heard Mary and Deputy Virgil Bone conversing in hushed voices.

The fact that Virgil was visiting with his wife in their kitchen didn't surprise Ray, since the deputy was a frequent guest to their table anyway, or had been until Catlin's arrival. Mary's and Virgil's families were quite close, tied together by both marriage and business, and the two had been friends since childhood. Yet something in the secretive way in which they spoke to each other aroused Ray's curiosity, and he didn't enter the kitchen immediately.

"Have you talked to Ray about this?" Virgil asked.

"No, I keep wanting to ask Ray to make him leave, but I just don't have the heart. He thinks Catlin will protect him. Imagine that!" There was a muffled sob, then, "Every time that man looks at me, I get a chill. I wish he'd die!"

Ray was stunned by his wife's harsh words. So was Virgil.

"Thunder! That don't sound like you, Mary."

She sighed. "I know. It's just that I want Catlin to pay for what he did to Sid, and I need your help. Remember that favor I asked of you last week?"

"Yeah, and I don't think it's such a good idea."

"Why not?" Mary demanded. "You were the one who started the rumor in the first place."

"Making it known that you're suspicious of somebody ain't the same as framing that somebody for murder."

"I don't want to hear any more excuses," Mary said. "Go back to Baby Head Bend, plant the evidence, and show it to the sheriff. He'll think Catlin killed Charlie and arrest him."

"Mary, that ain't gonna work, I tell you. Cat was with us when we found Charlie's body, so even if I planted the evidence at Baby Head it would be inconclusive. Besides, me and Sheriff Luger already combed the place for evidence. He might think it was sort of funny if . . ."

"Do it anyway," Mary snapped. "It's time to act. You said yourself people are talking it up about Catlin and that saloon woman and how they both showed up in Griffin at the same time Charlie's body was found."

"Well . . ."

"We couldn't ask for better timing, Virgil. And don't tell me you wouldn't like to get back at Catlin for all the mean things he's said and done to you in the past," she added.

There was a brief interlude in which Ray heard only the hollow clunking of the deputy's boots as he paced the kitchen floor.

"Oh, all right," Virgil said finally. "I'll do it."

Mary clapped her hands together with relief. "You won't regret this!" she promised.

"I hope not. If Sheriff Luger ever found out . . ."

"He won't find out as long as you're careful. Trust me." Mary paused, then said, "I hear Beth crying again. You'd better go."

"Sure thing. If Cat bothers you, Mary, just give me a holler."

Ray heard the outside kitchen door open and close, and he sagged against the wall, unable to believe what he had just heard. So many questions, worries, and doubts were running through his head that his brain felt suddenly very tired and slow.

He wasn't sure how long he had been standing there, dumbfounded, when he heard Mary walk back into the kitchen. Without thinking about what he was going to say or do, he pushed the door open and looked at her with hollow eyes.

Mary turned away from the cookstove, dirty pots and pans in hand, and spotted him standing in the doorway. Ray noticed that her eyes were red from crying. He shut the door behind him.

"I heard everything," he blurted. His voice sounded foreign to his ears, a stranger's voice.

Mary's face clouded. She turned away from him and placed the dirty cookware into a dishpan of hot water. "You hadn't any right to listen to our conversation."

"Hadn't any right!" Ray exclaimed. "My God, Mary! We're talking about people's lives here. My brother's life!" He stepped toward her. "Mary, look at me."

She faced him, arms folded in front of her, her left eyelid jumping wildly.

"Why are you doing this?" he asked. "Don't you realize the trouble you could get into if Sheriff Luger ever found out what you and Virgil are planning?"

"It would be worth it," Mary stated.

Ray's mouth fell open. "You hate Cat that much?"

"Yes, I do. He's the reason Sid went to prison. He's the reason Sid's dying."

"Mary, think about what you're saying. Cat was the one who braced Sid and got him arrested, but it was Conrad, Wyman, and Fletcher who turned state's evidence against him. They're more to blame than Cat."

"I know," Mary replied coolly, nodding. "And did you see me shed any tears at Charlie Conrad's funeral?"

Ray stared at his wife, shocked, remembering she hadn't shed a solitary tear, and he understood why now. She didn't care that the man had been murdered.

"Is that how you feel about me, too?" he asked quietly, for although he never testified against Sid, he didn't try to help him either. "Do you want me dead, too?"

Mary pressed her palm against his cheek and kissed him tenderly on the lips. "Of course not," she said. "Nothing will happen to you, honey. I'll see to that."

"How?" Ray asked, frowning.

She shook her head. "I can't tell you."

Shoulders slumping, Ray sighed gloomily. He felt deflated. "You'll confide in Virgil, but you won't confide in me, your very own husband. I thought you loved me."

"Oh, Ray, I do love you!"

"Then tell me what's going on. What's the big secret?"

Refusing to answer, she looked away from him, chin and bottom lip quivering.

Ray was at a loss. He didn't know how to reach her. He thrust his fists into his trouser pockets and gazed dismally down at the scrubbed floor.

"If you won't talk to me," he said, "then at least listen to me. Leave Catlin out of this mess, Mary. He has enough problems of his own without you and Virgil bringing on more."

Mary's features altered in a way that frightened Ray. Her face paled. Soft, heart-shaped lips twisted with fury.

"You're taking his side over mine," she said bitterly.

"Mary, please . . ."

"Your brother is morally dead," she continued. "He's a drunkard and a womanizer. Aunt Cora told me how he tried to force himself on her. Yet you take his side!"

"Mary, all he did was kiss her on the cheek!"

"I don't care. It was vulgar, and I don't want him around our daughter."

"But he loves Beth," Ray countered. "He'd never hurt her."

Mary shook her head, eyes filling with pity. "Ray, are you really so blind? Catlin doesn't know how to love." She turned away and began vigorously scrubbing on a pot, as if she were taking her frustrations out on the dirty dishes. "I want him out of our home tomorrow," she said at length. "Either he leaves or I do. Take your pick."

Ray sighed. "You'd leave me?"

"Yes."

"But . . ."

"Let's not argue anymore," she interrupted. "I assume we're still going to the church picnic tomorrow, and I have a hundred things to do before we leave."

"Maybe we shouldn't go."

"We'll go. We have to keep up appearances."

Staring at Mary's back, trying to think of something else to say, wondering if he should beg her not to leave him or walk out and slam the door, Ray was struck by how much she reminded him of Sid Lane. Imperious, deceitful, almost cold.

It was a side of his wife he never dreamed existed.

CHAPTER EIGHTEEN

Still pondering on what to do about Mary, Ray walked back into the store and found Catlin just finishing up the task of shelving the canned goods. Considering Cat Myers was a man who spent most of his time with a deck of cards in his hand, it seemed strange to see him doing respectable work. Ray wondered how long he could keep him here.

Unbeknown to Catlin, Ray's hired man had not hurt his back at all but was simply taking a paid vacation at his boss's request. This gave Ray an excuse for keeping Catlin close to the store. Unfortunately his brother was easily bored, and it was a daily challenge to find something new for him to do.

Ray drew up beside him just as he plunked the last can on the shelf and realized he didn't know the meaning of organization.

"You've mixed the cans of tomatoes with the canned milk," Ray complained, feeling rather testy anyway.

Catlin jumped as if someone had stabbed him in the back. "Damn! Don't do that!"

"I'm sorry," Ray apologized, realizing he had walked up on Catlin's blind side. "I thought you heard me come in."

"What difference does it make if the tomatoes sit on the same shelf as the milk?"

"No one can find what they're looking for."

"Well, hell, all they have to do is read the labels."

Ray sighed, wondering why he was quibbling over something so trivial when his whole life seemed to be crumbling down around his ears.

"Cat, will you do me a favor?"

"Depends on what it is."

"Stay away from Zella Moreno."

Catlin eyed him narrowly. "You look sort of peaked today, Ray. You got a headache?"

"Don't change the subject. I want you to stay away from the Moreno woman."

"May I ask why? Or is that none of my business?"

His sarcasm wasn't lost on Ray. "It's for your own good," he said sternly. "Virgil Bone's been spreading it around that you and Zella have something to do with Charlie Conrad's murder. He knows that she tried to hire you two years ago to avenge Eddie McCall's death."

Catlin had been lounging against the counter, and he slowly straightened now. "Bone's trying to point the blame at Zella, too?"

Ray nodded. "She's going to get you into trouble if you don't keep away from her," he warned.

Catlin shouldered past him and made for the door.

"Cat, wait! Where are you going?"

"To find Bone."

Grabbing his hat, Ray hurried after his brother, then remembered he hadn't locked up. Turning back, he closed and locked the door, and jogged across Third Street. He caught up with Catlin in front of the hardware store and gripped his shoulder.

"Don't do anything foolish, Cat."

Catlin shrugged free of his grasp. "All I'm gonna do is talk to him. Where would Bone be this time of morning? The jail?"

"I guess so. We can look."

They crossed main street to Fort Griffin's log jailhouse. A Roman-nosed buckskin gelding was standing three-legged at the hitch rail in front of the jail, and Ray recognized it as belonging to the sheriff. He noted with relief that Virgil Bone's horse was nowhere in sight.

Although the county seat had been moved to the town of Albany in '74, Sheriff Luger deemed it necessary to spend the majority of his time here in Fort Griffin, this being where the county's most unsavory characters preferred to congregate. The jail door was flung wide open to let in some fresh air, and Ray followed Catlin into the tiny front office.

R.D. Luger was hunkered over his desk, shuffling through a pile of wanted dodgers. Hearing them, he looked up.

"Howdy do, fellas."

Ray nodded. "Good morning, Sheriff."

Catlin planted both hands on Luger's cluttered desk and leaned toward him. "Where's your deputy, R.D.?"

When R.D. glanced his way, Ray frowned and shook his head.

The sheriff leaned back in his chair and clasped his hands behind his neck. "Oh, Virgil's out and about, I reckon," he replied casually. "Why, Cat? Do you have a bone to pick with him?" He grinned at his accidental pun.

"Tell me where he is."

R.D. heaved a sigh. "Why don't you talk to me first?"

"Bone's been shootin' off at the mouth about Zella Moreno," Catlin said. "I don't give a rat's ass what kind of lies he spouts about me, but you tell him to leave Zella out of this."

"All Virgil's doing is following up on every lead he can think of," R.D. said, his tone patient, soothing. "That's what makes him a good deputy. Right now, the whole county's breathing down our necks, pushing us to arrest somebody for Charlie's murder. It puts a strain on us."

"Well, it's starting to put a strain on me, too," Catlin said, and he straightened up from R.D.'s desk. "You tell that horsefly deputy of yours to lay off."

R.D. nodded. "I'll have a talk with him."

"Cat was with me when Charlie was murdered," Ray said. "We were riding in from El Paso. How could he be in two places at the same time?"

"Beats me." R.D. smiled. "I bet you even Virgil ain't figured that one out yet."

Catlin stepped toward the little stove in the corner of R.D.'s office, the rowels on his spurs chinging against the floor, and helped himself to a cup of coffee.

"Any suspects?" he asked. "Besides me, I mean?"

"Oh, just about two dozen horse thieves, twice that many cow thieves, and a coupla gun-toting toughs from up around Injun Territory." R.D. jetted a stream of tobacco juice into the waste basket near his chair. "Me and Virgil have questioned five gents so far. If I don't make an arrest pretty soon . . ." He left the conjecture dangling and brushed a forefinger against the gold star pinned to his vest.

"You'll lose your job?" Ray asked.

"Most likely."

Catlin sipped his coffee. "Maybe you need a new deputy," he suggested wryly.

No sooner had he gotten the words out than Deputy Bone burst into the office.

Catlin wrinkled his nose. "Speak of the devil."

"Bad news!" Virgil exclaimed. Panting, out of breath, he handed R.D. a scrap of paper. "Frank Wyman found this note pinned to his front door this morning."

His features tightening, Sheriff Luger read the note aloud: " 'I am a man more sinned against than sinning. You will pay dearly for your transgressions against me, Frank, just as

Charlie Conrad and Ben Fletcher have paid.' "

Ray felt as if he might pass out.

"Bastard's got a way with words," Catlin remarked.

"More Shakespeare," Ray said, and he looked across at the sheriff. "He's killed Ben Fletcher."

R.D. rose, picked up his rifle, and headed for the door. "Let's find out."

Following the sheriff, Virgil Bone, and Catlin out of the office, Ray noticed a man wearing a large sombrero, a dirty white shirt, and striped trousers loitering on the boardwalk nearby. At sight of the four men, the Mexican ducked his head and turned half around. He flicked a corn shuck cigarette into the street and started to walk away.

Catlin stopped so suddenly that Ray almost crashed into him.

"Hey, you! Eladio Moreno!"

The Mexican hesitated, back stiffening.

"You looking for me, Moreno?"

Eladio Moreno slowly turned. Sweat beaded his forehead. He glanced across at R.D. Luger, who was standing beside his horse and watching Catlin.

"If you kill me, *Gato,* the sheriff, he will arrest you."

"Zella tells me you're the one who wants to kill me," Catlin said. One corner of his mouth lifted in a smile. "Are you feeling lucky today, Moreno?"

Sheriff Luger stepped up on the boardwalk. "Cat, how about you boys take this fight out of town. A stray bullet's liable to hit some pillar of the community, and your tail'll be in a crack sure enough."

"My bullets don't stray," Catlin replied, never taking his gaze off the Mexican.

Moreno licked his lips, quick eyes darting from Catlin to the sheriff. "Not today, *Gato,*" he said finally. "Maybe some other time." He began to edge away and suddenly took off at a fast walk down the street.

Before Ray could prevent it, Catlin dashed after the man, caught up with him in three strides, and swung him around by the arm. Eyes wide with panic, Moreno started to tilt up the sawed-off shotgun that was looped to his belt.

"Cat, watch out!"

Grabbing the shotgun, Catlin jerked it free and took a swift step back. He aimed the blunt double barrels at Eladio Moreno's chest. Unarmed, Moreno hiked his arms into the air, and Ray's stomach tightened with fear.

"Myers, drop it!" Virgil Bone drew his sidearm. "Drop the gun!"

Disregarding the deputy's order, Catlin broke Moreno's shotgun open, ejected two shells from the breech, and very calmly proceeded to whack the empty weapon over the hitching rail. Moreno stood by and watched in open-mouthed dismay as pieces of his shotgun flew off into space. People stopped in the street to observe the unusual sight.

Breathing hard from his exertions, Catlin finally flung what was left of the shotgun at Moreno's feet.

"Unless you want me to do the same thing to you," he said, "stop following me around and leave Zella alone. She doesn't want you anymore."

Shoving his hands into his pockets, Eladio Moreno backed away from Catlin, muttered something in Spanish, and walked away. His broken gun still lay on the boardwalk. Ray exhaled, relieved that the shotgun was the only casualty, and wiped the sweat from his face with his kerchief. His lungs ached, and he realized he had been holding his breath. He and Sheriff Luger exchanged harried glances. It had been a close call.

R.D. and Virgil urged the crowd of onlookers to go on

about their business, and Catlin jerked his head at Ray.

"Get your horse," he said. "We're going with R.D."

"What was that all about?"

"A personal matter," Catlin replied and smiled, seemingly unconcerned that he had just caused a major disruption in the town's ordinary day.

Ray didn't question him further. Eladio Moreno was either Zella's husband or a relative, and he wasn't sure he cared to find out which.

Hurrying to the livery stable, Ray and Catlin saddled their horses in silence and met the sheriff and Virgil Bone at the river crossing north of town. Frank Wyman, a pale-eyed man with curly, carrot-orange hair, galloped toward them seconds later with coattail flying and one hand clamping a gray derby on his head.

The five men splashed their mounts across the river and pointed them roughly eastward.

Ben Fletcher, retired and recently widowed, divided his time between the domino hall and the fishing holes. He lived in Albany but also owned a small cabin on the north bank of the Clear Fork where he stayed during his frequent fishing excursions. The cabin was only a mile or so from Fort Griffin.

"I saw old Ben just yesterday," Virgil said, breaking the silence. "He was buying liver from the butcher's to use for bait."

A jumbo grasshopper flew up from the weeds and clung to Sheriff Luger's shirt sleeve. He swiped it away with his hand. "Ben must be gettin' lazy," he remarked. "He used to use hoppers for bait. He told me once they were the best for catching channel cats."

"Guess he got tired of running 'em down," Catlin said. "Damned perch steal your bait more often than not anyway."

R.D. nodded. "That's a fact. I sure would like to dip a

hook in the river, though. Have a good fish fry before winter settles in."

Riding ahead of the others, Virgil Bone twisted around in the saddle to frown at the sheriff and Catlin. "How can you two talk about fish fries at a time like this?"

"What do you want us to talk about?" Catlin asked. "Headless corpses?"

"Good Lord." Frank Wyman fanned his red, sweaty face with his derby. "Ben picked a thorry time to go fishing," he lisped.

Catlin glanced at Ray and smirked.

A horse had kicked Frank in the mouth several months ago, knocking out five of his front teeth, and he now had trouble pronouncing his s's and z's. Ray reflected that only his brother was immature enough to find it humorous.

"There's the cabin," Virgil said abruptly, pointing.

Ben Fletcher's little cabin was almost invisible, tucked away among the tall, shady trees and covered on one side by some sort of wild-growing vine. Yellow beams of sunlight slanted across the cabin's shingled roof. Sniffing, Ray caught a faint whiff of woodsmoke. Nearby the cabin was Fletcher's buckboard wagon.

"Maybe Mr. Fletcher's all right," he said.

R.D. cupped his hands around his mouth. "Hello the house!"

A wild turkey gobbled in response, but there was no other sound, save the jingle of bridle chains and an occasional snort from one of the horses. Ray saw Catlin lift his Winchester from its customary position on the saddlehorn. He balanced it across his lap, fidgeting, jiggling the rifle's lever with his forefinger.

R.D. tried again. "Ben! You around?"

Silence.

147

The five men dismounted and approached the cabin cautiously. A chill shinnied up Ray's spine, for dangling from the door knob was a short length of rope knotted into a hangman's noose.

Virgil drew his gun. "This don't look so good," he whispered.

Sheriff Luger knocked on the door, and it creaked open. Ray peered over his shoulder to look inside and found the cabin's single room empty. The bunk was neatly made and covered with a patchwork quilt. Fletcher's camping gear lay in a corner of the room, cooking utensils and tins of cornmeal and coffee had been unpacked and set out on the rough-hewn table. A scattering of live coals glowed among the ashes in the stone fireplace, accounting for the smoke Ray had smelled earlier.

"If his buckboard's here," Virgil said, "then where's his horse?"

Sheriff Luger cast a final glance inside the cabin. "No sign of a struggle," he observed. "Split up, boys. Dead or alive, Ben's around here somewhere. He may be pulling one of them big channel cats out of the river right this minute."

Ray rather doubted that, but went through the motions anyway, searching the trees for movement, hollering the old man's name. Farther away, Catlin ranged this way and that, slowly working his way to the river bank. He squatted down occasionally to study the ground, searching for tracks. A few minutes later, Ray heard his brother's shrill whistle.

He followed the others down to the river bottoms and saw Catlin standing beside Ben Fletcher's black mare. She had been tied near the water's edge, her lead rope weighted down by a rock. Ben Fletcher's cane fishing pole was jabbed into the wet sand. There were a pocket knife, extra hooks, and some other odds and ends lying nearby on a boulder's flat surface. A colony of ants had discovered the beef liver and were busily transporting it bit by bit to their nest.

"Well, we've got his horse," R.D. said. "Now if we could just find Ben."

Catlin stroked the mare's glossy neck and tipped his head slightly, gesturing down river. "He's over there."

Ray didn't see anything at first. He shaded his eyes against the sparkling glare of sunlight on water.

"Thunder!" Virgil exclaimed.

Stumbling forward over the rocky bank, Ray saw Ben Fletcher then, or part of him at least, and groaned, clamping a hand over his mouth.

Impaled on Fletcher's very own walking stick at the edge of the Clear Fork of the Brazos was the old man's head.

CHAPTER NINETEEN

Ben Fletcher's body lay half in the water and was partially hidden by a tree's overhanging branches. Virgil Bone and Frank Wyman dragged the body onto the bank. Grimacing, Sheriff Luger pulled the end of Fletcher's cane out of the mud, head and all, and laid it gingerly beside the corpse.

Weak in the knees, nauseated, Ray sought out a shady spot on the river bank, tripped over an exposed tree root, and fell, tearing a hole in the knee of his trousers. Virgil helped him to his feet and offered him a handful of Dr. Bristol's Neutralizers. Shaking his head, Ray listened to Virgil's teeth crunch the tablets and to Frank Wyman puke up his morning coffee.

Sheriff Luger scratched his jaw. "Poor old Ben. Never had a chance."

"At least we found him before the buzzards and coyotes did," Ray heard himself saying. His voice sounded small and far away, as if he were speaking through a very long tunnel.

Virgil sighed loudly. "I think I must have a stomach ulcer," he said. "I've read about 'em. Nasty things. All this mental strain seems to be stirring it up considerable."

"Can't you think of anything besides your aches and pains?" Ray snapped.

Virgil shot him a startled look and said no more.

Leaving the two lawmen to search the scene of Fletcher's murder for clues, a sick Frank Wyman sat in the shade, and Ray looked around for his brother. Catlin had never been the squeamish type, so he was surprised to see him still standing alone upstream with the old man's horse. He was smoking a cigarette and staring into the water.

Eyes squinted, Sheriff Luger followed Ray's glance. "What's the matter with Cat? Got a weak stomach today?"

"I guess so."

Squatting beside Fletcher's body, R.D. gave him a hasty examination and rose. "Shot through the heart and beheaded," he announced. "Same as with Conrad. My guess is he was killed late yesterday afternoon. Virge, have you found anything of interest?"

"An empty bullet casing," Virgil replied and tossed it to him. "Fifty caliber and reloaded. Why would the killer leave the casings behind if he likes to reload them?"

"In a hurry, I reckon."

"Yeah, but he took time to wipe out his tracks," Virgil pointed out. "I ain't seen nary a footprint . . . Hey, wait a sec. Sheriff, take a look at this!"

Alerted by the deputy's excited voice, R.D., Ray, and Frank Wyman hurried to see what he had discovered.

Clearly outlined in the smooth mud at the water's edge was a single boot print. The track was quite small for a man, and Ray noticed a star pattern in the heel. He frowned slightly, staring at that print, and suddenly turned to the sheriff.

"The killer wears Lone Star boots," he said. "It's a new type of cowboy boot made by a company in Austin. I know because I ordered a shipment of them."

Frank Wyman nodded. "I know the brand," he said. "I ordered a few pairth of them mythelf for the emporium. They haven't come in yet, though."

"Ray, can you remember who all's bought these boots from you?" R.D. asked.

"I haven't sold a single pair so far," Ray said. "Most of the cowhands around here only want custom-made boots. But I had a pair stolen from me while I was out of town."

"Stolen?"

Ray nodded. "I've been having a problem with thieves."

Frowning, R.D. lifted his Stetson and mopped his head with a red bandana. "Damn it all," he muttered. "Nothing but dead ends."

Casting about for more tracks, Virgil suddenly bent down and pulled something out of the tall grass. Ray saw it was a canteen with a carved wooden stopper and a woolen, sun-bleached covering. Stenciled into the cloth on one side of the canteen, faded, barely legible, were the letters, CSA.

Ray felt his heart start to pound. The canteen looked exactly like the one Catlin had been carrying during the long ride from El Paso! But how did it end up here? Unless . . . He cast an accusing glance at Virgil Bone, remembering the conversation he had overheard earlier between Mary and the deputy.

Sheriff Luger inspected the canteen. "Confederate States of America," he said thoughtfully.

There was more, smaller lettering beneath this, hand-written in ink, and assuming it was Catlin's name, Ray held his breath while the sheriff and his deputy squinted at it, trying to make out the scrawled, faded out script.

"It's somebody's name, I bet," Virgil said.

"Bradford L. Gilley."

At the sound of Catlin's voice, Ray turned to look at him, puzzled, not sure what he was up to. It didn't take him long to figure it out. Catlin strode past him and started to grab the canteen from Virgil Bone's hand. Twisting away from him, the deputy yanked it out of his reach.

"Hands off, Myers. This is evidence."

"Like hell it is. That canteen belongs to me."

Dismayed, Ray lifted his gaze heavenward.

Virgil stroked one end of his black handlebar mustache and glanced sideways at R.D. Luger. "You hear that, Sheriff? He says it belongs to him." A triumphant gleam came into his eyes. "I don't guess we have to look any further for our killer."

"For God's sake!" Ray exclaimed, stepping forward, shoving past Frank Wyman. "That's a bald-faced lie, and you know it!"

Sheriff Luger interceded with customary coolness. "Simmer down, Ray. Let's take this slow and easy. Cat, if this canteen's yours, what's it doing here? Any ideas?"

"Not a one."

R.D. contemplated that, sighed, scratched his head.

I've got an idea or two, Ray thought, and the words were on the tip of his tongue when he remembered his wife, and fear overtook him, muted him. If he exposed Virgil Bone for framing Catlin, he must also expose Mary. He found himself in a no-win situation.

"Myers didn't have the canteen with him when he wath looking for Ben," Frank Wyman remarked.

Virgil nodded in agreement, finding an ally. "Tell me, Myers, who's Bradford L. Gilley?"

"None of your damned business," Catlin replied. His voice was quiet. Too quiet.

Just now seeming to comprehend what all this was leading up to, he stood perfectly still, frozen in place, his gaze locked on the deputy, his face tense and unreadable. Ray recognized the stance, the look, and was frightened by this— the calm before the storm. He sidled toward his brother until he was almost touching him, hoping to prevent him from doing something rash.

"Who is Gilley?" Virgil persisted. "Your accomplice?"

"Let's not get carried away," R.D. said. "So far, this is the only evidence we've got against him."

"The only evidence?" Virgil's mouth fell open. "Sheriff, everything points right at him! What more do we need?"

"Good point," Wyman chimed in.

"So y'all think I'm the killer," Catlin said, his voice still quiet, restrained. "If I was gonna kill somebody, I wouldn't waste time writing silly ass threats sprinkled with quotes from Shakespeare." He glanced at Ray hovering behind and a little to the side of him. "And what about Ray? Do you think I'd kill my own brother?"

A smile lurked beneath the shade of Virgil's heavy mustache. "Did Cain slay Abel?" he asked slyly. "You ain't got a conscience, Myers. I think you'd kill just about anybody if the pay was good."

A tremor passed through Catlin's body. Ray felt it and moved closer, clutching his brother's arm.

"As for the threats," Virgil continued, "maybe that was your lady friend's doings."

"Virge, that's a'plenty," R.D. warned.

"No, sir, it's just now gettin' interesting." Virgil pointed to the boot track in the mud. "See that footprint, Myers? Mighty small, ain't it? Maybe it ain't a man's footprint a'tall."

Ray looked at his brother, caught the wicked glint of that one green eye. The storm clouds were darkening.

Virgil handed the canteen to Sheriff Luger and took a slow step toward Catlin.

"You know what I think, Myers?" he asked softly. "I think that footprint was made by a woman . . . Zella Moreno."

"Virgil!" Sheriff Luger's voice cracked like a whip. "Enough!"

The deputy ignored him. "How about it, Myers? Was your

little hot tamale with you when you bumped off Ben Fletcher? Did she help you cut off his head?"

Catlin thumbed the butt of his cigarette into the river, and the storm erupted with silent, lightning fury.

CHAPTER TWENTY

Even expecting it, Ray was not prepared. Catlin lunged at Virgil Bone, tearing free of Ray's grasp, and dove into him with such force the watching men heard the impact and the whoosh of Virgil's breath as Catlin landed on top of him. Punching, thrashing, grappling, the two men rolled over and over down the gently sloping embankment to the river.

Ray started toward them, but Sheriff Luger caught him by the shoulder, stopping him, shaking his head.

"Let 'em go at it," he said. "As long as they're using their fists and not their guns or knives, it'll be all right." He sighed and dug into his vest pocket for his chewing tobacco. "Maybe they'll get it out of their systems."

Watching the two men fight, Frank Wyman said, "Before they do, you'll have a dead deputy."

Ray worried he might be right. He stood on the river bank and watched Catlin and Virgil slug away at each other. They were in the water now, sopping wet and muddy, and it was crystal clear to all of them—possibly even to Virgil Bone himself—that this would be over in short order.

Quick as a wink and strong despite his slim build, Catlin was in the process of beating Virgil's head off when he suddenly slipped in the mud and went down. Not inhibited by prize ring rules or referees, Virgil took advantage of an unexpected opportunity and swung a chunk of driftwood at him. It struck Catlin hard on the left shoulder. He swung again, but Catlin was ready for him this time, and he grabbed Virgil's wrist, tugging, twisting, wrenching, and dragged the man down into the river with him and into deeper water.

Seizing a fistful of Virgil's hair, Catlin dunked his head below the water's surface. Virgil wrestled his way back up, arms and legs flailing, and gasped for air. He was fighting the river now instead of Catlin, and Ray caught a glimpse of his white, panic-stricken face an instant before his head disappeared again beneath brown water.

"Sheriff . . ." Ray began.

But Sheriff Luger was already hurrying forward, moving fast for a big man, Ray not far behind him, both of them intent on saving one drowning deputy. As it turned out, there was no need.

Treading water easily a short distance from the floundering Virgil Bone, Catlin took a quick breath and reached the man in three strokes. He managed to get his arm around Virgil's neck, at the same time dodging his threshing limbs, and swam to shallow water with the deputy in tow.

Ray and Sheriff Luger splashed into the river, grasped Virgil beneath the arms, and dragged him onto the bank. Choking, spluttering, mouth gaping, he lay there and pressed his thumb and forefinger against closed eyes.

Catlin sat on a rock and poured the water from his boots. His nose was bleeding profusely, rich red drops dripping from his lips and chin. Ray handed him his white kerchief.

Sheriff Luger broke the silence. "You know what I oughta do?" he asked, his voice edged with anger. "I oughta slap handcuffs on the both of you and cart you off to jail! Make you share a cell for a damned week!"

Catlin tugged his boots back on, repositioned his eyepatch, and picked up his hat. "Your fine deputy's the one started it," he said. "All I did was finish it."

"The thame way you finished Charlie Conrad and Ben

Fletcher?" Wyman asked. His pale, lashless eyes bulged with suspicion.

Catlin scowled at him. "Keep it up, you baby-talking bastard. Just keep it up . . ."

"And you'll do what?"

Pressing Ray's handkerchief beneath his bleeding nostrils, Catlin cut that green eye over to look at the redhead. "I'll kill you," he said, "and tell God you died."

Ray jabbed Catlin sharply in the ribs.

"Frank," R.D. said, diverting his attention, "go hitch Ben's horse to the buckboard and fetch a coupla blankets from the cabin. Plumb indecent, lettin' Ben lay there on the ground like that."

Frank Wyman cast a final, bug-eyed look at Catlin, turned quickly, and tramped off to get Fletcher's horse.

"R.D., if you're finished with my canteen, I want it back," Catlin said.

Sheriff Luger shook his head slowly, almost regretfully. "Can't do that, Cat. Not for a little while."

"Why? You think I killed Fletcher?"

Recovering from his scare, Virgil Bone sat up, waiting impatiently for his boss's response.

R.D. spat tobacco juice and watched a hawk wheel in slow circles high above them in a cloudless sky. "It's like Virge told you," he said after a moment. "The canteen's evidence." He finally met Catlin's intent gaze. "I can't just ignore it."

"Ha!" Virgil slapped his thigh.

Catlin seemed about to say something, then changed his mind and left them without a word, striding up the slope, disappearing finally from their sight among the trees and underbrush. A moment later, Ray heard the dull pounding of Chico's hooves.

"About time he left," Virgil commented. "The air's

cleaner already." He staggered to his feet and checked for loose teeth, gently wiggling each one. "Thunderation, that chunkhead's got hard fists."

R.D. nodded. "Cat always was a holy terror in a tussle."

"Well, next time . . ."

"There won't be a next time."

". . . It'll be with a gun and a pair of handcuffs," Virgil finished.

"Don't you even think about it."

"Somebody needs to! Crazy fool tried to drown me."

"He pulled you out of the water," Ray reminded him.

"Because he had witnesses." Virgil peered at Ray through puffy, bruised eyelids. "You didn't see the look on Myers's face when he pushed me under the water. He knows derned well I can't swim."

"Don't get yourself all worked up again," R.D. said. "What's done is done. Right now, we've got two murders to solve."

"They're already solved!" Virgil scowled at the sheriff and at Ray, smoothed his wet hair back, and clapped on his hat. "I've had a belly full of you two tippy-toeing around Cat Myers like he's somebody special. He ain't nothing but a cold-blooded killer, and you both know it!"

Virgil left in a huff, and seeing a chance to speak with the deputy alone, Ray started to follow. Sheriff Luger stopped him.

"Do me a favor, Ray. Find out from Cat who Bradford Gilley is, will you?"

Ray sighed. "I'll try."

"And be careful."

Something in his tone of voice made Ray wonder. "You don't honestly think . . ."

"I don't know what to think," R.D. said, cutting him

short. He tugged absently at a long, black hair growing from his left nostril. "Cat's a loose cannon. Always has been. So don't get too comfortable around him just because he was your baby brother once."

"Maybe . . . maybe somebody's trying to frame him," Ray suggested cautiously.

R.D. shrugged. "Maybe."

Ray didn't think he sounded very convinced.

Deeply worried, he returned to the place where they had left their horses. Virgil Bone had just tightened the cinch on his saddle and was about to untie his horse when he heard Ray and looked around. One of his eyes was now swollen entirely shut, the other very nearly so, and his lips were broken and bloody.

"What d'you want?" he demanded.

Ray ambled toward him, feeling his soggy socks squishing within waterlogged shoes. "I want to know how long you think you can pull the wool over Sheriff Luger's eyes and get away with it," he said.

"I don't follow you."

"Don't play games with me," Ray snapped. "I heard you talking to Mary this morning. I know what you're up to."

Thrusting the tip of his tongue into the gap between his two front teeth, Virgil dropped his gaze to the ground and kicked at a tuft of grass with his bootheel.

"I guess this was more convenient than leaving Cat's canteen where Charlie Conrad was murdered, wasn't it?" Ray continued, his voice rising along with his temper. "If I wasn't afraid of getting Mary into trouble, I'd tell Sheriff Luger everything. I'd make sure you lost your badge!"

Virgil gaped at him, shaking his head, seemingly surprised. "But I didn't plant the canteen!"

"You're a liar, too, I see."

160

"No!" Virgil cast a quick look around to make sure Sheriff Luger and Frank Wyman weren't within earshot and turned back to Ray. "Look here, I never laid eyes on that canteen until a few minutes ago. I swear it!"

"We'll see about that. My wife will tell me the truth."

"She'll tell you exactly what I'm trying to tell you now." Stepping closer to his horse, Virgil unbuckled the flap on one of his saddlebags and drew out a crinkled, dirt-smudged envelope. He thrust it toward Ray. "Mary went through your brother's stuff and found this letter. It's from Zella Moreno. Mary told me to leave it at Baby Head Bend . . . as evidence."

Ray accepted the letter and turned it over in his hand, reading the bold, flowing script, unconsciously comparing in his mind Zella Moreno's handwriting to the killer's writing. There was no resemblance. He suddenly realized what he was doing and loathed himself for it. I'm getting as bad as Virgil Bone, he thought. The letter had been sent to Catlin in Tres Alamos, Arizona, and was postmarked El Paso, Texas, June 1, 1877.

"I read the letter," Virgil said. "There's nothing incriminatin' in it." The deputy touched his mangled bottom lip and examined his findings, frowning at the blood on the tip of his finger. "The letter's all Mary gave me. I swear it," he said. "I told her it was a fool idea. Didn't want no part of it, but she . . ."

"If you didn't somehow plant Cat's canteen here," Ray said, "then who did?"

Virgil looked at him as if he had just uttered the most simpleton statement he'd ever heard. "Don't you see?" he asked incredulously. "Your brother dropped it on accident when he murdered Ben Fletcher!"

Frowning, Ray studied the deputy's beat up face. He had known Virgil Bone for years, long enough to think he would recognize if he was telling him a whopper, and looking at Virgil now, seeing the man's gaze hold his own without wavering, he suspected Virgil Bone was not lying. He had not planted the canteen.

He watched the deputy turn and swing into the saddle. "Where are you going?"

"Back to town." Virgil smiled sheepishly. "To the doctor. Don't want these wounds to get infected."

CHAPTER TWENTY-ONE

There seemed to be nothing left for Ray to do now but return to town and wait in dread for the other shoe to drop. He rode part of the way with Virgil, neither of them saying a word, an uncomfortable silence that was thankfully broken when Ray spotted Catlin's horse grazing near the river. He broke off from Virgil and rode toward the bay gelding, ducking low beneath overhanging tree branches. Chico's head flew up at Ray's approach, tufts of grass sticking out the corners of his mouth, and he nickered a soft greeting.

Ray left his horse with Chico and wandered down to the river in search of Catlin. He found him sitting in the sunshine at the edge of a steep drop-off overlooking the water, legs dangling off the side. Hearing his footsteps, Catlin looked around, at the same time lifting his Winchester rifle, bringing it to bear on him with one hand before he realized who it was.

"Announce yourself next time." He set the rifle aside and faced the river again. "Good way to get shot."

Searching the ground for stickers, bugs, and cow patties, Ray flopped down beside Catlin, taking care not to sit on his blind side. He watched his brother remove the cylinder from his Colt .45 and carefully wipe it dry with the only part of Ray's white kerchief that was not soaked in blood.

"Instead of drying your gun off," Ray said, "you ought to be drying yourself. You look half-drowned."

Giving no indication he had heard, Catlin proceeded to tear a corner off the handkerchief and run it through each of the cylinder's six chambers with a stick.

Ray picked at the frayed tear in the knee of his trousers. "What are you thinking about, Cat? Talk to me."

"I'm thinking that jackass deputy broke my nose."

"Let me see." Ray inspected Catlin's red, swollen nose and ran his forefinger up and down the bridge of it. "It's not broken," he concluded. "Anyway, Virgil looks a lot worse than you do."

"Good. How much you want to bet the first thing he does when he hits town is head for the doctor?"

"As a matter of fact," Ray said, "that's exactly where he's going right now."

Catlin nodded. "Puny bastard."

"He's not too puny to arrest you," Ray warned. At Catlin's puzzled look, he explained: "Virgil said it would be with a gun and handcuffs next time."

"I should've let him drown."

"I wouldn't mind drowning both of you."

Catlin glanced at him but made no comment.

"If you'd only kept your mouth shut, nobody would ever have known the canteen was yours," Ray went on. "To top it off, you threaten to kill Frank Wyman! That's the worst thing you could've done under the circumstances."

"I was just joking."

Ray made a face. "Yeah, you were a barrel of laughs all right."

He fell silent, trying to think what to do, what to say, what not to say. He felt inside his suitcoat pocket for Catlin's letter and wondered whether he should tell Cat about Mary and Virgil's foiled scheme. He didn't know who to trust any more.

No matter how hard he tried to ignore it, the seed of suspicion Virgil had sown was starting to take root in not only Sheriff Luger's mind, but in his own, as well. It occurred to him that Catlin might, in fact, be involved somehow in the deaths of Charlie Conrad and Ben Fletcher, perhaps indirectly, but still involved. How else could his canteen have ended up at the murder scene?

Sitting beside him, watching him assemble his gun with deft fingers, Ray wondered, *Is Virgil right about you? Would you kill me?* Catlin glanced over at him. "Somebody's trying to set me up," he said, almost as if in answer to Ray's unspoken questions.

"Who?" Ray asked. "The killer?"

"I don't know. You see, there's only one person . . ." He hesitated, casting a cautious look at Ray, and finished lamely, "I don't know."

"Only one person," Ray repeated. "Who?"

"I said I don't know, so stop saying who! What are you? A damned hoot owl?"

Ray sighed, noting the sudden roughness of Catlin's voice, so much like their father's. "Listen, Cat, let's stop keeping secrets from each other, all right? There's only one person besides you and me who has easy access to your belongings, and that's my wife. Is that what you were going to say?"

Catlin appeared surprised, but he didn't deny it.

Ray nodded. "That's what I thought, too, at first," he said, and he drew the letter from his pocket and gave it to Catlin. "But not any more. Mary's not at fault."

Frowning, Catlin looked from the letter to Ray. "Where'd you get this?" he demanded.

Starting from the beginning, taking a chance with his own honesty, Ray related the conversation he had overheard between his wife and Virgil Bone, then went on to recount his later argument with the deputy over the canteen.

When he had finished his tale, Catlin stared at him a moment, poker-faced, and idly slapped the letter against his thigh.

"I don't believe him," he said finally. "The son of a bitch left my canteen there . . . just like he was gonna leave this letter at Baby Head."

Ray shook his head. "He wasn't lying, Cat."

"How can you say that? You heard him and Mary making plans for me." Catlin took off his hat so the sunshine could dry his hair and gave a soft, humorless laugh. "Mary said she'd make my life hell if I stayed in Fort Griffin. She wasn't bluffing."

It was Ray's turn to be surprised. "Mary threatened you?"

"Yeah. The day after we got back from El Paso. I showed her . . ." He paused, thinking, frowning a little. "I showed her that threat you got, and she went nuts." He snapped his fingers. "Just like that. It was almost like she recognized the handwriting or something. When I asked her about it, she turned on me. Told me if I didn't leave town, she'd make trouble for me."

Ray heaved a gusty sigh, gazing miserably at his clasped hands.

"I didn't think too much about it at the time," Catlin went on, "but now I think maybe Mary knows something. She's protecting somebody, Ray."

"The killer, you mean?" Ray scoffed at the idea. "Don't be absurd! Mary would never do a thing like that!"

Catlin swore. "You're blinder than I am," he declared. "What do you call trying to frame me for murder?" When Ray didn't answer, he continued, "She's up to something, I tell you. Like last night. Where did she go last night?"

Ray looked at him. "What are you talking about?"

"It was after midnight when I got in," Catlin explained, "and there was Mary, fully dressed, like she'd gone out."

"But I didn't hear her leave my side all night," Ray protested.

"Yeah, well, you sleep like the dead." Catlin drew a pouch of soggy tobacco from his vest pocket, scowled and dumped it into the river. "I bet she's in on this up to her eyeballs. Think about it, Ray. Sid's coughing up his lungs in prison and now all of a sudden the very people who caused him to be sent to Huntsville in the first place are getting bumped off left and right."

Ray stared at him in astonishment and the beginning of anger. "How can you make accusations like that against my wife?"

"Open your eyes, Ray. She may be protecting whoever it is that killed Conrad and Fletcher. And I'll tell you something else. That footprint Bone found today looks just like some prints I found outside your store a while back. When I showed them to Mary, she raked her foot over them, like she didn't want anyone to see 'em."

Scowling, Ray jumped to his feet. "That's ridiculous!" he exclaimed. "Do you really expect me to believe Mary would put my life in jeopardy to protect a killer?"

Catlin gazed up at him. "Look, I don't know much more than you do," he said and shrugged. "Maybe that threat you got was just a ploy of some sort, a way of keeping us from suspecting Mary's involvement. Hell, I don't know."

"Or maybe it's a way of keeping me from suspecting you!"

Catlin frowned. "What's that supposed to mean?"

"It means I don't trust you as far as I could throw you," Ray retorted, too mad now to exercise any pretense of caution. "Two years ago, when Zella Moreno tried to hire you to kill the vigilantes, did she want you to kill me, too?"

"Now you oughta know better than that," Catlin replied, the frown on his face deepening. "And don't drag Zella into this. It wasn't two days after she tried to hire me she'd already changed her mind. She told me she couldn't go through with it."

Ray studied his brother, trying to decide if he should believe him or not, his mind a muddle of conflicting emotions. Catlin, unlike Virgil Bone, was an accomplished liar, always had been, the type who could look you square in the eye, tell you the moon was purple, and make you believe every word.

"Who is Bradford Gilley?" Ray asked abruptly.

Catlin's features tensed a little, a subtle tightening of the lips and jawline, and Ray glimpsed a shadow of sadness far back in his brother's eye an instant before he averted his gaze.

"Who is Gilley?"

"A friend," Catlin answered hoarsely. He cleared his throat. "A friend from when I was in the Army."

"Is he here?"

"No."

"Where then?"

Catlin was silent for perhaps half a minute, head bowed slightly. When at last he answered, his voice was barely audible.

"He's in Mississippi."

"Are you sure of that?"

"I'm sure."

"Why were you carrying his canteen?"

"Because I like it." Catlin glanced up at Ray standing over him with his hands on his hips. "Why?" One side of his mouth twitched upward in a halfhearted, faintly mocking smile. "You think he's my accomplice?"

Ray had no answer for that. "Mary gave me an ultimatum this morning," he said at length, changing the subject. "I have to choose between you and her. I've made my choice, Cat. I want you out of the house before the end of the day."

He didn't wait for a reaction. Walking to his horse, he felt he had handled the situation in a responsible manner. While he still didn't know who to trust, who to believe, his one consolation was that Mary would feel more comfortable with Catlin gone, and Ray reminded himself that his first obligation was to his wife and child. That Catlin could sit there and accuse Mary of . . . Good Lord! Accuse her of protecting some brutal savage who chopped off the heads of his victims! It was unthinkable!

Killing was Catlin's line of work, not Mary's.

Even as these thoughts coursed through Ray's mind, he remembered again his wife's words, her voice breathy, urgent: "Nothing will happen to you," she had assured him. "I'll see to that."

But how?

Ray had just reached the horses when Catlin caught up with him and jerked Chico's reins loose. He stepped into the saddle, swung the bay around, and looked down on Ray, his face cold, unforgiving.

"You'd better start carrying a gun," he said and pitched him his Winchester rifle, using more force than was necessary. "Else you might get to find out the hard way who the real killer is."

Catlin slapped the reins against Chico's neck and galloped away, leaving Ray in a swirl of dust and confusion.

CHAPTER TWENTY-TWO

He was sitting crosslegged among the mesquites and catclaws on a high bluff overlooking the Clear Fork of the Brazos, a slight, pale-skinned man with a short, neat mustache and goatee, both well-streaked with gray—prematurely, for he was not yet forty. Elbows propped on knees, he raised his collapsible spy glass to a red-rimmed eye, taking care to shield the lens from the sunlight so it would not glare and give away his presence, and he watched with acute interest the actions of the five men less than a quarter mile away.

He knew all of these men: the sheriff, his deputy, the red-headed Frank Wyman, Ray Myers. Bumbling idiots, all of them, and easily manipulated, his own cast of characters acting out a tragic drama for which the climax was yet to come.

Eyes narrowing, lips pursed, he settled the glass on the fifth man. He recognized this one, as well—rangy, sandy-haired, wearing an eyepatch—a dangerous character but recklessly so, and steeped in sin. The perfect scapegoat.

"Cat Myers," he whispered. "So good to see you again."

A dust devil whisked past him, whipping the mesquites with invisible force before it dispersed into nothingness over the edge of the bluff. He wrapped his jacket more tightly around him, chilled in spite of the sun's warmth cloaking his shoulders.

"They found Fletcher yet, or are we gonna have to go down there and point it out to 'em?"

He listened to the voice behind him, softly southern,

drawling, the voice of an East Texas cotton-picker most likely. Poor white trash.

"Your old friend discovered the corpse," he replied and lowered the spy glass.

"Myers is with them?"

"Yes. You wanted to see him . . . Here he is."

He glanced over his shoulder at his companion, Lee Riddick, watched him slink forward, crouching low, limping. He sank to the ground, stretched his game leg out in front of him, and peered through the telescope at the five men.

"The one with the eyepatch?"

"Yes."

"He hides his blind eye?"

"Of course. He's vain."

Riddick nodded. "Likes to look at hisself in the mirror, I bet." A faint smile played about his lips. "After all these years . . ." he murmured. "I want him, Pony. He's mine."

"That wasn't part of our deal."

Riddick glanced at him out of the corner of his eye. "It is now," he said. "The one thousand dollars you promised me and Cat Myers's stinking, lowlife hide nailed to the wall."

The little man called Pony hid his annoyance within himself, smothering it, realizing his limitations and his dependency on Lee Riddick.

Had he known Catlin Myers intended to return to Fort Griffin, he might have chosen someone besides Riddick to assist him in his quest for vengeance. Riddick's insane obsession with Myers was becoming a problem and liable to wreck his well-devised plans.

Taking the spy glass from Riddick, he waited and watched with growing impatience the movements of the men below him, irritated by their dawdling stupidity. Mouth pinched tight, he waited, waited . . . At last, the deputy, Virgil Bone, stumbled onto the little gift he had left for them, and matters suddenly came to a head quite rapidly. Satisfied, he passed the glass back to Riddick.

"Now there's a cow-country dustup if ever I seen one," Riddick remarked, watching Myers and Deputy Bone fight. "Wonder what started it?"

"Bone found the canteen."

Riddick scowled. "You mean, you left it behind? I told you . . ."

"I know what you told me," Pony cut in. "But Mary found the canteen with the rest of Myers's gear, and not many men carry old canteens like that anymore. I knew someone would recognize it as belonging to him . . . no matter whose name happens to be written on it."

Riddick peered through the glass again, not responding, and massaged the muscles of his left thigh with work-roughened fingers.

Pony studied him momentarily. Except for the whiplash scars crisscrossing his back and the callouses on his hands, six years of prison and hard labor had left no telling marks on Lee Riddick. He was a tough, taut, hatchet-faced man, unshaven just now, with very short, dull brown hair and intense, blue eyes. He lived in constant pain, an old war wound. It showed sometimes on his face, in the lines across his forehead and around his eyes, but he never complained.

Pony knew little about Riddick's past, except that he and three other men had attempted to hold up a train on the Houston and Texas Central in '71. The heist had not been successful.

"The sheriff's lettin' Myers go," Riddick observed.

Not surprised, Pony nodded. "I expected him to. Luger's careful. It'll take more than a canteen to convince him Myers is guilty." A rare smile crossed Pony's thin face. "By the time

Ray Myers and Frank Wyman are dead, he'll have no doubts. Cat will be arrested, tried, and hanged."

Riddick grimaced, shaking his head. "I don't like this set-up of yours, Pony. I ain't liked it since we got here. It's too risky, too slow." He licked his lips and cast a sidelong look at his friend. "And too damned bloody."

Pony sighed wearily, laced his fingers together, and glanced down at the dried blood spatters that stained the right sleeve of his jacket. Ben Fletcher's blood. In his own way, Pony was a fastidious man, and the blood stains offended him. He must remember to ask Mary to get him a clean jacket.

He was offended, too, by Lee Riddick's ingratitude. Of all the men he could have chosen to side him, he had chosen Riddick, not because he owed him the favor, but because, of them all, Riddick had seemed worthy. He was, at the very least, passably intelligent, he was capable of surviving in the harshest of environments, and he was eager to take and carry out orders.

So why was he acting balky all of a sudden? He had known from the beginning what he was stepping into.

"Have I asked you to dirty your hands in any way?" Pony asked, with forced patience.

Riddick shook his head. "That ain't the point. I'm as guilty as you are, the same as if I was the one that's doing the killing, 'cause I'm helping you." He absently pushed the collapsible telescope open and shut, his face thoughtful. "I've killed a number of men," he admitted, "either in battle or in self-defense, but never anything like this." He cast a furtive, almost resentful look at Pony. "I never butchered nobody like you done Conrad and Fletcher. Makes me think you got some Comanch' blood swimming around inside you somewheres."

Another gust of wind whistled through the brush, kicking particles of dust and grit into Pony's eyes. He fastened the top button on his jacket and watched, in the distance, the two men loading Fletcher's stiff, headless corpse into the back of a wagon. He couldn't be sure of the men's identities without the spy glass.

"I told you what my motives were," he said after a moment. "I want these men to fear for their lives the way I fear for mine. I want them to look upon those mutilated bodies and know that the same fate awaits them, too, very soon."

"You're crazy." Riddick wiped his sweaty face on his shirt sleeve. "The sun's addled your think box." He started to rise, then hesitated, something still weighing on his mind. "I want Cat Myers, Pony. I mean it. I don't want him thrown in jail."

Pony ignored the comment, withdrawn for the moment into his protective shell.

"You hear me, Pony? I've got to face him. Man to man."

Pony raised pale, bleak eyes to look at his partner's anguished face, disgusted by the emotion he saw there, the human weakness.

"Cat Myers will kill you if you confront him," he said evenly. "Now stop wasting my time with your endless whining and saddle my horse. I'm ready to go."

Riddick left him, and Pony sat alone, head lowered, chin tucked within his jacket collar. He was tired. Worn out from his exertions of the last twenty-four hours. It was hatred alone that kept him going, that stoked the fire within him and kept him from fizzling out entirely. A bitter, all-consuming hatred, rage, and need for revenge. He felt a little twinge of fear. Once his mission was accomplished, what would become of him then? Would the fire burn out forever?

Pony tried not to think of that. He closed his eyes, resting, and listened to the insects buzzing around him and the soft rustling of the prairie grasses. He breathed in the heavy, syrupy scent of the sunflowers. It was good to be home.

CHAPTER TWENTY-THREE

Saturday night and no sign of Catlin. It wasn't like him. He had been a regular at the Beehive ever since Zella began working here, so his absence tonight left her feeling anxious . . . and just a little disappointed, though she tried not to dwell on that.

The barroom gossip going around about him was not good, and Zella had already told off a few of the prime busybodies. If Catlin's canteen had been found at the sight of Ben Fletcher's murder, it was not he who had left it there. Granted, Catlin had killed many men, but if nothing else, his kills were at least swift, clean. Mutilation and torture were not his style.

It occurred to Zella that Catlin might have left Fort Griffin, but the thought was only fleeting. Typically, Catlin ran when it was in his best interest to stay, and he stayed when it was in his best interest to run.

Throughout the evening and into the night, Zella served drinks and kept a close eye on the door, sure any minute Catlin would saunter in with that devil-may-care look on his face, pull up a chair at the nearest draw poker table, and tell jokes and order drinks to keep the players in a jovial mood while he fleeced them. She had seen him do it a hundred times and still wondered how he managed to keep from getting himself killed. Someday, somewhere, he was going to flimflam the wrong sucker.

Time passed, and while Catlin never showed up, Eladio Moreno did. Already half-drunk, he wove through the Saturday night crowd on unsteady legs and propped himself against the bar. He watched Zella's every move with melancholy, bloodshot eyes. She ignored him at first, refusing to take his order or even look at him, until her boss, Mike, finally noticed and rebuked her for it.

She drew up in front of Eladio, expressionless, without warmth. "What do you want?"

"Tequila and you," he slurred. "What you think, Zella? We go and take a walk down by the river, yes? See what happens?"

She poured a shot of tequila and slid the glass across the bar to him. "I can tell you what would happen," she said quietly. "I would stick a knife in your belly and you would bleed to death."

"Ah, Zella, you still have a sharp tongue." He knocked back his drink, smacked his lips, and passed his forearm across his mouth. "Maybe I cut your tongue off someday and take you back with me to El Paso."

Zella thought about that and regarded this man, her husband, with unveiled contempt. The fact that he wanted her back meant nothing to her. He was ten years too late.

To look at him now, it was difficult to believe that Eladio Moreno had once been considered handsome, at least from a little distance away. As a girl, she had looked forward with innocent pleasure to the Friday night *bailes* when the flashy young Eladio Moreno would sweep into town with his *compañeros*, riding fast horses they had stolen from the Americans, though she did not know this at the time. They would dance together and take walks along the cool, dark Rio Grande to "see what would happen," as Eladio so slyly put it. Those had been happy, carefree times.

Zella's father disapproved of the attention shown her by Eladio. Wiser than she, he saw the obvious flaws in him that Zella's sixteen-year-old eyes refused to acknowledge. After they were married, however, reality soon smacked her in the face and awakened her from her girlish dreams.

Eladio often left her without warning and stayed gone for days, even weeks, stealing horses and cattle from the Mexican *rancheros* and selling them to the Americans, or the other way around. Eladio and his friends were not particular about whom they stole from.

The first time Zella complained about it, Eladio gave her a black eye. She hit him back, socked him square in the nose with her fist, and he retreated to the nearest cantina where he stayed until his money ran out.

They had many more fights after that, some of them violent, most of them over money . . . or the lack of it. The money he brought home from selling stolen livestock was thrown away on tequila and probably other women, though she never caught him. When he was home, he complained because he could find no job, blamed her because the children were hungry or ill, or because the roof leaked above their bed.

Thinking it would please him, Zella began taking in laundry and teaching some of the neighborhood children to read and write in return for a little flour or cornmeal. But Eladio cursed her for that, too. What are you trying to do? he would ask. Shame me?

He abandoned her shortly after the smallpox outbreak killed their daughter and two sons, at a time when she needed him most, and now when she needed no one, he was trying to force himself back into her life. Zella resented the intrusion.

Eladio lifted his second shot of tequila to his lips and peered at her over the brim. "I saw *Gato* Myers today."

"I heard about it," Zella said. "You're lucky he didn't kill you."

"No, this was later. I saw him go into a boardinghouse. I watch all day, but he never come out again." Eladio tossed off his drink and gave her a sly look. "I think his mind is troubled."

Zella's brows lifted. "Oh? Why do you think that?"

"He's alone," Eladio replied. "Nobody much wants the *Gato* around. Like he's poison." He leaned toward her. "I know these things because I listen and watch and don' say nothing. I know somebody here who wants the *Gato* dead. I think maybe me an' this somebody have much in common, see?"

Zella saw it clearly. Eladio Moreno would not take on a difficult task by himself. Like a parasite, he would attach himself to someone with a little more iron in his blood, a little more brains and backbone than he, and together they might very well pull this off.

Zella served another customer, frowning slightly, and then turned back to Eladio. "Who wants Catlin killed here in Fort Griffin?"

"Eso no importa."

"But it does matter," Zella insisted. "Tell me who it is. Prove to me you're telling the truth."

Eladio shrugged. "I don' know his name, but I see him go to the house of *Gato's* brother late last night and talk to a woman there."

"What did they talk about?"

"She gives him something—I can't see what it is in the dark—and he tells her *Gato* will be finished soon."

"Is that all you heard?"

"It's enough," Eladio replied and continued in Spanish, his words rushed. "*Gato* will be killed, Arnet Phillips will pay me what I am owed, and I will take you away from this place . . . to Mexico perhaps, and I will buy land and cattle and horses, and many men will work for me . . ."

"¡Basta!" Zella exclaimed. "You're all talk. The same as

before we were married. Oh, you were going to do great things. You! You were nothing then, and you're even less now."

When she started to turn away from him, Eladio grabbed her by the arm and jerked her around so hard she fell against the bar.

"You think you're better than me, uh?" He gripped her arm, fingers gouging into her flesh. "That killer gringo takes you to bed, and now you think you somebody." He slapped her across the face with the back of his hand. "Cheap whore!"

Zella twisted free of his grasp just as Mike rushed to her rescue. Reaching across the bar, he grasped a handful of Eladio's shirt in a meaty hand and rapped him a solid lick above the ear with an ax handle. Eladio's eyes rolled back in his head as he slid out of sight on the other side of the bar. Zella didn't see him again that night until two cowboys got tired of stepping over his sprawled body and dragged him outside.

Mike went back to work as if nothing had happened, and Zella did likewise. Having already seen him use his improvised club on another man who had tried to get too familiar with her, she wasn't shocked or disturbed by his brutal efficiency. Mike Forgerty didn't tolerate unmannerly drunkards.

It was nearly two in the morning before business slacked off enough for Zella to leave. She walked home alone tonight, for the bartender who normally took her place hadn't shown up for work, and Mike couldn't leave the saloon unattended.

It was a cool, moonless night, making the stars appear very bright and almost close enough to touch. Her high-heeled, button-up shoes sounded hollow on the boardwalk. Tired from standing on her feet for hours, she walked slowly and inhaled the fresh air.

She liked working in the Beehive, enjoyed the people and

the rowdy atmosphere and the knowledge that she was playing a part in something remarkable and exciting and, more than likely, short-lived. Most boomtowns were.

Fort Griffin was a tough place and not a suitable environment for the fainthearted. When she and Eddie McCall had owned the Starlight Saloon, Zella often found herself serving whiskey to some of the most dangerous men in the West, among them Doc Holliday, John Wesley Hardin, and of course, Cat Myers.

This last one took her breath away, then and now. He possessed a sort of boyish charm that was both disarming and pleasant, and Zella had felt drawn to him from the moment she first laid eyes on him. But the charm, she found out later, could be turned on and off at the slightest whim. Sometimes he made her laugh and feel happy, and other times he was so distant she despaired of ever reaching him.

Every few months or so, he would grow moody and restless and start cleaning that big gun of his, the Sharps .50, preparing for another job. He would leave her then, kiss her goodbye and ride away, and she would spend the weeks that followed worrying, waiting, alone. During these times, she chastised herself for being attracted to no-good men.

Tonight, walking home from work, Zella remembered again her conversation with Eladio. He had mentioned seeing Catlin rent a room at one of the boardinghouses. Catlin had been living with his family, Zella knew, and she wondered what had prompted him to leave. Even more, she wondered why he had not ventured from his room all day. Ironically, given his penchant for violence, Catlin Myers was a sociable sort, and it was not like him to remain holed up by himself somewhere unless he was sick or hurt . . . or on a binge.

The latter seemed to Zella the most likely explanation. At her urging, Catlin had cut down on his drinking during the two years they were together, and it saddened her to think he might be backsliding.

She approached the front entrance of the whitewashed Occidental Hotel, thankful to have made it there without incident, for the Flat was not safe during the day, much less at night. Rummaging around in her leather handbag for the key to her room, she stepped into the lobby just as a barrage of gunshots crackled somewhere on the other side of town.

The night clerk looked up as she walked in and gave her a sleepy smile. "You're braver than me," he told her. "I wouldn't set foot out there tonight if you paid me."

"I guess I'm used to it," Zella replied and stifled a yawn. "Good night, Harry."

"Good night, ma'am. Pleasant dreams."

Zella walked down the dimly lit corridor to room six, unlocked the door, and stepped inside. The sharp smell of tobacco smoke filled her nostrils, and she immediately knew someone had been in her room. Or still was.

Hardly daring to breathe, eyes straining to penetrate the obscurity surrounding her, she reached inside her handbag for the small, pearl-handled derringer. Her fingertips touched cool metal just as a match flared on the opposite side of the room.

"You're late, Zella."

CHAPTER TWENTY-FOUR

The intruder lit his cigarette, and the match's flame reflected off the bones of his face. Zella felt her muscles start to relax. Exhaling slowly, she closed the door.

"Catlin, what are you doing here?"

"Waiting for you."

"How did you get in?"

"Snuck past the clerk and picked the lock."

Her fright changing to mild irritation, Zella fumbled around in the darkness for a box of matches and started to light the wall lamp nearest the door.

"Keep it low," he said.

Not sure what difference it made, she lowered the wick nevertheless and turned to look at him.

He was lounging in an armchair, one foot propped on the opposite knee, idly twirling the rowel of his spur with his fingers. She noticed a dark purple bruise on his cheekbone, suggesting he had been in another fight today. No surprise there. He watched her watch him and finally gestured to the chair opposite him.

"Make yourself at home." His teeth flashed in a brief, gently mocking smile. "I won't bite."

She remained where she was. "Have you been drinking, Catlin?"

"Why are those always the first words out of your mouth every time we see each other?"

"I'm concerned about you." She bent over to unbutton

her shoes, kicked them off, and straightened up, leaning against the door frame and wriggling her toes. "I heard you moved into a boardinghouse today."

He gazed at her, silent.

"Eladio told me," she went on. "He's been spying on you."

Still no response.

Zella regarded him reflectively, studying his tan, fine-featured face in the bad light. She wished the room was brighter.

"How is your family?" she asked, trying to feel him out.

He shrugged and looked away. "Fine, I guess."

He sounded touchy. Zella combed her fingers through her long hair and tied it in a knot in back to keep it off her face and watched Catlin smoke. He seemed content to simply sit and stare at the wall. Zella suspected he had been drinking off and on all day and into the night. Though he was not a large man, he held his liquor well and rarely showed any outward signs of intoxication if he drank slowly over a long period of time. Zella's only clue that he had been drinking tonight was his stony silence.

"Do you want to talk about it, Catlin?"

"Talk about what?"

"Whatever's on your mind. I doubt if you're here to admire the wallpaper."

He met her gaze. "They're trying to pin these murders on us."

"So I've heard."

"It's all because of that business two years ago with the vigilantes," he said, "after they lynched Ed McCall."

"I know." Zella moved toward him, took the cigarette from his hand, and drew deeply on it, inhaling the pleasantly pungent smoke. She closed her eyes a moment and said, "I

184

wish I'd never involved you in that. It was a mistake."

Catlin shook his head. "It doesn't matter about me. But I want you to go back to El Paso. I'll buy you a ticket while you pack, and you can be on the first stage out of here before sunup."

"I'm not ready to leave. I like it here." She took one more drag on his cigarette before rubbing out the butt in an ashtray. "I'm sure Sheriff Luger will find the real killer. I don't think he's the type of man to let lies and rumors interfere with his work."

"Don't bet on it."

"You don't like him?"

"R.D.'s a sheriff, a sheriff's a politician, and politicians do whatever it takes to stay in office."

Zella smiled, amused by his candor. Catlin had as much regard for politicians as he did for rats.

"I want you to go home," he said.

She considered his request. He was right; it would be wise to return to El Paso for her own safety, but she was reluctant to leave him here by himself. It was just as Eladio had stated earlier. Catlin was alone in this town. Though he had grown up in the valley of the Clear Fork, he was an outcast among his own people, his own family even, and it was unlikely anyone would come to his aid should he need it.

A lot of bad men passed in and out of Fort Griffin, but a considerable number of the people who lived and worked here were stable and hard working. The Myerses tallied among this particular segment of Griffin's population, making Catlin a black sheep of the family and a black stain on the community in general. He had thumbed his nose at quite a few people here besides, important people with money and long memories.

Eladio Moreno wasn't the only man who bore a grudge against him.

"You're the one who needs to leave town," she said at length.

"I can't."

"Perhaps you should find a way. There are people here who want to make trouble for you. Your sister-in-law, for instance."

"What do you know about Mary?"

"Enough to distrust her," Zella replied, and she went on to tell him how Eladio had overheard Mary and a strange man talking about him the night before.

Catlin didn't seem surprised by her story. "Did he know who Mary was talking to?"

"No, but I'm sure he'll do his best to find out. Eladio thinks this man will help him kill you."

"Well, whoever he is, he's probably the one who left my canteen by Fletcher's body."

"That's what I thought."

Catlin gave her a dour look, his face appearing unnaturally taut in the dim light. "Go home, Zella."

She shook her head and turned away from him. Going to the little dresser where she kept her hairbrush, perfumes, and toiletries, she took off her necklace and opened the locket's tiny clasp. She touched the three silky coils of hair tucked inside and looked past her image in the dresser mirror to that of Catlin. He was sitting with his head resting against the chair's back and staring up at the ceiling. Strong, dexterous hands lay idle across his groin.

"You can sleep here tonight," she said. "I'll make a pallet for you on the floor."

"On the floor?"

Zella snapped the locket shut and placed it tenderly in its

small, felt-lined box. "If that's not good enough for you, then I guess you'll have to go somewhere else."

"You're awful high and mighty all of a sudden."

"It's late, I'm tired, and you toss and turn so much when you've been drinking that I can't sleep."

"I won't bother you. I promise." Rising, he drew up behind her and passed his arms around her waist, propping his chin on her right shoulder and gazing at her in the mirror. "Please don't make me go."

His pathetic, childlike entreaty tore at her heart, and she fought a silent battle with her emotions. A short time ago, it would have been easy to fall back into the old groove again, go on as if nothing had happened between them and pretend she was happy. Not any more. He had walked out on her, not the other way around.

Reaching down, she pried his arms from around her waist. "Catlin, you make me feel like your mother when you act this way."

"My mother?" He looked at her in surprise. "Why? Because you're older than me?"

Zella frowned at him, irritated by his reference to their slight difference in age. It was a sensitive subject for her but had nothing to do with the problem at hand.

"We need to make some changes," she said.

Ignoring her, he slipped his arms around her waist again, sensual this time, and pressed himself against her back and buttocks, hands roaming up and down her body while he kissed her neck.

Zella didn't respond to his advances, thinking surely he would get the message and back off, and watched their images in the dresser mirror. It wasn't easy, with his hands all over her, and his warm breath caressing her skin. She could feel the heat from his body through her clothes and breathed in his familiar scent, the smell of leather and tobacco, mixed tonight with that of whiskey. She gripped the edge of the dresser.

Cupping his hands beneath her breasts, Catlin kissed her behind the ear and spoke softly: "Would I do this to my mother?"

"I certainly hope not."

"Let me stay the night, and I'll show you something else I wouldn't do to my mama."

"I thought you didn't fool around with other men's wives."

"I've had second thoughts."

"I've had some second thoughts, too," Zella said. She turned in his arms so that she faced him and pushed him away. "We can't be together any more, Catlin. Not until you change."

"What are you talking about?"

"In some ways," she said, "this separation from you has done me a lot of good. I've had time to think about things, and I've made a decision."

She paused, building up her courage before taking the plunge. "I want you to stop hiring out your gun. If you don't, we're finished. I can't live this way anymore."

He stared at her, listening to the words she had rehearsed over and over in her mind, his face very still, almost stiff.

"Do you understand me?" she asked.

His chest rose in a deep breath, nostrils flaring slightly. "Yeah, I understand. You're just like everybody else." He looked away from her, the anger that was building inside him showing in the hard set of his jaw. "As soon as things get a little rough, and I need you the most, that's when you turn your back on me."

Zella shook her head. "That's not . . ."

"Don't deny it! My own damned brother thinks I'm

whacked out in the head! So why should you be any different?"

Realizing there could be no sensible discussion with him tonight, Zella started to walk away from him. He thrust his arm out, blocking her path and trapping her between himself and the dresser.

"It's because I told you about killing Johnny Keaton, isn't it?"

Zella gazed up at him, seeing the hurt on his face, the wrath. "I'm glad you confided in me," she said.

"But it turned you against me."

"I haven't turned against you at all! Can't you see that?" She touched him, smoothing one of his sideburns, gently stroking his bruised cheek with the tips of her fingers. "I was always afraid that you'd kill the wrong man, an innocent man," she confessed. "But my worst fear of all is that you'll be killed, and I'll never see you or hear from you again. I'm tired of being afraid."

Catlin shook his head, his expression softening a little. "This is the only life I know, Zella."

"Then learn something new. I can help you. We'll do it together."

He sighed, shook his head again, and turned away from her. "I'll leave. Put out the light, will you?"

"I'm not through talking to you."

Refusing to even look at her, he retrieved his hat and drew up to the side of the room's single window. "Unless you want somebody to see me sneaking out of your room, douse the light."

Zella reluctantly did as he told her and heard him draw back the heavy drapes and raise the window. Crossing the darkened room, she gripped his arm as he slung a leg over the window pane.

"Please think about what I've said." She waited for a response. When none came, she continued, "Will I see you in the Beehive tomorrow night?"

"No. I don't think we should be seen anywhere near each other in public." He pulled free of her grasp, slipped out the window, and dropped silently to the ground. "You take care of yourself, Zella." His voice was low, almost husky. "I wish you happiness."

His words sounded final. Zella leaned out the open window, straining to see him in the darkness, but he was already gone. She listened for his footsteps but heard only the crickets and distant voices and laughter and piano music.

Kneeling on the floor in front of the window, Zella gazed up at the Milky Way. I'm better off without him, she thought. She repeated the words aloud, speaking with force, as if she meant every word. The ache in her heart didn't lessen.

CHAPTER TWENTY-FIVE

Catlin rented a team of horses and a wagon from Hank Smith's Livery Stable early Sunday morning and drove to his brother's store. Fending off a drummer hawking Yankee notions to people on the street, he cupped his hands around his eyes, peered through one of the display windows, and spied Ray standing near the counter with his back turned to him. Catlin banged on the door.

Jumping in alarm, Ray whirled around, saw who it was, and frowned.

"Open the door!" Catlin hollered.

Still frowning, Ray snapped back the dead bolt and opened the door a fraction of an inch. "I don't think . . ."

"I don't really give a flip what you think," Catlin said. He pushed the door open, nearly smashing Ray's nose, and barged in without waiting for an invitation. "I forgot and left my slicker in my room yesterday. I wish you'd get it for me. It'll end up at the next murder scene if I ain't careful."

He and Ray glared at each other for perhaps half a minute before Ray left to get the slicker. Waiting for him, Catlin selected a few canned goods and tried to think what other provisions he and his father might need during their stay at the farm. Not sure how many days Ocie wished to remain there, he decided to play it safe and bought small quantities of flour, cornmeal, red beans, and similar items. Remembering his father's fondness for tea, he got some of that, too, and a tin of Chase and Sanborn coffee for himself.

Ray returned after a moment with Catlin's yellow oilskin slicker. Handing it to him, he looked at the supplies piled on the counter.

"What's this?"

"Groceries. Add it up."

"I don't do business on the Sabbath."

Catlin swore softly. "I forgot you were so pious." He nodded toward the goods. "Tell me how much, or I'll take it without paying."

Ray regarded him with a wooden expression on his face, making no move to comply, as if daring him to carry out his threat.

When Catlin started to gather the sacks and cans into his arms, Ray spoke up. "If you tote that stuff out of this store without paying for it, I'll go to Sheriff Luger."

His temper flaring, Catlin dumped the supplies back onto the counter, flipped out his .45, and leveled it at Ray with casual facility.

"Do you want to make this into a surefire robbery, Ray?"

Ray backed off a step and licked his lips. "There's no need to go to extremes."

"Then tell me what I owe!"

"All right, all right!" Ray lifted his hands, palms turned outward. "Just put that thing away for God's sake!"

Satisfied at having wiped the holier-than-thou look off his brother's face, Catlin lowered his gun and dropped it into its holster.

"What in hell's going on in here?"

Ocie Myers's hard voice hit Catlin like a fist and left him feeling sick inside. His gaze shifted toward the back of the store where the skinny, white-haired old man stood watching him with stern eyes. Sure that Ocie had seen him draw a gun on Ray, Catlin half-turned and began edging toward the door. While he wouldn't have shot Ray, it had been foolhardy to point a gun at him even in jest, and the old man was sure to bawl hell out of him for it.

"What's all the damned hollering about?" Ocie demanded. "You got Beth to squalling again."

Relief washed over Catlin. He glanced at Ray's rigid face, sensed he might be about to spill the beans, and beat him to it.

"Sorry, Pa. Me and Ray were just exchanging sentiments of brotherly love," he said and grinned at his own jocularity. He felt Ray glowering at him but pretended not to notice. "How you feeling this morning?"

"I feel like I need some fresh air." Ocie stole Catlin a conspiratorial look. "Nice day out."

"Yeah, it's that, all right."

Ray loosened his collar with an unsteady finger and cleared his throat. "Pa, are you sure you don't want to come with us to the church picnic?"

"I'm sure. I can get chewed on by mosquitoes as easy here in town as I can down by the river."

"They aren't as bad as they were," Ray said.

"Yeah, just like needles with wings is all." Ocie shuffled toward them, leaning heavily on his cane. He wrinkled his nose at Catlin. "You smell like you been dipped in a whiskey barrel, boy."

"Do tell!" Ray began sorting through the goods on the counter, calculating the total in his head, and glanced at Catlin beneath lowered brows. "Maybe that explains his ungodly actions this morning."

"Oh, get off your high horse," Catlin lashed back.

Ocie scowled. "Y'all don't act no different than you did when you were pups. If I wasn't so damned used up, I'd cut me a green willow switch and whip the tar outta both of you."

That said, he left them and disappeared into the family's living quarters.

"I wish he'd seen you," Ray murmured.

Catlin rested an elbow on the counter and leaned toward him. "You tell Pa what happened here, and I'll break your head."

"And I'll do like he said and lay into you with a willow switch. Your backside could use a good whaling," Ray declared. "You owe me eleven dollars and fifteen cents. Pay up and get out."

His teeth clenched, Catlin slapped his money down, loaded his supplies into a gunny sack, and left without a parting word or a backward glance. He heard the dead bolt snap behind him.

Another locked door.

If the underlying cause for this morning's spat with Ray wasn't so serious, it would have been almost comical. Catlin, however, could not forget his brother's suspicious insinuations of the day before. The whole affair baffled him. Ray had practically begged him to come home, hoping he could somehow protect him from a bloodthirsty killer, and now he seemed to believe Catlin was the killer, or in close association with him at the very least.

Catlin guessed when it came down to the draw, it was easier for Ray to point the finger at his own brother than at his wife. He and Ray had never been close, after all, so maybe it was an understandable reaction.

Catlin drove his rented team and wagon up the street a short distance and parked near the intersection of Griffin Avenue and Second Street where he got down to check the fastenings on one of the harnesses. Climbing back into the wagon's wooden seat, he opened a can of peaches, propped his elbows on his knees, and speared the juicy slices into his mouth with his pocketknife, gratifying his sweet tooth while he killed time.

Ocie had made it clear to him Friday night that he didn't want to leave until Ray and Mary were out of the house, thereby avoiding a squabble. Catlin figured they wouldn't have to wait much longer. Already, folks in and around town were heading for the river, families with children mostly, riding in wagons, buggies, and buckboards and loaded down with covered baskets of food for the church meeting and picnic. There wasn't the laughter and gaiety one expected to see on such an occasion as this. The murder of Ben Fletcher seemed to have dampened everyone's spirits.

Catlin remembered going to camp meetings when he was a boy. They had been few, but occasionally a circuit-riding preacher would risk getting ventilated by Comanche arrows and stray into the Myerses neck of the woods to preach sermons and perform baptisms and marriage ceremonies. An old hard-shelled Baptist was usually the only preacher willing to brave the hundred-mile trip west from Weatherford. Upon his arrival, word would spread, and neighbors would gather together in a camp and stay sometimes several days. Revival services were held under large brush arbors.

Summer camp meetings had been a welcome respite in the hard, lonely lives of the settlers and fun and games to the children. True to his nature, Catlin always managed to get into some mischief. He would end up becoming the minister's deterrent example of what could happen to youngsters not properly educated in the Word of God, and later, Ocie would educate his butt with a leather belt. Even so, Catlin looked back on those days with a touch of nostalgia. They hadn't been all bad.

Catlin ate peaches and watched the people on the street, particularly the young women, all dressed up in their Sunday best. Ray and Mary Myers passed by him presently in a shiny black runabout pulled by a high-stepping sorrel gelding. Ray stared at him as he drove past but that was all, and Catlin noticed Mary took special pains not to even glance his way. Fearful she might turn into a pillar of salt, no doubt. She was holding Beth in her arms and shielding the baby's eyes from the sunlight with her hand.

Catlin thought about Beth, picturing her innocent little face in his mind. He hoped his niece didn't grow up to be a snob like her mama.

Draining the syrupy peach juice into his mouth, Catlin tossed the empty can into the bed of the wagon and took up the leather reins. He waited for an opening and swung the wagon around in the middle of the street.

Dread pressed down on him like a welterweight as he headed back to Myers's Mercantile. He could never seem to do or say anything right in his father's presence, even when he tried, so the prospect of spending a few days alone with his old man didn't exactly overwhelm him with joy. He just hoped Ocie didn't get too riled at him and drop dead from a heart seizure.

He had a feeling if Ray knew about this little jaunt to the farm, he'd already be making their father's funeral arrangements.

Ocie was waiting for him when he pulled around to the back of the store. He stepped out the kitchen door with a small bundle tucked under one arm and his checkers set under the other.

"Ready to go?" Catlin called out.

"I was ready five months ago."

Catlin jumped down from the wagon and took his father's clothes bundle, the checkers set, and his cane. He was about to help him climb into the seat, but Ocie knocked his hand away, grumbled something under his breath and climbed up on his own.

Catlin handed Ocie his things and stood looking up at him with his hands on his hips. "Oughtn't we to leave Ray a note so he'll know where you're at?"

"He ain't my mammy."

"No, but he's a worry wart," Catlin said. He gazed up at his father while gently feeling of his nose, still painful from yesterday's fight with Virgil Bone. "You want me to write him a note?"

"Suit yourself. But I doubt he'll be able to read it. As I recollect, your ma was the only one of us who could ever make sense of your chicken scratchin'."

Zella can read it, Catlin thought peevishly. He walked into the kitchen and hunted around for a pencil and paper. Finding both, he leaned over the kitchen table and proceeded to compose a message to his brother. His brow furrowed in concentration, and the tip of his tongue stuck out the corner of his mouth. Writing had always been a strain on him.

Finished, he scanned his brief note:

Ray,
    I took Pa to the farm. He wants to stay there awile. I'll bring him back when he's done and want leeve him by himself.

                                  Cat

He frowned a little. A couple of words didn't look quite right to him, but he didn't have time to experiment with them; Ocie was yelling at him to hurry up.

They headed north on Griffin Avenue, making for the river crossing at the edge of town and the old wagon road that would take them across the five miles of mostly open prairie to the Myers farm. As they neared the Red Light District, a woman carrying a ridiculous pink parasol attempted to cross the street in front of them and spooked the horses.

Catlin felt his neck pop as the team broke into a hard gallop, and Ocie grabbed the seat with both hands to keep from toppling backwards. Half-standing, cussing in explosive bursts, Catlin sawed on the reins and managed to slow the horses just enough to avoid trampling the good lady and her confounded parasol into the Texas dirt. She shrieked as they careened past her amid a rolling cloud of dust.

By the time they reached the river crossing, Catlin had his team under control. These rental horses didn't possess a lot of vigor. They forded the Clear Fork without much difficulty and plodded on as if nothing unusual had occurred.

Ocie looked back toward town and shook his head. "That little gal was using language not befitting of a true lady. Are you still consortin' with them Jezebels, Cat?"

"I've never consorted with a Jezebel in my whole life."

Ocie snorted. "I guess you expect me to believe you never told a lie before either. You keep it up, boy, and you'll get the clap one of these days and something you hold near and dear to you's gonna rot and fall off."

Catlin grimaced and gave his father a sidelong glance. This was going to be a very long five miles.

CHAPTER TWENTY-SIX

The road Catlin and Ocie took out of town was well-traveled and deeply rutted, it being the main route to forts Belknap and Richardson. Catlin looked around him at the familiar countryside. He admired the gently rolling prairie, the grassy meadows, the low, rocky hills. He had ridden many miles over the years, had crossed whole states and territories and had seen some beautiful sights, but this land spoke to him in a way no other ever could. It brought back a deluge of memories, both good and bad, and evoked in him a feeling of homesickness and a yearning for his lost childhood.

Catlin was thankful he was not the sentimental type. If he was anything like Ray, he might have gotten teary-eyed and embarrassed himself in front of his father.

He made it a point to look behind him every now and then, thinking it would be just like Eladio Moreno to follow them to the farm. Catlin doubted the man had the guts to confront him again, but get some liquor in him, and he might just take a potshot at them out here where there weren't any witnesses. The possibility made Catlin's skin prickle with uneasiness. He glanced again at their backtrail.

Ocie looked, too. "What you expecting to see back there?" he asked. "Ain't nothing but dust, far as I can tell."

Catlin nodded.

"It's these murders," Ocie concluded. "Got everybody to looking over their shoulders." He paused a moment, then, "I know about Ray being threatened."

Catlin looked at him in surprise. "You know?"

"Seems to me like a body'd have to be blind and deaf not to. It's all they ever talk about in the barber shop these days. You and Ray've been all tight-lipped for nothing." His face screwed up in a ferocious scowl. "Mary told me last night there's rumors going around about you being in on this killing business."

An unpleasant bitterness rose up in Catlin like bile. "What else did Mary tell you?" he asked in a low voice.

"She thinks you're a danger to Ray."

"Do you believe her?"

Ocie considered that, lips pursed slightly, face thoughtful. "When you and Ray were kids," he said finally, "Ray wouldn't dast play with you 'cause you played so hard and rough, he feared you'd break his neck. You almost did a time or two.

"But do you remember when that bad grass fire come up, and Ray got trapped in the little tinderbox shanty we were living in at the time? I'd gone to Weatherford when it happened, but your mama told me about it. You were a mean one even back then, Cat, but she said you damn near killed yourself gettin' your brother out of there before the fire got to him. It made me and Rena think there was a dab of goodness in you, after all."

Ocie looked at him, a gleam of hope shining in his eyes. "I'd like to think you'd do the same now. I'd like to believe there's still some good left in you. Ray may need you again in the days to come, Tom Cat."

Catlin shook his head and stared at the road ahead without really seeing it. "Ray don't need me. He thinks like Mary. He thinks I'd kill him."

"Then prove him wrong," Ocie said. "Ray's had some schooling, and I admit he's better at storekeeping than farming, but town life's made him soft. That's why I want you to go back to Griffin as soon as you drop me off at the old house. Go back and stick by your brother."

"I can't leave you there alone!" Catlin protested.

"You can and will."

"I'll be damned if I will!" Catlin frowned in consternation. "Go back to town," he mumbled. "Hell. Ray'd have me shot on sight if I left you alone." He reconsidered. "Ray's liable to have me shot anyway."

Ocie let it lie for the time being.

It touched Catlin to know that, in spite of his bad reputation and Mary's tale wagging, his father was willing to give him the benefit of the doubt. Too bad Ray wasn't that charitable.

He felt it was getting about time for him to have a serious talk with Mary Myers. She wouldn't squirm her way out of this one.

The road forked, and Catlin took the cutoff, a less traveled road whose twin wheel marks were barely visible through the weeds. Half a dozen leggy, wild-eyed longhorns were grazing near the road. Alarmed by the rattling wagon, they turned tail and ran, making for the thorny brush.

An old spotted cow with one cropped ear and a myriad of brands scarring both hips stood her ground and tested the wind, wild as the buffalo and deer that shared this range with her. Catlin noticed her bag was swollen with milk. She had a baby calf hiding somewhere in the grass, he bet. She lowered her head and backed off a couple of steps as they passed by her.

Watching the cows instead of the road, Catlin didn't notice the wash-out until the front wheels dropped down, jarring him so hard he cracked his teeth together and bit his tongue. He immediately slowed the team so the back wheels didn't jolt as badly going down and cast a concerned glance at his father.

"You all right, Pa?"

"If you ask me that one more time . . ."

Ocie didn't bother to finish. His face appeared very pale and drawn beneath the battered straw hat, more so than usual, and a thin film of sweat made his skin shiny white whenever the sunlight touched it. Catlin had noticed him massaging his left arm and shoulder ever since leaving town and wondered if that was yet another bad sign. He hoped not.

He had never realized just how rough this old road really was. He became conscious of every bump, every pothole, sure he must be pounding Ocie to death without laying a finger on him. He decided the wagon seat didn't have an ounce of spring left in it whatsoever. It had all been bounced out.

He reined in the horses.

Ocie wiped away the sweat that had collected above his bushy white eyebrows. "Why are you stopping for?"

"Think I'll water a weed," Catlin replied casually.

He didn't feel a strong urge to relieve himself at all, but rather an urge to relieve Ocie from the bouncing, lurching, and jiggling. Standing beside the front wheel, he listened to the meadow larks' clear whistles and concentrated on getting the waterworks started.

"Pa, why don't you get out and stretch your legs?"

"Why don't you quit dillydallying around and take me home?" Ocie countered.

There was no helping some people. Catlin buttoned his pants, taking his time, and climbed back up beside his father.

After another torturous mile, they neared the line of tall cottonwoods, elms, and brush that flanked Plum Creek, so named because of the wild plum thickets found in concentrated masses up and down its course. Catlin guided the team and wagon across its shallow bed. Muddy water rippled ankle-deep around the horses' feet.

Plum Creek was generally dry half the year, except for a good-sized water hole to the northeast where the little tributary intersected the Myerses' thirty acre pasture. Catlin and Ray used to swim and fish there when they were boys, and it had been Catlin's chore to take the work horses to the watering hole every morning and evening, excepting Sundays when they would be let out in the pasture to graze. He couldn't remember the water hole ever going dry.

Ascending the gentle rise on the north side of Plum Creek, Catlin looked out across the place where he had grown up and was stabbed by another pain of nostalgia.

There was the Myers home, a one-story, L-shaped house with three rooms constructed of native limestone. The fourth room, a later addition, was built of pickets. When they first settled here on the north bank of Plum Creek, they had lived for a time in a small house made entirely of pickets. When it burned down in a prairie fire, Ocie rebuilt with stone, for by this time, he and his family were here to stay.

To the east was the barn, no larger than necessary and made of the same mellow gray stone as the house. The adjoining corral was built of mesquite poles stacked horizontally between pairs of knobby posts set into the ground and tied with rawhide thongs. Catlin well remembered helping Ocie cut mesquite timber from the breaks for the corral. It wouldn't have surprised him if he still had a thorn or two embedded in his hide from that job.

Beyond the barn and picket lean-to sheds and the corral, he could see the uneven rock wall that fenced in the pasture to the east. It was low and crude but had been good enough for holding in two overworked plow horses and his mother's milk cow. To the north, the one hundred thirty acres of land where Catlin, Ray, and Ocie had cleared the brush and grubbed up stumps so many years ago were freshly plowed, the fields of corn and oats having already been harvested.

All of this he had helped to build, much of it when he was still a boy, the rest after he returned from the war. It seemed ages ago.

He reined the team around the horseshoe drive in front of the house and stopped. Vacant for only five months, weeds were already beginning to creep up around the house, and the place appeared lonely and abandoned.

Ocie drew a deep breath, looked around him with a smile in his eyes, and gestured to the hand-dug well within the circle of the drive. "I've missed our well water," he said. "Want some?"

"Not yet. Let's go look at your mama's grave first."

Catlin drove the team between the house and outbuildings, making for the northwest corner of the pasture. Here, shaded by two huge live oaks, were the graves of Catlin's mother, Rena Myers, and Ray's first wife, Lucy.

Catlin helped his father climb down from the wagon seat and followed him to Rena's grave.

Ocie gazed down at the stone marker. "Forty-four years old," he murmured. "She died long before her time. Worked herself to death for us."

He bent stiffly to pull up a broomweed growing at the base of the marker. Even this small effort left him breathless, and it took him a moment to recover.

"Don't tell Ray I told you this, but Rena was always partial to you," he said at length. "I never knew why. From the day you were born, all you did was give her trouble."

Catlin nodded, feeling awkward and unhappy.

His mother's untimely death had hit him very hard. Frail, never fully recovered from giving birth to Catlin, she fell seriously ill while he was in the Army. This, coupled with the death of Brad Gilley, prompted him to desert and head for home. He arrived too late. Rena died without him getting a chance to see her one last time and tell her he loved her. He never got a chance to apologize for causing her so much worry and trouble.

It seemed to Catlin he always managed to bungle things when he least wanted to.

"I'm ready," Ocie said finally. "Let's go back."

CHAPTER TWENTY-SEVEN

Catlin drove his father to the house, unhitched the horses, and turned them loose in the corral. The farmer who had leased Ocie's land sometimes left his work stock penned in the corral, and Catlin found a little musty hay and some oats stored in the barn. The oats, cut just last June, looked more appealing than the hay, and he dumped a bucketful into the wooden trough. He could pay the farmer for it later. Filling the other trough with water from the well, he hung the harnesses up in the barn and went to the house.

He found Ocie wandering from room to room, looking things over, running a finger along the fireplace mantel, or touching some familiar piece of furniture made by his own hands. Most of the family's furnishings and household items had been left behind when Ray and Mary moved to town. Mary didn't like hand-me-downs.

"It's dusty, but it's home," Ocie said, and he smiled with pleasure.

Catlin started a fire in his mother's Black Prince cook-stove, thinking he'd fix something to eat, an intention that was abandoned when he found mouse pills on the kitchen counter. He immediately began a vigorous search for the rodent's point of entry into the house, found a crack at the bottom corner of the front door with gnaw marks in the wood, and stuffed a rag into the opening. Lunch forgotten by now, he sterilized every kitchen utensil, every cup, plate, and pot he could find, in boiling water, and scrubbed the counters and swept the floor.

Lounging at the kitchen table, Ocie smoked his pipe and watched Catlin's feverish house-cleaning in quiet amusement.

"Boy, you missed your calling," he remarked finally. "You should've been somebody's wife."

"Damn rats."

"Mice," Ocie corrected him.

"Same thing. One's just bigger is all."

Ocie shrugged. "I doubt a little mouse juice ever killed anybody. Since when did you get so nasty nice?"

"Nasty nice? Hell, Pa, a rat'll eat might near anything. Even people. During the war, I saw them . . ." He didn't finish, not caring to go into the gory details.

Ocie pointed his pipe at him. "I know what your problem is, Tom Cat. You seen and done too much at too early an age. A fourteen year old tadpole ain't got no business fightin' in a war. It was a dumb stunt you pulled, running off like that."

Catlin found no argument there.

"Still, you never should've deserted," Ocie went on. "I never figured you for a shirker till the day you come sneaking home, skittish as a wild colt and half-starved." He shook his head. "Once you start something, you're supposed to finish it. It was your duty, and you failed."

Catlin wondered how many times he had heard his father utter those same words, over and over again. Biting back the sharp retort that lay like acid on his tongue, he finished sweeping and put away the broom. His brief flash of anger and shame burned on his face and neck.

After a meal of canned beans, fried bacon, and fresh tomatoes picked from Mary's abandoned garden behind the house, Ocie retired to one of the back rooms for his afternoon nap. The bedroom he would be sleeping in during their stay was the same room Catlin and Ray had shared as children.

The same bed, too, for that matter. Covering the straw tick mattress with blankets brought from town, Catlin remembered how Ray used to press his cold, clammy feet up against him every night. Just like sleeping with a toad frog. Catlin had invariably kicked the snot out of him for it.

He wondered what Mary's reaction was.

Finding some mouse traps in the shed, Catlin baited them with leftovers from lunch, set them in various promising locations throughout the house, and went outside.

Walking to the barn, Catlin hitched the two rental horses to his father's breaking plow, and starting at the far end of the corral, he began plowing a fire break around the outbuildings and the house. It was a job Ocie had been asking Ray to do for some time. Wild fires were commonplace in this part of the country. Weeds and prairie grasses, allowed to take over and grow tall over the summer months, would burn fast and hot, particularly after the year's first killing frost.

The rental horses had never plowed before. They kept turning their heads to look back at the contraption of wood and steel that was dragging behind them, and it took much patience on Catlin's part to keep them in line.

He walked behind the plow and breathed in the warm, earthy smell of freshly turned sod. Ocie had first started him plowing when he was ten years old, and he guessed, like swimming, reading, and walking, one never forgot how. Though the day was hot and humid, it felt good to be plowing, a strange sensation for a man who had once loathed the farm and everything associated with it.

Ocie said it was the Spanish and French who first explored this country in search of God, glory, and gold—not necessarily in that order—but it was the farmer who settled the land and made it America. There were, however, a lot of folks who didn't see it that way. Cowhands used to poke fun at

Catlin and Ray when they were boys, calling them fodder forkers and making pointed remarks as to which end of the mule they faced at work all day. Catlin had once been sensitive to such bantering, but not any more. He was finally beginning to understand just how good his life had been, living and working here on his father's farm.

Catlin had plowed four rows around the buildings and was working his way in the direction of the corral again when a slight movement off to his right caught his attention. He glanced toward the creek and saw a man standing alone at the edge of the trees.

"Whoa, boys."

The horses drew to a halt, and Catlin stared at the motionless figure leaning against the pale trunk of a cottonwood tree. He wore a blue shirt, dark trousers, and no hat, but that was all Catlin could be sure of from this distance. Judging by his stance, he didn't appear to be threatening.

"Hello there!"

The man neither moved nor said a word. Catlin grew edgy. He tipped the plow over on one side, and in an unhurried manner, looped the lines over the plow's wooden handles. He started walking down the gentle slope to the creek bottoms. At his approach, the stranger pushed away from the tree trunk, wheeled around, and disappeared into the underbrush.

Catlin broke into a run. He reached the cottonwood where the man had been standing, pressed his shoulder against the rough bark, and peered into the trees. He caught a glimpse of the man sliding down the bank and into the water. Crouching low, Catlin hurried after him. He could hear the man's feet splashing as he ran across the narrow channel.

Thrashing through the elbowbush and white shinoak, Catlin caught sight of the stranger again as he was scrambling out of the creek bed and up the opposite bank.

"Hey! What are you running for?"

The man paused to look back at him and kneaded the muscles of his left thigh with his fingers. Their gazes held briefly, a flitting glance, and an eerie feeling stole over Catlin causing the hair to stand up on his arms. There was a wary, almost frightened look in the other's eyes, the look of a hunted animal, and then he was turning, climbing, digging his toes into the earth. Loose dirt and gravel spilled into the water as he reached the top of the bank. He ducked into the trees and out of Catlin's sight.

Still stunned and not sure why, Catlin started to follow him, stubbed his toe on a tree stump, and fell flat on his stomach. The fall gushed the breath out of him. Gasping, he jumped to his feet as the dull thud of a horse's galloping hooves sounded through the trees. Flushed from cover by the running horse, a covey of quail burst into the air and circled overhead.

Catlin heard it then, a fiendish Rebel yell, low at first, then rising, rising, growing stronger, an outburst of pent-up fear, hatred, and exultation. The last note wavered, carried astray by a gust of wind and a fast horse, before it faded into silence.

Yet Catlin believed he could still hear it. The familiar, high-pitched battle cry rang in his ears, and he stumbled backward through the brush and deadfall, wanting to escape the sound but not sure which way to turn. The sound grew in volume, roaring inside his head, a thousand voices lifting in unison and coming at him from all directions.

He took off running. He ran, fell down, got back up again, and ran blindly, recklessly on. He crashed through the undergrowth, seeking refuge from the dreadful voices.

Halfway between the creek bottoms and the barn, Catlin dropped to his knees amid the grass and buckwheat and scratchy weeds. He clapped his hands over his ears and squeezed his eyes shut. Rocking to and fro, his breath huffing in and out to the wild beat of his heart, he waited for the demons to leave.

His senses returned with grudging slowness, his vision cleared, and he cast a cautious look around him. It was quiet. The horses stood several yards away, watching him with ears pricked forward, still in harness the way he had left them, the plow hitched behind and tipped to one side.

Lowering his hands, he looked back toward the trees where he had first noticed the stranger. Birds twittered in the bushes, and cottonwood leaves slapped together softly, stirred by a light breeze. All was peaceful and undisturbed.

He felt as if he had just seen a ghost, and this made him wonder: Was the man he saw here real or imagined? Suddenly he wasn't sure, and his confusion frightened him. He began to think he hadn't seen or heard anything, that it was all a figment of his distorted senses, just as the voices had been. Bewildered, he dragged a shaky hand down his face.

"What the hell's wrong with me?" he whispered.

Sucking in a deep breath, he rose at last, walked back in the direction of the wooded creek bank, and retrieved his hat where it had fallen. He stared toward the cottonwood tree. There was one surefire way to find out if he had, in fact, chased a flesh and blood human being down to the creek. Ghosts and hallucinations didn't leave footprints. He stood motionless, stalling, and finally turned and walked back to his plow.

He didn't want to know.

Talking softly to the horses, Catlin unfastened the traces and looped them up. He grasped a handful of the nearest horse's mane and jumped, throwing his belly across the animal's broad back, and clambered aboard. Leaving the plow in the field and the fire break he had begun unfinished, he rode to the corral and saw Ocie walking out to meet him.

Afraid his father might have seen him tearing out of the trees like a madman, Catlin gave him a tentative little smile and slid to the ground.

"I didn't finish," he said. "Spent half the afternoon breaking these two jugheads in to pulling a plow."

"What was that goshawful noise a few minutes ago?" Ocie asked. "What were you doing?"

Unbuckling a harness, Catlin's fingers froze, and he peered at Ocie over the backs of the horses. "You heard it?"

Ocie nodded. "Gave me chill bumps, just listening to it. Kind of reminded me of an Indian war whoop, only it wasn't like any Indian I ever heard before." He studied Catlin curiously. "Was that you?"

It was a good question. Catlin pondered it in silence as he tended to the horses.

Once, when he was courting Mary Lane, she had wanted to hear what a Rebel yell sounded like. He had refused to mimic the battle cry for her, knowing full well he lacked the proper motivation to make it sound right, namely terror. His thoughts were of love, after all, not war.

Well, I'm wound tighter than a bedspring now, he thought. I bet I could raise a holler that'd curdle your blood.

He glanced at Ocie, aware of the old man's hard, probing stare. Perhaps he already had.

They walked to the house in silence. Ocie shot him several looks but didn't question him further, probably chalking it up as just another one of his younger son's peculiarities. He possessed a passel of them already, so it was nothing new.

CHAPTER TWENTY-EIGHT

Following supper of the same day, Catlin took the kitchen chairs outdoors, and he and Ocie sat and enjoyed the cool of late afternoon. They listened to the noisy chatter of several scissor-tailed flycatchers that were swooping, diving, and squabbling at each other in mid-air and watched a dozen or so cows and calves trail single-file down to the creek.

Catlin reflected that some of these free-ranging cattle might belong to Ocie and Ray. They had been buying a few head here and there over the past couple of years, slowly building up a herd. The cows were too far away for him to tell whether or not they bore the Running M brand.

Ocie jerked his thumb over his shoulder, indicating the heavy, dark blue bank of clouds to the northwest. "I bet we get a thunderstorm out of that," he said.

Catlin grunted a response and rolled a smoke.

Ocie glanced over at him. "You ain't said five words all afternoon. Something on your mind?"

"No, sir."

"Empty-headed as usual, eh?"

One corner of Catlin's mouth twitched upward. "I guess so."

"Before you leave for town here in a little while, there's something I been meaning to talk to you about."

"I'm not going back to town."

Ocie frowned but went on as if Catlin hadn't spoken. "I've been thinking a lot about this place here," he said. "What do

213

you think ought to be done with it, Tom Cat?"

Catlin looked at him in surprise. "Ray would have more to say about that than me."

"I've talked to Ray about it already. He's through with farming. Mary, she wouldn't let him go back to it even if he wanted to."

"I expect so."

"She's even been griping about us gettin' into the cow business. Ray'll probably sell our little herd here pretty soon."

"Probably."

"Ray made a suggestion a few days ago," Ocie continued. "He said to make it fair, you should be entitled to half of this place, and he should be entitled to half. He said he'd be willing to sell you his share if you wanted it."

Catlin digested this slowly. He turned his head to the side and spit out a shred of tobacco. "You're pulling my leg, right?"

"Like I said, it was his suggestion, not mine," Ocie insisted. "I told him you wouldn't want it. You couldn't wait to get away from here when you were younger."

Studying the burning tip of his cigarette, Catlin wondered how he should respond.

"Well," Ocie said impatiently, "do you want it or not?"

"I don't deserve it."

"No, you don't," Ocie agreed, "but you're still my boy. One of these days, if you don't get yourself killed first, you may decide to settle down. If you do, this place would be waiting here for you. So what do you think?"

"I think I'd be proud to own it."

The words spilled out of Catlin's mouth before he could really think them over, and he was astonished by his own answer.

Ocie appeared astonished, too, at first, then pleased. He

reached over and slapped Catlin on the leg. "The only thing I ask is that you give your brother first shot at buying the place back if you decide to sell it someday."

"It's a deal."

"Good. Soon as you and Ray shake on it, it'll be final." He gave Catlin a sidelong glance. "Ray tells me you won't have any trouble coming up with the money to buy his share."

"No, sir."

"Death must be a profitable business."

Catlin gave him a blank look and pretended not to know what he was talking about.

Ocie saw through that trick. "Don't play dumb with me," he said and shook his head, appearing suddenly very tired. "What's the matter with you, Cat? What drives you to do the things you do? Me and Rena tried to give you a Christian upbringing, tried to teach you right from wrong. What more could we have done?"

Catlin leaned forward, resting his elbows on his knees. "It's nothing you did or didn't do. It's me. I was twisted the wrong way when Mama was trying to have me, and I guess I just stayed that way."

"Maybe so," Ocie said. "I don't know. If Rena was alive, she'd blame the war, the Army, herself, anything but you. Sometimes I wonder. Maybe she'd be right to blame the war. It changed you."

Catlin considered that. The Army taught him how to kill, but it was he who had continued to do so long after the war ended. He still remembered the first man he ever killed for money, still remembered the stunned look on his face the instant before he died, still remembered his name. Jacob Heath.

Heath had murdered and robbed two prospectors who were working a claim in the Sierra Nevadas. Catlin was in California at the time, twenty years old, broke, and searching for work. When he learned that friends of the two murdered prospectors were offering a cash reward to the man who killed Jacob Heath, he thought to himself, Why not? He owned a good hunting rifle. And Heath deserved to die.

Two weeks later, Catlin found his man bellied up to a bar in a shabby mining camp near Virginia City. Just so no one could say he shot Jacob Heath in the back, Catlin hollered a howdy to him and when the man turned around, he nailed him square between the eyes. Easy money.

That had been the start of it all. One job always seemed to lead to yet another, and another, until he lost count of the men he had killed and lost belief in his ability to do anything else.

He finally spoke up, breaking the silence. "Pa, I know you don't think much of me but . . ." He paused, searching for the right words, wanting to make his father understand. "But the jobs I take on are for the good," he explained. "The men I've killed were killers themselves, or rapists, or . . ."

Johnny Keaton's youthful face flashed in his mind, and he stopped, unable to finish, realizing the fallacy of his words. Keaton's death had been wasteful, needless.

Ocie sighed and rubbed his eyes. "Well, you make it sound good, at least. I guess you'll keep it up as long as there's fools willing to pay you for your time and bullets, won't you?"

"I don't know. I've been studying on that some the last couple of months. Maybe it's time for a change."

Ocie regarded him hopefully. "You could do a lot with this farm here, Cat. You could add on to it, buy some cattle or horses. When you were a boy, you used to talk about raising horses, remember?" He swept his right arm in a wide arc. "Look at that grass. Bluestem, grama, curly mesquite. This land was made for horses.

"When we came out here in '57, we came with everything

216

we owned crammed into a covered wagon pulled by a high horse and a low mule, and we built this place from the ground up. You're younger than I was when we first settled here. Think of all you could do, Tom Cat, if you'd put your mind to it."

"It's something to think about, all right," Catlin admitted. "If I could ever see my way clear of this mess that's going on in Fort Griffin right now . . . Well, it'd make it easier to decide what to do. Stay here or leave."

"It's your bad reputation that's got you into this mess in the first place," Ocie said. "You'll have to work hard to make regular folks feel easy in your company again. Until you do, they'll mistrust you and shun you."

Catlin nodded. How well he knew it! His own brother had made that perfectly clear to him.

The sun dipped behind the trees, and the shadows lengthened. Mosquitos swarmed. They soon drove Catlin and Ocie indoors. Not ready for bed, Ocie positioned his chair before the screen door and watched the gathering dusk. From here, he enjoyed a sweeping view of the countryside.

"I wish you'd go on back to town," he said once. "I don't need a keeper."

Catlin rubbed his sore shoulder, the same one Eladio Moreno had peppered with lead, and stretched his arms and back. His muscles weren't accustomed to plowing. "If you're that worried about Ray, I'll ride to town first thing in the morning," he promised.

"You do that."

Catlin picked up his bedroll and tucked it under his arm. He fidgeted around a minute, then said softly, "Pa."

"Huh?"

"Thank you."

Ocie waved his hand at him, and Catlin left him alone

with his thoughts and his pipe.

He spread his blankets on the living room floor, tugged off his boots, and stripped off his shirt and dusty pants. He lay on his back on the floor and gazed up at the ceiling. He was too stirred up to sleep.

Ocie's offer came as a complete surprise to him. He had always taken it for granted that the land and everything on it would go to his brother. Ray was the oldest son, and he had worked, sweated, and bled on this farm long after Catlin had hightailed it out of here. Of course, were it possible, Ocie would have bequeathed his holdings to the family dog if it meant keeping it in the Myers name, but Catlin didn't care. The fact that his father had chosen him over the dog was what mattered.

He wondered what Zella would have to say about this unexpected turn of events. Would it make her happy if he traded his guns for a plow? Moreover, would it make him happy?

Catlin jerked awake. Thunder rumbled overhead, rattling the glass in the windows. He lay on his side and stared into the darkness, not sure where he was at first. Raindrops tap-danced on the roof. Rising, he groped his way across the room and lowered the windows. Lightning flickered, and he could see the jagged, fast-moving clouds. Tree tops tossed in the rising wind.

Something snapped, the sound of metal striking wood, and Catlin remembered the mouse traps he had set out.

"Got your ass," he murmured triumphantly.

Fumbling around in the darkness, he found a candle, lit it, and walked into the kitchen. He stooped down to look at the sprung trap, holding the candle's feeble flame close to the floor. The bait was gone and so was the mouse. He shook his head. It was a sad day, indeed, when a dirty mouse could out-smart a man.

He started to lower the kitchen windows when another bright flare of lightning lit up the room, and he spotted Ocie still sitting by the front door with his head slumped over his chest. He had fallen asleep in his chair. Easing toward him, Catlin laid a hand on his shoulder.

"Pa." He gave his father's shoulder a gentle shake. "Pa, you'd better go on to bed."

The old man didn't stir. Catlin shook him a little harder, spoke a little louder. Still no response. He felt his stomach ball up into a hard knot.

"Pa!"

The candle went out, extinguished by the wind blowing in through the screen door, and Catlin dropped it and gripped Ocie by the shoulders. He shook him as hard as he dared.

"Damn your hide, old man, don't you leave me now! Wake up! Wake up, damn you!"

His curses went unheard. Ocie Myers was dead.

CHAPTER TWENTY-NINE

Eladio Moreno touched the knot on his skull and staggered out of the livery stable with bits of hay and dried horse manure stuck to his clothes and hair. He didn't recall how he had made it here to the stables to sleep off the effects of the tequila and a sore head, only that he had been here quite a while. Already the sun was setting. The hostler who had shaken him awake moments ago told him this was Sunday.

One thing Eladio did remember painfully well was that he had lost his temper with Zella the night before and then the bartender hit him on the head. Everything after that was lost to his memory.

He ate his first meal of the day in a small, gloomy restaurant run by a woman who had once worked the cribs on River Street. She was greasy and unkempt, and when she banged Eladio's plate of food down in front of him, he noticed beneath her fingernails was black with filth. He ate heartily, not minding her dirt as much as he minded her dirty looks. She didn't like Mexicans, and he suspected she had spit in his coffee. He drank it anyway, and afraid not to, politely asked for a refill. She was a very large woman, and he didn't think he could bear another bump on the head.

It was dark outside when he paid for his meal and walked outside. He felt inside his pocket and jingled the gold and silver coins. He didn't sound as prosperous as he had a couple of weeks ago. The money Arnet Phillips had given him was running low, and he considered sending a wire to Tucson to

220

ask for more, a sort of advance on what Phillips had already promised him upon delivery of Cat Myers's scalp. Perhaps he would do that tomorrow.

Feeling much better with his belly full, Eladio walked down Griffin Avenue and peered into the open doorway of the Beehive Saloon. He saw Zella behind the bar, but the one-eyed *Gato* was nowhere in sight. He continued down the street.

He loitered in front of Myers's Mercantile. There were lights burning in the building's back rooms. He remembered the snatches of conversation he had overheard Friday night between the man and woman. "Cat Myers will be finished soon," the man had said. His words were music to Eladio's ears.

He realized now that the woman he had seen here that night was *Gato* Myers's sister-in-law. But who was the man? Would he come here again tonight?

Eladio hoped so. He wanted to meet this person whose hatred for the *Gato* was equal to his own.

Taking care not to be seen, he slipped into the pitch blackness between Myers's Mercantile and the restaurant next door. The store building was designed in the shape of an L. Hugging the wall, Eladio peered into the lee of the L where he had seen the man and woman talking that night. The area was lit-up by lamplight slanting through the windows. He could hear voices within. Taking a chance, he neared one of the open windows.

Gato's brother, a man with thinning, light brown hair and a mustache and short-clipped beard, was sitting at the kitchen table and rubbing his temples. He was heavier than the *Gato,* and his face and hands appeared very soft, pink, and well-scrubbed, like a baby's butt.

"I suppose Pa will be all right staying there one night," the man was saying. "But like it or not, he's coming home tomorrow."

A blonde-haired, nicely dressed woman sat across from Myers, her back turned to Eladio so that he could not see her face. "Ask someone to go with you," she said, and Eladio recognized her voice from Friday night. "I don't like the thought of you riding out there alone."

"Mary, do you really think Cat would . . . would kill me?"

"Yes, I do, and the sooner you come to accept it, the better."

Myers's face sagged with sorrow. "It's all so hard to believe. Here I asked him to come home, thinking I'd feel safe with him around, and now I'm more scared than ever."

Standing outside the window, Eladio nodded, glad to know he was not alone in his fear of the *Gato*.

"But Cat didn't kill Charlie Conrad," Myers went on. "I know that for certain. He's not working alone. If only I knew who this Bradford Gilley person is!"

"Sheriff Luger will sort it all out in time," Mary Myers assured him. She rose to her feet and scooted the chair beneath the table. "Come now," she said briskly. "Kiss Beth goodnight and let's go to bed. We have a long day ahead of us tomorrow."

Eladio didn't tarry to hear more. He stole toward a small storage shed standing nearby where he could clearly see the kitchen door and squatted on his heels in the deepest shadows.

He thought about the woman, Mary Myers. Was it possible that she had hired someone to kill the *Gato?* If so, then wouldn't she also want proof of his death, just as Arnet Phillips wanted proof? Though this posed only a minor problem, it worried Eladio. Cat Myers, after all, possessed just one scalp. He wondered if Phillips would settle for an ear.

Eladio pondered these things, scratched, yawned, and fought boredom by drinking small sips from his pint bottle of cheap, rotgut whiskey. All the lights, by this time, were out in the Myerses' living quarters, leaving the surrounding yard dark. Eladio eased into a more comfortable position, leaning against the side of the shed, and watched sheet lightning play along the northwestern horizon. He could hear no thunder; the storm must still be miles away . . .

Eladio's eyes suddenly flared open. He had fallen asleep! He sat up and looked around him. The air felt oppressive and so still he could hear his eyelids popping as he blinked the sleepy haze from his vision. A light was burning in the Myerses' kitchen.

Thunder rumbled across a black sky. Fearful of storms, Eladio pushed himself to his feet and sought shelter inside the storage shed just as someone stepped out the kitchen door. It was the woman.

"Where are you?" she asked, her voice tremulous, hushed.

"I'm here, Mary."

A man's shadowy form emerged from the darkness, and Eladio's eyes widened with eager anticipation. He recognized the thin, straight figure, the cultured voice. This was the same man who had predicted Cat Myers's finish!

The woman half-sobbed. "Oh, I'm so glad to see you safe!"

"Shhh. I'm all right."

Outlined against the lighted window, their silhouettes merged as they embraced.

"Did you get my supplies?" the man asked.

"Yes. Everything you asked for."

Lightning cracked very near. The blinding flash, booming thunder, and smell of charred wood and brimstone overwhelmed Eladio's senses. He quaked inside and glanced up at the sky, then turned back to the man and woman and strained to hear their conversation over the storm's angry rumblings.

". . . I got his rifle," Mary Myers was saying. "Will that do?"

"Perfect. I'll have Riddick plant it near Frank Wyman's body before morning."

"When . . . when did you kill him?"

"About three hours ago. Riddick and I pulled it off without a hitch."

Eladio held his breath. Who was Riddick? And Frank Wyman?

"Then it's done," Mary said.

"Not quite."

"Oh, please, no. Not Ray!"

"He must pay for his treachery. How many times do I have to explain this to you?"

"But Ray didn't do anything!"

"My point exactly."

"Oh, just leave him alone. At the very least, think of what you'll do to me and Beth if you kill him!" Mary buried her face in her hands and began to sob. "When Ray told me he had been threatened, I couldn't believe it. I couldn't believe you'd kill him until I saw the note and read your words."

"Mary, don't cry. Please . . ."

"Then promise me you won't harm Ray. Promise me!"

The man bowed his head, seemingly moved by Mary Myers's tearful pleading. "Very well," he said finally. "If all continues to go smoothly, I'll spare the fool's life."

"No more cruel threats?"

"No more threats." He laughed softly. "I believe Ray has already died at least twice anyway."

"What do you mean?"

"Haven't I told you, a coward dies many times, whereas a brave man dies but once?"

Thunder roared again, and Eladio missed the woman's response. The wind was beginning to stir. He tried to think what to do. Should he simply walk up to them and introduce himself? Fear cautioned him against such a bold move. There was obviously much more to this matter than he had at first thought, and the bloodthirsty little man intimidated him.

"I'll soon have to pay Lee Riddick," he heard the man say. "He's been a great help to me."

"Yes, I know. I've already spoken to Aunt Cora."

"What did you tell her?"

"I told her Ray couldn't pay off some debts and was too proud to ask for a loan," Mary replied. "Aunt Cora agreed to withdraw the one thousand dollars. I hated to tell such a horrid lie but . . ."

Eladio decided he had heard all he needed to hear, certainly enough to convince him these two people were not the answer to his problem. They hadn't mentioned Cat Myers even once, and the storm was increasing in intensity so that he couldn't concentrate on their conversation anyway.

He was thinking about bedding down here in the storage shed when the wind struck Fort Griffin with sudden and frightening strength, carrying with it a wall of blowing dust. Wind roared between the buildings and whistled through the cracks in the shed. This was no place to ride out a bad storm.

He peered outside and saw the kitchen light go out. Except for brief flashes of lightning, the night was black and filled with flying trash and dust and racket. The man and woman were gone, he supposed, driven their separate ways by the wind.

Eladio left, too. Clamping his sombrero on his head with both hands, he dove into the storm and instantly slammed against something. Or someone! Eyes wide, heart thumping, he veered sharply to the right. A piece of paper blew into his face, caught on his nose, and clung there. In a panic, he struck it away, and certain someone had just grabbed him by the nose, began punching the air with both fists.

Eladio's knuckles grazed flesh and bone. Lightning flickered, and he caught a glimpse of a man with a bandana covering his face standing less than four feet away from him!

Before Eladio had time to react, a bony fist smashed into his lower jaw. His head snapped back, lights burst inside his brain, and the next thing he knew, he was sprawled on his back in the dirt. He was vaguely aware of a pair of rough hands feeling him over for weapons, and then he was hauled to his feet and hustled across the yard and into the alley.

Here, lightning revealed another man and two horses awaiting them. Eladio recognized the thin little man who had been talking to Mary Myers and knew he was as good as dead now.

"Got him, Pony!"

The little man gave no indication he had heard. Coughing violently in the blowing dust, he stepped into the saddle.

Eladio's captor gripped his arm with steely fingers, took up his mount's reins, and led them both up the alley, following the man on the horse. No one spoke. It began to rain. Cold, hard drops pelted Eladio, creating mud on his dusty face.

They emerged from the alley and came to a narrow side street dimly illuminated by lantern light from a nearby saloon. The little man pointed to a horse standing with its tail to the wind at the hitching rail.

"Ride that horse!" he said, shouting over the storm.

Eladio's captor shoved him forward, waited for him to untie the animal and mount up, and lashed his hands to the saddlehorn with a short length of rawhide.

They rode out of town by way of the side streets and alleys, Eladio's horse being led by the man who had punched him in the jaw. Eladio swayed in the saddle. His head had begun to ache again, and he felt as if he might pass out. He didn't fight the feeling, preferring insensibility to terror, and sank blissfully into oblivion.

CHAPTER THIRTY

"I swear, I never seen a grown man faint before. Always thought that was a woman thing."

At the sound of the drawling voice, Eladio opened one eye, then the other. Someone was standing over him. Eladio focused with difficulty on the face. It was lean with a wide mouth and a crooked nose and earnest, sky-dyed eyes that were not unfriendly. The man smiled, and the deep crow's feet at the corners of his eyes spread their toes.

"Hey, *amigo*."

Eladio blinked up at the man's face without answering, and suddenly the face was gone, and he was looking through the dripping tree tops at a gray sky. Voices murmured nearby, and farther away was the trickling sound of flowing water. Eladio didn't move. He had expected to wake up dead and wondered now if perhaps this wet, dismal world was purgatory. Just in case it was, he crossed himself and whispered the Hail Mary.

The face appeared above him again, closer this time, and a warm, pleasant aroma filled Eladio's nostrils.

"Coffee?"

Coffee in purgatory? Not likely. Eladio raised up on one elbow and gratefully accepted the dented tin cup.

"Do you speak English?"

Eladio nodded and slurped his coffee.

The man spoke over his shoulder to someone: "He savvies."

228

Eladio looked to see who the tall, hatchet-faced man had addressed, and his heart dropped to the pit of his stomach and made him feel ill. He set aside his coffee and watched a small, light-haired man wrapped in a blanket walk toward them. His erect, military bearing brought Eladio to attention. He sat up.

"What is your name?" the little man asked.

"E-Eladio Moreno."

The little man peered down at him without speaking. Eladio found it impossible to hold his gaze but couldn't resist stealing a furtive look at him now and again. The man's face and hands were thin and bloodless, his eyes the color of ice. Eladio remembered the man was called Pony—because of his small size, he assumed—but didn't think the nickname fitted him. It was much too innocent. With his cold, colorless features, he could have passed for one of the devil's hellish host, if not *Diablo* himself.

Even that green-eyed assassin, Cat Myers, paled in comparison.

"So you understand English," Pony mused. "Then I assume you heard an earful last night."

Eladio realized his blunder too late. Had he pretended ignorance, they might have let him go. Now they would kill him for sure. He glanced around at the trees and at the river flowing a little distance away, looking for a place to run and hide should the opportunity crop up any time soon. He had no idea where he was.

"Look at me when I'm talking to you!" Pony snapped.

Eladio obeyed, centering his unwilling gaze on the little man's nose.

"You said your name is Moreno. Are you acquainted with Zella Moreno?"

"*Sí*. She is . . . she is my wife."

Pony nodded. "Mrs. Moreno's poor taste in men is consistent, I see." He gave Hatchet-face a sidelong glance. "She's Cat Myers's woman."

Hatchet-face regarded Eladio with renewed interest.

"Why were you eavesdropping on me last night, Moreno?" Pony asked.

Eladio didn't know what eavesdropping meant but figured it had something to do with his spying last night.

"*Señor,* I wasn't . . ."

"I don't tolerate liars, Moreno."

Eladio ventured as close to the truth as he dared. "I did not mean to hear," he said. "I was looking for the *Gato*. For Cat Myers."

Pony and Hatchet-face exchanged glances.

"I will kill him soon."

"Because of your wife?" Hatchet-face asked.

Eladio nodded. It was not the whole truth, but he thought he saw a trace of sympathy in the man's eyes and decided to keep his motive simple.

"Cat Myers stole my wife," he explained. "I think maybe he deserve to die for this, yes?"

"Yeah," Hatchet-face murmured. "Yeah, I think maybe he does."

"How do you expect to kill a man like Cat Myers when you carry no weapons?" Pony asked.

"I had a shotgun but . . ."

"A shotgun, eh? Let me show you a real weapon!"

Pony walked to the other side of their small, sheltered camp and came back carrying a rifle, only it was unlike any rifle Eladio had ever seen. He looked at the profuse floral scrollwork and engraving on the breech and buttstock. It was the most beautiful gun he had ever set eyes on.

"This, my friend, is a weapon," Pony said. "It uses fifty

caliber ammo, weighs twenty-five pounds, and has a thirty-six inch barrel. It takes a real man to handle a gun like this." Letting his blanket slip off one shoulder, he lifted the rifle up. "Just look at that stock. Walnut inlaid with engraved ebony and staghorn."

"She is *hermosa*," Eladio whispered.

Pony's ice cube eyes glinted. "It was given to me by a French nobleman following a successful bison hunt which I hosted five years ago. I have friends in high places all over the world, you see."

He returned the rifle to its leather case, drew one side of his blanket back, and from a hip scabbard, pulled forth a shining sword similar in style to the rifle. He held it out for Eladio to admire.

"This also was a gift from Count Beaumarchais."

Without warning, Pony took a swift step forward and thrust the sword's sharp tip toward Eladio's throat. Eladio gasped in surprise and cringed against a tree trunk, sure any moment the blade would be driven clean through him and into the tree.

Hatchet-face appeared just as startled. "Pony, what's got into you, man? The poor fella's already scared silly."

"French revolutionaries practiced decapitation during the 1700s," Pony said. "Of course, they used the guillotine, but I don't have that luxury, nor do I need it."

He caressed Eladio's throat with the sword's shining, curved blade, his touch feather-light. Eladio felt something warm and wet tickle his neck.

"I could cut off your head in less time than it would take me to draw a breath."

"Pony, come on. Let him alone."

Eladio squeezed his eyes shut and prayed harder than he had ever prayed in his whole life.

Several dragging seconds passed before Pony withdrew his sword and slipped it back into its steel scabbard. Beads of sweat broke out across his forehead. Hatchet-face, who had been squatting on his heels near Eladio, rose quickly and stepped toward him.

"Pony, you all right?"

The little man's face changed from white to red. His eyes bulged. Hatchet-face thrust a bottle of brandy into his hand, and he tipped it up and drank. His hands shook. Mystified, Eladio watched him and saw the precious liquor dribble from one corner of his mouth and soak into the ground. Eladio licked his dry lips.

Lowering the bottle at last, Pony closed his eyes a moment, breathed deeply, and his face faded to its usual pasty hue.

"All right now?" Hatchet-face asked.

"Yes. Fine, thank you." Pony wiped the sweat from his face and neck with a white kerchief.

Eladio was sweating, too. He felt it trickling down inside his shirt and touched trembling fingers to his throat. He was horrified when his fingertips came away crimson. It was not sweat, after all, but blood.

"I'm not going to kill you," Pony stated and shook out his damp kerchief. "You owe me something for my tolerance."

Eladio wiped his bloody fingers on his striped trousers and nodded.

"Good," Pony said. "I'm glad we agree. I'll think of something useful for you to do once we've eaten breakfast. Something to bring about the death of Cat Myers perhaps. Would that suit you?"

Eladio felt his spirits lift slightly. "*Sí,*" he whispered. "That would be ver' good."

"Then it's settled." Pony's lips receded backward in a smile, revealing pale gums and small, square teeth. "Of course, if you betray me, I'll kill you, but not because you failed me, nor because I believe you know more than you should. Understand?"

Eladio didn't understand at all. "Why you kill me then?" he asked.

"Because you stole a man's horse last night."

"But you said to take the horse," Eladio objected. "I did what you tol' me to do."

"If I told you to jump into the river and drown yourself, would you do it?" Pony asked. "No man makes another man do anything. You could have refused to take the horse, and I would have respected your wishes."

"You would have let me go, *Señor,* if I had refuse?"

"No, I would have killed you. It's better to die with honor, Mr. Moreno, than to live in shame."

He started to turn away. Hatchet-face stopped him.

"Pony, why do you want to get him mixed up in this? How do you know he won't rat on us?"

"Because he knows I would hunt him down and kill him." The little man stroked his silvery goatee and gazed down at Eladio. "Make no mistake, Moreno. I can be the best friend you've ever had, or I can be your worst nightmare. It's your choice. Are you with me?"

The choice was clear. "I am with you," Eladio answered and rose unsteadily to his feet. "One little thing, *Señor.* I would like . . . I would like *Gato* Myers's scalp."

Pony's eyes narrowed. "Why?"

"For a sakekeep."

"A keepsake, you mean?" Pony loosed a harsh bark of laughter that ended in a spasm of coughing. He quickly downed more brandy and wiped his mouth on the back of his hand.

"*Gato* Myers, as you call him, will be hanged shortly," he said at length, "but only if you do as I tell you. When he's dead, I'm sure Riddick here would be glad to help you dig up his body for souvenirs."

Almost faint with relief, Eladio shook Pony's bird-claw hand. He suspected the bloodthirsty little man was *loco*, and at that moment, feeling those chilly eyes on him, he would have gladly jumped into the river and drowned himself if Pony had told him to.

CHAPTER THIRTY-ONE

" 'Yea, though I walk through the valley of the shadow of death, I will fear no evil: for thou art with me; thy rod and thy staff they comfort me . . .' "

Catlin listened to Brother Stegall without hearing his words and gazed upon the coffin bearing the body of his father, soon to be laid to rest by the side of Rena Myers. He stood motionless, a tall, solemn-faced statue in a dark broadcloth suit and polished boots. To the left of him was his sixteen year old cousin, Bessie Thorpe, to his right was Ray. Both were crying.

" 'Thou preparest a table before me in the presence of mine enemies: thou anointest my head with oil; my cup runneth over . . .' "

Ray's tears ran over, too. Head bowed, shoulders hunched, he softly sobbed. Embarrassed for him, Catlin nudged him in the side with his elbow.

"Get a hold of yourself," he whispered.

It didn't help. If anything, Ray sobbed harder. Mary peered around her grieving husband at Catlin and shot him a look that would have dropped him dead in his tracks had it been a bullet.

" 'Surely goodness and mercy shall follow me all the days of my life: and I will dwell in the house of the Lord forever.' "

The morning was muggy and still, and Catlin was suffocating inside the unfamiliar confines of a suit and tie. He felt out of place standing here amid these gloomy men and weepy women all dressed in black, and was relieved when the services ended. He shook hands with Brother Stegall, and Ray thanked the preacher for his comforting words.

Though graveside services for Ocie Myers were open only to the family and a few close friends, there was still quite a number of people in attendance. Catlin didn't know or recognize but a handful of them. Even the members of his own family were strangers to him, for he hadn't seen most of them since his mother's funeral, and there were others he'd never seen at all. His family was not close-knit, so he guessed it was a good thing one of them died every so often; otherwise, they might never see each other.

Young Bessie Thorpe turned to Catlin and dabbed at her eyes with a handkerchief. "I'm sorry for your loss, John."

Catlin winced at her use of his first name. No one had ever called him that but his mother.

"Papa says you've been home a few weeks now," she continued. "It's good you came back when you did."

She smiled up at him through her tears and shyly patted his arm. Catlin wondered what else "Papa" had told her. Walter Thorpe, her father and Catlin's uncle by marriage, had settled with his family in the Clear Fork valley shortly after the Myerses. He had been trying to pawn one or another of his daughters off on both Catlin and Ray for years. Now that Ray was married again, Catlin remained the sole target.

Bessie was the last in what seemed to Catlin an endless string of children born to the Thorpes, most of them daughters, and the fact that Walter would try to push her on him was offensive.

Seeing Walter's wrinkled, snuff-stained face grinning at him over Bessie's shoulder, Catlin let his restless gaze wander elsewhere. He spotted a dark-haired woman in a white blouse and buckskin riding skirt standing beside her horse a short distance away. Zella Moreno! Catlin excused himself and walked past the little crowd of mourners, past the open grave that defaced the prairie like a raw, gaping wound, and joined Zella beneath the shade of an oak tree.

"Hello, Catlin."

"Zella . . ."

"Before you jump down my throat for coming here," she said, "I just want you to know how sorry I am about your father."

"I appreciate that."

"This must be difficult for you."

"I've had happier days."

She nodded and fidgeted with her horse's reins. "Your brother seems to be taking it hard."

"Ray's a milksop. He takes everything hard."

Zella gave him a gentle smile. "He doesn't hold his sorrow inside him. That's a good way to be, sometimes."

"I guess, if you don't mind making a fool of yourself."

"Is there anything I can do?" she asked.

Catlin gazed past her at the plowed fields. A breath of wind stirred his hair and cooled his damp forehead. He loosened the black string tie around his neck and let the ends dangle.

"Everything's done that needs doing," he said at length. "It's just a matter of planting Pa in the ground now." He smiled wryly. "Appropriate for a farmer, huh?"

"I guess so. Well . . ." She turned toward her horse, then stopped and looked back at him. "Catlin, I realize this isn't the best timing, but I thought you should know that Frank Wyman is missing. No one's seen him since Sunday afternoon."

Catlin mulled that over, scraped mud off his boot with a stick, and glanced up at Zella. "One more reason why you shouldn't be hovering around me."

"It doesn't matter . . ."

"It does matter. Go back to El Paso, Zella. Stay as far away from me as you can get."

He left without waiting for an answer. He didn't want to hear her refusal and wasn't in the mood to argue with her. It wouldn't do any good anyway. Zella Moreno had a mind of her own. It was a trait he found both admirable and exasperating.

Catlin thought about the lisping, redheaded Frank Wyman. Shot and decapitated probably, just like the others. Too bad. He guessed he was the prime suspect, and Ocie, the only person who could back up his alibi, was unavailable for questioning.

Following the burial of Ocie Myers, Catlin walked slowly back to the house with four of the Thorpe cousins, big, hairy men wearing homespun clothes and possessing their father's coarse manners. They found the house crowded with people and food and bustle. Several men and women were taking turns holding little Beth and cooing over her like passenger pigeons. Catlin pitied the poor kid. Not feeling very sociable, he sat alone on the front step to smoke a cigarette and was joined a moment later by Walter Thorpe and Ray.

Like Catlin, Ray had no appetite for food or conversation, but Walter was happily uninhibited. His plate was heaped two stories high with chicken-fried steak, gravy, cornbread, and black-eyed peas picked fresh from the garden behind the house. Catlin watched Walter shovel it in, amazed. If he hadn't known better, he would have sworn this was his uncle's first square meal all year.

"Say, Cat." Walter chewed with his mouth open and stabbed his fork at him. "Ray tells me you come into some money."

"A little."

"Got a nice big house in El Paso, Ray says."

Catlin frowned. "Not too big."

"Ocie musta been right proud of you."

Sitting on a tree stump a few feet away, Ray cast a sidelong glance at Catlin. "I don't think proud is quite the word for it," he mumbled.

"Makes me no never mind how Cat got the money, long as he worked for it," Walter said. "How you like that gal o' mine, Cat?"

"Which one?"

"You know. Bessie."

Catlin yawned, hoping Walter would get the hint and shut up.

Walter didn't take hints. "She's marrying age," he declared. "I always did say any gal that ain't jumped the broom by the time she's sixteen ain't ever gonna jump a'tall."

"Mary was twenty-four when we got married," Ray said defensively, "and she had a lot of suitors, too."

Walter nodded. "Your wife comes from a rich family. Rich folks can afford to take their time and be partickler." He turned back to Catlin. "So how about it, boy? You want my Bessie? Lots of folks marry their first cousins. Ain't no shame in it."

"No thanks, Walt. Think I'll pass."

Walter stopped chewing. "How come?"

"She's too damned skinny," Catlin replied.

Ray made a choking sound inside his throat, but Walter didn't take offense at Catlin's remark. He scraped his plate clean and spoke around a mouthful of black-eyed peas.

"Wish to hell I'd knowed you liked 'em fleshy. Opal, my second youngest, was fat as butter. I married her off to a preacher boy over to Jacksboro." He shook his head with regret. "That boy's too poor to pay attention."

Setting aside his empty plate, Walter hobbled out to his wagon, reached under the seat, and returned carrying a gallon jug of moonshine.

"You boys look to me like you could use some cheering up," he announced.

He offered the jug to Ray, who declined and passed it on to Catlin. Uncorking the jug, Catlin wiped Walter's snuff off the mouth and took a big swig. His uncle's home brew kicked like a Missouri mule. He sucked in his breath, and Walter laughed with pleasure and slapped him on the back.

"Nothing like that white lightning, eh, boy?"

Walter's sons came outside presently, and they all passed the jug around. By the time it visited Catlin a third time, he was feeling much better. By the fifth round, he was perfectly giddy with joy. Walter was right. All he needed was a little cheering up.

Sitting beside him on the front step, Walter slung an arm around his neck. "That damn Yankee gov'ment in War-shington's trying to put me out of the whiskey making busi-ness," he lamented. "A deppity U. S. marshal rode out to the place the other day and said if I didn't pay an excise tax, he'd come back and bust up my still."

Clem Thorpe cut loose a thunderous fart and grinned. "Tell Cat what you said, Pa."

"I says, 'Mister, you lay a finger on my still, and I'll shoot your Yankee-loving ass so full o' buckshot, your friends'll melt you down for bullets!' "

Walter clapped Catlin on the back again, and he and his sons roared with laughter. Catlin giggled drunkenly. He thought it the most comical tale he'd heard all week.

Hearing their laughter, Catlin's Aunt Emily stepped out the door with her eyes and face red and puffy from crying and gave them all a good chewing out.

"Shame on y'all! Drinking and carrying on while my poor brother lies yonder in the cold ground!" Hiking up her black skirt and petticoats, she booted Walter in the butt. "Shame on you!"

When she had gone back inside, Ray rose and regarded Catlin with disapproval. "I couldn't agree with her more."

"Listen to little Miss Goody-Goody," Catlin said, smiling, feeling the moonshine stirring up the ugliness inside him. "Mama's little cream puff. Ray, drop your pants and show Walt and the boys the pretty lace on your drawers."

The Thorpe cousins snickered.

Ray's cheeks flushed with indignation. He slung his suitcoat over his shoulder and started to go inside when a small book fell from his coat pocket. Catlin snatched it up before Ray could stop him.

"Hey! What's this?"

Catlin leaped to his feet, holding the little book out of Ray's reach, and read the title. It was *The Pocket Book of Poems.*

"Poetry!"

Walter spat a string of snuff into the mud and said, "Read us something, Cat."

Dodging Ray's reaching hands, Catlin flipped to a dog-eared page and read aloud the opening lines from George Wither's "Shall I, Wasting in Despair:"

" 'Shall I, wasting in despair, / Die, because a woman's fair? / Or make pale my cheeks with care, / 'Cause another's rosy are?' " He looked up from the page. "Damn, Ray, do you really like this flowery bullshit?"

Ray glared at him. "What in God's name is wrong with you?" he demanded. "It looks to me like you could at least pretend to feel some guilt today instead of acting a fool!"

Catlin's smile faded. "Guilt over what?"

"It's your fault Pa's dead," Ray accused. "You brought

him out here when you knew good and well he was too sick!"

"Pa told me to take him home. It's what he wanted."

"Pa told you to do a lot of things!" Ray's chin quivered. "Why did you have to pick this one time to obey him?"

He jerked the book of poetry from Catlin's hand, squeezed past Walter, and slammed into the house. Catlin stared after him.

"Cat, don't pay him no mind," Walter said. "He's just blue is all, and that woman of his has got him to acting uppity these days, I notice. You know where Mary's mama and daddy hail from, don't you?"

Catlin shrugged indifferently.

"Boston, Massachusetts," Walter replied. "Say, that reminds me of a good joke. A New England lady's traveling through Texas and gets plumb disgusted by the people's back'ards ways. So she huffs to a cowboy: 'In Boston, breeding is everything.' And the cowboy says: 'Why, ma'am, we do it out here, too, but it ain't everything!' "

Walter and his boys slapped their legs and laughed till tears rolled down their leathery cheeks and wet their beards. Grinning, Catlin hefted the gallon jug and swallowed another swig of moonshine. The mule kicked, but he didn't feel a thing.

CHAPTER THIRTY-TWO

Zella Moreno walked her horse toward the stone house and saw Catlin sitting on the front step in the golden glow of late afternoon. Balancing half a watermelon between his knees, he turned his head to the side occasionally to spit out the black seeds. Zella was sure he had spotted her the moment she crossed Plum Creek, for he never looked up from his watermelon, not even as she rode into the yard. Catlin might have only one working eye, but he missed little.

She stopped a few feet in front of him, and he spoke without looking at her. "You could have been well on your way to El Paso by now."

"I could have," she admitted.

He glanced up at her, his mouth full of watermelon, and didn't say anything.

Deciding he wasn't going to invite her to dismount, she did it anyway, tied up her horse, and stood in front of him.

"How are you, Catlin?"

"I'm tolerable." He gestured to the other half of melon with his spoon. "Have some?"

"No, thank you."

She watched him jet watermelon seeds across the yard, remembering how he had appeared this morning during his father's graveside services. So serious and reserved. So handsome in his black suit and tie! He had shed the suit and was wearing jeans with white stains of sweat ringing the waistband, scuffed, mud-caked boots, and no shirt. His back, stomach, and upper arms, normally stark white compared to his face and hands, were burned red by the sun.

"What have you been doing?" she asked.

"Patching the barn roof."

"Patching the roof? Today?"

"Too muddy to finish plowing." Catlin spit out another wad of seeds and wiped his mouth. "Why are you here, Zella? Have they found Frank Wyman?"

"No, they're still searching." She shrugged. "I saw your brother and some of your family when they drove into town this afternoon. I thought you might need some company." She hesitated, then said, "I'll leave if you want me to."

"Sit down. I'm tired of bending my neck back."

Smiling faintly, she gathered up her riding skirt, sat beside him on the step, and noticed his silver whiskey flask protruding from his hip pocket.

"You have company already," she said dryly.

At his questioning look, she slipped the flask from his pocket. "Your little friend."

"If you think I'm drunk, think again. I sweat it all out working on the barn."

Zella frowned. "I'm surprised you didn't fall off the roof."

Unscrewing the cap on the flask, she sniffed the contents, took a small sip, and choked. Catlin grinned and watched her wipe her watering eyes.

"My uncle's moonshine."

"*¡Es terrible!*"

"Don't tell him that. It'd break his heart."

They fell silent, and Zella watched her horse crop grass and stomp away flies. She had come out here half-expecting to see Catlin sprawled out on the floor in a drunken stupor. Family secrets didn't keep long in a small town, and she had heard that Ray blamed Catlin for their father's death. As if he didn't have enough on his mind! Catlin could get into trouble easier than anyone she had ever known, even when he wasn't asking for it.

"I've got a piece of news," Catlin said suddenly.

"Oh? What is it?"

He set aside his watermelon and rested his elbows on his knees. "Pa told me I could have this place here if I wanted it."

Zella lifted her eyebrows in surprise.

"Poor Pa." Catlin tapped his temple with a forefinger. "Lost his marbles and kicked the bucket all in one day."

"Does your brother know about this?"

Catlin nodded. "He was the one suggested it."

"And did you accept?"

"Yeah. Crazy, huh?" He picked at a hang nail on his thumb, his face thoughtful. "I've been going over and over what you told me Saturday night and some things Pa said the night he died. Y'all are right, you know. It's time I tried something different. Past time."

To keep from throwing her arms around him, Zella hugged her knees instead and turned her face away to hide the happy smile that tugged at her mouth and eyes.

"I'm glad for you, Catlin."

"What do you think of this place?" he asked quietly.

Zella gazed around her at the prairie and the plowed fields and the shady green creek bottoms. She imagined rose bushes in full bloom around the old stone house, pretty curtains in the windows, and wildflowers, herbs, and fruit trees growing in the yard. All it needed was a little care.

She turned to Catlin and smiled. "I think it's beautiful."

Her response seemed to please him. He squeezed her hand, got to his feet unsteadily, and caught himself against the screen door. Zella quickly rose.

"I don't think you sweat out as much of your uncle's

moonshine as you thought you did," she scolded.

"I'm sober." He slapped at a mosquito and opened the door for her. "Let's go in before we get sucked dry."

She preceded him into the house. With the sun gone, the kitchen was dim, and she heard Catlin stumble over something behind her. Lighting the lantern, she saw it was a pair of cracked, run-over brogans sitting just inside the doorway. Catlin picked up his father's shoes, sank into a kitchen chair, and covered his eyes with his hand. He hugged the old leather shoes against his stomach. Drawing up behind him, Zella rested her hands on his shoulders, felt the tightness in him.

"We were just starting to get along," he said. "First time in my life . . ." His voice cracked and trailed off.

"I know, Catlin."

He drew a slow breath. "I'm not talking about him giving me the land. I mean, we were getting along, Zella. I finally felt like I could talk to him, sort of." After a moment of silence, he murmured, "It's my fault he's dead."

"You know that's not true."

"It is true. Hell, I knew how weak his heart was, and what'd I do? I drug him out here and killed him!"

"You didn't drag him anywhere. Your father came here because he wanted to." She pulled a chair toward her and sat down in front of him. "He could have gotten anyone to take him home, Catlin, but he wanted you to do it. He needed your help, and you gave it. That's all that matters."

Catlin lifted his hand from his face and gazed at her, dry-eyed. "Ray don't see it that way."

"Forget him."

He sighed again and stared out the window. "It's gettin' dark," he said at length. "I guess you'll be going back to town."

"Yes, I'd better. I'm already late for work."

"I'll ride back with you," he offered.

"There's no need. I brought my pistol with me."

She stood up, smoothed her skirt, and studied him a moment, reluctant to leave him. She noticed his face appeared slightly flushed in the lantern light. Frowning, she pressed her palm against his forehead.

"*Dios mío,* you're so hot!"

"It's just a sunburn."

"Your face isn't burned." She touched cool fingers to his cheeks. "You have a fever. Why didn't you tell me you were sick?"

He passed it off. "A touch of the ague, is all. I'll live."

"It's the watermelon," Zella declared. "I told you they caused fever and ague,* but do you listen? No!"

Catlin gave her a skeptical look. "I had the ague off and on all during the war without ever lapping a lip on a watermelon."

"Then you must have caught it from someone who did. Come now. You're going to bed."

He gave her only mild argument. In the bedroom, she waited for him to undress and draped his dirty jeans over the back of a chair while he lay down and stretched out. A pleasant breeze blew in through the south window, and he shivered when it touched him. Zella drew the covers over him and picked up the lantern.

"I think I saw some willows growing down by the creek," she said. "Willow bark will help your fever. I hope I can find them in the dark."

---

* Some early physicians actually cautioned against eating watermelons in the belief that they caused fever and ague. Still others claimed the illness was caused from breathing the night air. In 1898, English scientist Sir Ronald Ross proved that the ague, known today as malaria, is spread by mosquitoes.

Catlin grasped her arm as she started to turn away. "Zella, hold on." He waited for her to look down at him. "Would you like to live here?"

Surprised by his point-blank question, she sat beside him on the bed. "Do you want me to?"

"You know I do. I was thinking . . . I was thinking we might get married."

Zella dropped her gaze, her heart filling with sadness as she remembered that awful night in El Paso and the anguish on Catlin's face when he told her, "What if I had asked you to marry me?" It had shocked her to learn that he had even given marriage a thought, that he truly loved her! And all for nothing.

"Have you forgotten about Eladio?" she asked.

"Divorce him."

"I can't. The Church forbids it."

He smiled in amusement. "No offense, Zella, but you and me have done several things the Church forbids."

"It's not that simple. Eladio would never accept a divorce. The way he sees it, we'll remain husband and wife as long as we're both alive."

Catlin's good eye narrowed. "I can fix that."

"No!" She shook her head vehemently, knowing what was in his mind. "No more killing. Promise me!"

Turning his head, he gazed up at the ceiling. "Well, I'll think of something. Don't worry about it."

Hearing the weariness in his voice, Zella tucked the covers under his chin and slipped his eyepatch off. When he raised a hand as if to cover his disfigured left eye, she smiled and pushed it away.

"Stop hiding it. It doesn't matter to me."

"Are you leaving?"

"Just for a few minutes. Try to go to sleep, all right?"

Zella picked up the lantern and left, quietly shutting the door behind her. She paused a minute outside the bedroom and thought about what he had said. No, she wouldn't worry. She didn't care if they were married or not. The fact that he still cared enough about her to suggest it was enough.

CHAPTER THIRTY-THREE

Yawning, Zella slipped Catlin's watch from the pocket of his jeans and checked the time by the light of a match. It was 11:35. If she were at work, she'd still have at least an hour and a half to go before quitting time, yet she was already tired tonight. She stripped down to her white chemise, lay across the foot of Catlin's bed, and gazed out one of the windows at the pale sliver of moon shining in the night sky.

With Catlin sick, she had intended to sleep on the floor, but he went berserk when he saw her spreading blankets down and told her there were giant rats in the house. He claimed they would eat her ears and toes off if she slept on the floor. To appease him, she finally promised to sleep on the bed. Catlin Myers had a thing about rats.

She glanced over at him. The willow bark tea seemed to have taken effect, and he was sleeping quietly. He suffered from the ague most often during the summer it seemed—a result of his fondness for watermelon and half-ripe fruit, Zella was certain—and he would sometimes shake so badly with chill that his teeth clicked together. Zella usually managed to keep the fever under control with a concoction of white willow bark and nettle root, and he would knock along as best he could until the illness wore itself out.

Rolling over onto her stomach, her head pillowed on her hands, Zella thought about Catlin's proposition. It would be good to live and work here with him, yet she feared it wouldn't last; Catlin was a born drifter with the itch in both feet. Still, in spite of his numerous flaws, she loved him. It was for that reason alone that she was willing to give him a chance. Perhaps someday he'd grow up.

Zella awoke two hours later to the sound of Catlin mumbling incoherently in his sleep, his body twitching and jerking, shaking the bed. A nightmare. Zella sighed, rolled out of bed to keep from getting kicked in the ribs, and lit the lantern. She was about to wake him when he cried out and sat bolt upright in bed. His eyes stared wildly into space, still seeing the visions that were locked inside his head.

"Catlin." She touched his shoulder, and he flinched violently away from her. "Catlin, it's just me. Calm down. It's over."

His chest heaving, he turned away, swinging his legs over the side of the bed, and Zella looked around for something with which to wipe the sweat from his body. After two years of this, she knew the routine. Finding a towel, she sopped his back, chest, face, and hair.

"Brad Gilley again?" she asked gently. When he didn't answer, she nodded. "I thought so."

"No. No, it was different this time," he whispered.

"Different how?"

He shook his head.

"Talk to me, Catlin."

"I was searching for Brad," he began slowly, "just like always, only I found him this time, Zella." He glanced up at her. "Brad was alive!"

"What happened?"

"He ran from me. I chased after him, but he just disappeared. I lost him." He heaved a shuddery sigh. "There were dead bodies all around. I looked down and saw Pa. I saw Pa's face . . ." He shook his head and closed his eyes.

Feeling him shiver, Zella wrapped a blanket around his

251

shoulders and slipped her hand beneath his arm. His skin was fiery hot.

"There were maggots in his eyes," he went on. "They were eating his eyes. I started looking around for something to kill them with, but when I got back to Pa, it wasn't him any more. It was Johnny Keaton, and he looked at me with the maggots in his eyes and said, 'Why did you leave me? You promised not to leave me behind.' That's when I woke up."

Zella rested her head against his shoulder. "Johnny Keaton. The man you killed in Arizona?"

He nodded. "I just left him laying there, Zella. Left him for the flies and buzzards. What if no one found his body?" He paused, his features still and pensive. "I did the same thing to Brad. I promised not to leave him behind if he got hurt or killed, and he promised to do the same for me. I failed him, Zella. The Yanks were closing in on us, I got scared, and I left him."

"But you went back," Zella reminded him. "You tried to find him."

"Yeah, two days later! What damned good was that?"

"Catlin, you did all you could do."

He looked at her, the doubt showing plainly on his face. "Brad wouldn't have left me behind. He wasn't a coward."

Zella didn't bother arguing with him. She knew from experience that there was no comforting Catlin after one of his night terrors. All she could do was listen to him and try to understand what he was going through.

For the longest time, he had refused to talk to her about the war, or about the nightmares that plagued his sleep and would become violently angry if she pressed him too hard. It was only last spring, as the nightmares began to recur with greater frequency, that he at last opened up to her. He told her about Brad Gilley.

252

"I have to go back to Arizona," he said abruptly.

"Why?"

"Because I've got to make sure somebody found Keaton. I can't live with another unburied body on my conscience. Not any more."

When she started to protest, he touched his fingers to her lips. "I've got to," he said. "I want to go back and see if I can find Keaton's mother. Arnet Phillips mentioned her. She's widowed and works as a laundress for the soldiers at Camp Grant. If I can find her, I'll give her some money, enough so she won't have to work any more."

Zella frowned. "What are you going to do, Catlin? Walk up to her and introduce yourself as the man who killed her son and hand her a fistful of money?" She shook her head. "You can't do that."

"No. I'll just send it to her. I'll make sure she gets at least some compensation. I have to."

Zella understood and appreciated his desire to help Johnny Keaton's mother but was afraid for him to return to southern Arizona so soon. It was far too risky.

When she told him as much, his only response was, "I'm going. It's settled."

Zella left him, not wanting to talk about it any more and walked into the kitchen. The pot of willow bark tea she had brewed earlier was keeping warm on the back of the stove, and she poured a cupful and returned to the bedroom.

Catlin took the cup from her hand and said, "Don't be mad, Zella."

"Shut up and drink your tea."

He obeyed, making his usual array of faces, and peered into the cup's murky depths. "Why is it this stuff always tastes like ground up piss ants?"

Zella laughed in spite of herself. "It's not that bad!"

Winking at her, he drained the cup, and his teeth rattled together in a sudden paroxysm of chills. Zella made him lie down, blew out the lantern, and slipped beneath the covers. Hoping to warm him up, she lay close beside him and held him tight against her body.

He sought her mouth in the darkness and kissed her. "If I didn't feel so down . . ."

"Go to sleep, Catlin."

". . . I wouldn't go to sleep," he continued.

She tweaked his chest hair.

"I'm glad you're here," he murmured. "You're the best friend I've ever had, besides Brad Gilley. Did you know that?"

Deeply moved by his confession, Zella smiled and brushed her fingertips up and down his body, feeling the familiar structure and contour of muscle and bone and sinew. She touched the mole on his side, just above his left hip, and ran her forefinger along the wispy line of hair that trailed down the middle of his stomach. She could have recognized his body by touch alone.

Lulled to sleep by her caresses, Catlin relaxed, and his breathing slowed finally, grew less erratic. Zella closed her eyes.

"You're the best friend I've ever had, too," she whispered.

CHAPTER THIRTY-FOUR

Catlin lay with his face buried in his pillow and listened to the rattle of trace chains and wagon wheels pounding the bumpy road, the racket growing louder by the second. He felt the mattress dip, then rise up again as Zella left his side, heard the rustle of clothing, the creak of the door being opened and closed, and at last, silence.

He opened his eyes and rolled over onto his back, too wrung out to bother with getting up. It had been an unpleasant night, cold one minute, hot the next, his very bones aching with fever. These recurrent onslaughts of the ague never lasted long, never pulled him down too badly, but they frustrated him just the same and left him feeling embittered. As a boy, he was rarely ill until the day he enlisted in the Confederate Army. The war, he felt, had weakened him.

He heard people talking in the adjoining room and held his breath, listening, straining to distinguish their voices. It was Ray and Mary.

Catlin groaned. Damn the luck.

Zella slipped into the bedroom, shutting the door behind her. "Catlin, it's your brother and his wife. They don't look very happy."

"Why? Because we're here together?"

She nodded, anger flashing in her dark eyes. "That Mary! Standing there with her perfect hair and her perfect clothes and her perfect nose stuck up in the air like this." She pushed her nose up with her finger and rattled off something in

Spanish that Catlin didn't understand. "Do you want me to tell them to go away?" she asked.

It was tempting. Certainly if anyone could do it, Zella could.

He looked at her with her long hair tangled from sleep, her loose white blouse slipping off her shoulders, revealing more skin than was considered decent by proper ladies like Mary Myers. She looked tired and probably was, having spent half the night caring for him. Yet Ray and Mary would think her disheveled appearance the result of something far less innocent. What a joke. The idea amused him.

"I told them you were sick," Zella said, "but Mary insisted it was a hangover. I'll tell them to leave."

"No, it's all right. I'll get up."

Catlin reached for his pants. He pulled them on, splashed water on his face from the wash basin, and tied on his eyepatch. Combing his hair down with his fingers, he followed Zella into the kitchen where Ray and Mary were waiting.

Zella was right. They didn't look happy.

"A little early for social calls, ain't it?" he said.

At sight of his partial state of undress, Mary's cheeks reddened, and she averted her eyes. Ray frowned.

"The least you could do is put on a shirt in front of Mary," he said, "and I for one don't consider 8:30 all that early."

Catlin rubbed his bare chest, straddled a chair, and folded his arms together over the back. "It's early for a couple of people who didn't get any sleep last night."

Ray and Mary interpreted that the way Catlin figured they would.

"We buried Pa only yesterday," Ray said, "and you're out here having a good old time in his house!"

Mary touched a gloved hand to Ray's arm. "Let's not

256

waste any more time," she said. "Tell him what we decided."

For some reason, Ray seemed suddenly hesitant, unsure of himself.

"Tell him," Mary prodded.

Ray sighed and examined his fingernails. "We, Mary and I, that is, have decided we'd like to keep Pa's land. I'll buy out your share for . . ." He paused, glancing at his wife.

"Go on," she urged.

"I'll buy your share for . . . for twenty-five cents an acre."

Catlin laughed.

"I don't see what's so funny about it," Mary said, her perfect nose sticking up in the air. "It's the same price your father paid."

"Yeah, twenty years ago, when the Comanches were paying us surprise visits every other week and before any improvements were made to the land." Catlin looked from Mary to Ray, still smiling, thinking surely this must be a joke. "Twenty-five cents an acre?"

Ray avoided his gaze.

They were really serious! Catlin shook his head, the smile dying on his face.

"Our lawyer assured us our offer is acceptable as long as both parties agree," Mary said.

"Well, this party don't agree."

Mary glared at him, her hands on her hips. "You're lucky we made an offer at all! We could have just taken it!"

"At a quarter per acre, you'd might as well have," Catlin retorted. "Besides, Pa told me y'all didn't want the land."

"We changed our minds," Ray said.

Catlin stared at him, gripping the back of the chair with both hands, feeling his body pulsating with the beat of his heart, the blood rushing inside his ears. He knew and accepted the fact that Ray didn't like him. He even accepted the fact that his brother had decided to go back on his word and take the land. But Ray was turning the whole affair into an insult, a slap in the face, and so soon after Ocie's death! This wasn't the same Ray he had grown up with.

Uncomfortable under Catlin's hard scrutiny, Ray turned his face away and gave his right earlobe an agitated tug.

"This place is worth at least ten dollars per acre," Catlin said quietly, "and you both know it."

Mary's lips pinched together. "Our lawyer said . . ."

"To hell with your damned lawyer!" he exclaimed and turned back to Ray. "I'll give you fifteen. In gold."

Ray looked at Mary. She shook her head.

"We want the land," Ray announced, "not your money. If that doesn't suit you, then we'll take it to court and see what a judge has to say about it."

Catlin exhaled slowly, his face impassive except for the nervous little ticcing of his jaw muscles. He felt Zella move up behind him, her hand going to his shoulder, digging her nails into his flesh.

"Well?" Mary said. "We're waiting for your decision."

"Take it. Hell, take it all. If you can live with it, I can live without it." His gaze settled on Ray again. "Just tell me one thing. Is a quarter an acre all Pa's land is worth to you?"

Frowning, Ray put on his hat and left the house without answering. Mary started to follow him, then paused at the door to look back at Catlin. Triumph burned in her eyes like a pale blue blaze.

"You really should have left when I told you to, Catlin." She cupped her fingers over the delicate ostrich feathers on her hat, protecting them from the breeze blowing in through the screen door, and gave Catlin a sugary smile. "I do believe the wind will blow today. Don't forget to put down all the windows before you leave my house."

"And don't you let the door hit you in the ass on your way out," Catlin replied.

She shot him a snooty look and left, letting the door bang behind her.

"My house," Catlin muttered, repeating Mary's words. "I oughta burn the son of a bitch to the ground just to keep her from having it. Tear it apart stone by stone and burn what's left."

"You're not really going to let them get away with this, are you?"

"The whole thing makes me sick, Zella. Reminds me of buzzards squabbling over a dead rabbit." He rose and crossed the room to look out the window. "The one thing I'll always remember is that Ocie wanted me to have this house, this land. That's enough."

Zella came to stand beside him, and he could feel the weight of her disapproval.

"You're just going to let them have everything?" she asked. "You're not going to fight them?"

"No." He passed his arm around her waist. "Don't worry. We'll still go through with our plans. As soon as I get back from Arizona, we'll find us a place of our own and make a fresh start."

Zella wasn't so willing to back down. "Mary put your brother up to this," she said. "I'm sure of it. Perhaps if you talked to him alone . . ."

Catlin shook his head. "This may have been Mary's idea, but Ray carried it out." He watched Ray turn his team and rig around in front of the house and was surprised to see a man sitting hunkered down in the back of the wagon. It was Ray's hired man. He was holding a shotgun across his lap.

"Nothing like a loving family," Catlin remarked. "Ray's so suspicious of me, he comes out here with an armed guard."

"Catlin, who is that?" Zella pointed, indicating two men on horseback emerging from the trees along the creek.

It was the sheriff and his deputy.

CHAPTER THIRTY-FIVE

Resting his arms on the window sill, his stomach tied in a knot, Catlin watched R.D. Luger and Virgil Bone ride toward the house. They met Ray and Mary on the road and stopped to talk for a few minutes, then rode on, approaching the house at a deliberate walk. Ray remained where he was, he and Mary twisting around in their seat to watch.

"Zella," Catlin said, "do me a favor."

She gazed up at him, worry lining her face.

"Go take a look out back and make sure nobody's sneaking up behind the house. And Zella? Get my gun, will you?"

She left without a word and returned a few seconds later with his .45. "I didn't see anyone."

Catlin took the gun from her hand, flashing her a careless smile as he did so, and shoved the gun's barrel down the back of his jeans.

"R.D.'s deputy isn't too fond of me," he explained.

She didn't say anything, and he knew she was thinking the same thing he was. They had found Frank Wyman's body, had made up their minds that he was the culprit and were coming here either to arrest him or shoot him. He figured R.D. would be generous enough to leave the choice up to him. Bone, however, might have other ideas.

Catlin chucked Zella under the chin. "Stay in the house and keep your eyes peeled."

He stepped outside and waited for R.D. and Virgil to draw

261

rein in front of the house. R.D.'s face was grim. He dismounted without waiting for Catlin's invitation, and Bone followed his cue, a sure sign that this was no casual morning outing.

Catlin looked down on them from the front step and kept his mouth shut, making no pretense of friendliness.

R.D. forced a smile. "Howdy, Cat."

Catlin nodded, glancing at the same time toward Virgil Bone. The deputy's gun was holstered, but the rawhide thong holding it securely in place had been slipped off the butt. Catlin doubted that this was an accident. The sheriff, however, was conspicuously unarmed.

"I never got a chance to tell you how sorry I am about your pa," R.D. said. "I liked Ocie. He was a good man."

When Catlin remained silent, R.D. sighed, grimaced, and scratched his armpit, his neck bent back so that he could look up at him. "We found Frank Wyman this morning," he said.

"Dead?"

"Like you don't know," Virgil growled under his breath.

R.D. shot his deputy a look of warning before turning back to Catlin. "We found him by the river. Same as before."

"Show him what else we found," Virgil said.

R.D. stepped toward his horse and pulled a beat-up Winchester rifle from the saddle scabbard. He held it up for Catlin to see, making an obvious effort to keep his hands away from the trigger.

"Does this look familiar to you?" he asked.

Catlin recognized it immediately. It was his rifle, the same rifle he had given to Ray that day by the river, following their discovery of Ben Fletcher's body. He hadn't seen it since.

R.D. shoved the rifle back into his scabbard. "First your canteen, now your gun," he said. "It's hard for me to believe that a man with your reputation could be so careless. In fact . . ." He paused to spit and repositioned the chaw of tobacco beneath his lower lip. ". . . I'd swear somebody was trying to set you up if it wasn't for the witness we got."

"What witness?"

"The one that came to my office late last night and told me he saw you kill Frank Wyman three days ago."

"Your witness is a liar. Sunday, I was here."

Virgil snorted in disdain. "Then you must have a twin running around here somewheres. Our man said it was you he saw. He took us right straight to Wyman's body this morning. Right where you killed him."

Catlin shook his head in sheer disbelief. "You gotta be kidding me. Who is this witness of yours?"

"Eladio Moreno," R.D. replied. "The same fella you had words with recently."

Catlin swore softly and heard Zella open the door behind him and step outside.

"Well, well, well," Virgil drawled. "Looks like we're gonna get to kill two birds with one stone today."

R.D. quickly doffed his hat. "Mornin', ma'am."

Zella gazed down at him, her face cold, expressionless. "Eladio Moreno is my husband," she said.

R.D. nodded. "Yes, ma'am. He told us that much."

"Then you should be able to understand why he might wish to make trouble for Catlin."

"That crossed my mind, all right," R.D. admitted, "but the evidence against Cat is stacked up a mile high." He looked from Zella to Catlin, genuine regret filling his eyes. "It pains me to have to do this, Cat, especially right after your pa's passing, but I'm gonna have to take you in for the murders of Fletcher and Wyman. I'm sorry."

There it was. What Catlin had expected all along. He didn't move or say a word, his gaze shifting to Virgil Bone. The deputy's hand was resting on the butt of his revolver.

"Zella," he spoke calmly, "would you get my shirt and boots for me?"

Sheriff Luger nodded, appearing relieved. "Please, ma'am. He'll need them for the ride back to town. I'd like for you to come along with us, too, if you don't mind."

Catlin frowned. "You're arresting her?"

"I didn't say that," R.D. replied.

He wasn't being up front, and Catlin didn't like the sound of it. It wasn't characteristic of R.D. Luger to be anything but straightforward.

Zella hesitated an instant, then turned and went inside. Catlin listened for the squeak of the bedroom door, making sure she was safely out of the way and rested his right hand on his hip. He smiled down at the deputy.

"How's your stomach, Bone? Still bothering you?"

Caught off guard, the deputy stammered a reply just as Catlin slipped his right hand behind his back and drew the Colt from his waistband. Seeing his movement, Bone grabbed for his own gun. He was too late. Catlin fired two shots between his feet, the bullets kicking up little clods of mud, and yelled a warning to Sheriff Luger.

"Get your hand off that rifle, R.D.! Now!"

Heaving a loud sigh, R.D. let the rifle slide back into the scabbard, eased away from his horse, and held his hands away from his body. Bone stood frozen a few feet from him with his long, skinny legs spraddled apart and his gun still gripped in his hand. Somehow, while jumping around to avoid being shot in the foot, he had tangled the barrel of his gun in his suspenders. At Catlin's bidding, he untangled it and laid the weapon on the ground.

Catlin's face relaxed, and he grinned at him. "Virgil, that was a cute little dance you did a second ago. What do you call it?"

"Thunderation," Bone muttered, humiliated. "I knew derned well . . . Sheriff, I told you we should take him by force! But heck no. No, we gotta treat him nice and gentle, like he's the gol'derned pope!"

"Virgil, damn it, shut up!" R.D. roared. He looked up at Catlin, his leathery face appearing a mite tensed and sweaty just now but not fearful. "Cat, there's some folks back in town told me I was a fool to go huntin' you with just one deputy," he said. "Like Virge here, they thought I should take you by force."

"Why didn't you?"

"Because I've known you since you were a little kid. Because I hoped we could keep this thing peaceful. I didn't figure I needed a gun or a lot of men backing me." He waited for a reaction. When none showed, he continued. "Don't make me eat my words."

"I didn't kill those men."

R.D. nodded. "All right. We'll talk about that. But Cat, I don't have no other choice but to arrest you. With a witness and all the evidence we've got . . ." He shrugged and spread his hands. "If you make a run for it, every able-bodied man in this valley will be after you. You'd never make it."

"I got no reason to run so far," Catlin said. He kept his gun aimed somewhere between R.D. and the deputy and looked past them to the road. He could see his brother standing up in the wagon now, watching. "Did Ray know you were coming after me?"

"Not until a few minutes ago," R.D. assured him. "Cat, put the gun down and let's try to work this mess out. I'll help you all I can."

Virgil's mouth fell open. "Help him? Are you serious?"

R.D. made no response, his attention riveted on Catlin.

"All right." Catlin nodded, his mind suddenly made up.

"I'll give myself up on three conditions."

"Let's hear them."

"Leave Zella out of this."

She spoke up from the doorway. "Catlin, no . . ."

"You leave Zella out of this," Catlin repeated. "Second, you listen to my side of the story for a change. And third, no jail cell. I want a hotel room. A room with a window," he added.

R.D. considered his request and said finally, "There's a lot of rumors flying around about you and Mrs. Moreno being in on this together, but so far all the evidence points to you, not her. As long as it stays that way, I won't arrest her. I can promise you that much."

"That's all I'm asking," Catlin said. "Listen, I know some things. I think I know who's setting me up." He cast an accusing glance at Virgil Bone, saw the deputy's eyes narrow slightly, and turned back to R.D. "Will you hear me out?"

"You can count on it." The sheriff suddenly smiled. "As for your room with a view, I'll have to give that one some thought."

Virgil shook his head in disgust.

R.D. moved forward and stretched out his hand. "Give me your gun, Cat."

Uncocking his .45, Catlin flicked the loading gate open, punched out the four remaining bullets, and placed both the ammunition and his gun into R.D.'s open hand.

"Hallelujah," Virgil muttered.

CHAPTER THIRTY-SIX

Catlin got the room but not the view.

Receiving permission from the owners of the Occidental to board a prisoner in their hotel, Sheriff Luger selected room three, clean comfortable quarters with a soft bed, two chairs, a washstand, mirror, and chamber pot. And no windows. He feared all that sunshine, fresh air, and freedom pouring in on his prisoner might prove to be too much of a temptation.

After escorting Catlin to his room, Virgil Bone emptied his pockets, taking away his matches, his tobacco and papers, and frisked and searched him from head to toe for the third time that day. Satisfied that he hadn't missed any hidden weapons, the deputy shackled his feet together.

Catlin endured these indignities in silence and sat down on the edge of his bed. Hooking his thumbs in his suspenders, Virgil started to say something to him, changed his mind, and walked out, leaving Catlin alone in his dim little room.

He sat and stared at the lamplight, mesmerized by the trembling, reaching flame, and listened to the muffled voices in the hall outside his door. Fearing a lynch mob, Sheriff Luger had spirited him into town as quickly and quietly as possible, but Catlin doubted his whereabouts would remain a secret for long.

He stirred himself after a few minutes and tested the strength of his handcuffs, disliking the cold steel encircling his wrists, restricting his movements. He had been thrown in jail in the past for being drunk and disorderly but had never suffered the shame of handcuffs and leg irons. He thought about his father, almost thankful Ocie was not here to see this. He had disgraced him enough over the years already.

Standing up, Catlin stooped over, slipped his hands down past his butt, and stepped clear of his bound wrists so that his hands were now in front of him and not behind. The chain linking his feet together made a hollow rattle on the wooden floor, and the door to his room opened a crack. Virgil Bone peered in at him.

"Sit down, Myers."

"Kiss my ass."

Scowling, Virgil started to open the door wider, but R.D. stopped him. "Leave him alone. He's all right."

The deputy slammed the door shut, and Catlin heard the voices pick up again, Virgil's and the sheriff's, talking about him, no doubt. He started to ease toward the door, wanting to hear what they were saying, but the rattling chains gave away his every movement. Tired and bored, he lay down instead, watched a spider crawl across the ceiling directly above his bed, and hoped it wouldn't lose its footing.

Time passed slowly. Catlin dozed off twice. He awoke once to see his roommate, the spider, descending toward him for a closer inspection. As the spider neared Catlin's face, he blew his breath on it and watched it climb back up its invisible thread of silk to the ceiling.

"Stay put," Catlin said, "or I'll smack you one."

He heard the door open and twisted his head around to see Sheriff Luger and Deputy Bone.

"Sorry it took me so long," R.D. said.

Catlin sat up slowly and yawned.

R.D. handed him a quart jar of pale gold liquid. "From your lady friend. Some sort of herb tea, I think she said. I didn't know you were feeling poorly, Cat."

"It's nothing serious."

"Just the same, I'll have Doc come in and take a look at you."

"No, you won't. You keep that sawbones away from me."

R.D. smiled patiently. "Don't like doctors, eh?"

"Zella's my doctor," Catlin replied. He sipped his tea, grimacing at the awful taste. "It was some damned quack that killed my mother. Puked, purged, and bled her dry."

"Well, you don't need no doctoring," Virgil said. "Be a waste of good medicine, seeing as how you're gonna hang for murder pretty soon. I doubt Doc Culver would bother with you anyways."

Catlin glanced up at the deputy. "Probably not. With you around, he doesn't have time for anybody else."

"Virge, why don't you go and get me and Cat a cup of coffee," R.D. suggested.

When the deputy had gone, R.D. looked at Catlin's manacled hands and feet, frowned, and dug a pair of keys from a pocket of his trousers. "I got a guard outside your door. I guess that's good enough."

He removed the cuffs and leg irons, and Catlin massaged his wrists while R.D. drew up a chair and sat across from him.

"Me and Virge had a little parley after we brought you in," R.D. began. "He told me your sister-in-law tried to talk him into planting false evidence so these killings would be pinned on you. Was that what you wanted to tell me?"

Surprised that Virgil had confessed, Catlin nodded and said, "Your deputy played you for a real sucker, R.D."

"Virge claims he didn't do it. I believe him."

Catlin turned away, his features hardening. "Then I guess you and me ain't got anything else to say to each other."

"We've got plenty to say," R.D. said gruffly. He reached inside his vest pocket and dug out two folded sheets of paper.

"A Texas Ranger dropped a bundle of circulars off at my office a few minutes ago." R.D. tossed the papers into Catlin's lap. "Take a gander at that."

Catlin unfolded the circulars and was startled to see a sketch of a familiar face glaring up at him from the top page. Above and below the artist's portrayal, in bold black letters, it read:

WANTED
SID "PONY" LANE

Shocked, Catlin glanced up at R.D., then read the smaller print. According to the circular, Lane and another prisoner by the name of Lee Riddick had escaped from the Huntsville State Penitentiary last June. Following this information was a physical description of the escapee and an offer of five hundred dollars to anyone who provided information leading to his arrest.

"So the little sawed-off son of a bitch busted out," Catlin remarked. "I'll be damned."

"I know," R.D. said. "I thought I was free of Sid Lane for at least eight more years."

He went on to relate what the Texas Ranger had told him. After Lane was stricken with consumption, he was kept in the prison infirmary for a time. Apparently, conditions were so bad there, he asked to be sent back to the work detail. Three days later, one of Lane's fellow jailbirds, Lee Riddick, overpowered a prison guard with the aid of a rock and his bare fists and stole the unconscious man's horse and riot gun. Several prisoners tried to escape on foot, and while the guards were busy chasing these men down, Riddick and Lane broke their chains with a sledgehammer and escaped together on the stolen horse.

"Lane's wife and kids are living with her folks in St. Louis now," R.D. continued. "The Texas Rangers and prison officials at Huntsville figured he'd head there. That's why they waited so long to send me word of his escape, I guess."

"He never showed up in St. Louis?" Catlin asked.

"Not that they've seen so far."

"He's here then," Catlin said quietly. "He has to be."

"Sid could be in Timbuktu for all you know." Virgil entered the room and handed the sheriff a cup of coffee. He had conveniently forgotten Catlin's. "Sid's smart," he said. "He knows St. Louis and Fort Griffin are the first two places the rangers would look for him. He won't come here."

"Then tell me why Mary's been acting so funny here lately," Catlin said.

"Why don't you tell us what you think," R.D. suggested.

Catlin looked from R.D.'s relaxed, deadpan face to the unfriendly visage of the deputy and felt as if he were already on trial for murder, guilty until proven innocent. He had no choice.

He told them everything he knew, starting with Mary's strange reaction when he showed her the anonymous threat Ray had received and how she had deliberately brushed out the footprint he found outside the store that morning, the very same footprint Virgil discovered at the scene of Ben Fletcher's murder. He told them about Eladio Moreno seeing Mary talking to an unidentified man late Friday night and what he overheard them saying. He even mentioned all the supplies that had turned up missing in Ray's store. Wasn't it possible that Mary might be the one taking these supplies and giving them to her brother?

"It all fits together now," Catlin concluded. "There's only one man in this whole world Mary would risk everything for. Her brother's here. He's here for revenge against Conrad,

Fletcher, Wyman, and my brother. And me."

R.D. sighed wearily, lifted his Stetson, and scratched his head. "If Sid Lane's our killer, how do you explain your canteen and rifle turning up near the bodies of Fletcher and Wyman?"

"Mary took them. She took them, gave them to Sid, and he left them there so you'd believe I was the killer."

"What about Eladio Moreno?" Virgil demanded. "He saw you kill Frank Wyman. He took us to Wyman's body. How do you explain that away, Myers?"

Catlin shook his head. He had no answer.

R.D. drained his cup of coffee and pushed himself to his feet. "I'll have a talk with Mary Myers and see what she has to say about this." He glanced at his deputy. "In the meantime, Virge, I want you to try to dig up something with Sid Lane's handwriting on it. We'll compare it to the handwriting on one of those anonymous notes and see if there's any likeness."

Virgil scowled. "You don't really think Sid's the murderer, do you. I mean, cutting off people's heads? Kind of barbaric for a gent like Sid, don't you think?"

"Two years ago, he hanged Ed McCall, an innocent man, had another poor fella beat to death when he tried to expose the vigilantes, and then he ordered his men to do the same to Cat here." R.D. jerked a thumb at Catlin. "Left him halfblind. If that ain't barbaric, then what would you call it?"

Virgil shook his head, not convinced. "Sid's ailing now, though. Plus there's our witness, Moreno, and don't forget his wife. Zella Moreno probably hired Myers to bump off Fletcher and Wyman to get back at them for hanging McCall. I'm telling you, Sheriff, Myers is our man."

Catlin watched Sheriff Luger, saw his slight nod of agreement, and turned away in disgust. They would never believe him. They didn't even want to.

R.D. followed Virgil Bone to the door and stopped there to look back at Catlin. "There's one thing you never explained to me," he said. "The name on the canteen—Bradford Gilley—who is he?"

"A friend."

"Are you covering for him, Cat? Did he kill someone? Charlie Conrad, maybe?"

Catlin gazed at the burning lamp, his jaw muscles tightening. "Brad Gilley's dead."

"But you told Ray he lives in Mississippi."

"I said he was in Mississippi. I never said he was living."

R.D. studied him a long moment. "Cat, you'd better get your story straight," he said at length. "And how damned long were you gonna wait before you opened your mouth and told me about Mary?"

Catlin didn't bother to answer. He lay down on his bed, turned his back to R.D., and heard the door close behind him.

He lay with his eyes wide open, staring at the wall. What good had it done to tell R.D. what he knew? He was still in the same predicament and destined to receive the death penalty. He realized he should never have given himself up. He should never have put any trust in R.D. Luger.

Yet Catlin knew one thing for certain: He wasn't going to sit here beneath the shadow of the gallows much longer. Just because he had surrendered this morning didn't mean he couldn't un-surrender tonight or tomorrow or next week even.

Sid Lane wasn't the only man who could break out of jail.

CHAPTER THIRTY-SEVEN

Catlin's fever and ague paid him another visit that afternoon. He drank as much of Zella's herbal concoction as he could stomach, collapsed on his bed, and awoke the next morning feeling as if someone had hit him in the head with a hammer. Even so, his first thought when he opened his eyes was of escape.

Virgil Bone came in with Catlin's breakfast, and he set the plate down on the small table beside his bed. Catlin noticed the deputy was wearing a red kerchief tied over his nose and mouth.

"What's with the bandana?" he asked.

"Germs."

"Germans?"

"No, germs," Virgil stated. "I'm blocking out germs."

"What are germs?"

"Something you're full of."

Catlin had no idea what he was talking about and didn't really care anyway. Virgil Bone was a strange one.

Knowing he needed to keep his strength up if he ever wanted to get out of here, Catlin forced down his breakfast. Once he got his appetite whetted, the food didn't taste half bad, though no one could beat Zella's cooking. Only two women had ever been able to put any fat on him—his mother and Zella Moreno.

Virgil leaned against the door and folded his arms across his chest. "If I was the sheriff of this county, you'd be sitting in jail with leg irons and handcuffs on."

"You're not the sheriff."

"I will be someday." He was silent a moment, watching Catlin eat. "You know, Myers, it's a weak man who can't admit when he's wrong, don't you think?"

"I guess. Why?"

"I was wrong about Sid not coming here."

Suddenly interested, Catlin looked up from his plate.

"I was in Doc Culver's office yesterday afternoon," Virgil said, "and the lady who comes in and cleans for him told me something curious. She said she'd overheard Mary asking Doc for laudanum and Stafford's Olive Tar. Do you know what people take Stafford's Olive Tar for?"

Catlin hadn't a clue.

"Consumption," Virgil replied.

"So Sid Lane is here."

"Was here," Virgil corrected him. "Me and Sheriff Luger had a talk with Mary. She finally broke down and admitted that Sid had been here. She said he hung around for a couple of days just to see her and rest up and then headed south, for Mexico."

"She even told you where he was going, huh? That was awful obliging of her."

"Unlike you, Mary knows right from wrong. She wants Sid brought back."

Catlin regarded Virgil in disbelief. How gullible could he be? Catlin didn't trust Mary any farther than he could throw a horse, yet here was this dimwit deputy believing every word she said just because she was a Lane. Everyone was so dead-set on placing the blame on him, they couldn't see the truth when it hit them square between the eyes.

"R.D. told you to compare Sid Lane's handwriting to the writing on those messages," he said. "Did you do it?"

"Didn't see any reason to. Sid wasn't even here when the

murders were committed. You were, though."

"I wasn't here when Charlie Conrad was killed. Neither was Zella."

Virgil tugged thoughtfully at his bandana and shrugged. "You've got an accomplice. That's easy enough. We just have to figure out who it is." He pushed away from the door and gathered up Catlin's dirty breakfast dishes. "Have fun, Myers."

The deputy left and Catlin drank his coffee in brooding silence and watched the spider that shared his room crawl down the wall on some mysterious errand. He wondered if it was poisonous. It might be fun to drop the spider down Virgil Bone's shirt.

He was contemplating how he could accomplish this when he suddenly noticed the two wanted circulars Sheriff Luger had left yesterday. He picked them up, scanned Sid Lane's write-up again, and then looked for the first time at the second circular.

This one was for the other escaped convict, Lee Riddick. Catlin studied the outlaw's roughly sketched features, and his pulse quickened. He recognized the face! This was the man in the blue shirt he had seen at the farm last Sunday, the same man who had run from him!

"I didn't imagine it after all," he whispered.

He stared at the sketch of Lee Riddick, absorbing every detail, reassuring himself that this was, indeed, the man he had seen that day, and the same eerie sensation stole over him again. He felt his mind start to slip away. A dreadful apprehension gripped him.

Catlin shot to his feet and paced around and around, faster and faster, his thoughts spinning like a whirligig inside his head. He caught a glimpse of himself in the mirror, paused to look at his wild-eyed image, and shouted in sudden rage. Wrenching the mirror loose from the wall, Catlin flung it across the room. He picked up the porcelain wash basin and smashed it against the floor, jerked the empty drawers from the little bureau and hurled them against the far wall, and struck the burning lamp to the floor.

Virgil Bone and another man burst into the room as bright yellow flames leaped upward from the broken lamp, and Catlin lunged for the open doorway and escape. Both men dove into him, their combined weights throwing him to the floor, and he lashed out with his fists and feet, struggling to free himself. Smoke filled his lungs so he could scarcely breathe.

"Somebody help!" Virgil hollered. "Help!"

Slipping silently past the kitchen where Mary was busy preparing the noon meal, Ray Myers hurried down the hall to their bedroom, glanced over his shoulder to make sure Mary hadn't heard him and went inside.

He approached his wife's dresser and slid open the top left drawer. Carefully sifting through Mary's girlhood keepsakes, family photographs, and pretty silk lace fichus, he found a bundle of letters tied together with a pink ribbon. Ray thumbed through the letters and found the one he was looking for, a letter addressed to Mary from Sid Lane when he had traveled to St. Louis with his wife and children three years ago.

Dropping to his knees, Ray unfolded the letter with trembling hands and studied his brother-in-law's handwriting. It was just as he had suspected.

Sid Lane's handwriting was identical to that of the anonymous threat he had received weeks ago!

"Ray, what are you doing?"

Startled by his wife's voice, Ray started to rise and bumped his head on the open drawer. Grimacing, he rubbed the top of his head and turned to see Mary looking at him from the open doorway. An odd little smile played about her lips.

"What on earth are you doing? I thought you were working." She drew nearer, saw the letter in his hand, and frowned. "Why are you reading my letters?"

Ray pushed himself to his feet. Unable to hide the terrible hurt inside him, he brushed the back of his hand across damp eyes and thrust the letter toward her.

"The handwriting's the same. Sid's the real murderer. He's the killer, and you knew it all along!"

Mary's left eyelid twitched. "Whatever are you talking about?"

"Stop lying to me! For God's sake, Mary!" He turned away from her and stared out the window, his vision blurred by tears. "You've lied to me, you've stolen from me, you've deceived me in every way."

"Ray, I haven't the faintest idea what you're talking about."

He turned to look at her. "You know exactly what I'm talking about. It all makes sense now. The Shakespeare quotes, for instance. Sid loved to read Shakespeare. He could quote him word for word. All from memory."

Mary's face stiffened. "You're talking foolishness."

"Am I? All right, what about when he strong-armed me into joining his vigilance committee two years ago? He made me swear an oath of allegiance and told me if I betrayed any other member of the committee, he'd make sure I paid for it with my life. Well, Conrad, Wyman, Fletcher, and I betrayed him, or so he thinks, and they're all dead except me!"

"Sid wasn't even here when those men were killed! He wasn't here! I've told you that!"

"You've told me a lot of things, Mary." Ray sagged into a

chair and sighed wearily. "Last night, I remembered something. I remembered the rifle and sword Sid gave you for safe-keeping until he returned from prison. There was also a sack of reloaded fifty caliber cartridges. I looked for them early this morning, Mary. They're gone."

"And you think I gave them to Sid so he could kill people and cut off their heads." Mary's tone was heavy with sarcasm. "Really, Ray, doesn't that sound a bit ludicrous?"

"If you didn't give the rifle and sword to Sid, then where are they?"

"Aunt Cora has them."

"No, she doesn't. I already asked her."

Mary's fists clenched, and her eyelid jerked wildly now, out of control.

"You see, Mary, I've figured it all out," Ray said quietly. He dragged a hand down his face and gazed at the floor. "You don't even care that Sid means to kill me. It doesn't matter to you at all."

"No! That's not true!"

Struck by the anguish in his wife's voice, Ray looked up at her.

"That's not true!" she insisted. "Sid promised! He promised he wouldn't hurt you! Sid always keeps his promises!"

She clapped her hand over her mouth, as if realizing she had said too much, whirled around, and fled from the room.

Ray stared after her but didn't follow. Never in his life had he felt so miserable and alone.

"Sid always keeps his promises."

He repeated his wife's words aloud and shuddered at the horrible truth of her statement. Sid Lane was keeping the promise he made to him two years ago with painstaking precision.

CHAPTER THIRTY-EIGHT

Ray saw Mary no more that day. She took little Beth and went to stay with her Aunt Cora, and Ray spent the afternoon alone with the curtains drawn, emerging only long enough to wander into the store and make sure his hired man was having no troubles, then retreating again to his darkened room to grieve for his father and his wife.

It was late afternoon when he finally put on his hat and suitcoat and ventured out of doors. A fine mist sprayed his face as he walked down the street to the Occidental Hotel. It had turned off cloudy and cool early this morning and had been threatening to rain all day, further dampening Ray's already soggy spirits.

Wiping his feet clean on the braided straw mat just inside the lobby doorway, he asked the little baldheaded clerk where his brother was being kept, walked down the corridor to room three, and saw Virgil Bone seated outside the door. He was engrossed in the most recent edition of the *Frontier Echo*.

Ray didn't have to guess what the deputy was reading, for he had already scanned the newspaper's front page article, the headline of which read: SUSPECT ARRESTED FOR BRUTAL SLAYINGS. It was filled with boastful quotes from Virgil Bone, telling how Catlin had drawn a gun on him and the sheriff while being arrested and how he had kept a cool head and talked the murderer into giving himself up.

"Rereading the lies you told the newspaper?"

Virgil looked up at him, smiled sheepishly, and folded his

paper in half. "I may have gotten a little carried away with the details."

"That's putting it mildly." Ray stuffed his hands inside his trouser pockets. "I heard Cat tried to break out this morning."

Virgil nodded. "Never seen anything like it, Ray. Derned chunkhead went nuts. Took four of us to finally pin him down. Mrs. Smith isn't too happy about the damage he done to his room, so I guess we'll be moving him to the jail, soon as Sheriff Luger gets back."

"Where did Luger go?"

"To Albany on business."

Ray frowned. "That's too bad. I'd hoped to have a talk with him about Cat."

"Guess it'll have to wait." Virgil jerked a thumb over his shoulder. "I've got your brother tied down pretty good right now, letting him cool off some and consider the error of his ways."

"How does he act?"

"Still mad as the devil," Virgil replied and shrugged. "I don't know what set him off so sudden-like this morning. One minute he's calm as can be, the next he's tearing hell up."

Ray sighed, dreading what he felt he must do. "I need to see him, Virgil."

"Sheriff Luger said no visitors."

"I won't tell him you disobeyed his orders."

Virgil studied him curiously. "Myers threatens to kill you, and you want to visit him? You oughta be out celebratin'."

"Just let me see him, Virgil, all right?"

"Well, if that's what you want. It's your funeral." Rising, the deputy dropped his folded newspaper in his chair and frisked Ray for possible weapons, apologizing at the same time for the necessity. "Can't take any chances," he said and opened the door to Catlin's room. "Do you want me to go in with you?"

Ray shook his head, shut the door behind him, and looked across the room at his brother.

Catlin lay on his back on the bed with his arms stretched above his head, his hands shackled to the bed's wrought-iron headrail. Someone had pulled his boots off and placed manacles on his ankles, as well, and a rope was stretched taut across his middle from one side of the bed to the other, further restricting his movements. Ray noticed Catlin's shirt was missing some buttons, and both sleeves had been ripped almost entirely off, but what was most prominent was the smoldering fury distorting his brother's face. If Virgil Bone thought Catlin would cool off in time, it appeared he had a long wait ahead of him.

Ray crossed the room, aware of Catlin's hostile gaze, and inspected the charred wall and bureau. Though the room had been tidied following this morning's fracas, broken glass and porcelain crunched beneath his shoes, and the air still smelled a bit smoky.

"Pa always said you were more destructive than constructive," Ray remarked. He met Catlin's blistering glare, tried to smile, and failed. "Pa was critical of us both, but it was only because he cared about us so much. You know, he never once told me he loved me, but I always knew he did. He loved you, too."

Catlin stared at him and said nothing.

Leaning against the bureau, Ray folded his arms across his chest. "Pa also used to say blood was thicker than water. I never believed him until today. Mary made me a believer."

He paused to gather his thoughts, lips moving silently, his gaze on the blackened floor. "I think Mary would do anything for Sid," he said at length. "She risked my life for his sake.

She helped him set you up so you'd take the blame for his crimes. She'd do anything for her brother. Lie, cheat, steal, you name it." He lifted his gaze to Catlin and shook his head with regret. "And what do you and I do? We fight each other every step of the way. We have a lot to learn, Cat."

Having finally uttered the words that had been eating at him all day, he watched Catlin's hard, unshaven face, saw no change there, and wished he would say something, anything. His silence was both uncharacteristic and oppressive.

"When Sheriff Luger returns from Albany," Ray continued doggedly, "I'm going to tell him everything I know. Everything." He sighed and rubbed his forehead. "He may not let you go even then, so I'll send a wire to a lawyer friend of mine in Jacksboro and see if he'll take your case."

"I don't need no damned lawyer."

Ray looked at his brother, relieved to finally hear him say something, and unfolded his arms. He stepped closer to the bed.

"It's your right to have a lawyer represent you."

Catlin turned his face away to gaze up at the ceiling.

Squatting beside the bed, Ray pried at the hard knots on the rope that was cutting into Catlin's belly, a small gesture of friendship.

"Just don't pull any more stunts like you pulled this morning," he said, "and I'll get you out of here. I promise."

He pulled the rope free and let it drop to the floor. Feeling there was nothing more he could say or do, he started to leave.

"Ray?"

He glanced around at Catlin and saw him stretch his hand out to him as far as the handcuffs would allow. Surprised, Ray hesitated, then finally thrust out his own hand and felt his brother's strong grasp.

"Watch yourself," Catlin warned. "Sid's got an escaped convict with him. He may not be through with you yet."

"An escaped convict? How do you know?"

"I saw him. And I saw his wanted poster, too. His name's Lee Riddick."

"Have you told Sheriff Luger or Virgil?"

"Luger's gone."

Ray nodded. "And I don't guess there's any use in telling Virgil, is there?" He put on his hat. "I'd better head home, Cat. I'll be back to see you in the morning."

A rakish grin crossed Catlin's face, reminiscent of his old self. "Don't count on it," he said. "If Bone slips up one time . . ." He snapped his fingers. ". . . I'm gone."

Ray didn't bother to voice his disapproval. What good would it do? He left Catlin alone in his room, and not wanting him to do anything rash, cautioned Virgil Bone to keep a sharp eye on him.

It was almost dark by the time Ray walked back up the street to his store, and he glanced around him uneasily as he fumbled in his pocket for the key to the door. He found his pocket empty and remembered then that Virgil had taken his keys before he entered Catlin's room and forgot to give them back to him.

"Confound the luck," he muttered.

Casting a cautious glance around him at the few passersby on the street, he stepped into the shadowy passageway between the store and Hatfield's Restaurant. A light rain had begun to fall, and water dripping from the eaves had created a tiny river between the two buildings. Ray bogged through the muddy water to the kitchen door and bent down to feel beneath the rubber welcome mat where there was a key hidden.

Clutching the key in his hand, he was about to rise when some slight movement caught his eye. He whirled to face it.

A shadowy form lurked among the empty barrels beside the storage shed. Ray's eyes widened.

"S-Sid? Sid, is that you?"

There was no answer. Ray tried to think what to do—run for help or try to make it into the safety of his house. The house was closest. Keeping his gaze trained on the stalker watching him from the darkness, he slowly raised his right hand, inserted the key into the lock . . .

The shadow leaped toward him. Ray yelled in fear, yanked up the welcome mat, and flung it at the dark form. Only then did he realize his attacker was a cat that had taken refuge from the rain on the leeward side of the shed. The frightened feline sprang clear of the empty barrels and vanished into the night.

Ray sagged against the door as the cold rain trickled down the back of his collar and seeped down his back. He chuckled with relief. Armed with a welcome mat, he had successfully fended off a stray cat!

Ray stepped into the safety of the kitchen, locked the door, and kicked off his muddy shoes. He groped his way through the darkened house and felt a cool draft of air. Ray followed the draft to its source, an open window in the living room. That was odd. He was almost certain he had shut all the windows before leaving the house.

Putting down the window, he felt for the lamp and struck a match. The match had hardly flared when it was unexpectedly extinguished, and a puff of warm breath fanned his hand. He froze, the smoking match still gripped between his thumb and forefinger.

"Who's there?" he queried tremulously. "Mary?"

Masked by darkness, his movements drowned out by pattering raindrops, Ray's uninvited guest struck from behind. Ray was jerked backwards by the neck, his feet almost lifting off the floor, his back arching. Gasping, choking, he twisted and squirmed and flailed at his assailant's body with his fists, but quickly realized the futility of it all when the taut arm around his neck squeezed harder, blocking the air from his lungs. He cringed as the chill, sharp point of a knife pricked the delicate inner skin of his left nostril.

A drawling voice spoke close to his ear: "Pony's been looking real forward to seeing you again, Myers."

CHAPTER THIRTY-NINE

It rained all night, a slow, steady drizzle that seeped, trickled, and dripped into every nook and cranny. By morning, Ray Myers resembled a drowned rat.

He had passed a seemingly endless night first in the saddle, then in strange, uncomfortable surroundings, and as the sky slowly lightened from black to gray, he looked around and found himself seated beneath a crude lean-to shelter. Its frame was built of green tree boughs, and over this was tied an old canvas tarp. Water leaked through the numerous gaps and rents in the tarp, and Ray's abductor, Lee Riddick, had placed pots and pans beneath the worst leaks.

A slow drip directly above Ray's head had proved to be particularly obnoxious. The lean-to was so crowded with saddle gear and supplies that he couldn't maneuver away from the leak, and no matter how he held his head, the drip always struck squarely on his bald spot.

Lee Riddick had risen from his damp blankets with the first hint of daylight and was now busily stirring about the camp, apparently not bothered by the rain. He had managed to build a small, sheltered fire, and the sizzling of bacon could soon be heard above the sound of the falling rain.

Bound and gagged and shivering in his wet clothes, Ray peered out of the lean-to at the motionless treetops and the heavy, gray clouds. The campsite was situated on a bluff overlooking the Clear Fork, and a small tent was pitched a few yards from the lean-to. Ray recognized the tent. It was just one of the many items that had turned up missing from his store in the past few weeks. Though he had seen no one enter or leave the tent, he was sure Sid Lane slept there, for during the night, he had heard his deep, racking cough—the cough of a man afflicted with consumption.

The fear that lived inside Ray increased in intensity as the morning grew brighter. He wondered what would become of him. Would anyone miss him? Not his hired man, who would find the door locked when he reported to work this morning and go fishing. Then there was Mary. She was so angry with him that it wasn't likely she would venture anywhere near the store, and even if she did find out he was missing, he doubted she would care.

That left only Catlin. Shutting his eyes, Ray sadly bowed his head. He was doomed.

"Good morning."

Startled, Ray jerked his head up to see Lee Riddick towering above him. The man bent down and lifted the gag from Ray's mouth.

"I've got breakfast cooking," he said. "You hungry?"

Ray tried to speak, but his tongue was like a stick of dry wood inside his mouth. He shook his head no instead.

"That's too bad," Riddick replied.

Ducking low, he crawled beneath the semi-shelter of the lean-to, sat down on his blankets, and smiled at Ray with a genuine warmth that was surprising, given the circumstances.

"I'm a pretty good cook," he said. "I learned how during the war. When the Yanks took me prisoner and sent me up to Camp Douglas, they damn near starved us all to death, so I learned to get real creative. Used to catch rats and fry 'em up in pork grease." He leaned closer to Ray and lowered his voice. "Pony don't know it, but the first square meal he ate when we escaped from Huntsville was fried rat. He thought it was squirrel."

Riddick's friendly chatter served to calm Ray's nerves somewhat, and his tongue loosened up enough to speak. "Is that what you call Sid?" he asked. "Pony?"

Riddick nodded. "One of the guards used to call him that. The name sort of stuck, I guess." He suddenly grinned. "Behind his back, we just called him the runt."

Ray glanced toward the tent. "Is he there?"

"Yeah. This wet spell has been real hard on him."

Riddick left to check on his breakfast, limping heavily, then returned a moment later to sit beside Ray. He was soaking wet but seemed oblivious to the fact, and Ray got the impression that his only reason for sitting beneath the lean-to was for companionship.

Riddick regarded him in silence, eyes narrowed a little, his expression serious now, almost melancholy. Ray squirmed beneath his piercing stare.

"So you're Cat's brother."

Surprised, Ray hesitated, then said, "Do you know Cat?"

"I knew him once. Or thought I did." He massaged his thigh, his gaze still riveted upon Ray's face. "Is it true what I've heard about him? Is he a hired gun?"

Ray admitted this was true, and hoping the fact might scare the man into letting him go free, added: "When Cat finds out I'm gone, he'll come for you and Sid."

Riddick only smiled. "I wish he would. I'd like to see him again. I'd like to . . ." His voice trailed off, and he looked away, staring off toward the river. "I saw Cat a few days ago," he said. "Your wife told us there was some oats for our horses at the Myers farm, so I rode out there to get 'em, and there he was. Surprised the hell out of me. Guess I just wasn't ready for him."

Shrugging off his moment of reflection, Riddick ran a

hand down his face and glanced at Ray. "With any luck, maybe I'll get another chance. Maybe I'll get to him before they hang him."

"When Sheriff Luger finds out about you and Sid, you two will be the ones to hang," Ray said.

"That ain't gonna happen, Myers. Besides your wife, you're the only one who knows the truth, and pretty soon you'll be dead." Riddick shook his head. "I'm real sorry for you, but that's the way it is."

"If you're so sorry, then don't kill me. Let me go."

His jaws tightening, Riddick stared down at his big, calloused hands. "I can't. I ain't got any say in this." He looked up at Ray, and the guilt that must have been chewing him up inside showed plainly on his face. "Look, Pony's the one does all the butchering. Not me. I never killed nobody that didn't try to kill me first."

He rose quickly and left the lean-to.

Watching him limp away, Ray realized he had touched on a very delicate nerve where Lee Riddick was concerned and sensed the man probably wasn't all bad. Likely, Sid Lane had promised to pay him well for his assistance, and desperate, Riddick accepted the offer. Now he was caught up in something too horrid for words. He wondered why Riddick didn't leave Sid Lane and go his own way.

Perhaps he feared the little man's vengefulness just as much as Ray did.

The dull beat of a horse's hooves sounded through the trees. Hearing it, Ray's heart and mind raced. Who could it be? Sheriff Luger? Virgil Bone? He craned his neck to see out of the lean-to.

A man and horse emerged from the trees, the man sitting hunched and wet in the saddle, the soggy brim of his straw sombrero flopping around his face. Ray was both surprised and disappointed to see who it was.

Eladio Moreno's shifty glance fell upon Ray, then flitted away when their gazes met. Riddick greeted him as he dismounted.

"How's it going, Ladio?"

"*¡Mecachis!* Bad night."

Riddick nodded in agreement. "Have some breakfast."

Moreno accepted Riddick's offer with a soft *gracias,* and sheltering his plate from the rain with his sombrero, he hurried toward the lean-to.

"Moreno!"

The Mexican stopped in his tracks. Startled, Ray looked past him at the tent, and a chill shinnied up his spine. Dressed in a yellow oilskin slicker, feet slightly spread apart, Sid Lane stood before his tent, regarding Eladio Moreno with keen distaste. Ray was shocked by his brother-in-law's thin, ghostly image.

"Why are you here, Moreno?" Sid Lane demanded. "Has something happened?"

Moreno nodded. "The *Gato* try to get away yesterday."

Riddick spun around to look at him. "Did he escape?"

"No. He jus' try."

Pale eyes glinting beneath his black slouch hat, Sid Lane stepped toward the Mexican. "You rode all the way out here to tell us that?"

"*Si.* And . . ." Eladio reached inside one of his trouser pockets and turned it inside out. "And I don' have no money," he said. "How you think I eat without no money?" He smiled weakly.

Sid Lane took a quick step forward and struck Moreno's plate of food from his hand. It hit the mud with a hollow plop.

"Get out of my sight!" he roared. "Go! Before I vomit from having to look upon your disgusting face!"

Moreno cringed away from the irate little man, but something was amiss. Ray saw it even before Moreno did. Sid Lane's face turned red, then purple, his features twisted, and he clutched his throat. Bending far over, he began to cough and choke and gasp for breath. Lee Riddick reacted instantly. Taking a brown glass bottle of medicine and another larger bottle of brandy from Sid's tent, he returned to his partner's side and forced him to drink from both bottles between spasms.

Witnessing his brother-in-law's agony for the first time, Ray realized more than ever the reason behind his bloody and brutal revenge. He was slowly dying and consumed with hatred for the men who had caused him to be sent to prison where his health deteriorated. He was merely a shell, empty but for the bitterness and hate that had driven him to murder those he blamed most.

Taking advantage of Sid Lane's preoccupation, Eladio Moreno crept toward Ray. Not sure at first if he meant to help him or attack him, Ray stared wide-eyed at the Mexican as he dropped to his knees beside him. Moreno's intentions soon became clear, however, when he began rummaging through Ray's pockets. He swiftly relieved Ray of his watch and money, transferred both items to his own pocket, and without giving Ray a second glance, left the lean-to.

Too frightened for his life to care about the loss, Ray watched the Mexican lead his swaybacked steed away from camp and picket him with the other horses.

Eladio Moreno's presence here solved yet another mystery. Moreno had lied, of course, about seeing Catlin kill Frank Wyman, and had done so most likely at Sid Lane's request. No wonder then that he had known where to find Wyman's body. Sid had told him where it was.

Just as in the old days, Sid Lane always managed to find a

fool to do his bidding. Ray realized that he, too, had been a fool the day he allowed himself to be sucked into his brother-in-law's quagmire, the Fort Griffin Vigilance Committee. What a mistake that had been!

"Feel better?" Riddick asked his partner.

Gasping, wheezing, Sid Lane nodded and inspected the flecks of blood on his white handkerchief. "It's getting worse," he murmured and glanced across at Ray. "Well, what are you gawking at?"

Ray quickly averted his gaze.

"Do you find something amusing?" Sid demanded. Still wheezing, he approached the lean-to and glared down at Ray. "Does it give you a glad feeling in your heart to see my suffering?"

"I never wished anything bad on you, Sid."

"Liar!" Sid jabbed a bony finger at him. "You'll pay dearly for what you've done to me, Myers."

Ray lifted gloomy eyes to look at his brother-in-law. "You promised Mary you wouldn't kill me."

"That was before you began snooping into matters that were none of your concern. You see, Mary came here yesterday to warn me that you had discovered the truth."

"She . . . she told you? Mary told you?"

"You act so surprised! Of course, she told me. She wanted me to make a run for it before you spilled the news to R.D. Luger." Sid sighed, his breath whistling through decayed lungs. "But I couldn't let you ruin my plan, Ray. Not after I worked so hard to set it up. If you had only minded your own business, you'd be out of harm's way."

"Does Mary know I'm here?" Ray asked. "Does she know you intend to kill me?"

"Not yet." Sid regarded him thoughtfully and stroked his goatee. "When she finds out, she may never forgive me, but that's a chance I'll have to take."

"If you cut off my head and display it on a stick like a trophy, Sheriff Luger will know Cat is innocent."

"Very true." Sid smiled thinly. "That's why I have something else in mind for you. Once this cursed rain stops, you and I will talk over old times, like how you turned your back on me during my trial two years ago, for instance. Then, my friend, I'll hang you from a tall tree and have Riddick here tie a weight to your feet and throw you into the river. You'll make a tender meal for the fishes."

Ray swallowed hard and gazed up at his brother-in-law's cadaverous face, feeling as if he were gazing upon Death itself.

"Cat knows about you. He knows everything. He'll tell Sheriff Luger, and they'll come looking for you."

Sid's laughter was harsh and humorless. "Do you really think anyone will believe that ne'er-do-well brother of yours? Hardly! No, you'll simply disappear. No one will ever know what became of you."

Another seizure of coughing drove Sid Lane to his tent. When he had gone, Lee Riddick retrieved his saddle from the lean-to and slung it over his shoulder. He gave Ray a pitying glance before leaving and spoke briefly with Eladio Moreno. Ray only half-listened to their conversation, too despondent to care what they said or to wonder at Lee Riddick's parting words.

"Ladio, you stay here till I get back," Riddick said. "If Pony needs you to do something for him, do it and don't complain. And don't drink up all his brandy."

"Where you goin'?" Moreno asked.

"I'm fixing to hunt me a one-eyed polecat."

CHAPTER FORTY

It was nearing 6:30 in the evening when Zella Moreno picked up her leather handbag and umbrella and left for work. Locking the door to her room, she glanced up and down the corridor and was surprised to find it empty. It was the first time since Catlin's haphazard escape attempt yesterday that an armed guard was not posted outside his room.

Already late for work, Zella decided a few more minutes would make no difference. She quietly approached room three, cast a quick glance up the corridor where it opened into the lobby, and tried the door knob. As she had expected, it was locked. Pressing her ear to the door, she listened for voices or movement, but the room was silent.

Zella tapped the knuckle of her forefinger against the door and spoke softly: "Catlin? Catlin, are you awake?"

"Zella?"

She smiled, glad to hear his voice, for they had been allowed no contact since his arrest.

"Yes, it's me," she said. "How are you?"

"Tied up. That damned deputy. The sorry asshole. If I ever get my hands on him . . . I'll kill him, Zella!"

"Shhh." Zella glanced toward the lobby and bit her lip, worried by Catlin's clipped, angry words. He sounded mad enough to follow through with his threat. "Catlin, don't do anything foolish. You'll only get yourself into deeper trouble."

"I've got to get out of here."

"I know, *querido,* but . . ."

Seeing Virgil Bone turn into the lobby, she broke off abruptly and moved away from the door.

"No visitors, Mrs. Moreno. I've already told you that."

"Has Catlin been allowed to talk to a lawyer yet?"

"He said he doesn't want one. No lawyers. No doctors. His words, not mine." The deputy sorted through the keys in his pocket, searching for the right one. "Sheriff Luger just now rode in from Albany," he told her. "He wants to move Myers to the jail first thing in the morning."

"Will I be allowed to talk to Catlin then?"

"Maybe." Virgil Bone eyed her coolly. "If Sheriff Luger decides to arrest you, you can talk to him all you want to until the day we stretch his neck."

Clutching her folded umbrella in her right hand, Zella was tempted to beat it over the deputy's head. It was easy to understand why Catlin detested him.

The deputy opened the door to look in on his prisoner, and Zella lingered in the corridor long enough to catch a glimpse of Catlin. He was laid out flat on his back and chained to the bed. Isolated and immobilized.

And ready to explode again any minute, Zella thought.

Leaving, she crossed the brightly lit lobby, opened her umbrella at the hotel door and stepped outside. Driving rain pelted her umbrella and wet her skirts, and though there would normally have been an hour's worth of daylight still left, the sky was almost dark and the streets practically deserted. Dreading the walk to the Beehive Saloon, Zella decided to hire a hack to drive her to work.

Trying not to muddy her clothes, she lifted her skirt and petticoats and picked her way around the side of the hotel, making for the livery stable at the back. She had gone only a few steps when a man's voice spoke close behind her.

"Zella Moreno?"

She stopped and whirled around, startled by the man's unexpected and silent approach, and drew her umbrella back a little to better see him.

He was tall, rawboned, and soaking wet, his blue shirt sticking to his chest and stomach, and water streaming from the curved brim of his hat. His face was partly hidden beneath the hat and the raised collar of his denim jacket.

"Are you Zella Moreno?" he asked again.

"I'm Zella. Who are you?"

He hesitated, glancing around him cautiously, then said, "I'm an old friend of Cat Myers."

Zella studied him with suspicion. "Catlin doesn't have any friends here in Fort Griffin." She took a small step backward and folded her umbrella, thinking to use it on the stranger if he dared follow her.

He held his hand out to her. "Don't be afraid. I need your help."

"You need my help? How?"

"I want to break Myers out of jail."

Zella laughed coldly. "The only people who want to break Catlin out of jail are the ones who want to lynch him."

"Would I come to you for help if that was what I wanted?"

Zella considered that. Was it possible this man was really here to help Catlin? Common sense told her it wasn't probable, yet he sounded sincere. And what about Catlin? As it stood now, he was destined to hang for murder. This might be his only chance.

Zella wiped the rain from her face with her hand and nodded. "All right. What is your plan?" she asked. "How will we get him out?"

Touching her elbow, the stranger drew her closer to the side of the hotel. "I heard he was being held here."

"You heard right."

"Is there any way for me to get inside the hotel without somebody seeing me?"

Zella thought a moment, then said, "Go to the other side of the building, and I'll open my window for you."

She started to walk past him when he gripped her arm, stopping her. "Don't double-cross me," he said.

Zella jerked free of his grasp and poked the sharp point of her umbrella against his chest. "That goes both ways, *senor*." Backing away from him, she spun around and hurried toward the front of the hotel.

The fact that he was as distrustful of her as she was of him made her feel better, more sure of herself. She ran up the steps and burst into the hotel. Several men were loitering in the lobby, smoking pipes and cigars and talking, and they turned to watch her as she pushed past them, clearly amused by her soggy appearance.

Leaving a trail of mud and water behind her, Zella darted down the corridor to her room. Once inside, she dug into her handbag for her .41 caliber derringer. Making sure it was loaded, she hiked up her skirts, tucked the weapon beneath the wide silk garter just above her right knee, and opened the window.

"I'm here," she said.

The tall stranger approached warily. "You alone?"

"Of course. Hurry."

As soon as he had crawled inside, she shut the window and lit one of the lamps, careful all the while not to turn her back to him.

Standing amid a puddle of water, the stranger took off his hat and fumbled with the brim, at the same time glancing around at her room, appearing ill at ease within the confines of four walls. He smelled like the outdoors, like rain and woodsmoke and horses, and the aura of him filled the room.

Seeing the stranger more clearly now in the lamplight, it took Zella only a moment to identify who he was, for she had seen his face on a wanted dodger posted in town. He was one of the prisoners who had escaped from Huntsville with Sid Lane! The realization left her breathless and afraid.

Lee Riddick detected the recognition in her eyes and shook his head. "I knew I was taking a chance coming to you."

"Why are you here?" she demanded.

"I'm here to get Myers out. Just like I told you. Who I am doesn't change nothing."

"It changes everything. You helped Sid Lane escape from prison."

"The man was dying. I felt sorry for him. Is that such a sin?"

Not sure how to respond to that, Zella gazed up at him, struck by his sober sincerity.

"Look, I risked everything to come here today," he said, "and I'll free Myers with or without your help, but it would be easier if we worked together."

"Do you believe he's innocent?"

"Innocent? Ma'am, innocent is one word that never fit Cat Myers. But that doesn't mean I want him to hang." He stared at her a moment, and a slow, friendly smile softened the sharp features of his face. "Ladio was right. You are pretty. Even wet."

Zella's eyebrows lifted. "So you know my husband. That gives me even more reason not to trust you."

"I just met him is all. He talks a lot when he's drunk. He told me all about you. He told me you were in love with Myers."

Riddick's smile faded, his expression darkened, and he reached out as if to touch her hair. When she shrank away from him, he quickly withdrew his hand and backed off.

"I'm sorry. After six years in the pen . . ." His cheeks became flushed with either shame or embarrassment, and he passed the back of his hand across his mouth. "I never was as lucky as Myers."

"He's not so lucky now either."

"No. No, I reckon not."

Strangely moved by this man, Zella found herself wanting to believe him, to trust him.

"If you're serious about doing this," she said softly, "then tell me what to do, and I'll do it."

"I need to know which room he's in."

"Room three." Zella moved toward the door, opened it a crack, and peeked out. "There's usually a guard or a deputy sitting outside his room, but I don't see anyone." She glanced over her shoulder at Riddick. "Catlin tried to break out yesterday, and they've got him in irons now."

Riddick frowned. "This ain't gonna be easy."

"No one said it would be."

"No. Well . . . here's what I need you to do. First, put those lights out in the hall there, then go and see if you can find Myers a horse. Any horse. When you find one, bring him to the back of the hotel where I left mine and wait there for us."

"His horse and saddle are in the livery stable," Zella said, and she threw her cloak around her shoulders and slipped on her gloves. "He'll want his gun, too."

"No gun."

Zella paused in her preparations to look up at him.

"Cat used to act first and think later," Riddick explained. "I doubt he's changed. I'd like to bust him out of here without somebody gettin' shot."

Remembering Catlin's angry threat against Virgil Bone, Zella didn't argue.

She eased the door open so it wouldn't creak, glanced outside, and drew back sharply when she spotted Virgil Bone walking down the corridor. Riddick stepped behind her to peer out, and together, they watched the deputy pause in front of room three. He shifted Catlin's supper to his left hand and dug into his pocket for his keys.

"He's the deputy," Zella whispered. "He'll have the keys to Catlin's handcuffs."

"Good for him." Riddick tied his bandana over his nose and mouth and drew his gun. "He's gone inside. Let's get this thing started."

Lifting her eyes heavenward, Zella whispered a fervent prayer, crossed herself, and hurried toward the lobby, extinguishing the wall lamps as she went, and she glanced behind her once to see Lee Riddick's shadowy form glide soundlessly into the darkened corridor.

She could only pray that he wouldn't deceive her.

CHAPTER FORTY-ONE

Catlin listened to the downpour outside. It sounded like a genuine frog-strangler, and he longed to be out in it, to feel the cold drops on his skin and breathe in the clean dampness and see the river roaring past Fort Griffin.

His room was stuffy. The spider had long since abandoned him. The steady rhythm of his own breathing, his own heartbeat, had become monotonous to him, and he felt at times as if he might explode into a million pieces. Like yesterday morning.

He regretted what had happened yesterday. His attempt to escape had been unplanned, spontaneous, an offshoot of his own violent actions. He wasn't even sure now what had prompted his sudden flare-up in the first place. The whole incident left him upset and confused.

Catlin heard a key being inserted into the lock and turned his head to look at the door with anticipation, for even Virgil Bone's visits were a welcome respite from the boredom. The deputy walked in with a tray of food, kicked the door shut, and glanced over at the smoking lamp.

"Wick needs to be trimmed," he remarked.

He set the tray on the table beside the bed, and gazing down at Catlin, singled out the key to his handcuffs.

"You know, Myers, if looks could kill I'd be bloated by now."

"Has Luger come in yet?"

Bone nodded. "Rode in about an hour ago."

"What about Ray? Have you seen him today?"

"No, but then, I ain't looked for him either. Hold your hands up."

Catlin obeyed and waited impatiently for the deputy to release him from his handcuffs, only the fourth time since yesterday morning that he'd been allowed any freedom. The deputy unlocked one of the cuffs, thereby freeing his hands from the iron headrail on the bed, and Catlin slowly pushed himself into a sitting position, wincing at the cramped stiffness in his shoulders and back.

Moving back to stand in front of the door, Virgil Bone folded his arms across his chest. "I'll give you fifteen minutes to get your business done."

"That's awful big of you."

"I can cut it to five if you start mouthing off."

Not doubting the deputy's word, Catlin held his tongue and swung his legs over the side of the bed. He stood up and took a few shuffling steps around his room, the chains on his leg shackles dragging between his feet.

Catlin thought about Ray and wondered if he would talk to Sheriff Luger about Mary and Sid. He had at first felt assured that Ray would keep his word, but as time passed, and his brother hadn't come to see him today like he said he would, doubt began to overshadow even this tiny glimmer of hope. By now, he was certain Ray and Mary had already kissed and made up and forgotten him entirely.

Scooting the chamber pot beneath the bed with his foot, Catlin washed his hands, splashed water on his face, and sat down to eat his supper.

"It's been a long time since Shackelford County had a proper, legal hanging," Bone commented. "I'm gonna take pleasure in seeing you hit the end of that rope, Myers."

"Always glad to be of service," Catlin muttered.

Bone shook his head. "You still don't believe it, do you?

You don't think it'll ever happen. Well, let me tell you something. No jury's gonna let you get off easy. Not after what you done."

Sopping up gravy with a biscuit, Catlin took a bite and eyed the deputy in detached silence.

Bone scowled. "You can set there and give me the stink eye all you want." Unfolding his arms, he dropped his right hand to his sidearm and tapped his fingers against the butt. "Go ahead. Stare. I don't care."

Catlin sensed the deputy's nervousness and was amused by it. Smiling a little, he scooped up a mouthful of mashed potatoes with his fork, and on sudden impulse, splatted it against the wall a few inches from the deputy's head.

"Hey! What'd you do that for?"

Cupping a hand beneath the mess to keep it from sliding down the flowered wallpaper, Virgil reached for the towel hanging by the wash basin just as Catlin let fly with another white glob. It plastered the deputy on the side of the face.

"Bull's eye!"

"Hey, now! Quit that, you derned idiot!"

Virgil started toward him, bent on putting a stop to this nonsense, when the door suddenly opened behind him. Startled, he half-turned.

Catlin hesitated only a second before taking advantage of Virgil Bone's fleeting preoccupation. Leaping up, he made a desperate lunge for the deputy's sidearm. The leg irons slowed him down, and Bone pulled his gun just as he slammed into him. They struggled briefly for possession of the weapon. Getting a stranglehold on Bone's neck with his left arm, Catlin sank his teeth into his shoulder, producing a hoarse shriek of pain, and wrenched the gun from his hand.

He and the man standing in the darkened doorway hiked

up their revolvers in the same breath and aimed at each other across the room.

Caught between them, Bone jerked his hands into the air. "Don't shoot! Don't . . ."

His words died with a strangled croak as Catlin tightened his hold on his neck. Keeping the deputy's rigid body between himself and the door, his breath labored with excitement, Catlin stared down the barrel of his cocked six-shooter at the stranger, watched him ease inside the room and shut the door behind him. His face was masked by a bandana, his eyes hidden by the low brim of his hat, and the hand that gripped the gun was rock-steady. He took a slow step forward.

"That's close enough," Catlin warned.

"Come on, Myers. We don't have time for this. Put your gun down."

"You first."

The stranger hesitated. It was a stalemate.

"Look, Myers, I'm here to bust you out. Zella Moreno's gettin' your horse for you right this minute."

Tensed and edgy, Catlin listened to his voice, his slow, easy manner of speaking, feeling as if he had heard it before. But where? He tried to match the voice to a face, a name, an identity, but his memory locked down and wouldn't budge.

"Who are you?"

"We can talk about who I am later," the stranger said. He drew a sharp breath. "I'll make a deal with you. I'll put my gun down if you'll put yours down. We'll do it together."

Realizing they might stand here all night otherwise, Catlin gave an almost imperceptible nod of his head, and he and the man in the denim jacket slowly lowered the muzzles of their six-shooters and eased the hammers down. The stranger holstered his weapon, and Catlin followed suit, shoving the barrel of his gun inside the front of his jeans.

Virgil Bone chose that moment to make a break. Tugging at the taut arm around his neck, he hooked his leg around Catlin's and gave a tremendous jerk that sent them both toppling over backwards. Bone landed on top of Catlin, knocking the breath out of him, and was about to roll clear when the cold barrel of his own gun jabbed him in the back. His body stiffened.

"Thunder. I can't believe this . . . ."

"You make one wrong move," Catlin gasped, "and I'll blow you to kingdom come."

"No killing, Myers." Catlin's benefactor opened the door a bare inch to peek out into the corridor and glanced over his shoulder at them. "Let's get out of here. Hurry it up."

Digging the keys from Bone's pocket, Catlin freed himself from his leg irons and tugged his boots on, careful all the while to keep a close eye on both men. Taking up the handcuffs, he shackled the deputy to the bedpost.

"You'll never make it," Bone told him. "We'll have a posse hot on your trail come daylight."

Making no comment, Catlin gagged Virgil Bone with a pillowcase and stepped toward the door.

"All clear?" he asked.

The stranger nodded. "The hall's empty. Let's go."

Guns drawn, they stole into the darkened corridor, and with grave misgivings, Catlin followed the man toward the back of the hotel, knowing in his gut this could all be a set-up, a plan for lynching him.

They stopped in front of room six. Zella's room. Going inside, Catlin saw it was empty. The lamp burned low. They quickly crossed to the window.

Parting the drapes, the stranger jerked his head at Catlin. "Go ahead."

"How do I know there's not a lynch mob waiting for me out there?"

"You're mighty distrustful, Myers."

"You damned right I am. You go first."

Hesitating only a moment, the stranger opened the window and crawled outside. Catlin heard his feet hit the rain-soaked earth with a soppy slap, and he cast a cautious glance out the window. Rain stung his cheeks and cooled his hot face. He could see little in the awful darkness. Lights glowed hazily in the windows of a nearby saloon and in a few houses on Parson Avenue, but that was all.

Straddling the pane, he slipped out the open window and dropped lightly to the ground.

"No lynch mob. What d'you know about that?" Catlin's liberator yanked the bandana from his face. "This way, Myers."

Catlin trailed behind him, running now, his head ducked low and the revolver wedged beneath his left armpit to protect it from the driving rain. He saw the dimly outlined forms of three saddled horses standing behind the hotel with their tails turned to the storm, and Zella beckoned for him to hurry. They embraced without a word, and she handed him Chico's reins.

The stranger grabbed up his own mount's reins and spoke harshly to Zella. "Go back inside!"

"I'm going with you."

"No, you ain't. You'll slow us down."

Bristling at the man's tone of voice, Catlin spoke up. "She's coming with me! If you don't like it, then ride on alone. Zella, mount up."

She ran to her horse, and Catlin turned toward Chico and grasped the saddlehorn. He had barely touched his foot to the stirrup when something struck him in the back of the head with sickening force. Zella's scream shocked him almost as much as the pain. He gasped and clung to the saddlehorn, stubborn, fighting to remain conscious.

"Run, Zella! Go!"

Chico sidestepped, and Catlin lost his hold on the saddle. He felt himself blindly falling, toppling, like in a dream in which he had stepped off the edge of a steep cliff. Only this time, he didn't awaken before hitting the ground.

CHAPTER FORTY-TWO

Catlin came to slowly and stared into the pitch-dark night. He lay with his right cheek compressed into the mud. Raindrops pummeled his back. His ears were filled with a rushing, roaring sound, and the musty smell of mold and wet, decaying weeds tickled his nostrils.

He pressed his palms against the cold mud and pushed, raising his upper body a few inches from the ground. Pain throbbed inside his head, and he imagined his brain pulsing, swelling, splitting his skull. The hurt was almost unbearable.

Groaning, he moved his legs, rigid with cold, and tried to get his knees under him. He never made it.

A twig broke near Catlin's face with a muffled snap, and a man's stiff-soled boot came down hard across his shoulders and crushed him to the ground. Digging his fingers into the mud, Catlin sucked in his breath. The pressure across his upper back increased as the man stepped on him, pinning him down.

"Keep still, Myers. You're not going anywhere."

Losing consciousness again, Catlin remembered no more.

When his eyes fluttered open hours later, the rain had stopped, but the roaring sound was still loud in his ears. He lay very still and blinked his eyes. He was lying on his right side, his good eye closest to the ground. Dazed, disoriented, he focused on the brown-gray leaves and twigs and the tiny blades of tender, green grass poking out of the mud in front of his face. A hand lay a few inches from his nose, fingers curled, nails dug into the mud. The thumb twitched, and Catlin realized the hand was his own.

Concentrating, working to set the gears of his mental processes into motion, he slowly raised his hand to his face. He touched the drooping upper lid of his blind eye, cupped his palm over it, a habitual gesture, and an image formed in his mind, a woman with warm, dark eyes gently brushing his hand away and saying, "Stop hiding it. It doesn't matter to me."

Catlin spoke her name aloud, a hoarse croak that grated in his ears and throbbed in his head.

There was a slight stirring nearby. "Don't worry about Zella Moreno. She's got spunk. She'll get along fine without you."

The voice startled Catlin. He carefully lifted his head. At first, he noticed only the Clear Fork of the Brazos less than a quarter of a mile away. Last night's rain had transformed the river's normally docile waters into a frothing, roaring monster. Closer to him, Chico and another horse grazed with their bridles and saddles still on.

Raising his hand to touch the raw wound on the back of his head, Catlin looked around and saw a man squatting on his heels a few feet away from him, his back resting against an elm tree, big hands dangling loose between his knees. Catlin stared dumbly at the man's narrow, sharp-featured face for almost a full minute before his memory kicked in, and he recognized Lee Riddick.

Catlin was attacked again by that awful sensation, that feeling of unspeakable foreboding, confusion, and torment, and his heart thudded against his chest. Riddick's features were agonizingly familiar. He felt sure he had known this man in another time and place far removed from the present. He stared hard at Riddick's face, concentrating, searching.

"Yeah, you know me," Riddick said softly.

"I don't . . . I can't remember."

Riddick took off his hat and scrubbed his fingers through short-cropped, mousy brown hair. "I've aged a good bit—more than you have, I reckon—but you know me. Think, Cat. Think back to May of '63, and if you've got any conscience left at all, you'll remember."

Catlin did remember. It came to him all at once, and the shock was like ice water down his back. Never taking his gaze off Riddick, he slowly sat up and thrust his hand out to brace himself against a tree trunk. A quivering that began in his stomach traveled outward to his legs and arms.

"Brad," he whispered. "Brad Gilley."

He looked into those intense eyes and knew he was right.

It was unbelievable. Staggering. He was seeing a ghost, the very ghost that had haunted his days and nights, tortured his dreams. But the ghost had indeed aged, no longer the fresh-faced youth he remembered. Deep lines creased Brad Gilley's forehead and spread outward from his eyes. Once good teeth were now crooked, gapping, ruined by poor diet.

"Brad. I thought you were dead. All this time . . ."

"Fourteen years." Gilley nibbled a grass stem and regarded him with narrowed eyes. "It's been fourteen years."

"That was you I saw at the farm a few days ago," Catlin said. "Why'd you run, Brad? Why? We could have talked."

Gilley shrugged. "Maybe I wasn't in the talking mood." He paused and gazed toward the river. "I stood there and watched you and it all came back to me, like I was living it all over again." He spit the grass stem from his mouth. "If I'd had a gun on me, I'd have shot you then and there."

When at last he looked at Catlin again, hatred burned deep in his eyes. "The only trouble was I wanted you to know it was me that killed you. And why."

Catlin drew his legs under him, tried to rise, as Brad Gilley pulled his revolver and leveled it at him.

"Sit down!"

His head swimming and stomach churning, Catlin wrapped an arm around the tree trunk to support himself and slid back to the ground. Expecting a bullet to crash through his skull any second, he found he didn't much care. If it would make things right, make Brad feel better, what did it matter?

He ground the side of his face into the tree's rough bark and closed his eyes, his thoughts reeling back to that terrible day of battle.

"I still remember the last time I ever saw you," he said quietly. "Covered in blood . . . all up and down your left side. You were barely conscious. The Union line was closing in on us, and our company, our whole regiment, was ordered to fall back. I didn't know what to do." Opening his eyes, he gazed past the gun aimed at his face to look at Brad Gilley. "I panicked. I ran. I thought I could come back for you after dark." He shook his head. "It was two days before I got a chance to double back. All I found was your canteen. I kept it . . ."

"Why'd you keep it?" Gilley sneered. "Thirsty?"

"Just to remember you by. It's all I had left."

"Well, while you were remembering, the Yanks were cartin' my ass off to a prison camp!"

"I'm sorry, Brad."

"Sorry ain't good enough!" Gilley rose clumsily, wincing, favoring his left leg. "They sent me to Camp Douglas in Chicago. That winter, it was so cold, men froze to death. Fifteen, twenty prisoners died every day, and no blankets, no overcoats. Nothing." He glowered down at Catlin. "And all you can say is you're sorry."

"How long were you there . . . in Camp Douglas?"

"Two years," Gilley replied. "Until I escaped."

At Catlin's urging, Brad Gilley briefly recounted his escape from Camp Douglas. During the two years he was a prisoner of war, he formed an unlikely friendship with one of the guards, a black man named Silas Johnson. They became such close friends, in fact, that on a crisp, spring night, Johnson looked the other way while Gilley and five other prisoners stole out of camp and broke for freedom.

"We killed a sentry and a Yankee officer outside the prison and took their horses and guns," he said, "then found out later Lee had surrendered that very day at Appomatox." He shook his head in disgust. "With the war over, the Federals decided it'd be fun to slap a murder charge on us."

Standing over Catlin, gun dangling at his side, Brad Gilley drew a slow breath, and his expression changed, turned bitter.

"When I got back to Texas, I found out I had a price on my head," he continued, "so I tried to keep a low profile. My folks were having a hard time of it and needed me at home. All I wanted was to be left alone, but East Texas was overrun with Northern soldiers and Carpetbaggers, and they got wind of me finally."

"But they didn't catch you," Catlin presumed.

"No. I got away. I changed my name. They wouldn't let me live honest, so I turned outlaw. The bastards didn't give me no other choice." Gilley paused, lost for a moment in the memory, and finally looked down at Catlin, met his gaze. "Funny how your one cowardly stunt messed up my whole life, ain't it?"

Catlin bowed his head. He didn't know what to say. Apologies and expressions of sympathy were just words with no power to heal or right wrongs. So he simply sat, silent, ashamed.

Reaching down, Brad Gilley grasped a fistful of his hair

and yanked his head back, forcing Catlin to look up at him. "What've you got to say for yourself, you stinking yellow-belly? Huh? More excuses?" He gave Catlin's head a rough jerk. "Come on, Myers. You always liked to work your jaws, so talk to me. Let me hear more of your excuses."

When Catlin refused to respond, Gilley's temper flared. Releasing him, he stepped back and kicked him in the side, catching him between the ribs with the toe of his boot, and cursed him in virulent tones.

"It's your fault! I blame you for all of it! For the whole screwed up mess that's been my life for the past fourteen years!"

He kicked him in the ribs again, harder than before, and the impact numbed Catlin clean to the shoulder, followed by a sharp, searing pain in his side. Yet this was nothing compared to the pain of Brad Gilley's words.

Inhaling short, shallow breaths, pressing his arm against his side, Catlin started to push himself to his feet. Gilley moved in close and backhanded him across the face, knocking him sprawling. He lifted his revolver and aimed it between Catlin's eyes.

"When Mary Myers told me and Pony you were here," he said, "I knew this day would come. I've wished for it many a time."

Lying on his back, Catlin bolstered himself against the ache inside him and looked up at this man he had once loved as a brother. When he spoke, his voice was quiet, steady.

"Then kill me. Get it out of the way and get on with your life."

Something flickered far back in Gilley's eyes, a trace of bewilderment perhaps, or surprise, for he couldn't have foreseen Catlin's stoic invitation. Lips pressed into a tight line, nostrils flaring, he curled his thumb over the hammer of his gun. The well-oiled metal clicked sharply as he cocked it back.

A fleeting thought crossed Catlin's mind. What did it feel like to die?

For a man of thirty years who had killed so many times, taken so many lives, even contemplated taking his own, it struck him as odd that he had never seriously considered the question. Would he feel the bullet and be aware of its swift propulsion through flesh and bone and brain matter? Or would it simply end in one big bang?

Propped up on his elbows, Catlin stared his soon-to-be killer in the eyes, calm, resolute, and waited to find out the answer to the mystery.

Yet nothing happened. Catlin watched Brad Gilley, wondering why he hesitated, why he delayed carrying out a deed he must have envisioned over and over since that day he lay alone and bleeding in a muddy ditch east of Vicksburg, Mississippi.

"Do it, Brad. Get it over with."

A barely visible tremor passed through Gilley's body. His gunhand trembled.

Impatience blazed up in Catlin like a flame. "Damn you, Brad, I said do it! Pull the damned trigger! Do it now!"

The shot exploded on "now", a hard, flat, angry blast that jolted Catlin to the bone. Bits of tree bark stung the left side of his face, and the bullet's concussion jarred his eardrums. It took him a moment to realize what had happened.

Shaken but unhurt, he looked from the splintered gash in the tree beside him to Brad Gilley's strained, sweaty face and spouted the most lame brain remark he could possibly have come up with.

"Shit, Brad. You missed."

"I didn't miss." Brad Gilley lowered his gun. "To hell with you, Myers." Backing away, he shoved the revolver into his holster and shook his head. "To hell with you."

He turned and limped toward his horse.

"Brad! Brad, wait!"

Catlin rose too quickly, staggered, caught himself against the tree that had taken the bullet meant for him, and watched Brad Gilley step into the saddle. Wheeling his horse around, Gilley jerked Chico's reins loose and looked across at Catlin.

"You ain't worth killing," he said in a low voice. "I got enough blood on my hands already."

He spoke roughly to his horse and struck out at a hard gallop, tugging the balky Chico along behind him.

CHAPTER FORTY-THREE

Catlin watched Brad Gilley ride away, watched him disappear from his sight behind a swell in the land and listened to the horses' fading hoofbeats until their rhythmic pounding was absorbed by the roar of the river.

He stood motionless a long while afterwards, staring in the direction of Brad Gilley's departure, unseeing, lost. A profound sadness overwhelmed him, stirred him, and he touched his tongue to his lower lip, tasted the blood there, and looked toward the river.

It took him several minutes to walk the quarter mile to the river's east bank. Weaving from one tree to the next, stopping every few steps to rest, he at last sank to his knees at the water's edge.

Fed by its numerous tributaries, the Clear Fork of the Brazos had flooded its banks, and the sound of the rushing, swirling waters filled Catlin's ears. He waggled the fingers of his right hand in the river. Leaning forward, he filled his cupped hands with the cold water and splashed it over his face, then drank deeply.

Catlin ripped the already torn sleeves off his shirt. Folding them together, he wet the makeshift compress and held it against the back of his head. He gasped at the coldness in the open wound.

Holding his breath, waiting for the initial shock to wear off, he felt his mouth fill up with saliva. His stomach rolled, convulsed, seemed to turn inside out as he vomited into the weeds.

He squeezed his eyes shut while dry heaves wrenched his body.

Later, crawling back to the water's edge, he washed his face and hands, drank again, more slowly this time, and collapsed exhausted on his back. He lightly brushed his palm back and forth over the lower ribs of his right side where Brad Gilley had kicked him. Live coals seemed to be smoldering there, just below the surface.

He gazed up at the cumbersome, gray clouds, thinking, Brad Gilley. Here. Alive! It was still incredible to him. After all these years of believing his friend was dead, believing he had left him to die. But no, he had left him instead to the Union soldiers and two long years in some godforsaken prison camp and a wrecked life. Which was worse?

Even as he thought this, he realized he was not solely responsible for Brad's postwar hardships. Most, if not all, Confederate soldiers and prisoners of war had returned home to ruin, poverty, and the injustices of Yankee reprisal. No one had forced Brad to turn outlaw, not Catlin, not the Yankees, and Brad had only himself to blame for his eventual imprisonment in Huntsville.

Catlin told himself this, but the cold, hard fact did nothing to ease the guilt and shame of his cowardly betrayal of his friend fourteen years ago.

He lay on his back a few minutes longer, taking time to collect his thoughts and gather strength, and finally pushed himself to his feet and walked back to where he and Brad had spent the night. He regarded the broken, muddy ground where the horses had stomped around, and followed Brad's fresh trail with his eye as far as he could see it.

Where had he gone? To rejoin Sid Lane? That the two men were here together in the valley of the Clear Fork was a certainty. What Catlin wanted to know now was why. Why would a man like Brad Gilley become mixed up with someone like Sid "Pony" Lane? To Catlin, who still persisted in re-membering Brad as he had known him, the alliance between these two men didn't make sense. The Brad Gilley he had known was no murderer!

Head lowered, gaze fixed on the horses' hoofprints, Catlin followed Brad's trail and hoped it would not rain anymore and obliterate the tracks. He needed to find Brad. Even if the man wound up killing him, he couldn't let it end this way.

Mud caked the bottoms of Catlin's boots, and he stopped every so often to scrape it off and lighten the load. He hadn't gone far when he was forced to make another of these neces-sary stops. While gouging the sticky mud off his bootheels, something, an extra sixth sense or mere instinct, stilled his hand and made him look up and around.

Hugging the river bank some distance behind him, a horse and rider appeared fleetingly through the trees. Instantly alert, edgy, Catlin ducked down and slunk into a shallow wash where he squatted on his heels to watch, hidden among the brush. The rider hove into sight again, closer this time and still coming Catlin's way, slowly walking his horse upstream.

Glancing around him, Catlin hefted a good-sized rock in his right hand and waited.

The horse and rider were within two hundred feet of Catlin before he trusted his glazed vision enough to be sure of the newcomer's identity. Relief swept over him like a warm wave.

Rising, stumbling out of the wash, he gave a short, shrill whistle and saw Zella Moreno's head snap around to look at him. She drew up sharply, startled at first by his sudden ap-pearance, then urged her horse into a hard gallop.

Drawing rein beside him, she dropped to the ground and melted into his outstretched arms. Catlin held her close for a long moment, until she eased back and tilted her head up to look at him.

"I was afraid I'd never find you."

Catlin kissed her forehead. "I'm damned glad you did." He stroked her hair, still damp like her clothes, and frowned. "How long have you been looking for me?"

"For hours! Last night, after Lee Riddick knocked you out, my horse spooked and almost got away from me. I was trying to calm him when Riddick lifted you onto Chico and took off." She shook her head, all the worry and fear of the past few hours surfacing in her eyes. "I lost sight of you in the rain. Catlin, I was so scared!"

"How'd you know which direction we went?"

"I had a . . . Oh, what do you always call it? I had a . . . a hunch that Riddick might go where there are fewer people, so I rode west from town until I reached the river. I was afraid to cross it. Then I heard a gunshot a little while ago. What happened? How did you get away?"

Catlin gazed southward, the direction Brad Gilley had ridden, and didn't answer, his thoughts straying from their conversation.

"I'm sorry, Catlin."

"Sorry?" He looked back down at her. "Sorry for what?"

"For trusting Lee Riddick. He told me he was an old friend of yours, and I believed him. He might have killed you!"

"He told you the truth. He is an old friend."

"Friends don't do what he did to you."

"He was just returning the favor, Zella."

"What are you talking about? Who is Lee Riddick?"

"He's Brad Gilley."

Zella stared up at him, searching his face, puzzled. "Brad Gilley's dead, *querido*."

"No, he's not. Riddick is Brad Gilley."

He explained how Brad had been taken prisoner by Union

soldiers, but Zella only frowned and bit her lower lip. Concern shadowed her features.

Catlin gazed down at her with narrowing eyes. "Why don't you believe me?"

"Because you're not thinking clearly right now," she said, "and it's not as if this is the first time you've imagined things."

Her reference to his occasional hauntings put Catlin on the defensive. "What is it? You think I'm crazy? Damn it, Zella, I know what I'm talking about! Brad's here with Sid Lane, and I've got to find out why. I've got to talk to him again!"

When he started to move past Zella to take up her horse's reins, she grabbed his arm, stopping him in mid-stride.

"Think about what you're doing!" she exclaimed. "Catlin, this person—Lee Riddick, Brad Gilley, whatever you want to call him—he's not your friend! He helped Lane escape from prison, and if he's with him now, then he must also have helped him kill those men. Even if he is Brad Gilley, he's not the same person you knew as a boy. He's changed, just as you've changed!"

"No. No!" Catlin broke free of Zella's grasp, anger at her words surging through him. "Brad's not like that! Not like me. Not like Sid Lane." He gripped her shoulders, looked deep into her eyes. "Zella, he proved it less than an hour ago. He had every reason in the world to kill me, but he didn't do it."

Zella wasn't impressed. "If you didn't have such a hard head, he would have killed you last night!"

At a loss, Catlin shook his head, backed off, and gathered her horse's reins. He mounted up, ducking his head to hide the pain, and pressed his arm against his bruised side. Something was almighty wrong there. A cracked rib maybe. Inhaling a slow, cautious breath, he kicked his left foot free of the stirrup and looked down at Zella. He held his hand out to her.

"Are you coming with me or not?"

Hesitating only an instant, Zella took his hand, stepped into the stirrup, and swung up behind him. Rearranging her burdensome skirts, she rested her hands on his hips.

"I got your rifle last night," she said, her voice toneless, almost sullen. "I put your ammunition in the right-hand saddlebag. If your 'old friend' decides to finish what he started last night, you may need it."

Catlin had already noted his Sharps .50 tucked safely away in its leather scabbard on the offside of the saddle. He had no intention of using it on Brad, however.

Spurring Zella's beat-out horse into a slow canter, he followed Brad Gilley's trail south and gritted his teeth against the shock waves that coursed through him with each fall of his mount's hooves.

Catlin judged they had ridden three or four miles when the trail suddenly veered right, toward the river. Following the tracks in the mud, Catlin neared the east bank and pulled up sharply. Standing alone on this side of the river, reins dangling loose at his front feet, was Chico.

"Well, look who's here," Catlin murmured.

Zella's chin bumped his shoulder as she looked around him at the bay gelding.

Scanning the trees for movement, making sure Chico was indeed alone, Catlin dismounted and spoke softly to the bay with hand outstretched. Expecting his morning oats, no doubt, Chico moved toward him, his hooves making sucking sounds in the boggy mud. He stepped on a rein, and stopped, ears pricked forward. Catlin slowly approached him and gathered the reins, and the gelding nibbled at his shirttail.

"What happened, you no account jughead? Didn't like Brad's company?"

The broken-up ground at the water's edge told the story plainly. Brad Gilley had crossed the river here, not a good crossing, the water deep from bank to bank and raging, possibly hiding any number of little whirlpools that could suck a man or horse underwater. Disliking the looks of the crossing, Chico had put up a fight.

More familiar with the Clear Fork's fickle nature than Brad, Catlin mounted Chico and ranged up- and downstream until he located a place where the banks had a more gradual approach to deep water, and a gravel bar provided firm footing for the horses. Chico was a good, strong swimmer, and Catlin let Zella ride him.

"Just give him his head and hang on," he told her. "I'll be right behind you."

She took off her shoes and stockings, mounted Chico, and walked the bay into the water. Holding his rifle up, Catlin followed them, keeping a watchful eye on Zella, and felt the rushing current lick up around his feet and ankles as they moved forward, the cold, muddy water climbing up his legs to his waist, pushing hard against his swimming mount.

Ahead of him, Zella glanced back once to look at him, her eyes wide and face pale with fear. Catlin yelled an encouraging word to her, but she didn't hear him over the roar of the river.

They made it across without difficulty, the horses scrambling up the slippery north bank a little downstream from where they had originally begun, long tails streaming water behind them. Shivering in his wet clothes, Catlin rode ahead to locate Brad's trail again, and they continued on, still moving roughly southward and parallel to the Clear Fork.

They were nearing a sharp bend in the river when Catlin

thought he smelled woodsmoke. Reining in, he dismounted and spoke in a hushed voice.

"We'll leave the horses here."

Tethering the horses and shouldering his rifle and saddle-bags, Catlin continued on foot with Zella close behind him. The trail was harder to see here, with the tall grass reaching almost to their waists.

He heard men talking before he saw the camp. Dropping down to hide in the grass, he listened to the men's voices, catching only snippets of their talk over the rush of water in the background, too far away to distinguish words or individual voices. He cautiously crept forward through the tall grass.

Tucked away beneath the deep shadow of towering pecan and hackberry trees and elms one hundred yards away was a small tent and lean-to. Horses grazed nearby the camp, picketed on long ropes, and two, no three, men milled about between the tent and lean-to. Squinting his good eye, Catlin studied the three men, instantly recognizing the tallest man in the denim jacket as Brad Gilley. He was fairly certain one of the other men was Sid Lane. The third wore a straw sombrero, and a red and brown poncho cloaked his shoulders.

"Eladio," Zella whispered.

"You sure?"

She nodded. "It's Eladio. I'd recognize him anywhere." She met Catlin's gaze. "He must be working for Sid Lane. That's how he knew where to find Frank Wyman's body."

"Looks that way." Trusting Zella's eyesight over his own, he asked, "How many men and horses do you see?"

"Three men. Four horses."

Four horses, meaning they either had an extra mount, or there was also a fourth man around somewhere. Catlin cast a wary glance around him, searching for movement among the trees and scattered thickets of chittam. Seeing nothing, he nudged Zella and pointed out a low spot in the ground a few feet ahead of them flanked by tangled brush and rocks.

She nodded in understanding. Bunching her soaked skirt and petticoats up around her thighs, crouching low, she followed him into the little wash-out. The grass was laid flat here by run-off water and the ground soggy, but the cover, at least, was good. Sinking down in the wet grass, Catlin rested his rifle barrel across his forearm and watched the camp through an open space in the brush.

"What are you going to do?" Zella whispered.

Catlin shook his head. He didn't know. All he really wanted to do right now was talk to Brad, but that wasn't possible with Sid Lane and Eladio Moreno in the way.

He watched Sid Lane crawl inside his tent, then come out a moment later with a coiled rope in his hand. He paused at the tent's entrance to cough, a deep, rattling cough that brought him to his knees. He was clearly suffering and so withered he looked as if a puff of wind might whisk him clean away, like a dry leaf.

Catlin watched the little man wipe his mouth with a handkerchief, stagger to his feet, and fling the coiled rope to Brad Gilley. He barked an order, and Brad tossed one end of the rope up and over a stout tree limb jutting out above their camp. Farther away, Eladio Moreno had saddled two of the horses and was leading them toward Brad.

"What the hell are they fixin' to do?" Catlin whispered.

Zella shook her head, frowning slightly, watching the camp. "There's someone sitting under the lean-to," she said suddenly. "I've seen movement there three times now."

Catlin looked but couldn't see anything. If there was a man under the lean-to, however, that would account for the fourth horse. He turned his attention back to Brad Gilley.

Having secured the rope to the tree limb, Brad was sitting astride one of the horses, looping the end of the rope, knotting it. Tying a hangman's knot!

"Somebody's gonna get lynched," Catlin concluded. "Wonder who?"

Not answering, Zella clutched his arm and pointed.

He followed her gaze, saw Sid Lane prodding someone out of the lean-to with his rifle. A man crept out of the makeshift shelter with his hands tied behind his back. Shouting at him, jabbing him in the butt with the point of his rifle, Sid Lane goaded the man to his feet.

When the man in the dark, rumpled suit rose unsteadily and staggered toward the dangling noose, Catlin swore softly and met Zella's gaze.

It was Ray Myers.

CHAPTER FORTY-FOUR

"Your brother," Zella whispered. "Oh, God, Catlin. They're going to hang him."

"Not if I can help it."

"If you confront Sid now, he'll just shoot Ray. You won't have gained a thing."

Catlin knew she was right. Sid Lane would have to be taken out quickly, without warning.

The gaunt little man shoved Ray toward one of the horses. Moreno stood nearby, observing the proceedings with mild interest, but Brad was gone. Catlin spotted him sitting by himself a little distance from camp. He appeared to be cleaning his rifle. Somehow, the fact that he was taking no part in the actual hanging of Ray relieved Catlin's mind to a small extent at least.

Easing himself into a more comfortable position, Catlin lifted the leaf sight on the Sharps .50, set it for one hundred yards, and pushed the rifle out in front of him. He pulled back the rear trigger and peered through the sights at Sid Lane and experienced an instant of panic. His vision was unfocused, fuzzy. His hands were not steady.

Zella stirred beside him. "Catlin . . . wait."

Eladio Moreno was moving into his line of fire, helping Lane boost Ray into the saddle. Catlin relaxed a moment, wiping his eyes, drawing a deep breath. He was shaking uncontrollably, chilled to the bone, and thought his fever might be taking hold of him again. Zella regarded him anxiously.

"Are you all right?"

Nodding, he ran his tongue over dry, broken lips and waited for Moreno to move out of the way. Ray was sitting in the saddle now, shoulders slumped, head bowed. Catlin frowned, wishing his brother would fight and show some spirit, but he seemed to have totally given up.

Moreno left Sid Lane's side, presumably to mount the other horse and place the noose over Ray's head, and Catlin lined up his sights on Lane again, knowing he must shoot him before Moreno got the noose in place, knowing he must bring Lane down with his first shot.

Sid Lane was standing sideways to Catlin, his rifle held loosely in the bend of his left arm, right hand on his hip. Blinking to clear his vision, Catlin settled the sights a little below Lane's right armpit, but before he could shoot, another fit of chills vibrated through his body, joggling him off target.

Moreno was mounted up and walking his horse toward Ray, reaching for the noose. Again, Catlin aimed at Sid Lane. Drawing a silent breath, he exhaled slowly, trying to steady himself, and squeezed the trigger.

The Big Fifty boomed like a cannon and kicked hard against Catlin's right shoulder. Swiftly jacking the lever, ejecting the spent shell, reloading, Catlin glanced up long enough to see Sid Lane reel with the bullet's impact and hit the ground on his side, wounded, writhing in agony.

Startled by the shot, Ray's horse half-reared and shot forward as if someone had stuck a prickly pear pad under its tail, and Ray toppled over backwards and landed like a sack of potatoes in the mud. Gaining his feet, he scrambled into the bushes. Moreno's horse had also spooked and was bucking and sunfishing around the camp in bounding, stiff-legged leaps, successfully dumping the Mexican off its back and into the smoldering coals of the men's cook fire. Moreno yelled in pain and frantically beat at his smoking poncho before clambering out of Catlin's sight behind the canvas tent.

A rifle cracked near where Brad Gilley had been sitting earlier, and the bullet whizzed very near to Catlin and Zella's hiding place. Catlin didn't return fire. More bullets caromed off nearby trees and rocks and whined into space. He pushed Zella down, trying to shield her with his body, and waited for the gunshots to cease.

Silence fell over the woods at last. Catlin peered through the rocks and brush. The only man in sight was Sid Lane, sprawled in the open where he had fallen, motionless now but still clutching his rifle in his left hand. Catlin thought he might have shot him in either the right shoulder or upper arm. Wobbly as he was, he was surprised he'd managed to hit him at all, and with Ray out of harm's way, he felt no desire to try finishing the man off. Let him suffer.

Seeing no other movement, no sign of Brad Gilley or Eladio Moreno or Ray, Catlin cupped his hands around his mouth. "Brad, it's over! Lane's done for! Can't we talk?"

Brad Gilley answered his request with a bullet. It kicked up a clod of mud a few feet in front of Catlin's face.

Undaunted, Catlin tried a different approach. "There's probably a sheriff's posse out hunting for us by now!" he hollered. "You keep shooting, and you're gonna draw 'em straight to us!"

Silence followed his words. Catlin waited, rubbing his face, feeling the coarse beard stubble on his cheeks and jaw. He glanced at Zella lying next to him.

"Do you think you could get Eladio to come out?" he whispered. "Maybe give himself up?"

She shrugged. "Maybe. I can try." She called out to her husband. "Eladio, it's me . . . Zella! What Catlin says is true, Eladio. Sid Lane is finished. If he lives, he'll go to prison.

Don't let him drag you down with him. Come out and we'll protect you!"

"*¡De ninguna manera!*" Eladio shouted. *"Es peligroso. ¡Tengo miedo de Gato Myers!"*

Zella translated for Catlin. "He says it's too dangerous. He's afraid of you."

"The dumbass," Catlin murmured. "He oughta be afraid."

Raising up on her elbows, Zella cupped her hands around her mouth. "Catlin won't harm you, Eladio! I have his word!" She paused, glancing at Catlin, then spoke again in Spanish, words meant solely for her husband.

Eladio didn't reply instantly, and Catlin heard Brad Gilley say something to the man, urging him to leave.

"Go on, Ladio! Nobody's stopping you."

"*Está bien,*" Eladio replied. "I'm coming to you now, Zella! Tell the *Gato* not to shoot. I don' have no guns!"

Catlin saw Moreno ease out into the open and sidle past the wounded Sid Lane, his hands raised above his head in surrender. And glimpsed something else, Sid Lane stirring, lifting his rifle, pointing it at Moreno's back.

Zella screamed a warning to her husband.

Taking swift aim, Catlin fired at Sid Lane but acted too late, the roar of the Sharps following on the heels of Lane's shot, and Eladio Moreno pitched to the ground. A few feet away from the fallen Mexican, Sid Lane's body went slack. His rifle slipped from his fingers.

"Cat, you hit Sid! I think he's dead!" Ray's voice was high-pitched with pent-up fear and excitement. "He's dead!"

"So is Eladio," Zella said softly. "My God, forgive me." Catlin looked at her, caught the stricken expression on her face an instant before she lowered her head and was rather startled by her reaction. He felt a pang of jealousy and fought against it, realizing he was being foolish.

"I told him I loved him," Zella said softly, and when she glanced up at Catlin there were tears in her eyes. "I killed him with a lie."

Slipping his hand beneath her damp hair, Catlin gently rubbed the back of her neck, moving his thumb and forefinger in slow little circles at her hairline. She sniffled and wiped her eyes.

"Lee Riddick's made a run for it!" Ray shouted.

Looking toward the sound of his brother's voice, Catlin saw him hurrying in the direction of the camp. He rose, using the Sharps to push himself to his feet, and swayed there a little, afraid he might fall flat on his face.

He called out to Ray. "Which direction did he go?"

"I saw him take off upriver! He's on foot!"

Leaving Zella to get their horses, Catlin walked toward the camp, reloading his rifle as he went. Ahead of him, Ray waited for him beside the lean-to, and his tired, muddy face broke into a grateful smile.

"Am I ever glad to see you!" he exclaimed. "Cut me loose, will you, Cat?"

First kicking Sid Lane's rifle into the weeds, Catlin found a knife in the tent and severed the rawhide string binding his brother's wrists. Ray flexed his hands, knelt beside Sid Lane's prone body, and glanced up at Catlin with a shocked look on his face.

"I was wrong," he said. "He's still breathing. You hit him twice, though."

Catlin stood over Sid Lane. The man's eyes opened slightly, icy slivers peering up at him from sunken eye sockets. Catlin pushed Lane's coat open with the muzzle of his rifle. As he had suspected, his first shot had struck Lane in the right shoulder, the large caliber slug practically tearing off his arm. From the second bullet wound in the center of Lane's chest, a crimson rose had blossomed and was spreading across the front of his white shirt. Catlin flicked his gaze back up to the dying man's face. "I know why you killed the others, but why'd you shoot Moreno?"

"He was a horse thief . . . and a coward." Lane's voice was weak, his words barely audible. "I did you a favor, Cat Myers."

"Yeah? How's that?"

"Moreno's wife . . . She's a widow." Lane leered up at him, smiling now, lips stretched taut over pale gums. "The shameless slut's . . . all yours. Trash for trash."

Even dying, Sid Lane managed to anger Catlin. His features fixed, inexpressive, Catlin let the barrel of the Sharps swing forward a little, the big black bore looking the man square in the eye.

Lane gazed up at him, unflinching. "Go ahead, white trash . . . Finish me."

Catlin's forefinger tightened slightly on the front trigger.

"Cat, no!" Reaching across Lane's body, Ray quickly lifted the rifle barrel clear of the man's face. "He's not worth it, Cat."

"Arrogant bastard," Catlin muttered. Exhaling slowly, his anger ebbing, he swiped the back of his hand across his mouth. "It's been a pleasure chatting with you, Lane, but I think I've had my fill for one day."

CHAPTER FORTY-FIVE

Catlin turned away from the cold-hearted little man who lay bleeding at his feet and saw that Zella had brought their horses into camp. She had found a blanket in Sid Lane's tent and was now shaking it out and spreading it over her husband's body. Saying nothing to her or Ray, Catlin mounted Chico, caught his breath as a sharp pain pierced his side, and reined the bay toward the river.

He headed upstream, riding slowly, scanning the ground and searching the wooded river bank for some sign of Brad Gilley. He could have gone anywhere. He might be watching him this very minute undercover, waiting to double back and catch one of the horses. Though if Brad was indeed watching him, Catlin thought it was more likely that he would just shoot him and take Chico.

Thinking this, he was startled minutes later when he saw Brad Gilley limp out of the trees ahead of him and seat himself on a rock near the river bank. Brad rested his rifle across his lap, massaged his thigh, and calmly waited for Catlin to ride up to him.

"Figured you'd show up sooner or later," he said, when Catlin drew within earshot. "I sort of thought it'd be later, though. You never could track worth a damn."

His tone of voice was neither friendly, nor unfriendly. Catlin dismounted a few feet away from him and let Chico drink from a small depression that had collected rainwater.

"Zella Moreno find you?" Brad asked.

Catlin nodded.

333

"She's something else," Brad remarked. "When I hit you last night, she drew her pistol on me. Would've used it, too, if I hadn't knocked it out of her hand in time."

This was news to Catlin, for Zella hadn't mentioned anything about drawing a gun on Brad. Her conduct didn't surprise him, however. Zella Moreno was not timid.

"I'm glad she didn't shoot you," Catlin said.

Brad studied him curiously. "After everything that's happened, how can you say that? I don't recollect you being that forgiving."

Catlin shrugged and didn't say anything for a moment. He squatted on his heels, twining Chico's reins around his fingers. Somewhere downstream from them, a lone coyote barked several sharp, choppy yaps.

"Brad, how'd you get mixed up with Sid Lane?" Catlin asked finally. "You don't have anything in common with him."

"I had plenty in common with Pony," Brad contended. "We were both sent to prison. We both wanted out. It was enough."

"You didn't kill any of those men, did you?"

"No, but that don't take away the guilt. Without me, Pony never would've killed anybody. He was too sickly." Brad sighed and gazed down at his clasped hands. "I never thought it'd get so bloody."

"Why'd you stick with him? Money?"

"Yeah, partly. Pony promised me one thousand dollars if I'd help him. All I had to do was make camp, cook, and run his errands. It didn't seem like a bad deal at first, and I figured with that much money I could afford to leave Texas and make a fresh start." He shook his head. "It wasn't his promise of money that kept me with him, though. Not after things got so gory."

"What did then?"

"I gave Pony my word I wouldn't quit him," Brad replied. "We were partners. Same as you and me used to be." He shot Catlin a frosty look. "But I guess that's something you wouldn't understand."

Catlin could think of nothing to say to that, so he held his peace.

"Pony shouldn't have killed the Mexican."

"He shouldn't have done a lot of things."

"Well, thanks to you, he won't be doing nothing any more. Kind of hard to believe he's dead."

"He's not dead yet," Catlin said. "Ray was a little premature."

Brad Gilley stared at him, appearing both surprised and upset. "So I deserted him, after all."

"I wouldn't take it too hard," Catlin said. "He was as good as dead long before I ever shot him."

"That ain't the point and you know it. I should've stayed with him to the end like I promised." The bitterness returned to Brad's voice and clouded his eyes. He met Catlin's gaze. "Damned funny thing. I went and pulled the same stunt I hated you for all these years."

They fell silent after that, Brad Gilley seemingly lost in thought, Catlin just feeling lost. He didn't know how to talk to Brad any more. Whereas he had once felt comfortable talking to him about almost anything, he now found it difficult to even look him in the eye. Brad's hatred and his own guilty conscience had destroyed the bond between them as much as the passing years had.

"So what now?" Brad asked at length. "You gonna sic the law on me?"

"No."

"Then I'd best get a move on."

So saying, he stood up and shouldered his rifle. Catlin rose also and felt Chico shove his nose between his shoulder blades, almost knocking him off balance.

"You need a horse."

"I'll run across one sooner or later."

Catlin turned to Chico, scratching the bay behind the ears, fondly rubbing the dark, velvety nose. "Take mine," he said.

Brad hesitated, caught between pride and necessity, and Catlin knew what he must be thinking. A man couldn't get much distance between himself and a posse without a horse, particularly a man with a bum leg.

Catlin gave Chico one final pat and held the reins toward Brad. "Take him. He's fast and strong. He'll get you to Mexico or wherever it is you're headed."

Brad gave in to desperation. "I'm obliged," he said and accepted the reins. "I wish I could offer to pay you for him, but I ain't got so much as a penny on me."

No amount of money could have compensated for the loss of the long-legged bay as far as Catlin was concerned, but he didn't say so. He watched Brad swing into the saddle.

"Chico's kind of touchy, especially with strangers, so watch him or he'll jump out from under you," Catlin advised. "Main thing to keep in mind is about the time you figure you can trust him, don't."

Brad nodded and smiled a little. "Sort of like his master, uh?" He gazed down at Catlin a moment. "Did you ever figure out why we fought in that war, Cat?"

Catlin considered the question, one he and Brad had discussed often as the war dragged on and the fighting and killing began to fray their nerves. They never came to any solid conclusion. Now, however, Catlin was able to look back and see himself and his motives more clearly. While others spoke of the Constitution and states' rights, his own personal reasons for serving the Confederacy were less complicated—a boy's yearning for adventure, the North's invasion of the South, patriotism. He found he could sum it all up in two words.

"We're Texans."

Brad nodded in agreement. "And Texans are damned good haters," he added. "I guess it's as good a reason as any."

Abruptly, Brad Gilley swung the bay horse around, pointing him south, and flicked the reins against his neck. Chico struck off at a brisk trot, then smoothed out into a ground-eating lope. Catlin saw him bob and toss his head, demanding more rein, and Brad let him have it. Man and horse soon passed from his sight.

Catlin wondered if he would ever see Brad Gilley again.

Later, plodding back in the direction of camp, he heard a shout and glanced up. Ray was riding toward him, elbows flapping at his sides like wings. Catlin squinted at him, puzzled by the way horse and rider seemed to be wavering before his vision, as if caught in a heat wave. Nothing seemed real to him. He broke out in a chilly sweat.

Stopping beside him, Ray glanced around them then looked back down at Catlin. "What happened to your horse?"

"He run off."

"Spooked, did he? You want to go after him?"

Catlin shook his head.

"Well . . . all right." Ray continued to stare down at him. "Did you see any sign of Lee Riddick?"

Catlin had already prepared himself for the question, which was fortunate. His head felt as if it were stuffed full of cobwebs just now, and he was finding it difficult to think his way through them.

"I saw Riddick try to swim across the river," he said. "Current pulled him under. He never come up."

Ray shook his head, grimacing. "Dern. What a way to go."
He clasped his hands over the saddlehorn. "Riddick wasn't
all bad. He had a conscience at least."

When Catlin didn't respond, Ray motioned him over.
"Let's go, Cat. You look about as worn out as I feel."

Handing Ray his rifle, Catlin climbed up behind him and
was thankful when his brother held his horse at a walk. He
didn't think he could bear any more bouncing around today.
Even then, he almost slipped off the horse's rump when he
looked down and saw the earth whirling beneath him in diz-
zying circles. He flung an arm around Ray, catching himself
just in time.

They were nearing the campsite when Catlin felt a cold
drop of rain splatter the side of his nose. He looked up at the
dark, heavy clouds as more and more drops began to fall,
harder and harder, drenching their already damp clothes and
plastering Catlin's hair to his head. Rain dripped off his eye-
lashes.

"I can't remember the last time I was dry," Ray complained. "I'm so shriveled up I feel like a prune."

Catlin did, too, but he suddenly felt happy, as well, almost
euphoric. The rain would wash away Brad Gilley's trail! Not
even the Texas Rangers could track him down in a gully
washer like this.

Laughing, he slapped Ray on the shoulder. "By God, let it
rain! I feel so chipper all of a sudden, I think I could swim
back to Fort Griffin!"

Ray twisted in the saddle to look at him. He didn't appear
convinced.

CHAPTER FORTY-SIX

The Myers Farm on Plum Creek: September 26, 1877

"I'm gonna miss the trees," Catlin said.

He and Zella were sitting their horses beneath one of the two huge live oaks that shaded his family's small burial plot. The morning was sunny and warm and so calm he could hear insects buzzing among the grasses and weeds. Above him, a grackle made rasping sounds in its throat and whistled shrilly.

It had been Zella's suggestion that they ride out here so he could visit his parents' graves before leaving for El Paso on the noon stage. Catlin could think of more cheerful ways to spend a nice morning like this. Ocie and Rena Myers weren't really here, after all, and seeing the bald mound of earth heaped above his father's body only made the loss that much more real to him.

He glanced up at the grackle teetering to and fro at the top of the tree. "Wish we had oaks in El Paso."

"We have other trees," Zella said.

"Yeah, but they're not oaks. I like oak trees."

Zella studied him thoughtfully. "It hurts, doesn't it?"

"What's that?"

"Not getting your father's land."

He shrugged. "After everything that's happened, I couldn't live here."

They rode their horses to the southwest corner of the pasture and stopped, dismounting. Catlin tethered the horses and helped Zella hoist herself up to a smooth spot on the top of the rock fence where she could sit comfortably. Even this small effort left him feeling shaky and weak.

For nearly two weeks, following his killing of Sid Lane, he had been laid up with the fever and chills and a couple of cracked ribs. He had lost both weight and strength and was put off by his own weakness, impatient to start feeling like his old self again.

Resting an elbow on the rock fence, Catlin listened to the creek trickling nearby and admired the way the sun shone on Zella's long hair, giving it a blue-black sheen.

He and Zella had spent the previous day discussing plans for their immediate future. They would travel by stagecoach back to El Paso where Catlin would leave her and make the long ride to Arizona to locate Johnny Keaton's mother. Zella was still annoyed with him for insisting on making the trip, but realized he could never put this matter behind him until he had at least made an attempt to find Mrs. Keaton. Money couldn't bring her son back to life, but it would help make her own life easier.

Thinking about Keaton reminded Catlin of the errand he had run bright and early this morning.

"I sold the Sharps rifle," he said.

Zella clasped her hands together beneath her chin. "Does that mean what I think it means?"

He nodded. "I'm through."

"That's all I ever hoped to hear you say!"

He looked up at her sitting on the rock fence with her legs dangling off the side and her face happier than he remembered seeing it in some time. He decided now was as good a time as any to try his luck.

His stomach fluttered as he reached into his pocket for the small, tissue-wrapped package. Opening the package, he took out a small circlet of gold, stepped toward Zella, and slipped it onto the third finger of her left hand.

Zella gave him a shocked look, then raised her hand and watched the slender gold band and set of pearls and garnets glint and flash in the morning sunshine.

"Oh, Catlin, it's beautiful," she whispered.

Standing in front of her, he smiled and rested his forearms across her lap. "I used the money I got for the Sharps to pay for it," he said. "It's all real, too. Won't turn your finger green or nothing."

She laughed with delight. "I never doubted it for a second!" Gazing at her ring and wiggling her finger this way and that, her expression sobered. "It's so expensive. Why did you buy this for me?"

"Because you're my favorite woman."

"I'd better be your only woman," she said and squinted one eye up at him. "Catlin, you have the same look on your face you had the time your horse trampled my rose bushes. Out with it. What have you done?"

"Nothing yet. I'll marry you, though, if you'll have me."

Zella didn't appear surprised, didn't seem to be moved at all by his statement, and Catlin thought perhaps she hadn't heard him. He considered repeating himself and was almost afraid to, dreading her refusal.

Zella brushed a strand of hair from her face and tucked it behind her ear. "So this is an engagement ring?"

"Well, yeah. If you'll agree to marry me. I mean, the ring's yours no matter if you want me or not but . . . ."

"Oh, I want you," she broke in. "I wouldn't have put up with you this long if I didn't. When would you like for us to be married?"

Amazed at how simple this had turned out to be, Catlin relaxed. "Today," he said promptly. "There's a preacher in town. He's probably drunk, but I bet I can get him sobered up enough to marry us before we leave for El Paso."

Zella shook her head. "I don't want to be married in Fort Griffin. Too many bad things have happened there." Her tone of voice was firm, uncompromising. "We'll have a proper wedding in El Paso where our friends are," she said and suddenly laughed. "My brother will be so relieved to see us married, he'll throw a week-long fandango in our honor!"

"All right," Catlin agreed. "El Paso then. I guess I can wait a few days."

"You'll have to wait longer than a few days. I won't marry you until you return from Arizona."

Catlin's spirits sank. He should have known this was far too easy to be real. Zella never made anything simple.

"It's because of Eladio, isn't it?" he said. "You're still feeling guilty about him."

"Eladio's death has nothing to do with it. I just feel you should take time to think this over and make sure you're ready to settle down." She gave him a knowing look. "I've seen the way you stare at other women."

"Looking ain't the same as touching."

"You're telling me you've never been tempted?"

Catlin frowned. "I guess maybe I've been tempted a time or two . . . or three. But that was when I was gone from home a long time and feeling lonesome. I've been faithful to you for two whole years, Zella."

Of course, there was the night he spent with the girls at Hunter's Hideaway on River Street, the first night of his return to Fort Griffin. Given the present circumstances, Catlin thought it wise to keep his one and only digression to himself.

His heart set on marrying quickly, he tried every possible argument he could think of to make Zella change her mind about waiting, but she wouldn't budge. In this instance at least, her obstinacy equalled his own.

"If an Apache buck stakes me out in the sun and carves me up like a side of beef while I'm in Arizona, you'll wish you'd married me," he said, irritated by her stubbornness.

"What a terrible thing to say!" she exclaimed.

Catlin had to admit this last argument was a scrape at the bottom of the barrel.

Zella slipped down from the rock fence and took his hands, interlacing her fingers through his and gazing up at him with those dark, perceptive eyes. He imagined sometimes that she could see clean through him to his very soul.

"Catlin, listen to me," she said softly. "I want to have the whole awful past behind us where it belongs the day we finally say our vows. And when we have children, I want them to grow up knowing you as their father and provider, not as a killer. This is my wish. Is it too much to ask?"

When she put it that way, Catlin couldn't argue the point further. They would wait.

Back in Fort Griffin, Catlin left Zella alone to finish her packing and paused outside the hotel to check his watch. He still had thirty-five minutes to piddle around before the noon stage departed for El Paso. He walked up the street to his brother's store.

This close to dinnertime, Myers's Mercantile was empty, and Ray was sweeping the floor. He glanced up at Catlin's entrance, propped his broom in a corner, and took off the white apron he always wore while working.

Hands on his hips, he gave Catlin a swift up and down survey and smiled. "You look like you might live, after all, Cat. How are you feeling?"

"Better." Catlin rubbed his tightly bandaged side. "Ribs don't hurt so bad."

"I'm glad to hear it." Putting up the CLOSED sign, Ray jerked his head toward the door leading to his family's living quarters. "Let's go in back and have a cup of coffee."

Catlin hesitated, not sure that was such a great idea.

"Don't worry," Ray said. "Mary's not here. She and Beth are staying with her Aunt Cora for a day or two."

They walked into the kitchen, and Ray poured two cups of coffee, passed one to Catlin, and sat across from him at the kitchen table. He rested his chin in his palm and watched Catlin dump several teaspoonfuls of sugar into his cup.

"Need a shovel, Cat?"

Catlin grinned. "I like a little coffee with my sugar."

"I noticed. I remember Mama saying you were part sugar ant." Ray sighed, appearing rather gloomy, and gazed out the window. "I wish we were kids again, don't you?"

"Yeah, sometimes." Catlin stirred his syrupy coffee and studied his brother's downcast face. "How's Mary?"

"Mourning Sid's death and hating you." Ray sighed again and shook his head. "Mary and I are going to try to work things out, though. We have to for Beth's sake."

"So Sheriff Luger's not gonna arrest her, huh?"

"No. The Lane name has saved her from that at least, though not from the town's disapproval, I'm afraid. She aided and abetted a murderer, and the people of Fort Griffin won't let her forget that for a long time. Possibly never." Ray gazed across the table at Catlin with a sad half-smile. "You know, Cat, for the first time since our marriage, Mary really needs me. It's a satisfying feeling to finally be needed by my wife."

"Maybe there's some good that came from this, after all," Catlin suggested.

"I hope so. How about you? Any plans for the future?"

Catlin nodded and sipped his coffee. "Me and Zella are leaving for El Paso."

"When?"

"Today." He suddenly smiled. "We're getting married."

"Married? Really?" Ray didn't sound overjoyed with the glad tidings. "Do you think that's a good idea, Cat? I mean, a white man marrying a Mexican woman? Folks frown on that sort of thing."

"They frown on us living together, too. Far as I'm concerned, they can frown till their damned faces fall off. We're getting married and that's that."

"Then what?"

"Zella's uncle and brother run a freighting company in El Paso," Catlin replied. "I'll get a job working for them, try to straighten myself out some, and see what happens."

Nodding, Ray frowned into his coffee cup and gave his earlobe a hard tug. "Listen, about Pa's land . . . If you still want it . . ."

"I don't."

"Well, if you change your mind, it'll be here waiting for you," Ray promised. "It's what Pa wanted."

"Forget it, Ray. El Paso's where me and Zella belong."

Ray shrugged and was silent a moment. "Lee Riddick's body still hasn't been found," he said at length. "Sheriff Luger's had men combing the river banks for days."

Catlin flashed his brother a careless grin. "Hell, man, Riddick's probably floating in the Gulf of Mexico by now."

"I rather doubt it," Ray said. He regarded Catlin with a touch of suspicion. "Why did Riddick come into town that night and help you escape, Cat? What was his motive?"

Catlin didn't bother to answer. It was the same question he had been hassled with for days by Sheriff Luger and especially Virgil Bone—ever since Zella admitted it was Riddick who helped him escape. His response to the lawmen's continued questioning was a stony, unshatterable silence, a reaction that baffled the sheriff and infuriated his deputy.

Ray was more patient. "Riddick wasn't his real name. That day by the river, you called him Brad."

"Did I? I don't remember that."

"Well, I do, and I'll tell you what I think. I think his real name was Brad Gilley. You two knew each other. Maybe you were friends at one time. That's why he freed you."

It was the closest anyone had come to discovering the truth. Lowering his gaze, Catlin rolled a cigarette, struck a match on his jeans, and lit up.

"You let him go, didn't you, Cat?"

Drawing deeply on his cigarette, Catlin exhaled blue smoke and met his brother's gaze, a tell-nothing expression on his face.

"I already told you what happened."

"Yes, you told me several things. You said Chico ran away, for instance, but I notice you haven't bothered to hunt for him. Is it because you gave him to your friend?"

Catlin thumbed the ashes from his cigarette. "Ray, you know what? You've been reading too many dime novels. They're startin' to warp your mind."

Blowing his breath out in a gust, Ray spread his hands in resignation and leaned back in his chair. "Maybe you're right," he admitted. "You know, I'd rather think about anything other than my problems with Mary. I guess my imagination's running overtime."

"Sounds that way." Catlin flipped out his pocket watch. "Speaking of time, I'd better go."

They rose, and Ray followed Catlin through the store to the front door.

"Try to get a seat in front of the coach," Ray told him. "It's smoother there and won't jiggle those bunged up ribs so bad. And do me a favor. Write me a letter once in a while!"

Catlin promised to keep in touch and shook his brother's hand, a single hard pump, but that wasn't enough for the emotional Ray. He threw his arms around Catlin and hugged him while tears ran unashamed down his cheeks and into his beard. Stiffening, Catlin endured the hug, clapped Ray on the back, and pulled free.

"So long, Ray."

"Goodbye, Cat. Take care of yourself."

Nodding, Catlin left the store and walked down the street to the stage station. He spotted Zella waiting for him among the other passengers and bystanders. Wearing a dark green traveling suit and a happy smile, she waved to him, the gold ring on her finger flashing in the sunlight.

"They've loaded our baggage, and the coach leaves in ten minutes," she said. "I'm looking forward to seeing El Paso again, aren't you?"

"Yeah." Hooking his arm in hers, Catlin grimaced. "I just dread that long, dusty trip we've got ahead of us."

"Don't tell me you're getting easily fatigued in your old age," she teased.

Grinning, he spoke close to her ear and slipped an arm around her waist. "When I get you home," he murmured, "I'll make you eat those words."

"I'm counting on it, *querido*."

Helping Zella into the coach, Catlin paused to take one final look at this place where he had grown up. A part of him, he supposed, would always long for the Clear Fork country, but he belonged also to a strong and loving woman, a woman who waited for him now to settle down by her side.

Not wanting to keep her waiting any longer, Catlin turned his back on Fort Griffin and climbed into the stagecoach.